Dizzlemuck

For more information visit
toddmichaelcox.com

Dizzlemuck

Love in the Time
of
Wee Folk

Todd Michael Cox

Sybil ◀ Press
Wisconsin

The characters in this book are fictitious,
and any resemblance to actual folk, full-sized or wee,
living or dead, is purely coincidental.

ISBN 978-0-9843661-7-0

For **Heidi**

always
everything

Dizzlemuck

Part I

Up the airy mountain
Down the rushy glen
We daren't go a-hunting
For fear of little men.
--William Allingham
The Fairies, 1850

1

Imagine a town, a simple little nice American town.

Imagine quiet neighborhoods with chalk-graffiti on the sidewalks, cars sleeping in driveways like tired dogs, dogs growling and hacking like tired cars, a Main Street of bank and barber and bakery.

Imagine all the events that take place in such a town, the parades, birthday parties, backyard cookouts, high-school football games, the gossip and proms, baptisms and funerals. Imagine, then, the people who live there, the bankers and lawyers and moms and dads, the dentists and used-car salesmen, the moody teens, the wizened elderly, the babbling bubbling babies. Imagine their conversations, their fights, their tears. Imagine everything they own and want to own. Imagine their dreams and nightmares.

Now, keep the image of this town in your head. Hold it. Examine it. Let it become a standard background for your thoughts. It is here where our tale is set.

Welcome, everyone, to Burghville.

*

On the evening of April 22, when the sun was saying goodbye to the horizon, Father Lee Preston was out for his nightly walk. He tried to walk at least five miles a day, a habit that had begun around the time he first considered entering the seminary a good ten years earlier. It was what he did when he had something to think about. Walking kept his mind focused.

He had started off from the St. Michael's Catholic Church with the sun blazing gloriously in the west, and by the time the sky was without any color but a smooth gray-blue he had walked three miles. He stayed away from Main Street, with its traffic and lights, keeping instead to the little streets that meandered their way through the backside of the town. The streetlights here were few and far between, and he was able to walk in shadow. Occasionally one of the lights would be dark until he walked underneath it, and then it would pop on and send its yellow glow down to him. He would think: *Ah ha! I just had a thought*! And then he would walk on, smiling at his little joke. Priests aren't allowed the liberty of many jokes so he had to take what he could, even if that meant enjoying a rather lame one all by himself on a Burghville side street.

At the end of one little dark street, just before it curved past the surrounding forest and continued back to town, he suddenly noticed a light at the second-story window of an older house, the very last house before the forest began. Other than this light the house was completely unlit, its entire yard bathed in ever thickening darkness. He stopped and stared up to that window. The shades were open, revealing a yellow room with a white ceiling. In the center of the room stood a young woman.

Father Preston swallowed as he stared up to her. He was standing directly in the glow from that window, which fell like a ray of Godly light in an old Hollywood movie.

The young woman was naked, though he could only see her from the waist up. She was dancing slowly to music he could not hear, her skin smooth and beautiful, still showing the remnants of last year's deep tan. Shadows played over her neck and shoulders, made intriguing designs on her round breasts. Her hair hung just past her shoulders, and now and then she would move her head in such a way as to make that golden hair dance on its own, flowing like water around her face.

Father Preston just stood there, staring, then began to smile. He knew the young woman. It was Helen Keller, with absolutely no relation to *that* Helen Keller, of course. An orphan, he believed... or at least he had never heard any mention of her parents. He wondered if she lived alone in the house, and he wondered how she could afford it. What did she do? Where did she work? What kind of life did she lead? What made her happy....

As she danced her healthy young breasts swung back and forth. They were enchanting, firm, fleshy, capped sweetly with tiny targets a shade or two deeper than the rest of her skin.

Father Preston turned his eyes from her only briefly, to glance back down the dark street. There were no cars and no pedestrians in sight. There was nothing but silence. Well, maybe the beating of his Catholic heart.

How many times have I walked past this house? he wondered.

Don't answer that, Lee, he told himself.

He looked back up at the window. The young woman continued to dance, breasts and hair following their own alternate rhythms. She appeared to have her eyes closed, those Asian eyes, so large on her fragile face. Her tight stomach, so smooth it was like a desert dune, caught his eyes and held them. A desert. Forty days alone in the desert. Your footsteps wiped away behind you by the wind, so there was no way to follow them back....

Helen Keller reached down during her dance, disappearing from view for a moment, and when she came back up she held a large snake in both of her hands. What sort of snake the priest could not tell. About four-feet long and two-fingers thick. She held it up, appeared to say something to the animal, and then began to dance with it. The tail fell like a living strand of dreadlocked hair to her shoulder and lay there twitching seductively back and forth. Other than that, the creature did not move.

The young woman moved for the both of them, her entire body swaying like a piece of grass manipulated by a breeze. Something at once natural and unnatural vied for possession of her movements. It was wrong what she was doing, and yet entirely right. She moved like something that wasn't human, like something fished out of the deepest recesses of the earth, out of the deepest darkest most forgotten corners of myth and legend. Those breasts, that hair, that snake. The reptilian tail resting on her smooth white skin.

3

Father Preston stood staring up at the sight framed for him in the window. He stood there a long time, until something like a heavenly breeze came along to tickle his cheek and tell him it was time to get moving. He obeyed that order, finally turning and walking down the quiet sidewalk, returning to the more well-lit part of town and his little home across from the church. Just before he went to bed that night he looked out his own window and wondered if he would dream. He did, and woke with two things: an erection, and an image burned metaphorically on his retinas.

*

That same night found Henrietta Pratt mucking around in her backyard garden. This was something she did often, ramble around among her plants long after the sun went down, weeding, exploring, twining her way through the vines and flowers. Her eyes adjusted to the darkness, she told anyone who asked, and besides, the night gave the growing plants and moist fertile earth a strange peace, a sense of quiet and purpose they did not have during the day. On this Spring evening she was on her hands and knees, moving between rows of not-yet-risen bellflower, asters, catnip, crawling along and within beautiful (and in this light, ghostly) bunchberry, trillium, lilies of various stripes, and her favorite, prairie smoke. This latter had recently come into its own, a flower of medium height and lovely delicate pink color which was always her first to bloom. She thought it interesting that until the flower was pollinated it hung down, as if drooping its head, but after pollination it sat straight and tall, damn near proud. It reminded her of her own first delightful experiences with sex. Oh good lord, she thought as she crawled around her midnight garden, where in the world is that dear sweet Juan Carlos now? The smell of the young and virgin flowers told her that life goes on, and that it comes back around, too, if one is patient. She thought of her younger self and smiled.

Henrietta Pratt's yard was large, and during the height of the summer growing season it threatened to invade her house: come July and August the bushes were thick, vines wrapped around the walls and windows, the trees were heavy with healthy leaves, the sun and shade came down in turns to help give life to everything, the native grass was lush, and on the sills of each window there sat a large variety of potted plants... as well as certain spices that she cultivated for her cooking. Everything was organic in Henrietta Pratt's house, and come summer a person could not look at any single corner of her property, at any single inch, without seeing vegetation of some sort sprouting happily. From some angles it was possible to not even see the house, only thick runs of elm, spruce, sunflowers. Your only hint that a domicile sat behind the foliage might be the many bird-feeders or the bird-bath at the center of the garden.

As this April evening darkened with every second, Henrietta crawled along, squinting to examine the little world below, searching for any non-native parasites that had made their way onto her property. Nothing non-native was allowed near Henrietta Pratt. Only alien birds were allowed to come around, because she had a kind heart and could not turn down a hungry creature.

But purple loosestrife might be hungry too and you just rip it out of the ground, someone might be tempted to say to her. To which she would reply:

Purple loosestrife may indeed be hungry, but it does not have a mind, and it does not have eyes that call out for compassion. And she would throw seed to pigeons and house sparrows and bits of fruit to starlings and say: So there.

She was just pulling herself along the moist dirt of her garden, imagining the life that was teeming underneath the ground, churning and aerating the soil, making everything ripe for plant growth, when she felt something odd with her one outstretched hand, something hard, but of a distinctive design and texture. She frowned and brought the object closer to her face, her eyes straining to take in whatever light this night provided. She hadn't realized how dark it was until this moment.

The object was of a familiar shape, but smaller than it should be, about two-and-a-half inches long. She brought it to her nose for a sniff, and her frown deepened.

5

It hurt her head to frown this much. She was used to being a happy, bright, joyful woman.

She brought the thing to her nose again, and sniffed once more. Yes, she was right the first time: it smelled of tobacco. Not any tobacco she had ever smelled before, something sweeter, perhaps a little more acidic, but tobacco nonetheless. Burnt tobacco.

Which made sense: after all, the object was made for such things.

It was a little wooden pipe, and it was warm.

*

Well into the evening, when the town was fully covered by a heavy shadow and most people were settled down in front of their televisions to watch the latest brand-new sitcom, there was love-making going on at the Buckthorn residence.

The Buckthorn's lived on the far Northwest side of Burghville, in a large and spacious house nestled back into the woods like a tick embedded on a dog. It was a beautiful house, all polished wood walls and doors, with a very large back deck that overlooked the forest. Between the patio and the open living-room sat a wall-sized window with remote-controlled shades, this window also over-looking the beautiful forest behind the house. There was never a need for those shades to be drawn, however: the Buckthron's had no neighbors and their property was protected by ADT, as the stickers on the front gate warned. Most mornings Dick Dick would go out on the deck, open the fly of his pajama-bottoms, and urinate freely down to the forest floor thirty-feet below. It was his way of welcoming the day.

Other interesting features of the Buckthorn home included a gorgeous basement recreation room with plush carpet, full bar, wood-paneled walls, pool-table, large-screen television, juke-box (for those contemporary country favorites), and two-lane bowling alley. Plus, seven large bedrooms, four bathrooms, a six-car garage (rendered four-car by the presence of Dick Dick's monstrous jet-black military-grade Canyonero SUV), the previously mentioned living-room (with another large-screen television, and a grand piano that neither of the Buckthorns could play), a formal dining room (with a serving wall that opened so that dishes could be passed to the kitchen), and another recreation room with yet another pool table and yet another bar.

It was a nice home, like nothing else found in Burghville, but what the hell, it was set back in the woods, behind gates and at the end of a long driveway, so it wasn't like they were arrogantly throwing their affluence in everyone's faces. At least, this was what Dick Dick had said to sell the home to a reluctant Betty those few years ago.

On this night they were in that upstairs rec-room. Betty was bent forward over the pool table, her breasts pressed against the smooth green felt, and Dick Dick was going to work behind her. She was not thinking about the big house around her at this moment, was in fact calling out to her savior.

"Oh Jesus!" she called out. "Oh Jesus God! Yes! Oh Yes!"

Music was on low in the background, coming from the hidden speaker system Dick Dick had installed at Christmas. It had been his gift to himself, and he thought it somehow completed the house.

When Dick Dick finished what he was doing he fell, sweaty and large, onto his wife's back. After he had regained his breath he kissed the nape of her neck and said:

"Oh God, Betty! I feel weak."

She listened to him breathe for a while, waiting, and then realized the show was over. She tried to stand up but his weight was too great. Dick Dick was not a fat man, but he was large, six-foot four and broad at the shoulders. He hovered over everybody and he liked it.

At last he stepped away from her and she was able to stand upright. She turned and looked at her husband.

"What music is that, anyway?" she asked, frowning at where she imagined the speakers to be. Dick Dick had not told her where the system's parts were located, so the music came forth from the walls like words of wisdom (or otherwise) from an oracle, mysterious and, she had to admit, rather creepy.

7

He smiled at her with his broad, toothy-smile. "You like it? It's music from the films of Arnold Schwarzenegger. I think this piece is from *Conan the Barbarian*. You like it?"

"It's very sweet."

He nodded his head for a while to the music (a deep, softly driving, resonant tune, music for those quiet before-decapitation moments) and then leaned down, took his wife by the shoulders, and kissed her forehead.

"I gotta get to bed, honey. Big day tomorrow."

"Really? You can't stay up and snuggle on the couch? Or...."

"No... no, I'd like to, but I have some important people coming by the factory tomorrow. Foreign investors."

She frowned and pouted her lip. "All right...."

He kissed her again. "You can stay up if you want."

"I'll curl against you when I come up. I know you get cold in the night."

He smiled. "Sounds good. But try not to wake me." With one more kiss on her forehead he was out of the rec-room and crossing the livingroom, his broad back and ass white and hairy.

"Oh, honey?" she called out.

He turned and looked at her, standing fully naked in front of that aforementioned wall of window, his body looming like a monolith.

"Could you turn this music off?" she asked. "I want to watch some TV."

"Sure." And then he was gone.

Once the love theme from *Conan the Barbarian* was gone from her ears, Betty Buckthorn retrieved her robe from behind the bar, where her husband had tossed it after their shower, and then lowered all the lights and sat down on the sofa. She picked up the remote control for the television but simply held it, not pressing any buttons.

She tried to remember the last real orgasm she had had... or, rather, the last one given to her by another person. It might have been ten years ago. Had it been by Dick Dick? No, it hadn't. It had been just before him, in fact. A nice, sweet, gentle man that had been. A writer.

8

They had gone out for a while when they were both undergrads, and then he had slipped off to Europe somewhere, never to be heard from again.

Her best sex ever? She thought about that for a while, there on the couch in the darkened livingroom of this giant house.

She decided it had been. The fellow had had nimble fingers. She chalked that up to all the typing. When they'd been dating he'd been writing a book on archaic aircraft, and it seemed all his time was spent at his typewriter. When he wasn't writing he took her out to do research... which amounted to flying around in his father's little airplane. He'd shown her the basics of flying and she'd let him find out what fellatio at five hundred feet was like.

She pulled her legs to her chest and hugged herself. She thought about this life she had here. It wasn't bad, but was it what she had wanted when she had been young? Was this what she had dreamt about?

It wasn't bad, was all she could think. There were, after all, more important things in life than orgasms.

Such as? she asked herself.

Oh shut up, she thought, and flicked the giant television on. A few minutes of meaningless images passed before her eyes and then she was thinking again:

Dick Dick was not a bad man. He was not even an overly selfish man. She could have demanded something for herself, maybe guided his big hands where she wanted them, but she understood, as a good wife should, what was best for her husband. Dick Dick Buckthorn was a busy man. An important man. And she understood that her job in this marriage was to stay out of his way. If she had to sacrifice the chance for an orgasm so he could get to sleep then so be it. A minor inconvenience.

Better to be a good wife. And she was, she knew, a very good wife indeed. And Dick Dick had never been real good with a woman's equipment anyway. His form of playing with her was like typing with gloves on, to bring it all back to that writer fellow.

After a while she reached under the center cushion of the couch and pulled out a rumpled pack of cigarettes and a lighter. She cocked a head to the rest of the house, all of it now dark save for the few scattered night-lights faintly glowing in the walls, and then stood and went out onto the back deck.

The Spring night was fresh and she inhaled the cool clean air deeply, tasting it on her lips. She stood leaning against the rail and then pulled out a rather bent cigarette, stuck it between her lips, and lit it. In a moment she was sucking on the thing and making its end glow bright, like a captured falling star. She stared out to the dark forest as she smoked, listening to the purring of frogs.

She sucked on the cigarette, held the smoke in her lungs, then blew it out with relish, watching the ghostly gray cloud float slowly into the air. Dick Dick did not know she smoked. He knew she had *once* smoked, but he thought she quit. And she had. Now the act was reserved for quiet moments such as this, a cigarette a week, maybe two, always out here on the patio, never inside. Dick Dick would never smell it because his nose was burnt out by the chemicals at his plants, but she couldn't risk someone else coming in and saying Gee, Dick Dick, I didn't know you smoked. He wouldn't be *angry*, she didn't think... he would just be disappointed. And a wife who disappoints her husband was not a good wife at all.

She inhaled and then looked at the cigarette. What the hell, she thought, it's just cigarettes, plain old Pall Mall cigarettes. It wasn't like it was *pot* or anything.

Although it *could* be, she thought. Maybe someone at Buckthorn Industries could supply her, in payment for a good word whispered in Dick Dick's ear come employee evaluation time. She hadn't smoked pot in years, not since back in her pre-Dick Dick days. She believed she could start to miss it.

She smiled there in the darkness of this cool night, smoking her cancer stick and listening to the life out there in the woods. Although there was no one there to see it, it was quite a beautiful smile. After the cigarette was done she went back to the couch, muted the television, opened her robe, and began to pleasure herself to the silent and unreal images on the big screen.

It was kind of funny, actually: the movie was Arnold Schwarzenegger in *Conan the Barbarian*.

Go figure.

10

*

On the very opposite side of town from the Buckthorn residence sat the reason for Dick Dick Buckthorn's money (and happiness and reputation and etceteras): the monstrous, solid-brick three-building plant called BUCKTHORN INDUSTRIES. It was a chemical plant specializing in high-quality pesticides and herbicides and whatever other -icides you could imagine. Its "Cicada-Be-Quiet" bomb was a particularly popular seller during the summer season.

Buckthorn Industries occupied almost the entire Burghville Industrial Park on the Southeast side of town. A few other minor factories also sat there, but Buckthorn Industries was by far the leading employer in Burghville. It was, some said, the single reason the town still existed. Once upon a time the town had served as a supply stopover for river and railroad traffic, but when those forms of transport had died off the town began to dry up, and a void threatened to grow over the workforce. Buckthorn Industries filled that void better than anyone... certainly better than the other minor factories in the Industrial Park. Among those minor factories were a glove factory (which, symbiotically, supplied Buckthorn Industries with heavy-duty industrial rubber gloves), a place where they boxed and shipped dry goods, and a factory that made burn kits and chemical-spill emergency packages, which was also a heavy supplier to Buckthorn Industries. Although these places were hanging in there and doing all right, they were quite simply overshadowed by Dick Dick's company, and their jobs were mostly filled by after-hours high-school students and college kids home for the summers. Buckthorn Industries employed almost everyone else, save those who commuted elsewhere or who owned small businesses on Main.

On the same evening that Dick Dick Buckthorn was physically expressing his love for his wife, Buckthorn Industries was dark, save for a few dim security lights. The barbed-wire fence that circled all three buildings was a twofold joke: first, who would dare break into the lifeblood of the town? And second, the front gate was left

11

open all the time anyway. There weren't even any motion-lights. So, on this particularly evening as on any other, it was quite easy for the person who had been hiding behind the dumpsters to stand tall and run across the parking lot up to the side of the largest building. No one saw, and because no one saw, no one cared. The town continued sleeping.

Actually, no one would have cared if they *had* seen: this was only Carol Slugg. She was one of Father Preston's flock, although she saw herself as a follower of no one but the Lord, Jesus Christ. Father Preston was just a conduit and clarifier of Christ's message... and, if you asked Carol Slugg, not a very good one at that. But he would do. Everything in this town would do for now, as a place to await the *true* kingdom that will be found only in Heaven.

Once she was against the side of the building she pulled from a pocket a single crucifix. Holding the crucifix firmly in both hands, she first kissed its top, then lowered her head and began to pray.

She prayed for Burghville. She prayed for Buckthorn Industries. She prayed for there to be always a continuous need for herbicides and pesticides. She prayed, in fact, for Biblical-sized plagues, for swarms of locusts and mosquitoes and flies and weeds. She prayed for there to always be a need for Buckthorn Industries to produce its products, so that the town and its people would always have work and therefore food, clothing, shelter. She would have prayed, too, for the millions of animals that made their temporary homes inside of Buckthorn Industries, the five-hundred thousand roaches, the million ants, the hundreds of rats and mice and raccoons and mosquitoes which the Buckthorn Industries' lab workers used to test their products. She *would* have prayed for those animals, if she had known they existed. She prayed that the townsfolk would all see the errors of their ways (their secret, hidden, wicked ways), for them to open up to the words of Christ, for them to see the path to true love and eternal light. She prayed, also, for them to understand and accept the things that she, Carol Slugg, believed and felt. She prayed that some day she would be allowed to stand every day at noon in the parking lot of Buckthorn Industries and pray for all of these things, without the snickers and finger-pointing

12

and jokes. She prayed that all of this would come true... sooner rather than later, though she would never think of rushing God.

She had, in fact, once tried to pray in front of the gate to this factory, but Dick Dick Buckthorn himself had come roaring out and told her to go away. He threatened to call Sheriff Sherman if she didn't leave.

It's a free country, she told him.

The spot of land you're on is *my* country, he thundered at her. And my country is not free!

So, at the end of her prayers, she always added a little extra one for Dick Dick. She prayed that he would someday use his over-sized body and larger-than-life presence for good. He was, she believed, a good man at heart. He just had business interests to look after. Carol had been told a possible explanation for his actions that day: her friend Mabel, who worked in the smallest of Buckthorn Industries' factories, told her that that very day Dick Dick had been showing a group of investors around. And, Mabel said, those investors had been from *California*, and you know they don't believe in God out there! So Dick Dick had been trying to prevent them from being insulted. It all made sense. Had those atheist investors seen God-fearing townsfolk praying in the parking lot, they might have pulled their money and Buckthorn Industries might have suffered.

So maybe it was all worth it, after all. And perhaps Dick Dick would not mind her praying for his factory in daylight, if no investors were around, but she wouldn't risk it. Not yet. Not until everyone believed as she did.

On this evening she finished her prayers and placed her crucifix back into her pocket, where it felt cold against her thigh. Such coldness reminded her of Jesus' immediate presence in her life, and she smiled. She knew He was around. She could sense Him.

She turned and looked at the night, which was quiet and still, peaceful. She waited a while, then started back across the parking lot. Once she was at the gate she hesitated and looked back at the factory. In this dim midnight it looked nearly Biblical, like some massive compound from ancient Israel. And, of course, there were

13

three buildings here. Everyone knew three was a sacred number.

Father. Son. Holy Ghost.

She felt something hot and bubbly stir deep inside of her at this realization, and then she smiled again and turned back towards town.

Which was when she saw the following:

Four small shapes, about a foot high each, running across the road in front of the gate. They were visible for only a brief moment, just flashes seen in the blink of an eye, and then they were swallowed by the darkness.

Carol Slugg frowned. Squirrels? she wondered. Cats? A pack of little dogs? Terriers gone feral?

She shook her head and continued on down the sidewalk towards Burghville. After a few steps she heard something behind her, a shuffling sound that echoed in the quiet. She turned quickly and saw nothing, just the gate and parking lot of Buckthorn Industries and the quiet gray strip of road that ran past them.

She turned back towards town and took a few more steps. Everything was good for nearly ten feet, and then she heard something odd:

A high-pitched, nervous little chittering laugh.

She didn't look back this time: she read her Bible, she knew the darkness was where Satan hid. It could be anything back there, anything at all.

She just walked on, silently mouthing a few Hail Mary's to guide her way.

*

About that same time Sheriff Leroy Sherman was sitting at his desk, eyes closed, brain slowly in the process of shutting down. This was a nightly ritual for him, staying at the station on Main Street as late as possible, waiting by the phone, if time permitted doing a little paperwork. At least, paperwork was what he told people he was doing: in reality, he spent his evenings going over his Plan.

Simply stated, his Plan was this: nothing less than the complete security and safety of the town of Burghville, to be obtained through a full-time police force patrolling the streets day and night, said force to be initially made up

14

of five officers on foot and three squad cars with two officers per car. This roving force was to be monitored by at least three officers at the station, one on the phone, one on the two-way radio, and a third as both back-up and jail-guard. Over time the force would be strengthened by both more officers and greater weapons. Sheriff Sherman envisioned an eventual SWAT team and at least one helicopter, plus all the assorted necessary toys like night-vision goggles and canine units. In this way, Burghville would be made safe both in reality and in the minds of its citizens. Such a strong and active police force would ensure the total security of the streets, at all times of day and through any emergency or situation.

This Plan was a pipe dream. And, to his credit, Sheriff Sherman understood as much. Still, this realization did not prevent him from planning every detail, from equipment needed to necessary budget. It was more than a hobby: as his wife would have said, it was an obsession.

And yet, pipe dream or not, he knew that it was also not *impossible*. All he had to do was convince enough people... and not even that so much as convince all the *right* people. If that could be done then the dream would become reality and he would be seen as the brilliant mastermind behind it. He would be known and respected the world over.

Burghville has no crime, his wife had said more than once.

Yes, he had answered, it has no crime. And the purpose of the Plan is to see that it stays that way!

She didn't understand. She was naïve. So be it. When the respect and the renown came she would not be part of it, he would leave her out of everything. And if she continued to be a negative force in his life he would just have to see what he could do about getting rid of her, just like he would get rid of the criminals and undesirables. She was certainly the latter, wasn't she? Undesirable. And you got rid of the undesirables, didn't you?

He nodded his head there in his office, pleased with the thought. But it was far in the future. Right now there was....

Right now there was nothing. The office was quiet. The phone was silent. Burghville was sleeping.

15

He put his feet back on the ground, then stood and walked over to the front windows. He peered out at Main Street, the lights of which were a soft yellow that did not push the shadows of night away so much as *shoo* them, like an overly-polite old lady shooing school children from her yard.

He walked back to his desk and looked at the thick blue binder sitting there. The contents of the Plan, thus far, were inside that binder. He had just been going over the proposed budget when he had fallen asleep. Numbers did that to him. He had little use for them, and he was convinced they absolutely hated him. He especially did not like them when they told him bad news, as they had been doing this night. He did not like numbers when they stared back at him and seemed to laugh, to mock him, to speak in his wife's voice and tell him that what he was thinking was stupid and irrational and unnecessary and expensive.

But the good thing about numbers was this: with a few little creative flourishes of the pencil they could be changed, they could be erased, they could themselves be rendered unnecessary.

He picked up the binder and replaced it in the personal safe he kept between the desk and the wall. Once the combination to that safe had been his wife's measurements, now it was his own birthday. Things change.

He sighed and walked to the back of the station, where the jail was. It was sad to see the cells empty. They looked lonely.

When had the jail seen its last occupant?

Sheriff Sherman did not want to think about it. Too long… years. And what good was a jail without the jailed?

Jesus, he thought. Nothing happens in this damn town!

He felt quite clearly that his talents as an officer of the law (and, ultimately, as mastermind of the world's first Ultra-Safe Community) were wasted here in Burghville. He was growing fat and useless. Look at him, once a healthy and robust running-back for the Burghville Browns, he was now slowly turning into a middle-aged mess: the gut, the softening facial features, the drooping eyelids, the

16

love-handles, the knees sore from inactivity. What was he becoming?

"Chief Wiggum," he whispered there near the empty cells. " Buford T. Justice...."

He knew what he needed, of course, and the sooner the better. He needed something big! Something exciting! Something dramatic!

He needed, in short, an incident of national proportions... or fuck it, of *international* proportions.

Only trouble was, nothing like that ever happened in Burghville. Of course, it *could* happen here, but there was one thing preventing it:

He was just not that lucky.

"Shit," he hissed through teeth clenched like the bars in front of him. His voice echoed in the empty cells, mocking him.

He went back to his desk. Within minutes, he was once more sleeping. Somewhere on the other side of town, down a quiet little side street, in a beautiful little home, his wife was also sleeping, untroubled by dreams, occupying the whole bed in a delightful fetal position.

*

Midnight in Burghville, and Burghville sleeps deeply.

Candy Cleaver was by this time well into her third hour of sleep. There was a faint odor of artificial orange to her breath, the sort of smell usually found on dust-rags and wooden banisters. She was the sole occupant of her bed, having never been married and, at thirty-five, not really thinking her prospects for matrimony were any good. And just as well, she usually thought: what man could meet her standards? Instead, she gave love and motherly attention to her dolls, and they repaid her with their non-judgmental silence. Was it all right for a grown woman to collect and care for dolls? It was certainly as all right as a grown man crying over a football game. And these were wonderful dolls, they really were: all sorts, from Raggedy Annes to ragged little wooden figures from the previous century. Candy Cleavers' house was like a mortuary for misfit toys, or a museum for midget mummies. She was, at this moment, lost in the deep well of a dream. In all of her

17

dreams she too was a doll, a tiny little version of herself struggling with the larger world around her, gigantic chairs and tables and books and huge open staircases looming like cavern walls. This dream was no exception. Her best friend, Tracey White, was also there, a tiny little Tracey White who looked absolutely adorable in her little miniature wedding dress and veil. In the dream Candy Cleaver was smiling, but in real life, this midnight in Burghville, what was on her face looked much more like a snarl.

Speaking of the Whites, they too were rounding their third hour of sleep, right across the street from Candy, the beautiful young Tracey and her new husband lying peacefully in their big bed, he fetal, she spooning him from behind. Around them their home settled, the floors creaking and pipes thumping melodically in the basement. Dreams of remodeling swirled like visions of sugar plums in their minds. They had had the house for roughly six months, and it still felt new to them, still retained its sense of wonder. It was, after all, *their* house, their beautiful little home, purchased right after they'd gotten back from Scotland, where they had gone to be married. There had been no logic in their choice of wedding location, it was simply a place they had each wanted to visit and so Scotland it was. A small service, only five people total, and of those five two were the Whites themselves; the other three (a registrar and two city employees acting as witnesses) had been complete strangers until that morning. After the ceremony came a long drive into the Highlands, exploring the gorgeous landscapes, soaking up the culture. It had been a like a trip back in time, the whole country so wild and undeveloped as to remind them of what America must have been like a hundred years ago, with jagged cliffs, open skies, thick forests. There was a primitive, untamed aura to those mountains and forests, a feeling of complexity and depth. Those trees hid secrets and mystery.

What'd you bring back? everyone asked them when they returned. And they responded:

A husband.

A wife.

Well, every marriage must begin with a half-truth. The Whites returned to start their new lives in Burghville with so much more than spouses.

Behind their new home, right at the edge of their yard, began the forest that surrounded Burghville, the same forest where the Buckthorn residence sat. Somewhere back there ran a little stream, and not too far from that stream sat a small rocky hill, the result (like all of the land here) of glacial movement eons ago. On the side of that hill was the very small entrance to a cave, which looked out at the forest like a solitary dark eye. No one knew of that cave, and even if they had no one would have been able to enter it: the entrance was only about a foot in diameter, barely big enough to pop a head into. The woods that surrounded both the cave and the stream had an open floor under a dark canopy. What little light came through fell to the ground like showers of gold, and on a midnight such as this there were trickles of moonbeam. Mushrooms grew big and fat here, and there were all sorts of little stirrings in the shadows, tiny creatures scurrying here and there, hunting or being hunted. This was a place few people ever ventured, and certainly a place Tracey and Timmy White had never explored. Their first half-year in their new home had been occupied by other pressing concerns: unpacking, buying furniture, having a house-warming party, going over each other's belongings to see what should be saved and what could be tossed, preparing their rummage-sale (which they were planning for the following weekend, in fact), and, maybe most pressing of all, lovemaking. They were still newlyweds, of course... still randy newlyweds after six months.

Both of them stirred in the darkness. Like many nights, this one had ended with a session of tender yet passionate sex. Afterwards they had laid there in bed, wrapped in each other's warmth, listening to their hearts and slowly slipping off to dreamland.

If not for the condom in the trash, it might have been a perfect evening.

This had been Tracey's last thought before dozing off, and she would actually not remember having it come the morning. To her, it may have been the beginning fragment of a dream. It may even have been brought on by

19

the overly-sauced pizza they had had for supper, which hadn't sat too well with her. It could have been anything... certainly not trouble in paradise.

No, most likely the pizza.

*

The last person awake in Burghville this evening, as it was every evening, was Helen Keller. Not *that* Helen Keller, of course: this Helen Keller could see and hear quite well. In fact, she could see and hear much better than any of us, and it was this which usually led her to the truth of things. Of course, this also tended to lead her into trouble.

She was sitting in the same upstairs room where Father Preston had seen her dancing earlier, but the light was dimmer now. She was sitting on the floor, covered in a very soft white robe. Her eyes were open, but she was motionless. Her hands rested palm-up on her crossed legs, but she was not meditating, she was not praying, she was not ending a session of yoga. She was watching her snakes.

There were four terrariums along the wall opposite the window, each of them three to four feet in length, two feet in height, and each of them occupied by a single reptile. The snakes themselves, one eastern garter, one eastern hognose, one milksnake, and one fox snake, were paying her no attention. In fact, only the milksnake was moving at all, the front half of its body rising up to test the limits of its enclosure. The other snakes were more motionless than the girl, lying there like beautiful hoses. Still, as Helen Keller knew quite well, there could be much to learn in their stillness and in the deep darkness of their unblinking eyes.

This was not her house. The owner of this place had been a good friend of hers, a very gruff, manly, yet gentle poet-slash-artist of some minor renown in other sections of the country, and they had spent much time together, teaching each other their various hard-earned lessons, their philosophies and theories. Helen had showed him the joy and delight and wonder and beauty to be found in the earth that surrounded them, and he had introduced her to his intricate and absurd world of words and ideas. They had gotten each other embroiled in friendly arguments almost on a daily basis, odd and sometimes deep debates about meaning and truth that usually occurred when he was preparing some fancy exotic dish. Those debates had ended four years ago when he dropped dead of a heart attack at what was, for him, the ripe old age of fifty-five. He had willed the house to Helen, and so she had promptly moved into it ... but only during the winter months. In the summer she chose to live out of a tent in the forest, preferring to stay close to the Mother that had created and nourished her, and to which she would someday return as nourishment herself. Now, with Spring in full bloom and the weather turning warm, she was starting to feel the urge to return to the arms of the earth, to its blessings of dirt and tree and bird and sky and snake, to its abundance of love and beauty and wildness.

She sat there on the floor this night in late April, studying her houseguests intently. When it was time for her to return to the wild, so would they. Perhaps tomorrow. In the meantime, she studied them, waiting for a bit of wisdom.

It was the milksnake that finally revealed it. As he continued to extend his head upwards, flicking his tongue at the terrarium's ceiling, poking at the screened lid, turning sideways to glance at the human across the floor, she realized what he was telling her, and a small smile crept onto her mouth. This is what his movements said to Helen:

Always search out the bounds of your enclosures, and always dream of what's beyond.

Helen Keller nodded in understanding. She agreed wholeheartedly, as she of course must: snakes do not lie, and their wisdom is among the most complete and true in all the world.

She stood, satisfied for now, and turned off the single dim light, leaving the snakes in darkness, with nothing but the final image of her smile to light their reptilian dreams.

21

2

After only five hours of sleep, Helen Keller woke with the sun. Just as that nuclear furnace was poking one fraction of its curve over the earth's horizon she opened her eyes a sliver, and for a moment, so brief it was sweet as candy, a fragment of dream followed her into waking life. She grasped at it, tried hard to pull it into the day, and failed. She bit her bottom lip and shook her head. There was much to be learned from dreams, much revealed in those seemingly illogical regurgitations of the subconscious mind, and she hated to miss what this one might have offered. Was it a dream of the forest? Animals? Stars? Something deeper, a bit of disturbing imagery from the most hidden recesses of her being? Perhaps a vision? She would never know.

Disappointed, she took a few deep breaths, then swung her feet off the bed and onto the cool hardwood floor. She walked to the window and peered out at the morning. The sun's light was golden-red on this corner of the waking world, giving her little segment of Burghville a lovely and warm tint. It was only at moments like this, when the town was silent and the warm and familiar rays of the sun were caressing it, that Burghville looked pretty to her. In these moments, when she was the only person awake, she would look out and think that yes, this had the potential to be a wonderful place, it had the potential to be all that it thought it was.

Otherwise, she knew too much about the people here.

She watched this sliver of Burghville for a while, and when she saw the little old lady across the street open her front door to let out a yapping little dog, she smiled sadly. She did not know the old lady's name and had never spoken to her, but she knew this: her husband had died five months ago and the dog had been his. That little poodle was now a proxy for the old man, something the woman could give her love to, something to keep her from being lonely.

She did not know why she knew this, but of course it would be ridiculous to always expect the world to give you reason and logic. Helen Keller just *knew* things, that was all. She could *see* them, as plainly as the average person can see their own hands. She knew many things before she ever had reason to, before she was ever presented evidence of their truth. For instance, she had never met the old woman and yet she knew her husband had died and that the little dog had been his and that at the funeral his sister had sent lilies when she knew damn well that the widow was allergic to them. Helen knew all of this, and more. Some call it clairvoyance, others simply the Sight. In fact, Helen herself preferred this latter, on the rare occasion when she called her talent anything.

She turned from the window, left the bedroom, and walked down the hall to the snake's room.

Her guests were awake now, save for the milksnake, which was coiled under a rock, sleeping. The others stared out at her, tongues flicking to greet the new day.

She walked over and knelt before them.

"Today may be the day," she said cheerily, smiling as she did her brightest most perky smile, the smile that had made so many people back in school ask her why she didn't go out for cheerleading.

The snakes stared at her intently.

"It all depends on the weather."

They gave no reaction to indicate their feelings at this news. Emotions were hard to come by in a reptile's face, although....

Helen leaned down to the hognosed snake's terrarium, nearly pressed her face right up against the glass.

On a floor of aspen chips the hognosed snake stared back at her. His round eyes, just slightly lidded by a subtle jutting of scale, seemed darker than usual, and deeper. She peered into them and frowned.

"You don't, huh?" she said softly.

The snake was still, though its tongue continued to flick in and out.

23

Helen smiled and sat up straight. "I don't know honey... you really don't belong with me." Then she smiled again and shook her head. "We'll see."

She knew, of course, that the snake had no way of understanding her, at least not in the conventional sense, since serpents lack ears and therefore cannot hear airborne sounds. However, there were other methods of understanding. Other conduits.

She stood and left the room, made her way downstairs to the kitchen at the back of the house, where she prepared her breakfast of tea and eggs and toast. It was a long and lazy breakfast and by the time she was finished and cleaning up the morning was full and healthy and the murmur of a well-rested Burghville was coming in through the open window above the sink.

*

Henrietta Pratt sat at her own kitchen table, a cup of lightly-creamed coffee sitting before her. Next to the cup sat the object she had found the night before.

The little pipe.

She wanted to assume that it had been part of a garden-sculpture, some little two-foot high garden gnome or fisherman someone had set out there once long ago to guard azaleas and roses. But there was the little matter of the tobacco smell it carried, that odd little sweet smell that reminded her of marijuana, although of a much more refined and delicate sort than any she had encountered in her youth.

She couldn't help but think that it was a real pipe, not some fake thing made to sit between the lips of a ceramic Ahab or a stone imp. And of course there was the other little detail:

The pipe had been warm when she'd found it, as if it had been recently used and dropped.

Ridiculous, she thought, sipping her coffee. She glanced first out the window over the table, which looked out on her blooming yard, and then at her airy kitchen. Potted plants of all stripes occupied nearly every horizontal surface, and spider-plants hung from suspended containers, draping their long tendrils almost to the floor. Through the

24

doorway into the livingroom she could see her cat Mr. Stinkels lying on a rocking chair. He was slowly cleaning himself, obviously relishing the act. It was nearly unbearable to look at, so she turned her attention back to the pipe.

It was a well-carved little piece of work, made of some wood she could not identify, and neatly polished with care. It was no cheap folk item.

She sipped her coffee and looked once more out to her yard. The morning sun had yet to fully fall over her property, and so the yard was still mostly washed in a rich and cool shade. There was to be no rain this day, but there had been plenty in the weeks past and her yard was promising to blossom like Technicolor wildfire.

She finished this cup of coffee and fetched another, returning to the table to stare out the window. She reflected on the luck that had befallen her, the luck that enabled her to spend all of her time tending a yard such as this without having to go out and work in some stuffy little office. Some people are made for offices, they love the feeling of being entombed within four concrete walls, they love the sound of heels on carpet, the clicking of computer keys, the printer puking out its endless reams of meaningless documents and reports. They love the smell of processed air pumped through cold and indifferent pipes.

Not her. She had done her duty in that war, of course, but that was many years ago, and though she understood the need for those sorts of places she also understood that if it was ever necessary for her to return there she would quite literally explode. She could not handle it. She needed this:

Her quiet and life-affirming yard, the soothing presence of soul-satisfying plants, this open house with its many windows and its quiet places in which to read. She needed all of it.

Which made her lucky, because what she needed was what she had, and how many people can say that?

Lucky indeed, but maybe it wasn't even her own luck so much as the foresight her husband had had to invest so well in so many things during their short marriage. He had also had quite the life insurance, so when he died (of a stroke in an office, ironically, dropping dead right there over his computer) she was suddenly allowed to spend all of her time doing the one thing she absolutely loved: tending to a garden of native vegetation.

She smiled at her luck and looked down at the pipe. With two careful fingers she picked it up and stared at it in the new sun's dusty glow.

And thought: What the hell...?

*

Most of the citizens of Burghville did not have the option to sit and contemplate such minor items of interest, since this was a morning like any other and life went on. People rose, ate quick breakfasts of frozen waffles, poured travel mugs full of coffee and took off for work. The day began at Buckthorn Industries' three factories promptly at seven, and those who did not work there had to open their respective stores on Main Street by eight or hit the nearby highway for the commute to one of Burghville's neighbors. So it could be said that the little town of Burghville was bustling by eight, churning out widgets and selling wicker chairs by the truckload. Most people could not imagine having each and every morning to sit and enjoy the paper and a slow cup of coffee, and a lot of them would not want to: they saw such a thing as either laziness or wastefulness. Real people got up and went to work, they believed. That was what kept America rolling. People who enjoyed their leisure time too much, or who had too much leisure time to enjoy, were damn close to un-American, if you asked them. There was sweat to be sweated, tears to be shed, backs to be broken, calluses to be callused, dirty nails to be further dirtied, bosses to be angered, conveyor belts to convey, trucks to be driven, boxes to be shipped, gravel to be crushed. There was, in short, the job of keeping America moving.

This was why most of them considered Henrietta Pratt to be slightly suspect. The only thing in her favor was that she was a woman (and a widow at that) and she was rather harmless. Had she been a man, an agitating sort of fellow with his nose in everyone's business, there would have been trouble.

26

This morning saw the whistle at Buckthorn Industries go off at seven, the stores on Main turn on their OPEN signs, and entire neighborhoods become silent and still as their occupants headed off for work. It was just another day here in Burghville, just another bright Spring morning with the sun burning nicely, as it would for a few billion years yet, and the color green exploding everywhere in rich dark tones. Eight hours later the air would be filled with the scattered sound of lawnmowers, since this would be the first time in a while they had had the opportunity to perform that most sacred of suburban duties: the chopping of the holy weed.

Most of those who pulled out their lawnmowers later that day would be in for a surprise, however, and quite a few of them would be downright shocked.

*

Dick Dick Buckthorn stood on his back balcony, smiling with pleasure as he carried out his morning piss. The look on his face suggested that he was either still asleep or in some sort of trance: he wore a strange smile, and his usually keen eyes were half-closed into slits. In front of him, beyond the golden arc of urine, the woods were hushed and dark. A few birds chirped to greet the morning, but that was all. When the sparkling stream trickled to its end, Dick Dick opened his eyes further and, still smiling, looked out at the trees. He thought there was something arrogant in those trees... something he could identify with. They were still and strong, having no need to move for anything, man or beast. They reeked of age and patience, yet their power was undeniable as well: it took either large saws or massive storms to even threaten to split them, and once split they would still flourish, growing beyond the scar to curve like ancient gods into twisted, forceful figures that spoke of might and will.

Dick Dick took hold of his penis and shook the few final drops of pee down to the forest floor. Then it was back into the boxers for little Dick Dick. This ritual done, he turned and entered his house.

Across the livingroom, his wife lay on the couch, still sleeping. He did not mind when she slept on the couch

27

because it meant more room for him on the bed, but still, was it good to have your wife sleeping in another room, especially after a night of screwing? How would it look?

He walked over to her and stood there for a time, staring at her. She was curled like a fetus, and her face was nearly without expression. He expected her to wake up, but she remained motionless.

He saw that her robe was open, exposing a single breast. She was a very pretty woman, still as gorgeous as she had been when he had first married her. A good wife.

After staring down at her for a while, he reached out and kicked the couch with a single mighty blow. Betty Buckthorn woke up startled, sitting tall and staring at her hulking man.

"Jesus!" she said. "What the hell's wrong?"

"I'm going to be late tonight," he said. "I just wanted you to know." He smiled at her with his wide salesman-boss-good-old-boy-Teddy Roosevelt smile. "Didn't want you wondering where I was." He turned to walk away. "Coffee's on," he called back to her.

She sighed and pushed the hair from her face. "Thanks..."

"Could you bring me a cup?"

She watched him walk off, a very large broad-shouldered man strutting through his big home like a proud gorilla, his ass a cracked mount of muscle beneath his checkered boxers, and she wondered what the definition of "good morning" was, for Mr. Dick Dick Buckthorn.

She straightened her robe and looked out the patio doors. Another morning, she thought. And ahead lay another day, like always, like forever. She took a deep breath and tried to regain her composure. She had been right in the middle of an interesting sex dream (a masked orgy) and all her secret parts were still tingling. Christ, from an orgy to Dick Dick kicking the couch, what a way to wake.

She heard the shower start to run and she stood and went to the kitchen. The smell of coffee greeted her warmly, and she poured two cups. She set one on the kitchen table and took the other to the bathroom, which was steamed up from the shower. She set this cup on the counter next to the sink and then stood next to the shower stall, behind the frosted door of which the blurred image of her naked husband could be seen, like an Impressionist's painting of a fleshy nude Goliath.

"Coffee's here!" she called out.

"Thanks honey!" came the response. Then: "Could you set out my schmoozing suit? I have those foreign investors today and I gotta look purrtee!"

"Of course," she said.

"You hear me!"

"Yes!" she screamed over the running water.

"Thank you! I love you darling!"

"I love you!"

"What?"

"I love you!"

"You love me?"

"YES!"

A wet arm came over the top of the stall. She reached up and took it gently. The big fingers squeezed back. Then, this little ritual finished, she turned and left the bathroom. Other, less pleasant morning rituals awaited her elsewhere.

First, she went to the bedroom and found her husband's "schmoozing" suit, which was ultimately more casual than one would have expected: a nice white dress shirt over which he wore a rather beautiful leather vest and, weather permitting, a brown suede jacket. Around his neck he strung one of those string ties, the sort a cowboy might wear out on the town, tied with a silver chunk of medal on which there was an etching of a steer. For pants he wore a clean and stiff pair of brand-new dark-blue jeans. Over his feet he would slip his silver-tipped cowboy boots, and on his head he might wear a brown cowboy-hat.

It was exactly the sort of outfit a Texas oil man might wear, and that was exactly why Dick Dick Buckthorn had chosen it: though he hailed from Michigan, Dick Dick had long ago adopted the personality of one of those rich sons of bitches from the southwest. He always said that that was the way a businessman should look and act.

"Why can't the Midwest have its larger-than-life characters?" he had asked his wife once, in private. "Why the hell not? Why couldn't a J.R. Ewing rise from the heartland?"

29

She had shrugged. Sure, why not. It wasn't like it didn't suit him: he was by nature an outgoing, arrogant, charismatic figure, big of body and voice. He was already the sort of man to walk into a board meeting clapping everybody on the back, why not go the whole way?

She drew the line, however, at his adopting of the Texan accent... and of his using words like "dagnabbit" and "pardner."

Once she had laid his outfit on the bed, she left the room for the kitchen, where she paused for a moment to sip her cooling coffee. Through the window above the sink she could see it was to be a beautiful day. A bright, clear spring morning was upon them, hinting at the summer to follow. Soon she would have to start preparing for all those summer parties Dick Dick dragged her to, which meant she would have to start practicing the following attributes:

Perkiness; politeness; an easy laugh; willingness to listen with feigned interest to the stories of people she despised; a phony friendliness and familiarity with the wives of Dick Dick's associates.

Jesus.

She took another long drink from her coffee and then wondered if she should prepare Dick Dick a breakfast. He had not said anything, and she suspected he would have to leave for work fairly quickly. But...

She stood there for a long time, debating what to do, listening to the steady hiss of the shower. At last, hearing that shower stop, she placed two pieces of bread in the six-slotted toaster, where they would be if he wanted them, then went to the garbage, pulled the bag out, and walked towards the back of the home. It was garbage-day today, she remembered. Sometimes that was the only thing that got her out of the house.

She stepped out the backdoor, and came into the connected garage. Dick Dick's massive Canyonero loomed there like a hunk of space junk, all jagged edges and no curves, lacking any style save that reserved for such autos: the style of a grunting, powerful, brute-like beast that would sooner bite you than allow you to pass. God but she hated the thing. It wasn't even a comfortable ride, and when had it ever been off-road? A waste of goddamn money.

She walked around the back of the vehicle, glancing only briefly at the three other cars in the garage. They were, for information's sake, a convertible sports-car, a large cruising sedan, and her own small little compact. All of these cars were dark blue, Dick Dick's favorite color. She had wanted her own to be green, but if Dick Dick was going to buy a car then goddamnit it was going to be blue. And not just any blue, but the most unnatural, dark, clotted blue you could imagine.

Betty shook her head and walked to the two large plastic garbage cans next to the garage doors. These cans were sitting on a cart, which was then to be wheeled down the driveway, through the gate, and onto the road. It was her own little chore, and she didn't mind it. She tossed the new bag into one of the cans, pressed a button on the wall next to her, and waited for the garage door behind the SUV to lift to the rafters.

Like a theatre curtain rising to reveal a set, the garage door lifted to reveal the new morning, all those rich shadows beginning their struggle against the sparkling sun. The driveway rested there like a black version of Dorothy's road, and after a moment's pause she took hold of the cart and pushed it down the drive.

Gray squirrels watched her pass from the forest floor on either side of the driveway. It was an interesting yard, the Buckthorn's: there was no attempt at the usual grass-covered lawn, rather it was like the house had been set smack dab right in the center of the woods, so that it was common to wake and see deer not far from the front door. There was a small flower garden lining the front walkway, but so far that was the only concession to typical landscaping that had been done. Still, this did not imply that Dick Dick was going to let the place retain *all* of its wildness: once every other week or so he went out there with a gas-powered chopper and cleared away the underbrush. The sound of the machine would rattle and roar through the woods as he chewed up the tiny bushes, the saplings, the various thorny-looking flowers that popped up here and there.

"You let a woods go crazy," he had said once, "and the bugs run rampant."

She had asked him why he didn't just put his faith in one of the insecticides or herbicides his factories made, and he had held the chopper up like an action-hero cradling a massive machine gun. Smiling at her, he answered:

"This here gets my aggressions out."

However, he was not above using his own products: once he had set out a particularly nasty pesticide, hoping to rid the garage of a group of marauding mice. The damn bomb (the MOUSE MUTILATOR) had filled the whole house like mustard gas. She remembered difficulty breathing, remembered her eyes swelling nearly shut, remembered a stench like the bowels of hell.

She remembered, most of all, the dead squirrels that had been scattered around the property, like victims from a rodent war.

"Collateral damage," he had said. "Won't see no more mice around."

She looked at the squirrels now, as she walked the cart down the driveway. They stared at her with their curious black eyes, tails jittery, their bodies suggesting energy restrained. Was it possible for them to remember that massacre? Did such creatures have the capacity for thoughts of vengeance? Did the image of their dead ancestors haunt them?

She looked at the closest squirrel and made a "chit-chit" sound with her tongue. The animal moved slightly, staring at her, and then suddenly bolted up to a higher branch.

Betty Buckthorn raised her eyelids and looked down the driveway. Through the open woods she could see the front gates. A moment later she was there, opening the gates by punching in a code on a keypad, then pushing the cart through and resting it near the road. The garbage truck came through around ten, so around noon she could come back to retrieve the cart. Such an exciting day she had planned. She looked up and down the quiet road, studied the woods around her, wondered when someone was going to build a subdivision out here. It was coming. Some day these woods would not be so quiet. Some day there would be children screaming and laughing and the sound of music blaring and the smell of charcoal on lazy summer afternoons. Some day there would be other wives knocking

32

on her door, inviting her to parties. They would tell her she didn't have to bring anything but she would bring over some wine and maybe a dessert, because that was the proper thing to do.

She was turning back towards her house when she heard the gates close. They were the sort of gates that slid apart, rather than opened like a door, and she heard the unmistakable *click* as they came back together.

She frowned. The woods were motionless. After a moment she walked over to the keypad on this side and punched in her code again. The gates slid open... half-way, and then promptly slid back shut.

"What the hell..." She re-punched the code. The gates opened all the way this time and she ran through them. "Stupid—" she began.

There was the sound of laughter. Unmistakable, that sound. Withheld laughter, like children in the back of a classroom.

She wanted to ask "Who's there?" but of course there could be no one... there was no place to hide.

Betty Buckthorn, you may be going crazy, she thought.

She started to walk up her driveway, knowing she was alone and yet feeling watched.

Dick Dick had enemies, she thought. Someone could try to kidnap her!

She walked quickly up the drive, not looking back. Through the open forest floor she could see her home, but she wondered how well Dick Dick could see *her*, should he happen to look out a window. Goddamnit, it was past time he got that chopper out! she thought. This place was like a jungle!

Her pace quickened, she felt the robe flowing around her like a cape, was aware that it was opening and that she was naked underneath, was aware, too, that she didn't care.

Laughter again.

She stopped, feeling suddenly cold, and looked to her right. Nothing there, of course, but....

From behind a small deadfall log she could see a wisp of smoke rising straight into the air.

"Who—"

She didn't let herself finish. This was ridiculous. No one could hide behind such a small log, no one at all. It was crazy.

She squinted over there and could no longer see the smoke. It had been a trick of the sun, perhaps in cahoots with her still waking eyes and mind. No smoke at all, just a play of light and shadow. And no laughter, either, just....

Betty Buckthorn turned and jogged back to her house.

*

Once her husband was gone to work, Tracey White set about organizing their garage for the upcoming sale. The trick with setting up a garage-sale was striking a nice balance between cheap crap you would normally throw away and less-cheap crap that you had not paid anything for (unwanted birthday gifts, say) and which you thought might bring you a buck or two. One man's crap is another man's crap, of course. Or, to put it another way, one will always buy crap if one believes that said crap is being taken at a bargain. This said, Tracey began to haul out the boxes of unnecessary belongings that she and Timmy had gone through, setting them on the two long tables that occupied opposite walls of the garage. Once she had the boxes in the garage she began to take out the items inside and place them on the tables. Her idea was to have everything laid out for the browsers, so it was unnecessary for them to dig through cluttered boxes. Tracey White was an orderly person. Her high-school yearbook had labeled her as such ten years earlier: "Tracey Stone: Most orderly." She had been hoping for "Most changed since Freshman year," because she saw herself as incredibly different from that younger girl, but alas, it was not to be. And, truth be told, the Freshman Tracey Stone had been entirely the same as the Senior Tracey Stone. In fact, in the ten years since graduation she had still not changed. She would be entirely recognizable to her old teachers and classmates.

Around nine in the morning her friend Candy Cleaver came over. She had brought along a few items she thought the Whites might like to include in the sale, and

34

together the two women set about organizing the garage as well as they could. Things must look neat and clean, they both knew. About ten minutes into this work Candy mentioned this year's Memorial Day parade.

"I heard Carol Slugg is going to haul a huge wooden cross down the street," she said.

Tracey smiled. "She means well."

"And Scooter Boober might be the grand marshal."

"Will we be able to see him?"

"Tracey White! That is not nice!" But Candy laughed anyway, one palm covering her mouth in mock shock.

Scooter Boober was the town's only dwarf. A nice fellow, kept to himself, though he'd been known to kick a few shins and crotches when the need arose and had never been considered an overly gregarious sort. However, a person might be allowed to be a little cranky when his entire lifetime is spent ass-level to everyone else.

The Memorial Day parade was always a big deal to Burghville, though no one quite knew why (it actually had to do with the fact that it once coincided with a now long-forgotten event known as Train Day, which had celebrated Burghville's one-time career as a railroad stopover, a career that had fed and nourished the town at a time when it could quite easily have gone to Ghost). It was the year's largest parade, larger even than the one on the Fourth of July, larger than the one for Labor Day. The damn thing had gotten to the point in the past few years where they had had to consciously limit the number of floats and marchers, lest there be more people in the parade than watching it. Someone had once joked that maybe the whole town could march down Main Street, while a video camera recorded it all from the sidewalk. That way, everyone could watch it later.

The thought of the parade had come to Candy Cleaver this morning because she was heavily involved with its planning, being as she was a member of the Jaycees, who were organizing the whole thing.

"It's too soon to think about," Tracey said.

"Not for us. We've been thinking about it for months now. There's going to be some surprises, you know. It won't be the usual run-of-the-mill parade."

35

"Really? Like what?"

"Like you'll just have to wait and see! All I can say is, it will be a purely American parade, celebrating tradition. The theme is..." She glanced sideways at Tracey. "Can I trust you with this?"

"Of course."

"The theme is: How America Has Marched On Through The Centuries."

"Sort of a mouthful, isn't it?"

Candy seemed puzzled. "No, it's beautiful."

"How about: America Marches On?"

Candy's puzzled look turned to one of annoyance. "No, that implies the future, and this parade is about the past. It's about the past, and how America can use the past to show the present how to... be a good future..." She let her voice trail off and fell silent.

"Well, it sounds very interesting."

Candy Cleaver began to sing "I Love a Parade," in a voice soft but out of tune. A few minutes later she pulled a ragged old doll from the bottom of one of Tracey's boxes.

"What's this?" she asked.

Tracey looked at the thing. It was more than raggedy, that doll: it looked like a dog might have used it for training duty once, its face faded, its neck loose, one leg hanging by little more than a thread. Stuffing was coming from a variety of wounds, like moth-bitten viscera, and there was a maroon stain running up the entire right-side.

"Little Sarah," Tracey said. "One of my first dolls."

"And you're *selling* her?"

"Of course. Look at it. It's a mess." Tracey looked into her friend's face, saw the way she was holding the doll. "Do you want it?"

Candy Cleaver's eyes widened and she nodded slowly. "I don't just *want* her, Tracey. I need her. And she needs me. I can fix her up again."

"I don't see how."

Candy looked into her eyes. "Trust me. She'll be just like new."

The morning went on and the work progressed slowly but steadily. Toward noon the two women both

36

stopped at the same time, as though communicating a single thought through telepathy:

"Lunchtime," Tracey said. She turned to go into her house.

"What's this?" Candy asked.

Tracey turned, expecting to see another old doll, and instead saw her friend staring down at the garage's cement floor. She walked over to have a look and found herself frowning at the drain there.

"What's what?" she said.

"Look," and Candy pointed to the area around the drain. There was a small pool of liquid there, perhaps a leak from the car.

Candy was pointing to a tiny set of wet footprints leading from this pool to the garage door. After three feet the tracks faded, but where they began they were clear enough.

They were the size of doll's feet... and though not bare, they were obviously humanoid, textured as if from very small moccasins.

Candy looked at Tracey. "Are you playing with me? Setting doll's feet down there. Very cute."

Tracey said nothing. She stared down at those prints for a moment, then looked into her friend's face.

"I'm sorry," she said, shrugging and smiling weakly. "Just a joke...."

*

For most of Burghville this was a rather uneventful day, with nothing about it to suggest that something was afoot. Spring was sprung, that was all. The grass was riz. They may have wondered where all the birdies is, but perhaps not. Even those who had had interesting things happen in the past twenty-four hours found the day falling toward noontime without anything out of the ordinary occurring: Henrietta Pratt donned her floppy hat to tend to her garden, and while she wandered through it, not looking for anything in particular (it was too early for weeds) she thought little of the pipe. Gardening was a mind-washing sort of exercise, of course, and it's hard to ponder other things while kneeling in dirt and examining shoots and

37

trimming bushes and smelling flowers. These were spiritual activities. Henrietta found herself thinking more about the subtle meaning of lady-bug colors, or whether the first blue-bottle fly was a harbinger of good rain or good sun. The pipe lay inside her home, safely resting in the drawer under the phone.

Betty Buckthorn contented herself with her day's smoke at exactly twelve-fifteen. She went down on that cigarette with a relish that only a secret nicotine-fellator could understand. Her morning had been spent tidying up the house, just in case Dick Dick should chance to bring his foreign investors home for supper, as he sometimes did. He liked to show off his home: Look at how successful I've been, and how successful my company could make *you*! She knew he would call around two if this was his plan, and between noon and two she found herself first talking on the phone with a friend from the city, and then lying on her bed, intending to nap but finding herself once more exploring her body. Her whole life, it sometimes seemed to her, had been spent exploring her body. There were no longer any new frontiers to investigate, and yet each exploration party she sent out came back with wonders more great than any Lewis and Clark had found. She had five orgasms in twenty minutes this afternoon, and after that was too awake to nap, so she took a shower and watched television.

Only Carol Slugg spent any part of this day thinking about what she had seen, or thought she had seen, the night before. She went to the St. Michael's Catholic Church around eleven and found Father Preston dusting the panes underneath the beautiful stained-glass windows. He had been humming an odd tune when she found him, one she had never heard before and one that sounded rather un-churchlike. A secular pop song, maybe, certainly something not found in the hymnbook. When she came up to him he nearly jumped, dropping his can of Buckthorn Industries Anti-dust Spray.

"Miss Slugg!" he said, smiling and retrieving the can. "Good morning! What a pleasant surprise." In fact, he could expect to see her at least twice a week, popping in as she did for her frequent confessionals, although her confessions were rarely confessional and tended to be like

38

mini-inquisitions, peppered by questions intended (he thought) to search out his own weaknesses of belief and moral stature.

"I'd like to go to confessional," she said. Her voice echoed in the empty church like the fluttering of bat wings.

Father Preston nodded and looked around the church. It was a beautiful building, with those gigantic windows filtering God's beautiful light into splendid rays of gold and red and green and blue. The wood of the church was kept immaculate and well-polished, and the whole place smelled of various Buckthorn Industries products. There were, too, the typical church-smell of incense and candles and stale air, although some might consider the latter to be the smell of serenity, of quiet, of holiness, of the presence of the Holy Spirit. Call it what you will: it was stale air, the product of heat and age and human sweat.

"Of course," Father Preston said, though he had been thinking of many options for word-choice. He had been enjoying a fine quiet morning alone, and now....

Carol Slugg smiled and led him to the confessional at the back of the church.

"Forgive me, Father, for I have sinned," she began, just as she always began. But Father Preston had learned long ago that Carol Slugg's sins were like no other sins he had ever heard: they were mostly minor variances from her own tough beliefs. She followed her own strict personal doctrine, and he knew that he himself would have failed in any attempts to follow them. She had expanded on the Church's official line on many matters, and as a result she made most of the nuns he had ever known look like heathens. Nice heathens, though, certainly friendlier than Carol Slugg.

He was thinking about a few of those nuns when he realized she had asked him a question.

"I'm sorry," he said softly through the latticed window that separated them. "I was thinking about the gravity of what you said previously. Could you repeat that?"

"I said," she said, miffed, "what credence should we give those things we see in the dark?"

He tensed. Those things we see in the dark? He thought of what he had seen in the dark. That girl. Helen

Keller. The slow rhythmic dancing, the sway of her young breasts. The coldly erotic movements of the snake.

"Things?" he asked, trying to keep his voice from shaking. "Things like what?" He tried to take his mind from *that* Helen Keller by remembering a joke about the *other* Helen Keller: Why did Helen Keller wear tight pants? So people could read her lips.

Carol Slugg paused. In her presence, silence was indeed golden.

"Things that..." she began, her voice suddenly thin. "Things that are unclear. Things that may be from the Lord or... or from Satan."

Father Preston frowned. The name Satan always made him do one of two things: frown or laugh. It was much the way those who fear clowns must feel when they hear the name Bozo: clowns may be fearsome, after all, but come on, it's *Bozo*!

"I'm not sure I understand," he said.

"Tell me what lives in the darkness, Father," she said, voice thinner now, almost ragged. Witch-like.

"What lives..."

"And how to stop it, if it comes from Satan."

What am I? he wondered. A vampire-hunter? He wanted to tell her to go out and put a stake through its heart, whatever it was. But then he realized the woman might really do that, and the demon she put a stake through might end up being some neighbor's dog that rattled its chain at night. Or it might be the neighbor himself. Anything could be Satanic, in Carol Slugg's world.

"What have you seen?" he asked.

Another pause, longer. "I cannot say," she said finally. "I cannot and I mustn't."

"Well I can't really help you, then, can I? I must know."

"What things have *you* seen, Father?"

He thought again of Helen Keller. Those breasts, that fall of hair, that snake....

Quickly, as an act of self-protection, he thought of another old Helen Keller joke: How did Helen Keller burn her ear? She answered the iron. Which was as stupid as it was old, of course, denying its own basic logic (how would Helen Keller answer the phone if she couldn't hear it?).

Anyway, it served its purpose, taking his mind from certain physical attributes of Burghville's own Helen Keller. Father Preston looked at Carol Slugg.

What are you hinting at, Witch? he thought, wondering if she had seen him watching the girl.

"In your life, have you seen anything that was from the foul womb of Hell?"

She was testing him. He leaned in close to the window, could make out her slight dark shape in silhouette. She was leaning close too, waiting for him.

"I saw..." he began, slowly and with a voice full of hesitant breath.

"Go on!" she said.

"I saw a dog that spoke in tongues!"

Silence.

"It was kept by a poor man in south Georgia. He kept it chained in an old rotted shed, but he'd bring you back there for a price. An old priest told me of it, he said that one goes to this dog and feels the earth's balance broken, smells the rotting breath of demons. You were to ask that dog a question and it would answer, but the old priest told me that one must not trust the answer, for the dog was a trickster, the voice of Hell."

Carol Slugg was so close now he could smell her breath. "What did you ask it?" she whispered in that ragged voice.

"I asked it how the rest of my life would be..." he whispered back, then paused.

"What did it say? What did it say?" She was nearly trembling with fear.

"It said...."

"Please Father! I must know!"

"It said: *Ruff*!"

Silence from the other side of the window. Then the figure there sat straight, her backbone like a board.

"Father Preston!" she said. "You... I don't... you..." Not finding the words, she stood and left the confessional, moving quickly, full of indignation. The big oak doors slammed shut as she left the church. Dust rose from the rafters... perhaps in joy that she was gone.

Father Preston broke out in laughter.

41

Dick Dick Buckthorn's foreign investor was busy going down on him. She was, in fact, no investor at all, foreign or otherwise, but her lips were damn close to exotic, like a strange flower opening for a bee, and that had to count for something. She had those fat full lips which he had always found ideal for the duty of fellatio. Such lips had the strength of pythons, wrapping around him and bringing him closer and closer to *le petite morte*. One did not need to be lost in jungles to experience the strange and pleasant sensation of constriction. Hell no, any old office would do. And this girl here, though possessed of those python lips, could in no way be mistaken for a loin-clothed goddess from the Amazon, despite the exotic way she had of teasing and tempting and squeezing. No sir, she was nothing more or less than the girl next door... albeit one dressed in a navy-blue power suit.

She licked her lips with relish when she was finished, and looked up at him with big doe eyes.

"You have something on the corner of your mouth," he said.

Her tongue came forth to lick it away and he smiled again.

"You're a magician," he said. "Do you know that? An absolute magician. The things you do..."

"It's what I was born to do," she whispered. "Some are born to greatness, some have greatness thrust upon them. And others," she batted her eyes coyly, "take greatness inside."

His smile (what his wife called his Teddy Roosevelt-smile) broadened into its full glory and he reached down to where she was still kneeling between his legs and pushed the hair back from her forehead.

"When will you be back?" he asked.

She kissed the little boss on the head one final time and then stood and crossed Dick Dick's office. Her purse was sitting on a chair there and she pulled a small black appointment book from it, flipped a few pages, followed something with her finger, and frowned in concentration.

Dick Dick zipped up and watched her expectantly.

"Actually, I can be back this way in about four weeks." She closed the book and looked at him. "One month."

His turn to frown. "Hmmm. That means you'd be here around the time of the parade...."

"Parade?"

"The Memorial Day parade. I don't know if that will work out. That's a busy time."

She shrugged and placed the book back into her purse, then crossed the office again and leaned down to him as he sat there in his leather chair, looking the part of the successful businessman behind his fat mahogany desk.

"That," she said softly, seductively, placing her face close to his, "is entirely up to you...."

He felt her warm breath on his cheek, smelled the equally warm odor of himself on her tongue, heard her soft voice in his ears like the sound of something both comforting and thrilling. Her lips parted and he could see beyond them into a mesmerizing cave where a man could fall and get lost forever. The soft tongue moved like a snake over the rim of her front teeth.

"Pencil me in," he said.

"Oh Dick Dick," she said, standing tall, "you are truly one of my favorites."

*

Not long after this encounter, upon seeing the young woman off at the front door, where she bounded perkily off to her next appointment (the owner of a major asphalt company three counties over), Dick Dick Buckthorn took a quick walking tour of Buckthorn Industries' three buildings. The building where his office sat was the largest and was positioned far from the others, so that none of the office workers needed to hear the running of the machinery in the other buildings. His office was the largest of the offices, of course, and it sat quite apart from the others. Dick Dick needed his privacy, for matters both professional and private. Point of interest: his office was lined with real wood, deeply stained, and there were the requisite plaques and awards on the walls, but the real focal point of the room was the great mahogany desk,

43

which had once belonged (or so he had been told) to Ross Perot, Texas billionaire and crackpot candidate for the Presidency. Upon receipt of that desk Dick Dick had gone through the drawers, searching for some little item the wrinkled old branch of a man might have left behind. Luck passes from rich man to rich man that way, you know. Most successful businessmen have some little artifact that had been owned by another successful (and therefore idolized) businessman. Dick Dick, however, had found nothing. He wondered if that meant he would never be a billionaire.

He had also wondered if old Ross Perot had ever been visited by someone like the lady who had just left Buckthorn Industries. Probably, he decided.

A word about that lady: in that purse of hers, in a side pocket, sat seven business-cards that each read POLLY ANDERSON, EXECUTIVE SERVICES UNLMTD. And that was about all that needed to be said.

When Dick Dick wandered about the factories he was always approached by managers asking questions and telling him things he already knew. This day was no different, and they were lucky, since he was in a good mood today and willing to joke around with them a little bit. It lifted the little guy's spirit to have the boss act like he was their good friend, and it did him no harm. He also liked to saunter up to a lowly worker on the line and ask him how it was going.

"How's it going?" he would ask.

"Good," would come the nervous answer.

"How do you like it here?"

"Good. Fine." Standard answers. And if there was a picture of a child or wife or husband posted at the work station he would nod at it and say:

"What a good-looking boy/girl/woman/man. Your son/daughter/wife/hubby?"

"Yep," would be the answer.

Dick Dick liked this sort of thing; it was fun to make them uncomfortable, and it made him feel like he was giving charity, acting like a regular joe, talking on their level. These were the people that worked for him, but he knew as well as most that they were doing him no favors: they had to work, and he paid well. If they didn't like it, there would always be someone else willing to do the work. In other words, he did not have to be nice. But why be a prick? Like the southern businessman he idolized, Dick Dick tried to be a slap-on-the-back kind of guy, someone people would like to drink a beer with, even if they would never get the chance. A boisterous good-old-boy, that was him, fond of nicknames and bawdy jokes.

So he wandered through his factories this day, pausing at random work-stations, even stopping assembly-lines to chat with everyone and gossip a little, ask them if they were excited for summer, ask if they were planning any vacations, ask if they would like to work on the Buckthorn Industries float.

There was, however, one person he had never stopped to talk with. This person worked in the third, smallest building, where he manned the labeling machine for the -BE QUIET line of bombs (CICADA-BE-QUIET, DOVE-BE-QUIET, CRICKET-BE-QUIET, etceteras).

This person was Scooter Boober, the dwarf.

There was nothing inherently wrong with the man, and nothing inherently wrong with being a dwarf (Dick Dick had, for example, never been attacked by a pack of them). It was just....

Well, truth be told, it went back to Dick Dick's childhood. In short, he had seen *The Wizard of Oz* when he was five and the munchkins had scared the hell out of him. That was all. Period. End of story. Dwarves and midgets just gave him the creeps.

On this day he passed Scooter Boober's station and when the little man looked up at him from belt-level, Dick Dick smiled, nodded, and moved on.

Munchkins, he thought, shivering....

*

One of the people Dick Dick talked to on his jaunt through his factories, one of the people he walked up to and clapped on the back (though there was no element of surprise in this, Dick Dick being a large man who could not saunter), was Timmy White. Timmy White was a line manager in the second building of Buckthorn Industries. While this may have sounded impressive on paper and in

45

polite company, it was really a glorified peon position. Timmy White managed one single line of herbicides, and mostly his duties consisted of making sure everyone else on the line was doing their job. If they weren't he ran the risk of losing his. *Manager* in this case signified very little: he himself had more bosses than he cared to think about, and on most days this feeling of being low man on the totem pole was magnified beyond proper proportions. The insignificance of the title *Manager* was made clear by the way Timmy had gotten the job: he had outlasted everyone else who might have been qualified, they all having moved on to better careers elsewhere.

Not long after Dick Dick Buckthorn clapped him on the back and asked him, for the one-thousandth time, what it was like to be married, Timmy White took a five minute break to call home. Since the cutesy phase of being a newlywed had ended he had rarely made such calls, but the urge to call his wife came strong and persistent this day.

What he wanted to tell her about was a dream he had had the night before. He was not the sort to assign meaning to his dreams, but this dream was bugging him mightily, and, he knew, for good reason. In it he had been tiny, barely six inches tall, and he'd been trying to avoid the normal-sized Tracey as she walked through their home. No matter how much he yelled she couldn't hear him down there, and she went about her day oblivious to him.

"Hello?" she said over the line.

"Honey...."

"Sweetheart! Is something wrong?"

"No... no... nothing's wrong. How's your day so far? How's the garage looking?"

"Good. Nearly in order." Pause. "Are you sure nothing's wrong?"

"Nothing's wrong." His own pause. "Is Candy with you?"

"She just left. Tim... why did you call?"

He paused again. Such pauses were not like him. He fancied himself a direct man, a man without hesitation. And still....

"Honey?" she asked softly, and he was aware he was scaring her. She might think he was injured, or calling to tell him he'd been fired. But this was nothing of the sort, this was....

"I think we should... go camping more often," he said.

"Camping?"

"Sure. I think it would be fun to get out somewhere this summer. I've been feeling like getting away for a while now. What do you think? We could use whatever we get from the sale to help fund a little trip."

"Sure. If that's what you want." She still sounded confused. He could almost picture the frown on her pretty face.

"I think I do."

"Is that all you wanted?"

Another pause, much more brief. "That's all. And to say I love you."

"I love you too, Shnooky! I...." Her turn to pause again, as if they were playing some strange game of aural chess. There was something in this pause that made Timmy White frown, perhaps the same something his own had contained.

And so they stayed like that for rather a long time, a young couple speaking in silences, communicating through what was really a stunted telepathy, revealing nothing to each other and yet maybe revealing much in the process. Perhaps their subconscious minds understood this quiet language. Certainly Helen Keller would have been able to read what was being spoken, had she been around. And perhaps, in their own way, Timmy and Tracey White knew that it was best, right now, that they *not* fully understand what was meant in these pauses. Not just yet. Each had something to say, and each thought the other might think them crazy. They may as well have been wanting to ask each other to do something new and kinky and quite possibly illegal in bed some night, something to spice things up.

But no, it was nothing like that at all.

"I love you," they each said finally, and hung up.

*

47

In the end, Helen Keller decided to release her reptile companions that afternoon. Had the sun been too hot she would not have done so, since her little friends would be forced to quickly find respite in the shade and she didn't think that was fair, to free them from the secure, if illusory, safety of captivity and send them into the wild world, where the first thing they would need to do is exercise perhaps rusty survival skills. No, much better to ensure a comfortable buffer between their winter world and this open and dangerous one of summer, so a mild, partly-cloudy day was deemed best. And, each of the snakes requiring a specific sort of environment in which to live, with a little overlap, she took them out into the forest in turns. First it was the fox snake, which she released in a meadow. Its coppery head glowed in the spring sun, and initially it hesitated, unsure of its new surroundings... perhaps expecting her to grab it again and place it back in a vivarium. But she did no such thing. The most she did was reach out to touch its coarse dry back, giving it one final caress, and as she did it slithered slowly off into the grasses of this meadow, which were at last standing tall, no longer bent by the weight of winter snow.

As its tail disappeared from view she thought she received a meaning from its movements. A word came to her, or perhaps it was just a sound. Either way, it was something. It was:

FALL.

She walked back to her winter home, her human's hibernacula, and took the milksnake out to the forest. This forest that surrounded Burghville was rather large and varied for one that sat so close to suburbia. Though it had seen its share of logging and other assaults it had retained a wildness that was unbroken for most of its length and depth: rivers crossed through it, meadows and prairies vied for space with kettles that rolled through hardwood and coniferous forest alike, and there were a few splotches of old-growth somewhere deep in the center. Most of the woods that sat close to Burghville were of the dark and wet sorts, with open ground decorated with mushrooms and rotted logs, though there were places where people had pushed the trees out to make those odd human attempts at fields, and of course the good citizens of Burghville had

48

made three parks at opposite ends of the town. These were typical parks: mostly open grass and parking lots, with a few trees at the edges and enough monkey-bars for the kids to climb... heaven forbid they climb those trees, it was better they got used to the smell of metal and plastic, those were forever, but trees...?

Helen Keller returned to a wetter area of grassland that bordered a marsh, and there she set the milksnake free. And what was gleaned from the slithering of *his* tail?

LOW.

The garter snake was returned to a place just on the edge of the forest behind her winter home, near a small pond. She had always liked garter snakes because they were hardy and ubiquitous, like coyotes and crows and raccoons.

A future world, when we humans are gone, will be filled with garters and coyotes and raccoons and crows and cockroaches. And will that be a bad world? She thought not.

The garter snake crawled off quicker than its two previous cousins. It went so quickly that she was worried she had missed something in its movement, another word or sound perhaps. But she knew, from a lifetime of knowing and understanding the things she did, that if she was meant to glean information from something, she would. It would come to her when it came to her, if it was meant to.

Last, and certainly not least, there came the hognosed snake. She was fairly certain that this critter had wanted to stay with her for the summer, and why not? She was good company, and its meals were guaranteed, yet she felt certain that keeping the cute little fellow was not the thing to do, no matter what it might wish. Besides, life in a tent was not conducive to having pets. Her life in the summer was one stripped down to its essentials. It was freedom in the truest sense, basic, elemental, raw, and there was no place for a serpent.

To compensate, to meet the fellow halfway, she released him not far from the site of her summer residence, which, as it turned out, was not far from where she had captured him, and which was ideal for his species: sandy hillsides bordering a small unmotivated stream. Hognosed

49

snakes favored toads for food, and here there would be plenty. And, if the mood ever struck, the snake could visit her when it wished.

She passed by her little tent, which was at the edge of the dry open woods near the sandy-soiled upland, just to show the guy where she would be. Then she marched to the very top of the nearest hill and lifted him from the terrarium. He wiggled in her hand and gave a little hiss before settling down, warmed by her flesh. His upturned nose was so cute she had to lean down and kiss it. His tongue flicked out in response, smelling her.

"Here you go," she said softly. "Home."

She set him on the ground and he just sat there, motionless save for that tongue. She squatted next to him and observed him for a while. A few minutes passed and then he immediately placed his nose to the sand and began to burrow down, slipping through the sand easily, as if it were water.

It came to her then, simply, without fanfare, like everything she was given to understand:

COURSE OF NATURAL THINGS.

"Course of natural things," she said. Not quite a sentence, certainly nothing prophetic or poetic. She thought of the other snakes.

LOW. FALL. Now, COURSE OF NATURAL THINGS.

And at last it hit her, as it always did:

FALL. LOW. COURSE OF NATURAL THINGS.

"Follow the course of natural things," she whispered to the spring day. It seemed like good advice to her.

She thought of the other night's message, revealed by the milksnake:

Always seek out the bounds of your enclosures, and always dream of what's beyond.

She'd thought it before, and she'd think it again: there was much to be learned from the movement of snakes.

At last there was nothing left of the hognosed snake aboveground but the very tip of its tail, and then that too was pulled down below the sand, with first a little wave goodbye... or so Helen thought.

She waited there a while, reveling in the subtle downward progress of the afternoon. The light was dimming gradually, gathering that dullness that signaled, to those sensitive to such things, the conception of evening. At last, not wishing to lose too much of the day's light, she stood and headed back to town. There was still some work that needed doing before she was completely moved out of her winter home and into her summer one. And when would that move be complete?

Not soon enough, for sure, she thought, inhaling the fresh air of this free and natural world and thinking about her tent in the woods, her real home, her place of identity and calm.

The sun followed her as she walked, like a friend. Like a long lost friend.

*

Everyone was happy to see the afternoon aging, and now that it was spring they were nearly elated to see the sun staying fairly high in the sky as well. The average worker begins to watch the clock somewhere around two in the afternoon, if not sooner, and by three no one is doing serious work. They hear the seconds ticking loudly, like a time bomb, like a voice in their heads saying "Soon, soon, soon."

Shortly before five, mere minutes before the workers began streaming from Buckthorn Industries, Candy Cleaver sat on her bed. She held the doll Tracey White had given her. Little Sarah. With expert hands, Candy had managed to spend an hour sewing up the doll's wounds. Now Little Sarah was left with barely visible scars, just tiny lines of stitching noticeable only because she had not had the exact color thread handy and so at a few places on the doll's body there were inch-long marks of discoloration. No big deal, Candy thought. They gave the doll character. We all have our scars.

Her house was filled with dolls: she had them on shelves in nearly every room, she had them propped on tiny chairs in corners, she had one sitting on a high-chair against

51

her kitchen table, she had some arranged neatly in her livingroom. Everywhere you looked you'd find yourself watched by the eyes of dolls. The paranoid individual would not find comfort in the home of Candace Cleaver.

She was not, however, simply a collector. She saw herself as a restorer of dolls, seeing no difference between herself and those who restore classic cars. The same zeal was there, the same careful attention to detail.

Someone, once, had called her a "doll nurse," and she liked that phrase as well. She did not simply gather dolls, she took broken and torn ones into her home and rehabilitated them. To this end, she had enough yarn and string and fabric to circle the earth, as well as nearly any tool required for such purposes. Fixing up Little Sarah (which Candy doubted was the doll's real name) had been easy, a matter of adding a little stuffing and sewing up the cuts. Nothing to it.

At this moment, holding the doll in her hand as she sat on the bed, she had the sudden and unmistakable feeling that she was being watched. Usually she was aware of the glass eyes that surrounded her, but this was different. Candy Cleaver understood quite well that those eyes did not see. Despite some of the vicious rumors she'd heard about herself, she did not think her dolls were real. And though she sometimes talked to them she did not believe that they talked back. There were definite psychological reasons behind her choice of hobby, but she was by no means crazy. Dolls were dolls, that was all.

No, this feeling of being watched was quite real. She looked up at the four shelves across the room, each of them occupied with at least ten dolls of various make. There were Raggedy Annes, Raggedy Andies, bizarre foreign creatures with bald heads, hand-made antiques, at least two kewpies, and an anatomical baby boy dressed in a blue jumper. This latter was one of her newest, and she remembered putting a hand over her mouth in mixed shock and glee when she lowered those bottoms and saw the curled little penis between the legs. What will they think of next? she'd wondered.

She looked over the dolls, then turned her head to the nearest window. That window was too high up for someone to be looking in, and who would look in anyway?

She was a nice woman, she kept to herself. There were many people in this town more worthy of being spied on, people offering greater interest, greater reward for the peeping tom's efforts. She was just a woman with dolls.

A woman with dolls and no husband. That rare thing in such an overpopulated world: an old-maid.

Only not so old and not so...

She frowned. She had to justify her life to no one, dammit! Sure, it might seem odd to some that she had never married, but good things happen to those who wait and some day her prince would come and happy endings are never too far away and....

Something moved somewhere. A slipping, a foot scraping on a floor.

She set Little Sarah on the bed and went to the hallway outside of her bedroom. Someday her prince would come, and what if today was that day?

She looked down the hall and saw no prince, just her house, her dolls.

"Tracey?" she called out.

Tracey White did not answer. *Nothing* answered. And then there it was again, a soft shuffling sound.

Mice?

"Oh for goodness' sake," she said, sighing and starting down the hall. Mice, of all things. Was any creature more un-American, more dirty, more useless? She marched down that hall full of indignation. She had had a mouse problem two summers back and had gone out immediately to buy Buckthorn Industries' most potent rodent-killer. That had seemed to do the trick, but now here they were again. She felt angry: she did not want to do another Mouse Bomb, remembering that for the first one she had had to stay out of her home for a full week.

"Scram!" she shouted to the unseen critters, stamping her feet. "Scram, you dirty devils!"

At that exact second, there was a horrible scream outside, and she froze.

*

Not so much a scream, though, as a shout. An angry shout, followed by another just a few moments later.

The shouts of men, as deep and resonant as the voices of opera singers, filling the cathedral of this quiet neighborhood.

Men have surely screamed like that before, usually at an uncooperative car part or a vandalizing animal or child. Such shouts have followed thumbs being hammered and toes being stubbed. Such shouts have accompanied great money loss, or sexual dysfunction, or a football game gone bad. But these screams, and there were a whole series of them now, followed from none of these things.

"What's wrong, Herb?" one passerby said to a man standing in his side-yard. Herb had given his shout, and then just stood there with his hands grasping handfuls of his hair, a mower resting quietly at his feet, like an obedient dog awaiting orders. "You okay?"

Herb said nothing. None of the other men who shouted this afternoon said anything, either. They screamed, hollered, and then just stood there like Herb, staring at what lay before them with eyes wide and mouths open in shock. The slanting sunlight came from the west and lay like golden dust on their yards, threw comforting shadows against the sides of their homes and over their backyard grills and patios. This picture would have been an ideal rendering of suburban comfort and tranquility had it not been for what the men were looking at:

Their lawns, full of thick and healthy grass this morning, were now mostly bare, with just a few squares like leftover sod scattered about, and the earth itself trampled, as if by the presence of large animals.

It wasn't every yard, but enough to fill this quiet early-evening with shocked screams as more people returned home from work and found their cherished mowing plans cruelly altered. Later, as darkness finally fell over the land, the rising moon found many lawnmowers still sitting in front of houses, looking lost and lonely on their sickly patches of ground, abandoned in the frenzy of anger and annoyance.

By morning, those patches of ground were spotted with thick white mushrooms, and the mowers had been emptied of gas.

3

There was something about being a young and good-looking priest, something that made others look at you differently than if, say, you were an elderly priest with arthritic hands, cloudy eyes, and a gnarled back. When people saw you and realized you were a priest, that you were a healthy young man who had dedicated his life to celibacy, they immediately, if only subconsciously, thought: *What a waste.* The human animal is a sexual animal, and it's hard for most to understand a person who is not ruled by their sexuality, who even *denies* their sexuality. He had been told while in the seminary that most of the problems he would encounter among his flock would be rooted in a carnal nature, whether it be trouble in a marriage or trouble among wayward teenagers. It all comes down to sex, he was told. In fact, he had been shocked by how much talk of sex there had actually been among his teachers, the nuns and Fathers and even the visiting Bishops. He had even thought he detected a tone of jealousy creeping into their conversations. The human critter is a sexual one, indeed, and those desires, he had come to believe, could never be fully controlled. And perhaps they *shouldn't* be. Maybe to deny them completely is to deny one's humanity. Maybe it was alright for a Father to look out at his congregation and think: *My, Mrs. Carter looks beautiful today.* Or: *Lord, the Williams daughter is sure starting to bloom*! Or: *Good Christ, to be wrapped inside those legs of Mrs. White*! Maybe it was all perfectly okay.

He was thinking these thoughts on this Saturday morning because he had woken early to work on the next day's sermon. Normally he wrote his sermons out weeks ahead of time, modifying them as needed but generally being ready by Friday night. Not this week. This week he had been distracted by outside events... or rather, by the lack of outside events.

Namely, the disappearance of Helen Keller from her home by the woods.

Though he didn't like to think about it, his walks every evening had been taking him past her house for some time now. He would start out telling himself that he was not going to go that way tonight, and then the next thing he knew he would be there, standing on the sidewalk like a peeping tom, hoping for a glimpse of the girl.

He thought of the Evening of the Dance. The image of her moving with the snake was burned onto his brain. He thought it was something he might take with him to the grave.

But, no matter how often he went back there, he had never seen the act repeated. In fact, only a few days after the incident her home had gone dark and quiet. Had she gone away? Had she moved to another town? Was she shacking up with a boy?

He had wanted to ask someone these questions, but of course he could not. Perhaps if she was part of his congregation he might have felt comfortable asking, but as it stood she was just a young woman he had seen dancing naked in a window. A young woman he had seen around town, maybe followed in the grocery store, a young woman he had been obsessed with for a long time now, ever since he had first set eyes on her.

He sat at a desk in the little home he'd been given across the street from the St. Michael's Catholic Church. In front of him sat a blank piece of paper. In his hand he held a pen. Between that pen and the skin of his fingers was a thin sheen of sweat.

For only seven years now he had been a priest, and for four of them he had been here, stationed in Burghville. And the town was a nice enough town, he liked it just fine, but just as there was something about a young priest, there was also something about a small town. What it boiled down to was this:

A small town was no place for a good priest. Why? one might ask. Father Lee Preston had concluded, quite early on in his time here, that it had to do with that smallness, that closeness the townsfolk felt toward each other. *Closeness*, keep in mind, had little to do with *friendliness*. To be a good priest a man must be trusted, must be part of the community, a warm and familiar, yet simultaneously unattached, part, someone people could come to with their problems, with their personal issues and spiritual concerns. But in a small town like this one, people felt that their neighbors were too close, that it was impossible to keep a secret, that the walls were too thin between houses, that what a person might say in the darkness of a confessional or the soothing light of his office might end up the next day as the prime topic of discussion at Joe's Joe on Main. In such a climate, where people are hesitant to tell the truth about their issues, it was nearly impossible to be a good, effective priest.

He'd had the same conversation time and again here:

Father, me and Carl are just... we're not communicating right now.

Communicating how?

Well (hesitantly)... we just want different things. He wants one thing and I want another and we don't see how we can find middle ground.

So, you want, like, a four-door car and he wants a two?

Well...

You want a new washer, he wants a new television?

Well...

He sighed now, thinking of such things. It was impossible to give guidance when people did not feel capable of opening up.

He had thought at first it was he himself that was the problem. Maybe it was the fact that he was young, much younger than the majority of his congregation. But no, he didn't think that was it, and had been told as much by none other than Carol Slugg.

"I don't want the things I tell you spread all over this town," she'd said when he first came to Burghville... when she was the very first person to march into his office,

57

in fact. "These people don't need to know everything I think. They're not worthy and they wouldn't understand."

He had assured her that whatever she said would stay with him and him only. Unfortunately for him, she had believed that: now he had to put up with her every time he turned around.

He assured her he would say nothing, that he would keep her privacy sacred, that nothing she told him, whether in the sanctity of the confessional or in simple conversation, would ever reach the ears of another.

I'm a good priest, he assured her. She had given him a sideways look, suspicious and untrusting, as if she found it hard to believe such a young and handsome man could be any such thing. Yes, there was just something about being a young and good-looking man of the cloth. It was a burden.

"I don't know if you should be a priest," the not-so-kindly and not-so-warm old priest who had been his first seminary counselor had said early on. "You ooze sex..." Dragging out *ooze*, of course, with lecherous relish.

"I'm a good priest," he whispered now, defiantly. "I'm a good priest."

He thought of the sweat on his hands, thought of the unwritten sermon, thought of the girl dancing naked with the serpent, thought of the erections he woke with whenever he dreamt of her. Those erections were like the worst sort of uninvited guests, for a priest anyway.

Maybe the best men of God are those who participate fully in life, he thought. Maybe it takes a married man to understand marriage, a father to understand parenthood, a fully functioning sexual being to understand issues of sexuality.

He swiveled in his chair and picked up the Bible that sat at the far end of his desk. He hefted the big book and flipped through its pages, randomly reading sentences. It seemed every phrase he came across had to do with sex. Good Lord. There would be no inspiration from the Good Book today. It was nothing but the Good Book of One-Handed Reading.

Could he just make up a sermon? Or recycle an old one?

Can't I just skip it? There would be those in the congregation who would welcome such an edit to the service.

He closed the Bible and set it on the desk, where it made a hollow yet intimidating *thump*. He looked out his window, where the morning sun was touching the front of the church with a golden polish. It was promising to be a splendid morning, warm and sunny, a tease for the coming summer. The smell of plants in bloom would fill the air, that moist and comforting musk of Earth's own sexuality.

He wondered where the girl was, this mysterious and beautiful Helen Keller, this woman of his dreams, of his nightmares, of his deepest darkest sweetest desires. She had disappeared last summer too, he recalled, only occasionally returning. Perhaps she had a boyfriend who lived elsewhere... maybe she was a seasonal worker employed out of town... maybe....

Leaving the empty paper and the unwritten sermon behind, he decided to leave his house and go for a walk. This beautiful morning beckoned, and unlike other things that beckon, it could do no harm to heart or soul.

*

There had been a minor run on sod at the Burghville Seed and Landscaping Store. On the morning after some in the town had discovered their lawns mysteriously cleaned of grass, the Landscaping Store was filled with agitated men loading sod and seed into the backs of pickups. Between disgruntled groans and pissed-off grunts there had been an attempt at conversation, at trying to solve this mystery.

Vandals, was the consensus, though a few souls suggested some sort of blight, a fungal parasite perhaps. Either way, no one had seen anything like it. The men filled their trucks with rolls of sod and bags of seed and drove off to their homes, unhappy to have this new chore but hating the sight of their bare lawns. It just looked bad, having yards like that. A large expanse of lush grass around a house was an American tradition, was damn near a fundament of patriotism. Some even frowned at Henrietta Pratt's yard, which was nearly grassless, save for

59

a sliver at the front which she claimed was some sort of native grass that needed less watering and even less mowing. Whatever. It takes all kinds to make the world go round. So the men drove home and went to work.

Some yards had it worse than others, but over the next few days people noticed that it seemed that *every* yard had it to some degree. This disappearance of grass seemed almost like a cancer, spreading from neighborhood to neighborhood. And then, to top it off, there were the mushrooms.

No one knew what sort of mushrooms they were, but they were ugly. Who wants such things in their yard? They were pale and cold to the touch, like dead skin, and probably poisonous, too.

Perhaps it *was* a fungal blight, then. People began to focus on the mushrooms as the source of the grass' disappearance. There had been a second run on a Burghville product: the anti-fungal powder called SHROOM-BLAST produced by Buckthorn Industries. This powder came with the following warning on its label:

THIS PRODUCT CONTAINS INGREDIENTS KNOWN TO BE TOXIC TO HUMANS AND DOMESTIC ANIMALS. USE SPARINGLY AND ONLY OUTDOORS. SEAL OFF YARDS, POST WARNINGS, AND KEEP CHILDREN FROM THE AREA. DO NOT EAT OR OTHERWISE TAKE INTERNALLY. IF INGESTED OR INHALED, DO NOT INDUCE VOMITING. DRINK WATER AND SEEK MEDICAL HELP. MAY BURN THE EYES AND SKIN AFTER PROLONGED CONTACT. MAY CAUSE MISCARRIAGES. MAY CAUSE SEVERE RASHES TO THE SKIN. STORE ACCORDING TO SIDE LABEL. KEEP AWAY FROM CHILDREN AND ELDERLY.

At this point the makers ran out of room and there was only the following statement:

SEE FULL WARNINGS AND PRECAUTIONS ON THE BUCKTHORN INDUSTRIES WEBSITE AT BUCKTHORN.COM.

The smell of the powder filled the air. In some neighborhoods it was like a fog.

*

Explaining the gas was another matter. Even lawnmowers that had been filled earlier that evening were found empty the next morning. People chalked this up to thievery, plain and simple, and the authorities were fully notified.

*

Sheriff Sherman saw Father Preston walking down the sidewalk this day and gave him a casual waive, friendly but noncommittal. He did not like to be too friendly when he was on duty, he felt it diminished his aura of authority. He was not your buddy when he was in uniform, he was an Officer of the Law, and therefore there had to be a distance between himself and the public, otherwise the whole system would break down. Who would respect him if he was always bumming cigarettes from people? Or gossiping about local issues? Or cracking dirty jokes at the expense of Burghville's hottest women?

He was out driving this morning only to pass the time and maybe, if he was lucky, find some trouble. Even some little kids smoking would be worthwhile, if only so he could flex his muscles (so to speak) as a uniformed policeman. Little kids were among the few people who were still rather intimidated by policemen, and he knew most of them by name, either through their parents or from his annual bike safety talks at the Middle School. If he saw any he would stop, tell them smoking was a deadly habit, urge them to stay off drugs and stay in school, and ask them if they'd seen anything that merited his attention.

Most likely they would say no to the latter, but it was worth a shot. Maybe someday one of them would spill the beans about their pot-smoking parents or the car their older brother stole from two towns over. Maybe. Some day. If he was lucky.

The young priest returned the wave and kept on walking. Sheriff Sherman watched him in the rearview mirror for a moment and then sighed and returned his attention to the street in front of him.

He could never put his finger on priests. They were just so... so...

61

Priestly.

"Elvis Priestly," he said, giggling.

He steered the cruiser down a quiet street, came to a stop, and took a right. He wanted to check out those yards where the grass had vanished. He'd been called the next day, once the gas was found siphoned from the mowers, but had been rather useless, he had to admit. If it wasn't absent-mindedness by the owners of those mowers, or the result of minds gone to mush with anger over the grass, it had to be theft. And though he had done what he could, there was really no way to track down stolen gas. Such a thing can be burnt off quite quickly... although, who would have taken it? Mixed with oil as it was, could you use it in a car? He thought not, but people will try anything. Maybe eventually a car will come to Miller's Auto Repair with a suspicious problem and the crime will be solved. Until then, Sheriff Sherman knew there was nothing he could do.

But it bothered him, the grass more than the gas. And those mushrooms, for crying out loud. The whole thing worried him, and not because he actually cared, but because it was exactly the sort of thing that, if it became a true plague, would make the news... maybe even the national news, like those deformed frogs in Minnesota. And, while there was nothing inherently wrong with this, it was not something he looked forward to.

See, it was the sort of thing that might make the national news... but which also had nothing to do with him. He could neither solve nor talk about the incident. It was beyond him. There was no place in such an incident for his particular talents.

He drove around secretly hoping for a crime of some sort. Nothing too big. A visiting serial killer. A rape. A school shooting.

Hell, couldn't that priest back there molest a choir boy or something?

Sheriff Sherman frowned at his thoughts. Okay, maybe not a molestation, but how about a *solicitation*? That would work. Something he could *do* something about. Really, was it too much to ask?

He passed by a house where a homemade sign in the yard announced a RUMMAGE SALE. A few cars were parked in the drive and along the street, and he saw people milling about in the open mouth of the garage. He slowed as he passed, wondering if they had anything good in there, and saw a glimpse of that young Mrs. White, the former Tracey Stone.

A very pretty lady, was she. Such legs. And she was in shorts today, it being a fairly warm morning.

He debated pulling the cruiser over and wandering up there, but decided against it. It wouldn't look professional, he decided.

He continued down the street.

*

"There goes Sheriff Sherman," Candy Cleaver said to Tracey White. They both watched him pass and then Candy leaned over and whispered: "Hope you have a selling permit for this, or he'll bust you."

Tracey smiled. Everyone knew how zealous the sheriff could be.

The sale was going good so far. It had started promptly at eight and now it was nearly nine and they had already had quite a few browsers. It was strange, seeing so many people going through items that had once been personal to her, that had once held meaning and importance. Even stranger was selling those items for pennies.

"Warm day," Candy said. "I'll go make some lemonade." And she disappeared inside the White's house, leaving Tracey to stand there smiling at the old ladies digging through boxes of knick-knacks and clothes.

It was an interesting crowd, those who go to rummage sales. As far as Tracey could tell, it was made of three types of people:

Those who come looking for bargains;

Those who come for curiosity, just to see what other people owned;

Those who came looking for obscure and maybe priceless artifacts.

Of the three types, she disliked the last the most. She felt that they looked at her like an idiot, expecting her to have some rare object she was too stupid to know the value of, that she would just throw in with the rest of the junk. They came, in other words, expecting to make her look like a fool. For a quarter they could buy a rare record or something and turn around and sell it for thousands of dollars. She despised them.

So far, one college-aged kid and a man in his mid-thirties had come, the kid going through her books, the older man carefully inspecting her jewelry. They had looked like they knew what they were looking for, and when she smiled at them she felt that they were inspecting her as well, trying to judge what sort of woman she was, how much she might know about their fields of interest, if she was the sort who would throw out, say, a Faberge Egg, thinking it was just some piece of crap Gramma had gotten while visiting an ostrich farm in Iowa.

She much preferred the elderly ladies who came looking for cheap but useful items for their households. Or maybe they were looking for things of the sort they might have had when they were younger but had lost in fires and floods. Whichever. They were friendly and sweet as they dug through her stuff, and they never tried to bargain her down from her already low prices.

"Shame about the yards," one of them said while she dug into her purse for seventy-five cents, the cost of an old candle-holder.

The lady who was with her shook her head and made a clicking sound with her obviously false teeth. Both women were slightly bent over, developing that old-woman hump that all young women feared. Tracey was amazed at how clean and neat these ladies looked, apparently not sweating even in the growing heat of the day. Here it was only late-April, and already the day was threatening to be a scorcher. These ladies, however, looked as dry as the desert, and their soft-colored dresses (shapeless, as is the fashion with old women) were so clean they looked as if they'd just been made.

"Horrible," the second woman said. She had a strange voice, at once grating and melodic, like sandpaper playing Mozart. "All that grass ruined. Everything looks like the Mojave. You expect to see cactuses sprouting up."

"Just ugly," the other agreed. "And those horrible mushrooms. Ed over at the hardware store told Martin that they might be poisonous. He said he saw something about them on TV once." She grimaced at the thought of this tragedy. "Just a sight, I tell you. I've never seen anything like it."

"Mushrooms," the other said contemptuously, again shaking her head.

Tracey took the first woman's seventy-five cents, thanked her, and offered them both a smile. She watched them shuffle out of her garage and down the drive and wondered how many children and grandchildren they had. Elderly people made her think in terms of generations. You look at an old woman and you see all the people that came after her.

Just the opposite with a baby: you look at one of them and you thought of all the people that had come before.

When Candy came out with a pitcher of lemonade and a stack of Styrofoam cups, Tracey told her to man the garage for a while, then she slipped into her house and went to the bathroom. Warm days made her have to urinate a lot. Which was interesting, because in Scotland last October, when the days had been on the cooler side, she had not had to stop for hours. In fact, it had been Timmy who had had to pee all the time, pulling the rental car over to nearly all the widely spaced little pubs they'd encountered, or to the sides of desolate roads when there were no towns anywhere and they were miles from any restaurants or petrol stations. He would wander up into the woods, or step behind a broken old brick barn and do his business while she laughed through her open window. Once he had had to pee on a moor, in the middle of nowhere, out in the open like a vagrant, telling her over his shoulder that she'd better not be looking. And of course she had, she couldn't help herself. One of the duties of a young wife was to annoy her husband.

Ironic, then, how the one time she *had* run off to pee in the woods....

She frowned. She wouldn't allow herself to think about that, despite all this talk of grass and mushrooms and tiny footprints on the garage floor. She just wouldn't. She tore off a length of toilet paper, hoping this act alone would erase what she was thinking.

When she wiped herself she saw blood on the tissue.

"Goddamnit," she whispered. With this whisper came a whole new slew of thoughts and feelings, some out front and others hidden in her subconscious, persistent as an itch she couldn't quite get, causing reactions in her which she couldn't recognize at the moment but which were strong nonetheless. Her period. Goddamnit.

She stood to fetch herself a tampon from the cupboard under the sink.

And found them gone.

How convenient, she thought. When Timmy wants a condom, there are plenty of those, but when I need a tampon....

She felt like crying.

*

Women would perish the day they lose their empathy for each other, Candy thought as she ran across the street to fetch some Kotex for Tracey. We rely on each other so much sometimes, much more than men do. Take this incident, for example: if they had both been men, and Tracey had come into the garage and whispered to Candy that she was in need of tampons, Candy the man would have laughed loudly and told Tracey to use something else, old underwear or bread or something just as equally absurd. She could imagine the jokes:

Use bread, just don't get a yeast infection.

Just go with the flow, dude.

And then, once the proper products were actually furnished, Candy the man would have held them just out of Tracey's reach, probably right in front of everyone at the rummage sale. It would have been just hilarious.

As it was, and as it should be, Candy came back from her house as quickly as she could with three tampons tucked safely and discretely in her pocket. She took Tracey inside and handed them to her. Tracey disappeared back into the bathroom and Candy went back to her post at the sale, thinking all the time about how men could never handle the things women went through all the time. The Lord God had been correct in giving all the real work to the women. Pregnancies and periods would be the death of men.

*

The crowd at the rummage sale was growing bigger all the time, cars lining up at the curb and people walking in from the sidewalk. The day, though warm, was clear and fine for such a thing as this, and whatever heat there was would be alleviated some by the lemonade.

Tracey came out and stood next to Candy, smiling and saying hello to various customers. Some congratulated her on being married and she wondered how long that would go on. Others asked her when children were coming. Just like that: When are children coming?

Tracey just shrugged and smiled and tried to look like a blushing schoolgirl. At one point three young women flocked around her at once and asked her the same question. These women each had twins and were known as the Twin Trio. They hung together as if having twins marked them as a clique or a cult or a street gang (the Twinners). And despite their attempts to appear calm and content, Tracey could not help but notice how pale and ragged they looked. They had that damn short style-less hairstyle that all young mothers get, apparently the day they leave the hospital, and their faces had gone puffy and slack as their once youthful fitness had disappeared with the demands of motherhood, but there was something else about them, too: they looked like they had had a sizeable chunk of themselves removed. It was in their eyes and the things they talked about. It was in the *way* they talked, in the way they walked, in the way they looked at the world. It was as if some sort of shark had taken a bite out of their former selves. Good God, look at Krissy Means there, she had been a very popular cheerleader in her time, and now, the mother of those twins, she looked dumpy and zombie-like, the latter the result of all that time spent with *Sesame Street* and whatever else passed for children's entertainment these days. A mother tends to lose her mind.

And mercy, how Tracey White envied them.

She felt this envy stir inside of her, as much a physical thing as the shedding of her uterine lining... and

67

not far from the same spot, either. It was like a twinge, a vibration, a rustling. There were things stirring inside of her that she did not fully understand.

The garage was getting full of people. They came up to the check-out table, where Tracey and Candy stood, and where sat the pitcher of lemonade and a big whicker bowl for money, and placed their treasures down. Tracey watched her earlier life as a single person flash before her eyes. And Timmy's too.

Old clothes, old books, old records, old jewelry, old silverware, old toys, old knick-knacks, old salt and pepper shaker souvenirs, old paintings in even older frames. She saw her childhood, her college years, her year spent as a single girl living in the city, she saw it all pass in front of her this day, replaced each time with no more than two dollars and fifty cents. It made her feel both sad and happy: she was watching her old life go out the window, and seeing her new one open with possibilities. She wished Timmy was here so he could be witness to the event, but he was....

She had no idea where he was. He had slipped off on what he called errands that morning and hadn't been back since. Perhaps watching his old life disperse out to the greater populace was too much for him to face.

She watched as their belongings were poured over and snatched up by the eyes and hands of the curious.

It seemed this sale was attracting the elderly in droves. They came in groups of three, and filled the place like chattering liver-spotted clones from Mars. One would think their conversations would be interesting, would be filled with history and wisdom... but one must not have spent much time with the elderly: their conversations rarely contain either. Instead, there is much talk of the trivial, and much misunderstanding, and much bitterness. What a drag it is getting old, indeed.

"Here you go, dear," one tiny little lady said, setting a pretty little fake-pearl necklace down on the table and smiling at Tracey. The woman pointed at the tag on the necklace. "What does this say?" she asked.

Tracey smiled and read the number. "One dollar."

The old woman nodded, started to dig inside of her purse, and, as if it were a Russian nesting doll, pulled out an even smaller purse. She opened this slowly and for a moment Tracey expected to see yet another tiny purse. Instead, the old lady began to count out some coins. She set down three quarters on the table and then went back to the coin-purse, searching.

"Oh no," Candy said next to Tracey, nudging her sharply in the side.

Tracey looked up, and through the milling group of elderly she saw a familiar figure coming up the drive.

It was Carol Slugg.

Of the three types of people that attended rummage sales, Carol Slugg was most definitely a member of the second: she went to see what other people owned, taking it as an opportunity to peer into their lives and see just exactly what sort of lives those were.

"Good thing I'm not selling my vibrators," Tracey whispered to Candy.

Candy put a hand over her mouth to cover her shocked laugh.

As Carol Slugg approached the open garage door, people parted to let her pass. She would probably have seen in this a Biblical image, but to the objective observer it looked instead like villagers stepping out of the way of the local monster. This said, though, it must be understood that no one present wanted to give her the impression that they were repulsed by her, and in fact she had a few friends here. Rather than show their feelings, however, those who wanted little to do with her simply smiled pleasantly as they backed away, offering her perhaps a pleasant and noncommittal "good morning" as they did. Those who might be considered her friends, whether secretly or overtly, wished her a good day and asked her how she'd been doing. She was a pillar of her church, it must be understood… or rather, *wished* she was a pillar of her church, and there were those who wished to graft themselves to her, however tenuously, should she in fact become a major force in church politics at some point in the future.

Most, though, saw her as something to be held at arm's length. Not feared, necessarily, but to be looked at sideways. You wouldn't want the attention of her full gaze, after all. Who knew what she might see? Who knew what one might *become*?

She was the closest thing Burghville had to a Medusa.

The little old lady with the fake pearl necklace found what she was looking for in her coin purse and held up a single quarter. Tracey held her hand out and the lady dropped the quarter into her palm.

With a smile, the old lady started to walk off.

Tracey looked down at the quarter in her hand and stared at it for a moment. At the same time, a young man in his twenties stepped up and asked:

"Do you have any CDs here?"

Tracey stared at the quarter a moment longer, glanced up at Carol Slugg, who was headed straight towards her, and then saw the back of the little old lady as she moved away.

"Excuse me!" she called out to the old woman.

"Do you have CDs here?" the young man asked again.

"Excuse me?" Tracey called. The old woman was pushing her way through the crowd, apparently on a collision course with Carol Slugg, who was approaching along the same line.

"Do you have—" the man started again.

"Excuse me!" Tracey said louder. This time the old woman turned back and smiled. She returned to the table.

"It's no big deal," Tracey said, feeling slightly foolish, "but that necklace was a dollar."

The woman continued to smile. "Yes I know," she said. "Thank you."

"No, I mean..." She held up the quarter. "You only gave me twenty-five cents."

Now the woman frowned. "I put the rest down. I thought you picked it up."

Tracey looked down at the table. "No... I don't think I did." She looked up at Candy, who was watching the approaching Carol Slugg.

"Well, I put three quarters right there," the old woman was saying. "Then I fished for the forth, and I thought you must have picked the rest up."

70

Tracey shook her head, then looked up into the slightly doughy face of this little old lady.

"Forget it," she said, smiling. "Either way, a dollar or twenty-five cents, it's yours."

The woman's smile returned. "Thank you dear," she said, and when she turned to leave the table she found herself face to face with the dour personage of Carol Slugg.

"Oh, Carol," she said. "How nice to see you. Enjoying your day?"

Carol Slugg nodded, and there might have been an attempt at a smile threatening the corners of her mouth.

"I enjoy every day the Lord grants me," she said.

"Of course." And then the old woman was off, moving quicker than she had been before, pushing her old arthritic bones into overdrive to get out of the suddenly uncomfortable garage.

Carol Slugg looked first at Tracey, and then into the face of the young man standing next to her. One could see in his eyes that he wanted to ask again about CDs, but when he looked into Carol Slugg's face the color left his own and he sort of slumped away.

Carol then brought her full attention to Tracey White, who smiled and said, pleasantly:

"How are we doing this morning?"

"*We* are doing fine. But every day presents its challenges which the Lord sets before us. And it's up to us to try and meet those challenges as best we can, in compliance with His wishes."

"I'm going to get more lemonade," Candy Cleaver said, and then she left the garage.

Tracey swallowed and smiled at the woman before her.

A no-man's land had grown around Carol Slugg as everyone moved away from her. It was sort of funny to see the majority of people gathered on one side of the small two-car garage, all of them sweating but none of them wishing to spread out and risk being closer to the Medusa in their midst. Almost at once everyone had found the boxes of old clothes across the room fascinating.

Tracey looked at the open area that had grown around this woman, and then at the woman herself.

71

It wasn't always interesting, what Carol Slugg wore, but it perhaps suggested the sort of person she was, if it isn't quite clear yet, that on this increasingly hot day she was dressed like an Amish woman: all in black, although her formless dress was sleeveless and she was showing more calf than normal. Her straight hair was hanging past her shoulders like weeds down a cliff, but two silver barrettes held thin fragments away from her ears and up over the top of her head. She wore no makeup, and her skin was pale and translucent. Visible blue veins were the only sign that she was made of the same matter as the rest of us.

"Can I help you?" Tracey asked... again, as pleasantly as she could. The image of this tiny woman carrying a cross down the street during the upcoming Memorial Day parade entered her mind and for some reason made her feel cold. Something stirred inside of her at this thought, something far from the stirring of her uterus... something, in fact, that might have the power to stop *that* stirring dead in its menstrual tracks.

"I believe you are the only person who can," Carol Slugg said. She held up an object for Tracey's inspection.

It was a painting in an old frame, and Tracey realized immediately, with a sick feeling, that this painting was one she herself had sold earlier that morning. It depicted a pastoral scene with naked picnickers. She believed it was a poor imitation of some classic work she could not name.

She swallowed dryly and tried to smile. "Two dollars," she said.

"Excuse me?"

"Two dollars. I sold that earlier for two dollars."

Carol Slugg's lips pursed. "I know you did, and that's why I'm here. You sold it to a lady named Dorothy Danning. I saw the poor old soul walking down the street with it, like it was some innocent post-card. Well, you can be sure I took it away from her immediately, told her the errors of her ways, and sent her off with a few suggestions for prayers of penitence. Now, far be it for me to suggest that it is my duty to be moral custodian of this entire town... but someone has to do it, and apparently no one else is stepping up to the plate. I don't think I need to tell you that displays of naked flesh are not something we want to see all over our good streets."

Tracey said nothing.

Carol Slugg stood tall and defiant. People were looking over at the scene cautiously.

"Is this the sort of thing you think you should be selling?"

Tracey's eyebrows raised and she considered the question. She was feeling increasingly confused.

"It was two dollars," she said.

Carol Slugg frowned, not liking the fact that her message was not getting through. She stepped back from the table and regarded Tracey suspiciously.

Candy Cleaver appeared for a moment in the doorway that led to the house, but when she saw that Carol Slugg was still there she turned and disappeared again.

"You should probably give Ms. Danning her money back, and throw this, and whatever else like it you have here, in the trash where it belongs." Slugg set the painting, objectionable side down, on the table.

Tracey nodded and reached for the whicker bowl that was holding the cash. She found one dollar, then another. When she brought them up she saw something strange:

Smoke was rising from between Carol Slugg's legs. It rose slowly, delicately, as if it were being formed by an artistically inclined breeze.

"And might I suggest," Carol Slugg was saying, "that you stop this sale until you've gone through all of your belongings, until you can be certain that there is nothing else... *inappropriate* here." There was a smug little smile on her mouth now, apparently the only sort of smile allowed to her frustrated facial muscles.

Tracey looked at that smoke and frowned. It looked familiar, somehow, rising as it did with deliberate artfulness, straight into the air but twisting over itself like a foggy strand of DNA.

Carol Slugg cocked her head. The smile left her face, replaced with a frown of her own.

"Are you listening to me?" she asked. "I've seen rudeness before, but...."

73

The smoke continued to rise from under the woman, right up the front of her black dress like a magical zipper of cloud. By now Tracey could smell it, sweet and spicy and tinged with memory.

Carol Slugg, offended, looked down at her dress. There was hesitation in the moment between her seeing the smoke and realizing what it was. When her mind registered that it was in fact smoke, she looked up at Tracey with wide eyes. Her skin, if it was possible, had gone a shade or two paler.

"Is it… is it a sign?" she asked, her voice suddenly weak… the same voice she had displayed in the confessional with Father Preston.

Tracey started to shake her head (*I don't know*, not *No*), when a man shouted:

"She's on fire!"

There were screams, some confused running, and then a middle-aged man was crossing the garage and tackling Carol Slugg. He brought her to the cement floor (she made a sound like *Umpff*! when she landed) and then began to roll her around.

"Stop drop and roll!" he shouted over and over like a crazy man, rolling her like one would roll a raw cookie in sugar. "Stop drop and roll!" He pushed her all over the floor, until her dress was covered in gray dust. She, for her part, kept her arms crossed tightly over her chest. Strange sounds came from her mouth. They might have been prayers.

After a time the man stopped rolling her around the floor and she stopped making sounds. Everyone gathered, hovering over her with curiosity. There was silence in the garage.

Carol Slugg was motionless for a moment, and then she slowly climbed to her feet, smoothing out her black dress and dusting it off as well as she could. She even attempted to straighten some now-wild strands of hair, in an effort to regain her lost dignity. She looked at the man who had rolled her around.

"Stop… drop… roll?" he said meekly.

"What if that had been a sign from God?" Carol asked, no anger showing in her voice at all, only a thinly masked fear.

He said nothing.

"Are you all right?" Tracey asked. She felt it was her duty to ask it, since this was her garage.

Carol Slugg looked at her and offered a strange ill-formed smile, punctuating it with a nod of her head.

"How did it happen?" someone asked.

Everyone was looking closely at Carol Slugg's dress, some of them kneeling down to have a look at where it hung between her legs. She, for her part, started to move around, attempting to avoid their eyes. This must have struck her as an invasion of privacy, to say nothing of modesty. In time, though, she herself looked down at her dress, obviously hoping (by the look in her eyes) that there was nothing showing. The sight of undergarments is the simplest doorway to Hell, she had once written in a pamphlet she passed out for Sunday school, the meaning of which was lost to the children.

There was nothing wrong with that dress, besides its lack of style: not one single burn mark, no damage whatsoever beyond a coating of garage dust.

Everyone was quiet, each of them considering what had just happened, each of them staring at Carol Slugg and, perhaps, each of them thinking about spontaneous human combustion.

Each of them, that is, except for Tracey White. She was looking around the garage, searching for something in and around the knees of her customers, something that might be hiding under the tables, or in the shadow-filled corners, or hiding on top of the open garage door. Something that might be, right this minute, laughing its chittering little laugh right behind her, always out of sight, seen only as a blur from the corner of an eye.

She saw and heard nothing.

Candy Cleaver came into the garage again, oblivious to what had happened, smiling as perkily, yet cautiously, as she could. She was carrying a fresh pitcher of lemonade. The garage was so quiet one could hear the ice in that pitcher clinking musically.

"Anyone thirsty?" she asked, before noticing that silence and the look in Carol Slugg's face.

"I'll have some of that," the stop-drop-and-roll man said. He walked quickly over to Candy.

75

"Yeah, me too," said someone else, following.

Soon everyone was sipping fresh lemonade… everyone except Carol Slugg, that is, who marched quickly out of the garage, down the drive, and back to where she came from.

The rummage sale went on without further incident.

4

As Memorial Day approached, the excitement for the parade grew. The meetings of the Jaycees were fevered events at which minor disagreements over parade routes and float order threatened to turn violent. This year's theme, HOW AMERICA HAS MARCHED ON THROUGH THE YEARS was found to be too cumbersome to fit properly on a banner, so it was shortened to AMERICA MARCHES ON, which Candy Cleaver suggested, telling no one that it had been Tracey White's idea. Some things people just did not need to know.

In the weeks leading up to the parade people still found their yards damaged, despite the sometimes copious amounts of seed they spread and nurtured, and those damn mushrooms continued to pop up, despite the anti-fungal powder that was spread everywhere like a rumor. There was a growing fear in Burghville that no one would have decent yards this year, that anyone driving through would think the good citizens of this little community did not care how their yards looked. At least one homeowner on Main Street had put up a sign that read:

MY YARD IS UNDER ATTACK BY A MYSTERIOUS DISEASE! DO NOT THINK I DO NOT CARE HOW MY PROPERTY LOOKS! I AM A PATRIOTIC AMERICAN!

The strange blight had spread all over town now, and it wasn't just grass either: at least one patch of tulips had been found decimated overnight. In fact, most spring flowers were affected in some way, either by having their petals shredded or disappearing altogether. Explanations for all of this were legion, but no one answer had been accepted. To channel their pent-up energies and frustrations, people turned their attentions to their AMERICA MARCHES ON floats.

For some reason, a trend had spread across Burghville to include flowers on the floats. You could look into almost any garage and see a wooden frame, set on a flat-bed trailer, being covered with dyed red and white flowers: tulips, daffodils, roses from the flower shop. And there were some beautiful floats, make no mistake. Award-caliber floats, really. The weeks leading up to the Memorial Day Parade were the most creative period the denizens of Burghville ever experienced.

Interesting to note, however, that most of the people we've met so far in this story did not plan on being in the parade, with three exceptions:

Carol Slugg, who was going to walk the length of the route carrying a large wooden cross, like her savior;

Scooter Boober, who was to walk the parade with a few choice animals from his hobby farm;

And Dick Dick Buckthorn. Although, to be truthful, Dick Dick himself did not plan on actually being in the parade, he simply planned on having a float in the thing. This float would represent Buckthorn Industries, and he was adamant that it be the best looking and most interesting float in the whole parade. To this end he personally selected those folks he felt were the most creative people in his company to work on it. He told these people of his selections himself, walking through his factories and pulling each of them aside to give the good news. At first they worked on it after and before work, and then, in the final week before the parade, Dick Dick pulled them from their work stations and assigned them to the task full-time. All of them were only too happy to do so, since the float was being made under nonexistent supervision in a far corner of one of Buckthorn Industries' warehouses, and those who wanted to could smoke out there as they worked.

77

Smoking was a no-no anywhere near the main buildings, you see: all those chemicals were, among other things, highly flammable.

The town's float-making activity took part in secret, especially in the last week. Few details were shared, new techniques were kept tight, materials were hoarded. Garage windows were darkened. Lips were sealed. Husbands and wives kept mum to their children, the children spoke little to their parents. Few things are more serious than float-making intrigue. Even Timmy White, tapped to work on Dick Dick's float, did not mention much about the project to his wife. In fact, they weren't speaking about much at all these days. There was a strange distance between them, brought about, ironically, by a secret bond they shared with each other. Timmy had still not told her about his dreams, Tracey had not told him about the footprints in the garage, or the incident at the rummage sale. They went through their days in near silence, as if there was tension between them, as if they had had a fight and had not yet made up. But there had been no fight, and there really was no tension. There was simply a single thought, shared between their two brains but not spoken aloud. As the Memorial Day Parade approached, Timmy began to spend more time on the Buckthorn Float, and Tracey contented herself with listening to Candy Cleaver effuse over the coming event. Once or twice, secretly, the White's each pulled down their Scotland photo album and stared at the pictures, frowning.

All in all, though, there were few strange occurrences in the time leading up to the parade. Among these few were the following:

While taking a long and relaxing bath one evening, Candy Cleaver again had the feeling that she was being watched. She sank down until only her nose and eyes were visible over the suds and gazed around her bathroom. It was by no means a large bathroom, so there was no place anyone could hide. But it could be something else, she knew. Ghosts, maybe. Or one of those little cameras people hide everywhere so they can watch you on the Internet. She leaned towards ghosts, in her mind, because she actually felt as if eyes were on her and did not think she would be able to sense a camera. Maybe it was the result

78

of living alone without a man, maybe it was from reading far too many trashy romance novels, but she couldn't help it either way: the thought of ghosts watching her wet naked body excited her to no end;

While walking through her growing and healthy yard one evening, enjoying the smell of fresh vegetation that rose through the air, Henrietta Pratt happened to glance over at her neighbors and see three five-gallon buckets of anti-fungal powder resting there, as if waiting for a massive outbreak of athlete's foot. She wandered to the edge of her property, parted the vines that clung to the trellis and studied the sight. No one had asked her about the blight that was affecting every yard save hers, and she wondered if she should give her opinion freely. But no, not yet. Soon. She turned back, crossed her yard, and went into her home. She made herself some green tea, then sat down in front of the television and found the nature channel. She watched a show about the African savannah for a while, until she sensed that some lions were getting ready to take down a young gazelle, and then she quickly turned the whole thing off. However, instead of silence she found her home filled with... laughter? A high, reed-like little trill of a laugh. And, just before it faded, she heard a tiny voice. The voice said: "Dizzlemuck." After that there was nothing;

A tampon was found on Main Street's North sidewalk by Sheriff Sherman, although at the time he didn't know what it was. It was out of its applicator, but unused. He picked it up by its string and saw that there was a tiny word sewn on its side. The word was NYE-THRESSA. "Litter-bugs," he whispered harshly to himself, placing the tampon into his pocket and moving on;

There was a grass fire in someone's backyard, just a small square of freshly-placed sod burning with an almost Biblical intensity one otherwise quiet night. This fire was quickly put out, but not before the children of the house were given a serious lecture about playing with matches;

Music was heard by many people, a strange percussion-based music that was labeled "African-like" and which was despised by all who heard it. It came from dark yards late at night, but when homeowners rushed out to complain they found nothing but silence and shadow. Again, the blame was placed on "kids";

A family was driving home after a dinner out one evening, the mother and father silent while the children slept deeply in the back of the mini-van. They were making their way through a tiny run of forest, the tires humming pleasantly on the asphalt, the dash lights comfortably faint and green, the whole van like a mechanized womb lulling them into complacency, when something ran across the road. It looked like a tiny person, but was in and out of the headlights so quickly it was impossible to say for sure. Father and Mother looked at each other, then at their sleeping children, then back at each other. Nothing was said. The incident was quickly forgotten. It may have been, after all, a shared delusion brought on by full stomachs and pleasant exhaustion. It may have been a raccoon;

There was a rash of small-time thefts across town, although few noticed and no one realized it was in fact a rash, since the items stolen were relatively unimportant and the result was nothing but minor annoyances all around. The stolen items included, but were not limited to: television remote controls, pens and pencils, balls of yarn, batteries, Scotch tape, cigarette lighters, Play-Doh, a few cereal bowls, safety pins, and some swatches of fabric. These thefts, if noticed at all, were chalked up to the usual disappearances that happen to household items. Certainly no one notified Sheriff Sherman or their insurance companies. The only person who thought something was up was the town's only dentist, who noticed that the gold fillings he kept around as a joke were missing. He suspected his assistant, though he had no proof;

Electrical appliances began to go on the fritz, apparently for no reason. When the utility companies were notified they found nothing wrong. When the cable man was dispatched to investigate seven houses on one single block, he too found nothing wrong... although he did find that he'd been locked out of his truck and had to call a colleague to bring an extra key;

On the Sunday before church, the bells in the St. Michael Catholic Church bell tower failed to produce a rich musical tone: instead there issued forth over the town a horrid dull *clunk* and *thunk* that made people wince and look skyward, as if expecting to see chunks of a Russian satellite hurtling to Earth. When Father Preston investigated he found the altar boy whose job was to ring the bells sitting on the stairs that led up to the tower. The boy said the door from the second landing was locked, prohibiting ascent to the belfry. Father Preston tried the door, found it open, and climbed the rest of the way to the tower. Upon examining the bells he found them in perfect shape, with one exception: their clappers were missing;

During one of her afternoon masturbation sessions, Betty Buckthorn (lying naked on her bed in a beautiful patch of sunshine) thought she smelled smoke. She sat up, inhaling deeply the air that surrounded her. It wasn't bad smoke she smelled, she decided: it was *pipe* smoke, of a sort. Keeping herself to one cigarette a day, she was quite attuned to the odor of tobacco. Leaving her pretty pink vibrator on the bed, she threw on a robe and walked through the large house, following the smell as it coursed into and out of every room. In time that smoke led her to the back porch that overlooked the woods. She stepped out there and smelled nothing but fresh leaves and wet earth. She went back inside and took a few deep sniffs, detecting only the usual odors of her home, dusting products and coffee and Dick Dick's cologne. She shrugged and went back into her bedroom, hoping to finish giving attention to the needs of her body. When she got there she found that the batteries to her vibrator were missing.

*

It was this latter incident that caused the most trouble, because it caused Betty Buckthorn to think one of two things: either someone was in her house, or she was going crazy and there had been no batteries in the thing in the first place. It caused a third response, too, which took on greater significance than anything: pent up with sexual energy, and feeling as frustrated as a homosexual bull, Betty Buckthorn needed, absolutely *needed*, to find orgasmic relief. Hoping to escape those two thoughts (that she was not alone or that she was crazy, neither of which were very conducive to the gentle art of jacking off) she

81

dressed and took her car to Buckthorn Industries. She would surprise Dick Dick in his office, seduce him as quickly as possible, then make him service her right there. Then they would go home together and he could make sure the house was not occupied by a stalker. She thought of that time when she had taken the trash out and the gate had locked on her. Perhaps someone *was* stalking the Buckthorns. It was a serious thought.

But not so urgent as the horniness of a healthy nymphomaniac.

She was nearly in a froth as she sped across town towards her husband's factory. On her way she lit a cigarette and sucked it off so quickly it was done before she'd gone two miles. She rolled down her window and tossed the butt out to the street. Just two seconds later red and blue lights filled her rearview mirror.

"Shit!" she hissed.

It was Sheriff Sherman.

She debated a high-speed chase, then decided against it and pulled over. The Sheriff pulled in behind her and waited a while, a long while, before he climbed his fat ass out and sauntered up to her window. She looked out at him with her prettiest smile.

"Good afternoon, Sheriff," she said pleasantly.

"Where's the fire?" he asked, his tone all business. There was a toothpick between his lips, bobbing up and down as he chewed it.

In my pants, she thought, but said: "Was I speeding?"

"Fifty-seven in a twenty-five."

She frowned. "Oh, well... see, Dick Dick called me from his office. He needed something from home, something important."

"Really? What?"

"His checkbook."

"His checkbook?"

"Yes. He... he needs it for... something business-related. I'm not really sure what it is."

"Oh." The sheriff seemed to think about this for a moment. "Important, huh?"

"Yes, very."

82

He nodded thoughtfully, staring over the top of her car to something in the distance. The toothpick went up, down, back up again. After another long while he looked at her.

"I'll give you an escort," he said, with such solemnity one would have thought he'd been waiting all his life to say those words (and one would be right).

She smiled and reached out to touch his arm. "Thank you!" she said.

"No need to thank me," he said. "Buckthorn Industries is the life-blood of this town. We can't have anything going wrong there, can we?"

"No," she agreed.

He went back to his cruiser and pulled away with his lights and siren blazing. She squealed out behind him and together they roared across town, a little pre-Memorial Day parade of their own.

*

"Mr. Buckthorn, your wife is here to see you!"

Dick Dick looked up at the intercom on his desk. He stared at it for a full ten seconds before he looked back down at the woman between his legs. For a moment he did not know which to give his attention to, the woman or the intercom, but finally the woman fellating him took her lips from his penis and smiled.

"I suppose you want me to stop," said Polly Anderson, she of the Unlimited Executive Services. She had come in a few days early, having found some free time in her schedule. Dick Dick said great, hang around town for a few days, see the parade, come to the office, it'll be good.

"Ummmm…" he said now, thinking… or trying to think.

There was a knock on the door and an attempt to turn the doorknob.

Polly licked him teasingly. "Well?"

Dick Dick's mind, so adept at quick business decisions, struggled and groaned like a crashing computer. It was almost possible to hear a motor running inside his skull, searching for a suitable response to this sudden crisis.

He looked from the door to the smiling young woman kneeling at his wilting penis.

And then he had a thought.

*

It was something you don't see every day, outside of the movies. Certainly it was something that Timmy White had never expected to witness:

As he was standing outside of the warehouse that was housing the Buckthorn Industries float, unpacking a fresh delivery of blue roses, he happened to glance over to the office building. From this angle he had a view of the wall of windows that marked Dick Dick Buckthorn's office. Usually when a person looked up there they did nothing but wonder who cleaned those windows, being as they were a good forty-feet above the ground. But that was not Timmy White's thought this afternoon as he stood outside in the bright sun. Not at all. *His* thought was:

Who the hell is the hot woman up there on the ledge?

She saw him looking at her. As she stood there casually, just as if she were standing on the ground taking a cigarette break, she gave him a little wave. The sort of wave that consisted only of seductively wriggling fingers.

Timmy White waved back sheepishly, then glanced around to see if anyone else was witness to this scene. There was no one.

He looked back at the woman (she was putting on makeup now; there was a flash of compact-mirror-reflected sunlight), then sighed and continued with his work.

*

These were the only strange occurrences in the days immediately prior to Burghville's Memorial Day parade. The rest of the time was full of the same normalcy that was Burghville's special forte: a rather mindless normalcy, an expectation of the mediocre. People lived their lives in Burghville expecting things to stay the same, expecting a comforting blanket of dullness, of predictability, to envelope every waking moment. This was the *reason* people lived in Burghville. They wanted nothing to happen, or, if things were bound to happen, they wanted them to be benign and non-threatening. Excitement was indeed enjoyed in Burghville, it was just that the townsfolk preferred it to be an excitement of the predictable and safe kind. The status quo was not only embraced in Burghville, it was expected. No one wanted anything to enter their lives that would upset the delicate balance between comfort and dullness that they had worked so hard to achieve.

This year's Memorial Day parade, however, was about to disappoint them.

5

Memorial Day. It started beautifully, the dawn clouds pushing out early and leaving a sky of heavenly blue in their wake. There had been a minor chance of rain but by midmorning all that was left to even suggest precipitation was a cooler touch to the air. The sun was bright and proud in the sky, and everyone woke feeling that this was going to be a perfect day for a parade. Not too warm, not too cold, not too windy. Just right.

Carol Slugg began her day, as she did them all, with a long prayer session at the side of her bed. She held a crucifix in her hands, clasping it as if it were a safety line and she a drowning woman, and wordlessly mouthed her plea to her lord. One of the things she did was thank Him for providing the strange blight that had befallen the lawns of Burghville, therefore ensuring the further economic security of Buckthorn Industries and, by turn, the town itself. With everything economically in line, she felt, it would be easier for the townsfolk to seek the one true path to salvation... the path she herself had already found. With

85

each increase in pesticide and herbicide production the town was one step closer to realizing she'd been right all along, that her way was the right way, the only way. When a soul no longer needs to worry about the necessities of life it can then have the peace of mind to worry about the necessities of the *afterlife*. So praise be to Him for the strange grass disease! Praise be to Him for the ugly mushrooms! Praise be to Him for the need to make chemical killers! Praise the Lord!

She made the sign of the cross, then smiled. Downstairs, right smack dab in her livingroom, sat her own cross, the one she would carry with pride down the streets of Burghville as a reminder to the good people of this town that they had responsibilities to the Lord Jesus Christ. It was six and a half feet long and weighed close to eighty pounds... and it had been lovingly polished, like a Victorian banister. She had done this work herself, humming favorite hymns as she did.

She rose from her knees, feeling happy and content. She went to her window and looked out at the clear morning. God's beauty lay over the town, falling as golden light on the grass-less yards across the street. She felt like crying, and then remembered the sign she had received at Tracey White's garage sale. A minor miracle, she had to admit, certainly not up there with parted seas and burning bushes, but more than most could claim. She had asked Him many times what the sign had meant but had gotten no answer. There was a chance, of course, that it could have been a sign from Satan. She felt it was completely rational to believe that God and the Devil would fight over a soul like hers. Would she know the difference when each of their voices called to her?

She made another sign of the cross, asking God for guidance and clarity of vision. And strength, too, that she may be able to carry her own cross as her Savior did His, that she might not stumble on her route... or, if she did stumble, that it be three times, like Jesus on the way to Golgotha.

Outside, there was a roll of drums. She looked out the window again, knowing it was only a quick little practice roll by a high-school drummer warming up, but searching anyway, just in case, for something else... the sight of a single white dove rising into the air, maybe, on the current of the Lord's breath. But there was nothing.

Just some squirrels scampering up a tree. Nothing Godly at all, she decided, turning away.

*

Besides the high-school marching band, there were other musical participants in the parade: the middle-school band, a very raw elementary school band (which preferred nose-picking to practice), and the Burghville Bagpipers. The latter were all older men, none younger than fifty, who for various reasons had taken up the pipes as a hobby. Prior to the start of the parade each of these groups of musicians sent a few notes into the air, as either quick practice or, in the case of the youngest players, as a form of aural vandalism. Particularly horrid were the attempts by the elementary trumpeters. It was, however, the sound of the bagpipes screeching melodically into the morning that woke Tracey and Timmy White. He rolled over and looked at her.

"I was dreaming about Scotland," he said.

Her eyes widened as if she'd been suddenly shocked and she sat up quickly and swung her feet from the bed. "Do you want coffee?" Before he could answer she was out of the room, as if she'd been awake all along and had simply been waiting for the sound of his voice before she got up.

We should talk, he wanted to call after her, but he did not. He put his head back down on his pillow and stared at the ceiling.

Across town, the bagpipes droned again, wheezing cheerily for just a moment before being replaced by the sound of moaning trombones. For a second, that split second when he first woke, he had actually thought he might be back in Scotland, freshly married, enjoying a vacation in a lovely and strange country. But no, he was here, in Burghville, good old Burghville. He closed his eyes and fell back to sleep.

*

87

Also waking this day to the sound of the pipes was Father Preston. The bagpipers were letting their instruments squawk like dying chickens only a block from his home, and the sound went through his skull, stirred his dream-thoughts into mush, and were then promptly altered into a ripe headache. He sat up and looked out his bedroom window. There, directly across the street, was the St. Michael's Catholic Church. He stared at it for a moment, trying his hardest to recall the dream he'd been having just before those pipes began to screech and moan. He'd been having dreams every night lately. Vivid dreams, too, probably too vivid for a priest to have. He knew very well that most of them were dreams of the girl, Helen Keller. He had not seen her at all since he'd found her house dark and silent, had not heard anyone mention her name. Sometimes he wondered if she had even existed. She could very well have been part of the most vivid dream of all.

This morning's dream proved impossible to recall. He sat there on the bed trying to conjure it for a few moments, then rubbed his eyes and stood with a groan. He sighed, yawned, and leaned back to stretch his spine. There was a symphony of vertebrate protests. He looked out the window again.

St. Michael's Church loomed there, not at all invitingly: a solid brick façade with heavy wooden doors, steep front steps, and thick stained-glass windows that might have been thought of as pretty in another era but which now looked cold and distant. There was nothing about those windows that would suggest to a passerby that this was a building worth entering, a place offering sanctuary. Rather, there was the feeling that what awaited someone beyond those doors was a reprimanding. A lecture. A sermon. The holy ass chewing.

Churches, Father Preston sometimes thought, ought to look like restaurants where you can get a nice homey meal. They ought to be warm and inviting, and comfortable as sin inside.

Instead, they were large and imposing and cold and you had to sit on hard pews that had been built not for comfort but to keep half-awake parishioners from falling back to sleep.

"Pains in the ass," he said softly to this morning. And then, aside from *that* discomfort, there was all the noise: screeching choir members, pulsing organs, the banging of the bells. At least for a while there had been respite from the latter.

An odd turn of events, that theft of the clappers from the church tower, although, truth be told, he could understand it. Probably it was some cranky neighbor, driven to said crankiness by the gonging and banging of those damn things. They were loud, too, those bells, you could feel them in your chest if you stood outside on the church's front steps. Someone was probably sick of being woken by them every Sunday morning. There were hard-working people in this town, and for a lot of them Sunday was the only day they had to sleep in. It was a day of rest, after all.

Father Preston had actually considered *not* replacing those clappers, but he was confronted by many members of his congregation who had asked him how much it would cost and if the church had enough funds or insurance and how soon, dear Father, before our beautiful bells could be fixed? He had no choice. He had called around to find a place where he could order them and had found something called the Quasimodo Bell Company. The person on the other end of the line had asked questions about the bells that Father Preston had not been able to answer, so he'd been forced to put the guy on hold while he ran up the tower to find numbers and sizes and whatever else the guy had requested. During this forced exercise he had realized how out of shape he had become. Walking was one thing, and walking was good exercise, but he knew he needed more. One of these days he would take up jogging. He would become known around town as the Running Priest, and there might be those who would frown at the sight. They could go to hell.

He stared at his church this morning and tried to regain his thoughts. Memorial Day. Did he have to do anything? Was there a need for those bells to ring today? He didn't think so. He turned and went into his kitchen. The house the congregation provided for its priest was small but nice, as comfortable a place as he had ever lived, and his favorite place was the kitchen, which was open and blessed with lots of counter-space.

He thought about this: he liked open kitchens but not open churches. Did this mean anything? He thought not.

Outside the trombones were groaning and someone did a quick roll on a snare drum. Father Preston's headache throbbed, and the first thing he did was swallow two aspirin. Then he wondered if he could simply stay inside his house all day, huddled under blankets while everyone else watched their grand parade. He wasn't needed out there, after all, this was not a holy day, he was not slated to ride in a convertible down Main Street, or sit atop a float, or waive from atop a fire truck. No one would know he was missing. He could not imagine a situation happening today where someone would need to utter the words: *Where is Father Preston?*

And really, that made it the best sort of day.

*

The Buckthorns took the opportunity this morning, at the instigation of Betty Buckthorn, to have a quick roll in the hay. Afterwards, while Dick Dick showered, Betty stepped out onto the deck for this day's cigarette. Her robe was not tied tightly and as a result opened with a morning breeze, exposing her naked breasts and stomach to the forest. She stood there smoking her cigarette and wondered what the woodland creatures thought, seeing her body this way. She wondered, as well, what a peeping tom would think. After she went to Dick Dick's office that day (where he seemed unusually enthusiastic to see her) they returned home and Dick Dick had gone over the entire house, searching for signs of intruders. He found nothing, though he frowned at the vibrator on the bed and mumbled something about how if someone saw that they would think he was less of a man. She told him that if his tongue could vibrate a thousand times a second, and was always around whenever she needed it, she would gladly toss that toy in the trash. He just shook his head.

No signs of an intruder. Why did that not comfort her? She wondered if she was crazy. Maybe there really *had* been no batteries in the damn vibrator. Maybe she'd been too damn horny to even notice. And what about the smell of tobacco?

Now think about that, he'd told her. Would an intruder break out a cigarette?

It wasn't a cigarette, she said. It was a pipe.

So would an intruder break out a pipe? Maybe you're just under stress.

He had actually said that: Maybe you're just under stress. She'd wanted to ask him just exactly what stress that was, but left the topic alone.

Now, out here on the deck with the woods below her, she stuck the cigarette between her lips and closed her robe. If there *was* a peeping tom, she would make the son of a bitch work for a view. She took a series of deep drags on the cancer stick, then buried the butt deep in a flower pot that was sitting there. Somewhere under all that dirt was a whole tribe of butts, one a day for the past month.

Just moments after she crushed the cigarette out Dick Dick opened the patio doors and came out onto the deck.

"Beautiful morning," he said, coming up behind her for a bear hug.

"Smells so fresh," she whispered.

He inhaled, then sighed. "I can't smell anything, honey. You know my nose is shot."

She turned her head so that he could kiss her cheek. She closed her eyes at the feel of him, a giant of a man, solid of chest and arms, a mountain of flesh and bone.

"I'm not sure what to wear," he said. "I want to dress like I own this town."

"Don't you?"

He smiled and kissed the top of her head. "Not yet."

"We're not *riding* in this thing, are we?" she asked.

"No, but I'll be pressing the flesh on the sidewalk."

"Will the mayor be there?"

Dick Dick smiled. This was sort of a joke: the mayor of Burghville was a man named Darrow who rarely came to town. He spent most of his time in Florida, in fact,

91

so was mayor in name only, but no one seemed to mind, not with things in Burghville running so smoothly.

"Mayor Darrow," said Dick Dick, "could be dead, for all we know."

"Does he even exist?"

"I've met him. Once. I think." He kissed the top of his wife's head again. "Listen, could you get the coffee started while I dress?"

"Sure."

"Good." Another kiss. "You are the best wife in the world."

"Really?"

"Absolutely. Stick with me and you're gonna go far."

After he went back into the house she stayed on the deck a moment longer. There was something about this morning, a certain slant in the sunlight perhaps, that was just a bit... odd, that was the word. Odd. She squinted out at the woods, searching for a glimpse of smoke rising from behind a log. There had been two instances related to smoke so far: first, the curls rising from the woods that day she took the garbage out (something which had not been repeated on subsequent trash days), and then that smell in the house. Maybe it was all the result of a brain tumor, and would that be better or worse than insanity? Better, she decided. A tumor was respectable.

She saw nothing in those woods below. And the strangeness of this morning could be chalked up to the anticipation of that day's parade. It was not, however, a *good* anticipation: she was not looking forward to it at all. Dick Dick might be a pro at pressing the flesh, but she was not. And parades had never been her thing. Just organized traffic jams, was how she saw them.

Memorial Day, she thought. What a crock.

She went back inside to make the coffee.

*

Candy Cleaver was running up and down the growing line of parade participants, smiling at everyone and saying "good morning" until it hurt her throat to do so. She'd been up early this morning. Much work to do, after

92

all. She and other excited members of the Jaycees were walking amongst the floats and bands and clowns, making sure everybody had what they needed and knew what they were doing. These women personified the term "bright-eyed and bushy-tailed." This flower-ridden, motley-colored physical realization of the theme AMERICA MARCHES ON, growing longer and longer as more floats and wagons pulled up curb-side, got them wide-eyed and weak-kneed.

"It's going to be a wonderful parade," Candy said to someone. Not five minutes later she said it to someone else: "It's going to be a wonderful parade." Then she added: "A long line of wonderful."

On this clear and fresh May morning, no one noticed the slight odor of chemical-enhanced pine on her breath. Or maybe they mistook it for mouthwash.

*

Also up early this morning was Henrietta Pratt, again wandering her garden as the sun rose. Her yard was doing well, if she thought so herself. The blight that had attacked everyone else's grass and flowers had still not set foot in her yard, and there wasn't a mushroom in sight. As the sun broke over the horizon like an egg, spilling its golden yoke over the town, birds flew to her feeders and began greeting her with song. She paused in her work to look up at them, offering them a bright smile. It was promising to be a beautiful day. She even liked parades, and planned on going down with a lawnchair and sitting in front of the library to watch the floats and marching bands pass. Something about a parade just *reeked*, pleasantly, of summer, and of course there was the delight to be had in seeing the library lawn, which was a native species of little bluestem she had had a hand in placing. Like her own yard, the library lawn was untouched as yet by the blight and mushrooms.

Only one thing kept the day from being completely pleasant, one thing buzzing in the back of her mind like a mosquito:

That word: *Dizzlemuck.*

Unlike Betty Buckthorn, Henrietta Pratt did not think she was crazy. She knew with certainty that there had been odd laughter in her house, knew with certainty that someone had uttered the word *dizzlemuck*.

But who? Children?

Most likely. Children could be a joy to behold, but she also knew they could be evil as well. Those who would pontificate on the pure innocence and unbroken wonder of childhood are living a delusion. The thing with children's minds is they are open... but they are just as open to evil as to good.

But if it had been children she had not found any. The little bastards could have snuck out before she could catch them, but if they came again she would be ready. There were, after all, many ways to skin a cat, and just as many ways to trap a kid.

Dizzlemuck. What was that, some hip new swear word?

She took hold of a handful of young renegade dandelions and ripped them from the ground with a sound like shredding flesh. When the sun was high enough to send the last of the evening's shadows running she sat back on her heels and admired her yard again. It was turning into a completely native wonderland, which was the plan all along, of course.

A cardinal sang to her, echoed by a flock of finches, and somewhere from her front yard cooed a mourning dove, a little chamber-orchestra of birdsong trilling a pleasant, lovely number. And then the bagpipes started up, suddenly silencing the birds. A moment later the trombones groaned. The marchers would be lining up already, all of them excited. Who didn't love a parade?

Henrietta stood tall, stretching her back. Through a small opening in her bushes she saw neighbor kids two yards over, running and laughing like typical seven year-olds. She walked to that opening to have a closer look, and saw they were throwing a small football around.

The sight of that little football reminded her of the pipe. Had it been the kids' as well? She thought not. At least, not kids *that* age. It could very well belong to their older siblings. But what had it been for? Not pot, she'd already decided it was like no pot she'd ever smelled.

94

Perhaps they had just snuck some of their dad's pipe tobacco and thought it would be cool to take a few drags. Then, after getting sick, they had tossed it into her yard. Possible, and yet...

It was so *tiny*, that pipe, so like a toy.

She watched the kids a moment longer, just to see if they ever looked her way, just to see if they had guilty faces, and then she turned and crossed her flowering yard.

Which was when she found the sparrow.

*

On a side street off of Main they lined up, a murmur of excitement growing along their ranks as coffee and nicotine and parade-buzzes kicked in. Thirty floats in all, the already-mentioned marching bands, the various clowns, the fire engines, the car made of wood (a favorite of everyone), the ten horses, the bag-pipers, the contestants hoping to be this year's Memorial Day Queen, the Knights of Columbus in their mini-cars, Carol Slugg with her life-sized crucifix, flat-bed trucks carrying local bands (two country, one old-time rock-and-roll), some brand-new John Deere tractors, a bunch of old men on riding lawnmowers, and a group of men and women dressed in Revolutionary War clothing. The only ingredient missing was Scooter Boober and his hobby-farm beasts.

*

Helen Keller was on her way into town when she spotted the dwarf and his animals.

She'd been marching along through the woods next to an old country road, preferring the feel of forest ground beneath her feet to the hard impersonal floor of asphalt, preferring as well the cool moistness under that canopy to the anger of the burning sun. After a time she looked over to that road, hearing the sudden jangle of bells, and saw three very large creatures walking there. She crept closer to the road for a better look.

One llama, one Holstein bull, and one strange-looking thing with insanely red hair and gigantic horns. The hair of this latter animal was long, especially on its

95

head, so that it hung over the eyes like bangs, as if the creature were a cross between a cow and a Beatle circa 1964. She'd never seen anything like it.

She watched the little man behind these animals, improbably controlling them with single leather leashes attached to each of their belled-collars. He appeared to be mouthing words to them, but she couldn't hear anything. It was a sight to see, really: this tiny man, barely four-feet tall, marching along behind these great beasts, any one of which could have flattened a man three times his size. But the animals never cast so much as a look back at him, instead walked down the road calmly, their feet making *clop* sounds on the asphalt. The little man, for his part, allowed just the barest amount of slack to develop between himself and the animals. He looked, aside from his size, like any other content gentleman farmer: new jeans, a clean white shirt buttoned all the way to the neck, and a tan cowboy hat.

Helen Keller did not know which sight was the oddest: the little man with the big animals, the sight of a llama walking along calmly with two cattle, the fact that one of those cattle was a *bull*, or that strange-looking red cow with the long hair. She wondered if the man had invented that breed himself.

She watched him for a moment as he walked, and then she realized something about him, her Sight revealing just two things with sudden clarity:

The little man hated his job at Buckthorn Industries and was planning on quitting that summer to dedicate himself to his hobby farm, and he had once been deeply in love with someone, a woman of normal height. Beyond this she could tell nothing. He had loved the woman, but Helen could not tell if the love was reciprocated. Some things stayed fuzzy, even for her.

She bit her bottom lip, looked back into the woods, and then stepped out and onto the old road. The sun was brilliant and sharp, and she was glad she had dressed as she had: khaki shorts with a dark green tank-top. Standing there for a moment, she took in that sun slowly, let it rest on her skin, tried to acclimate herself to it as if it were a bath of hot water. Then she put some loose strands of hair behind her ears and walked out to the little man and his animals.

"Hello!" she called.

He looked up at her. Nodded.

"Are you in the parade this year?" she asked.

He nodded again.

She squinted towards the sun. "You'd better hurry. It's pushing ten-thirty."

He said nothing.

She walked alongside him for a time, watching the three furry ass-ends in front of her. Each of them wiggled distinctively: the llama primly, the bull cockily, and the shaggy red cow deliberately.

"How do you keep that bull in line?" she asked. "I thought they were supposed to be ornery."

He cocked his head a bit, considering the question. Then he shrugged.

"It's a matter of respect," he said in time, his voice high-pitched yet pleasant. The bull turned its head to glance at the little man with a great black eye.

Helen nodded. "You listen to him, in other words."

"And he listens to me."

"That's how I am with my snakes."

He looked up at her. "Snakes?"

"I like snakes," she said simply, watching the animals.

He nodded and readjusted his leashes. The sun was glinting off tiny shards of glass on the road, as if they were walking a path of diamonds.

"My name's Helen," she said finally.

He nodded.

"Helen Keller."

He took all three leashes in one hand and offered her the free one. "Scooter Boober."

She shook his hand, then looked back down the road. "What if someone comes?"

"They go around."

She nodded. "So... a llama, a bull... and what do you call this other girl?"

"Jennifer."

"Jennifer..."

97

He looked up at her. "Her name's Jennifer."

*

Sheriff Sherman pulled up in front of Henrietta Pratt's house and killed the engine of his cruiser. This was a strange lady, he thought. And yet pleasant enough, never trouble. Like most people in this boring town, never trouble.

He found her in her backyard, which looked to him like a movie where the plants had started to rebel: they were everywhere, on every surface. The little square of grass she had was not like any grass he had ever seen, and though she claimed to abhor weeds it looked to him as if there was nothing here *but* weeds. Most people tore out plants like these, ugly scratchy-looking things that seemed more appropriate for deserts and old fields. It was a cluttered yard, not to his taste at all. Could she even *mow* that strip of yard? It was too small to make even three passes with an average-sized mower. Maybe, he thought, she just came out here with scissors, got on her hands and knees, and started clipping away. To each her own.

"Sheriff!" she said as he approached her. In one hand she was holding a pair of clippers, with the other she removed her straw sun-hat and pushed a loose curl of hair from her forehead.

Curls, thought the sheriff. A woman her age should not have hair like that: wild, curly, free. It wasn't right.

He nodded in his professional way. "Morning, Miss Pratt. You called?"

"Yes. Absolutely. The poor thing. This way," and she turned and led him through a group of tall ragged-looking flowers and over to a small patch of open lawn. The smell of flowers and leaves was heavy in this yard, thick with a spice like none he had ever smelled before. Sheriff Sherman had a thought:

Henrietta Pratt was a sort of hippie-ish woman... what exactly *does* she have growing here?

He looked around, searching for anything unsavory. Trouble was, it *all* looked unsavory to him... even the savory growing in the pot in her kitchen would

98

have looked unsavory to him. Any of these plants could be exotic narcotics he had never heard of, right here, under his nose. Oh, she could be brash, she could be brash indeed. A major supplier of drugs right here, under the façade of this innocent little woman.

"You sure got a lot of interesting plants," he said suspiciously.

She ignored him: "Here he is."

He looked down at the bird lying there.

It was a house sparrow, obviously dead. Equally obvious was the cause of death: there was a small arrow through its chest.

Sheriff Sherman frowned. "What the hell...?"

"I don't know if this is relevant," she said, pulling something from a pocket. "But I found this a while back, too. Out here."

He took the object and his frown deepened. It was a little pipe.

"It smelled like tobacco," she said.

He brought it to his nose, smelled nothing.

"Seems to be a lot of tiny little things around this Spring," he said, mostly to himself.

"What do you mean?"

He brought out his own object, which had been sitting in a pocket of these pants since he had found it a week ago. He held it in his palm for her to look at.

Henrietta Pratt put her hand over her mouth, stifling a giggle.

He frowned. "What?"

"Do you know what that is?"

He thought about it. "No."

"That there, Sheriff, is what you might call a feminine hygiene product."

He looked down at it, saw nothing that would suggest it owned such a long name, it was just a small cylinder of cotton with a string hanging from one end. "A what?"

"A tampon."

He immediately dropped it to the yard. "Oh Jesus!"

Now she giggled openly. "What on earth were you doing with it?"

99

He looked sick. "I found it on Main Street. I thought... I thought it... oh hell, I don't know what I thought. Jesus, 'scuse my language, but Jesus H. why don't they label those things better?"

"*Label*? Better?"

"Yeah, there's a label on its side."

Henrietta Pratt bent and picked up the tampon.

"Hey, don't!" he said.

"Relax, Sheriff. It's unused." She held it in her hand and looked at it closely. Sure enough, on its side, was the word: NYE-THRESSA. "Now what in the world is that?" she whispered.

"Don't they all look like that?"

"Sort of," she said, looking at him. "But most of them don't have words *hand-stitched* on them."

"Hand-stitched?" He bent over her hand, studying the stitching.

"Hand-stitched. Remarkable work, really... but why?"

He sighed and shook his head. Standing tall, he gazed across her yard and into an unseen distance. "Crazies out there, Miss Pratt. They're starting to come into town." He thought of his Plan. "Someday we'll have to do something about that, and in my opinion we'd do best to act sooner rather than—"

"This is weird," she said. She looked down at the bird. The tiny arrow, about five-inches long, stuck straight up from under its feathers, like a flag pole from a courthouse lawn.

"Not as weird as it's gonna get," he said, still thinking of the Plan... lost in it, in fact, as one would be lost in a dream of rivers and hills.

"Pipes and tiny craftworks are one thing, Sheriff," she said, offering him the tampon and, when he refused, taking her pipe back. "But I won't have anyone killing my birds. I invite these creatures into my yard for sanctuary and food, I won't stand for anyone abusing that for cheap and sick thrills."

He nodded. "Of course... of course." He bent down and picked up the bird, tried to remove the arrow. When he could not, he looked at Henrietta Pratt. "I'll look into it."

"Please." Then she smiled prettily and he was taken aback for a second. She really was a lovely woman, despite her need to keep such a strange yard.

He nodded. "Enjoy the parade, Miss Pratt," he said, and then he was gone, carrying the dead sparrow to his cruiser, placing it on the seat next to him, and wondering, just briefly, if this could be a sign of something major afoot. He could hope, could he not?

*

"You know, I never knew it before, but there's a lot of wisdom in the ass-end of a bull," said Helen Keller. "All of sudden, just looking at all that muscle, I realized that there's a lot of dignity in being a purely physical animal. I mean more than sex, of course, but sex included. What do you think, Mr. Boober?"

"Do you see any balls?" he asked.

She frowned, considering the question and its implications (did he mean, like, *ever?*) and then looked back between the bull's legs. Nothing dangled there, just a stalk-like lump dangling from a thick copse of coarse hair, the holster for his great cock.

"No," she said. "I guess I don't. You're saying he's no longer a sexual animal."

"I'm saying," he said slowly, "that you are right, there *is* nothing wrong with being a purely physical being. This bull is indeed sexual. I'm also saying it's perfectly natural to be interested in things even when you don't exactly have the capacity to act on them."

She nodded and walked in silence for a while before deciding on the right words and the right tone with which to say:

"You were once in love with someone. A woman of normal height. Who was she and what happened to her?"

He looked up at her from under the brim of his little cowboy hat, then suddenly pulled his three animals to a stop, removed that hat to reveal sandy-colored hair, pulled a kerchief from a pocket, and wiped at his forehead. The kerchief away again, he looked back at her.

"You're an interesting girl," he said. Then, the hat back on his head, he prodded his beasts onward.

Helen put her hands in the back pockets of her shorts and looked once more down the road. It lay stretched behind her as straight as a belt, dull gray and uninviting. There were reasons aplenty why she avoided traveling on such things. Imagine, she thought to herself, some people drive for hours on asphalt strips each day, never utilizing the freest and most wonderful mode of transport of all: their own legs. Sad.

She looked back at the man and his animals. They were making good and steady progress towards town, the little man in the middle of the road with the three beasts in front. They all moved smoothly, without fuss, like figures in a fairy tale book. She watched the four until there grew a rise of shimmering heat between herself and them and then she ran down the road to catch up.

"So who was she?"

"Who was who?"

"The woman you loved?"

He said nothing for a moment, then brushed a fly away and smiled. "That was a long time ago. An old story. And the oldest stories are the least interesting."

"That's not true. The oldest stories are the ones with the most to offer."

"You are a very different sort of girl." He gave a gentle little tug on the ropes to speed his animals up. Amazing the way he did this: intuitive, instinctual. Helen thought there was magic in the way he worked them. She fell back a pace again and just watched the four of them. A strange tableau.

After some time he looked up at her and shrugged. "She loved me back, which is the tragic part. It was her family that broke us up. They didn't approve of me."

"That's a shame."

He shrugged again. "Few people like that which is different from them. Few realize how rare and wonderful it is to be different. I can tell you do." Then he fell silent.

"I'm not so different, you know," she said after they had walked some distance in this comfortable silence.

He said nothing. From this angle she could see only a bit of his face, but she knew what he was thinking: he wanted her to talk so he did not have to.

"I mean," she continued, "maybe compared to society, sure, I'm different. But who wants to follow society? Societies form from people who need structure, who need to be told which paths to follow, who need to be told how to think and feel. I've never needed those things."

She wiped sweat from above her eyes and looked around at the landscape they were passing through: fields stretched out on the right, on the left spread the cool shadows of the forest. On the far side of the fields, past broken fences, she could see old dilapidated farms. Struggle was everywhere. Like joy, too. And happiness. And sadness. And death. And life. Everywhere.

"But that's an old story," she said. "Society versus the individual. Hardly worth mentioning, actually. An ancient topic. And the benefit of being an individual and going against the grain can be seen, in fact, from before Man was able to even fathom such a thing as *ancient*. Think of evolution as being evidence of the benefit of individualism. I mean, primordial sludge would never have evolved into more complex life forms had not at least a few of those early bacterium had the balls and gall to become worms. And those worms would never have gotten anywhere had not a few of them said fuck it, I want to be something else, a fish, perhaps, or whatever. And then there's the great ancestor of our fishes today, who looked out at the dry world above the water line and dreamt of what lay beyond. These were all individuals, going against the grain of their societies. In that sense, it seems to me the best people today are those who follow different drummers."

She looked at him. He just kept walking the same way he'd been walking all along, but at last he looked up to her.

"A person shouldn't *try* to be an individual, though," he said. His voice had a coarseness that made her think it must have a fine bluesy quality when he sang. A reedy voice hardened and enriched by hard liquor. "If you have to try to be different, how different are you really?" He looked back at his animals, adjusted his straps. "A

103

person should be themselves. If you're different, then so be it. If you're not, if you're a sheep, then so be that."

She agreed. "The world needs sheep. I'm just saying a person should not be persecuted because they're different. They should be celebrated, even envied. When Mankind evolves, it will be those people who will lead the way."

No sound for a while but that of their shoes on the old asphalt. They climbed a hill and saw the town beyond it, good old Burghville lying like a tumor between the fields and the forest.

Finally Scooter Boober stopped his animals again and looked up at her. She studied that face, found it a handsome one: lines around the eyes gave him character, and his mouth was firm and strong, as was the chin it set upon. She thought he resembled a shrunken Robert Redford, in his heyday. Maybe a shrunken Brad Pitt, a Brad Pitt that had been placed in a dryer for too long.

"I said you were an interesting girl," he said. "I wasn't judging. It was a fact. And it was a compliment."

She nodded as she stared into his eyes. "All right. Thanks."

He returned the nod, even tipped his hat cowboy-style, and then once more urged his animals down the road.

*

They made quite the sight coming into town: the beautiful young girl in the very short khaki shorts and the apparently shrinking tank-top, and the dwarf farmer behind his animals. In fact, when first seen from the front it simply looked like she and she alone was walking alongside the beasts, Scooter Boober being hidden behind their massive bodies. Heads turned indeed when they came down the road where the parade was lined. Eyes went from Helen Keller's tan and muscular legs to the patiently marching creatures she was in company with, and when at last the man could be seen those eyes widened at the sight: such a small man controlling such beasts (and a *bull* nonetheless!) with effortless ease.

They walked alongside the resting parade until he came to where he was scheduled to be, right at the front of the procession. Clowns were in place behind him, ready for poop detail with shovels and scoops. Nobody said anything to Scooter Boober as he took his place, they simply made room for his beasts.

Helen waved goodbye to him and continued on alone, walking past the gathered paraders and making her way to Main Street. She saw Candy Cleaver walking around making last-minute checks with a clipboard in hand, and the two women smiled at each other.

It was five minutes past eleven. Parade time.

*

First there were sirens, as one of Sheriff Sherman's deputies pulled slowly out in his squad car, preparing to lead the parade on its route. The red and blues of his bubble lights spun weird designs on the houses he passed and sent psychedelic swirls into the eyes of the parade-watchers. As he turned the first corner onto Main Street there rose a thunderous applause from the audience, which he responded to with another blast from his siren. People stood to clap and shout their excitement and approval.

Then there was music. First, the high-school marching band, playing an Edward Elgar march right behind the cop car. They were an okay band, as far as high-schoolers go. Some bad notes, some missteps, much lack of interest in the whole thing. Their music teacher marched alongside them, looking just as petrified as they did, if not more so. There were rumors that he still partook of the wacky weed now and then. If you were a high-school music teacher, wouldn't you?

The band played its song and marched onto Main Street, and many parents began to take pictures from the sidewalks and curbs.

Following the band was the first of the day's floats: a gorgeous red white and blue thing that was supposed to represent the Statue of Liberty but which looked, in fact, like a giant pistol resting on its barrel, due to a lack of head and arm definition. A sign on the side of the float said HARRIS HARDWARE.

When the band quieted down so that only its drummers were playing, pounding out a steady rhythm

105

designed to keep everyone's feet moving, there were cheers from the crowd.

After this float came the first of the clowns, tossing candy to the crowd. The clowns walked goofily along the curbside, making babies cry and shaking the hands of parents. One of them carried helium balloons, which were passed out to the youngest children. The sky was soon filled with strange and fat rainbow-colored birds.

The parade slowly snaked around that first corner and came onto Main Street. As is typical of any parade, there were moments when the whole thing stopped so someone could do a little show: in this case it was first the raising of the fire engine's ladder, then a demonstration by the Knights of Columbus in their little cars. During this latter a clown was nearly taken out when one of the Knights attempted a too-sharp turn. The clown mouthed something that may have been "fucker" and there was an attempt at a middle-finger extension, which was impossible to do with big white clown gloves, however, and when the clown brought his hand up children waived at him. He caught himself in mid-bird and waived back cheerfully.

A parade is a strange thing: it moves so slowly it becomes oddly hypnotic, so that after the first bit of hysteria passes the audience simply sits or stands back and stares with dull eyes as each new segment passes. People watch parades the way they watch TV.

Slowly it came this day, this largest and most grand of Burghville's parades, unwinding onto Main exactly like a great python unwinding onto a rock. The image of parade-as-snake was not lost on Burghville's resident snake-lover, Helen Keller.

She walked the parade route, not yet taking a place, instead watching the audience. Men and women alike turned their heads almost instinctively to look at her as she passed among them. She was a strikingly beautiful young woman, of course, but it was more than this that attracted attention to her. She radiated warmth and energy in a way no one else in town did... in a way, in fact, that few people on the planet did. Working within her was a marriage of earthly beauty and unearthly liveliness. One could look at her and think that there was not blood and bone beneath her tan skin, but the power of supernovas, the chemical reactions that give birth to solar systems. Also, of course, when she looked at you there was a strong feeling of *knowledge* in her eyes. What did she know? people wondered. Can she read my mind? When they looked at her they saw a living mirror, a humanoid pool of energy and insight.

She moved through the audience this day full of friendliness, smiling at every one, occasionally patting the head of a child or two. Her tight khaki shorts revealed enticing valleys and crevices that moved like dunes as she walked.

At last she took her place on the lawn of the library, not too far behind Henrietta Pratt, who was stationed near some children. The youngest children were bringing Henrietta dandelions and she was telling them about the flowers, holding them under their little chins to see who had boyfriends and girlfriends.

The library sat on top of a hill, so the lawn rose up above the sidewalk and street below, giving a good view of both the parade and the audience. Helen found what she thought was both the highest and best point, then sat there with her legs outstretched in front of her. She kicked off her shoes and let her toes enjoy this day's sun. The library lawn, unaffected by the blight that had fallen over town, was full and healthy and soft to the touch.

As soon as Helen sat down the first of the clowns began to pass and she smiled. The children down below cheered and ran out for candy.

It wasn't truly fair, Helen knew, to call a parade snake-like, for in fact the two things moved entirely differently. A snake is much more ordered and graceful, lacking the parade's jerky movements. And a snake is an entirely more beautiful entity.

However, parades had their charm. Not, however, for the parade itself (at least not for her), but for the audience that gathered along its route.

It was observing this audience that Helen Keller enjoyed the most. She sat back and looked at everyone, seeing on this side of the street the backs of heads, on the other smiling shiny faces, everywhere a multitude of stories.

107

This was her chance to catch up on the town's inner workings. She stared down at them and like lines of poetry it came to her: she saw love, fear, worry, happiness, pure unadulterated joy. She saw what she needed to see, and no more. Except....

Except, for just the briefest moment she saw the ghost-like image of a different sort of parade, sketched faintly against the real images before her: a great herd of animals, from insects to raccoons, marching down Main Street. She saw it briefly, though clearly, and then one of the clowns tooted a toy horn and it was gone.

"Hmmm...." she said. She'd had visions before, but this one was different. How, she could not tell.

"Hmmm....."

*

He didn't need to see this.

Father Preston had decided to go to the parade at last, to leave his little home and get out among the people. It was, he decided, his duty as a representative of the Church. So he dressed as informally as he could while still staying what he considered "priest-like" and walked down to Main Street.

And almost immediately he saw her. The girl. Helen Keller. She was moving among the people like Christ, with everyone parting for her and a glow seeming to rise from her body like an all-over halo.

Father Preston stood staring at her, until he realized his mouth was gaping and that this was no pose for a priest to be seen in. He abruptly snapped shut that mouth and turned away from the sight of her. It was too late, however, for him to stop the reactions his body took at her image: he began to sweat and breathe deeply and there may have been a tightening of his pants, a sudden rush of blood to his neglected nether-regions. He put two fingers inside his collar to loosen it and let in some air, then looked around the crowd for someone to talk to, for something else to occupy his mind before hope sprang eternal and he looked like he was enjoying the parade *too* much.

He settled on the father of one of his altar boys.

"Hello, Father!" this man said, offering his hand.

108

"Helen," Father Preston said. The man apparently did not notice the mistake.

*

Things started slowly. The first few floats rolled down Main Street without incident, and they were wondrous to behold:

The YUNOCH RIVER RIFLE CLUB's float was a very detailed replica of the American flag, done in roses and violets;

The DAHMER GROCERY STORE chose the Liberty Bell, also in violets;

The GAHBEL REAL ESTATE COMPANY had actual people dressed as soldiers from various American Wars, these people standing amidst a replica of Mount Rushmore. Across the base of the Mount were the words BURGHVILLE MARCHES ON! The actual significance of this imagery was lost to all, even the float's designer.

Then came horses (and poop-scooping clowns), the car made of wood, the contestants for Memorial Day Queen (all riding in the backs of convertibles, back seats being familiar and comfortable to them all), the first of the flat-bed bands (the country band, playing a song about Alabama, which no one in town had ever been to) and the bagpipers. The bagpipers weren't bad, really, as far as bagpipers go. "Amazing Grace" droned and wheezed down the street like the last song of a dying pterodactyl, but this was the nature of the instruments: they were designed to carry across harsh and ugly landscapes, tools of war designed to annoy people into a vicious froth.

Dick Dick Buckthorn, walking along the sidewalk, towering over everyone and shaking hands and clapping backs, heard those bagpipes and winced. He smiled at one of his managers, took the smaller man's hand in his own, and said something about tortured cats. There were laughs all around.

Betty Buckthorn, walking beside her husband, smiled and adjusted her sunglasses. She did not want to be here and yet she didn't want to be home, either, so, this dilemma playing uncomfortably inside of her, she resigned herself to smiling and shaking hands and accepting hugs

109

from people she did not trust. She did not want to disappoint her husband. She was a good wife.

Helen Keller (who loved bagpipes) looked down at Betty Buckthorn and detected instantly the sadness inside the woman. That was not a woman who loved her life, and yet she was also not a woman who hated her life: she was stuck between poles of emotion, lost in the land of *Numb*. She was also something else: she was unsatisfied. Deep inside, she may have also felt she had settled. Settled for her life or settled for her husband?

That Helen could not tell. She looked away from Betty and set her eyes, for just a moment, on big Dick Dick Buckthorn, Burghville's most prosperous man, a larger-than-life character of energy and drive who stood out from the crowd like poop from diamonds.

She didn't like what she saw, so she turned away, enjoyed the bagpipers as they played. She thought there was something organic and earthy about bagpipes. The music of the Spheres, no, but maybe the music of the earth, the sound the world makes as it evolves. And would such a sound be pretty in the traditional sense? No, the world moves and changes with squeaks and groans. Evolution is efficient but rarely graceful.

It was at this moment that the first of many things went wrong:

The helium balloons, being carried in a great bouquet by a blue-shoed clown, began to pop one after the other, loud retorts like gunshots blasting across the street. The clown flinched violently and the children around him scattered. It looked, briefly, like Kennedy's assassination being reenacted by a children's theatre troupe. Perhaps there was a second popper on the grassy knoll. Of course, closest to the grassy knoll was Helen Keller, and she saw nothing, not one single soul anywhere with a blow-gun or a slingshot.

Once the popping was finished and everyone's ears were ringing, the clown looked at the limp strings in his hand, each ending with a brightly-colored bit of viscera. Being a good clown, he looked at the audience, shrugged in an exaggerated style, and quickly did a series of cart-wheels down the road. Everyone cheered.

Then, not a minute later, one of those tiny Knights of Columbus cars went careening down the road, speeding to beat the devil. The driver's face became a mask of terror as he struggled to control the little automobile. Clowns scattered (the clown who had nearly been run over earlier took off one of his gloves this time and gave the bird properly) and horses reared up, threatening to toss their drivers. There was a brief shout of surprise and fear from the audience, until the little car hit a curb head-on and came to an abrupt stop. A second later a little billow of smoke rose from its engine.

Dick Dick Buckthorn, from the sidewalk, shook his head at this sight. "Maybe we should have breathalyzers for those guys," he said to Sheriff Sherman, who was standing nearby. The people around Dick Dick laughed, some raising their own plastic cups of beer in salute.

Sheriff Sherman stared out at the scene of the accident and nodded to himself… just a brief nod. He was thinking that maybe that wouldn't be such a bad idea, breathalyzers. Why should a safe community tolerate drinking and driving on its roads under *any* circumstances? In his Ultra Safe Town there would be absolutely no tolerance for such things, and anyone driving any mode of transport in a parade, horses and little cars included, would be tested before they hit the road.

Dick Dick shook some hands, pointed in greeting at a few more managers of his, and continued on down the sidewalk. His wife followed in his wake, again accepting hugs and handshakes from people she did not know or did not like. With Helen Keller now positioned on top of the library lawn, away from the rest of the crowd, it fell to Betty Buckthorn to be the woman who made heads turn. And she was an attractive woman, of course, not a trophy bride in the classic sense but pretty of form and face. She had her admirers, let's say. Many people wished they could be Dick Dick Buckthorn, and she was one of the main reasons.

Out on the road the Knight of Columbus climbed out of his smoking wreck and shrugged to his companions, who shrugged back and continued along the route, spinning around in circles and zigzagging in and out of each other to

111

please the crowd. The fallen Knight got help from some members of the audience in pulling the car up onto the sidewalk.

The next thing to go wrong was that Mount Rushmore float: it, like most of the floats, had been designed to sit atop a trailer, and this trailer was being pulled by a Ford pick-up. At about the halfway mark of the route the trailer suddenly dropped an axle, the thing simple fell off and the float toppled sideways. The people on the float dropped their ancient rifles and grabbed for something to hold. One of them slipped and fell to the asphalt with a dull thud.

Again, a sound of surprise rose from the crowd. The driver of the pick-up, hearing this, stopped and climbed out. The damage was irreparable, and the people directly behind this float (the car made of wood, as it turned out) began to honk in mock-anger. A fist came through the wooden window and was shaken at the sky.

The driver of the Ford pick-up shook his head at the broken float, then looked at the men in the wooden car.

These men, friends all, exchanged mock gestures of anger, and then the wooden car gave a roar and drove around the lame float.

The rest of the parade was momentarily stopped, since the two horses behind the wooden car were frightened of the Mount Rushmore made of flowers and would not pass it. Men rushed out from the audience to help pull the dead trailer to the side of the street.

"Where's your float?" someone shouted to Dick Dick Buckthorn. To which he responded:

"Good things come to those who wait!"

The next thing that happened was that the Liberty Bell float began to lose its flowers. They simply fell to the ground or floated off on a breeze, and soon the float looked like it was partially decomposed, with half of the bell stripped down to its chicken-wire skeleton.

Passing clowns pretended to slip on the flower petals, to the delight of the crowd.

The parade was allowed to continue for a time after the Mount Rushmore float was pushed to the side of the road, its former riders now piling into the back of the pick-up. The horses finally calmed enough to pass as well, and then:

One of the brand-new John Deere tractors that were creeping down Main Street blew a tire. This sound was much louder than the sound of the popping balloons, and everyone jumped, not just the children. It was such a forceful explosion of air that it blew a swirl of dust up from the pavement. The giant tractor came to a halt, and the driver climbed out. He stared at his flat tire for a long while, perhaps willing it to refill with air.

Dick Dick Buckthorn, close to this accident, again shook his head. He felt good this day, looming over everyone and feeling just like those Texas businessmen he admired. He was wearing a leather vest over a white shirt, and on his feet were silver-tipped cowboy boots. He was not wearing a hat, but there were shades over his eyes. He didn't need people to see his eyes when he was out and about: he charmed them with his smile.

"Good lord!" he said loudly. "Maybe we should have gotten disaster insurance! It always pays to be prepared!"

Everyone laughed.

"And where's the Buckthorn Industries' float?" someone asked.

Dick Dick smiled down at the man. "You hold on to your hat when you see her," he said. "She'll knock you flat on your ass!"

Carol Slugg was next in line behind the tractor, and she only paused for a second when the tire blew. Frowning, she gripped her massive cross firmly and marched around the big green machine.

Father Preston, seeing her coming down the street, shook his head. One thought crossed his mind:

Quick, someone get the nails...

And then he smiled at some other members of his congregation, who offered him a soda from a cooler.

Carol Slugg carried the cross well, it must be said. She didn't struggle too much as she dragged it along, the cross beams over one shoulder and the foot end of the crucifix on the road. She chose this method of carrying it because it was how Christ carried the cross in all the paintings. She was thinking that everyone should carry a

113

cross like this, once a year at least: it was the best way, short of actual crucifixion, to actually feel what Jesus had gone through, and the best way therefore to *know* Him.

Helen Keller, watching from her place on the library lawn, wondered if Carol Slugg knew that there *were* people in the world who actually had themselves crucified in order to better experience (theoretically speaking) Jesus' love. They were tied to crosses and nails were driven through their palms, then the crosses were raised and the "victims" were allowed to hang there, experiencing Rapture with their excruciating pain, along with (she had to assume) a touch of embarrassment. Helen decided it would be for the best if Carol did *not* know this, at least for her sake. Let her carry the cross instead, if that was what she needed to do. It was harmless.

A few minutes later there rose a murmur from the crowd. Heads turned to see what was up.

It was the Buckthorn Industries' float, and it was massive. At least, so spread the word among the crowd. The people near Helen could see nothing but the lame John Deere tractor and, passing around it now, clowns, the flat-bed rock and roll band (not playing at the moment... apparently having trouble with their instruments), the old men riding lawnmowers, men and women dressed in Revolutionary War outfits, and Scooter Boober and his animals.

Of all the people in the parade, Scooter Boober looked to have the most control. His animals were well-behaved, and they walked down the street calmly. He had only to follow them, sidestepping the occasional dropping or two, but for the most part making slow and steady progress along the route. Little children did not know what to be amazed at, the llama, the great red shaggy creature with the intimidating horns, or the dwarf leading them all. The adults wondered if the Holstein bull was going to go crazy any moment and run rampant through the crowd.

"Is that legal?" someone asked Sheriff Sherman.

He pondered the question as he watched the little man and his animals. He could not think of a law against it.

"Is it safe? Should he be allowed to do that?"

114

Ahh, thought the Sheriff, these were other questions indeed. In an Ultra Safe Community, of course, it would be against the law to have potentially dangerous animals in a parade. A bull in particular was an angry and mean old beast, as anyone with any sense well knew.

And then there was that *other* thing, the red cow with the horns and the hippie-bangs over its eyes. What in the world was *that*?

"What if that bull goes mad and runs the crowd down?" someone asked.

The Sheriff looked at this person and patted his sidearm. The black revolver gleamed in the sunlight of this bright afternoon.

"Think you could take it out?"

Sheriff Sherman did not smile. "Yes," he said.

Helen Keller watched the man too, and without fear. She knew how the man was with those animals, she knew he understood them. Watching him control the beasts was like watching a master artist working a piece of marble or a pallet of paints. The man knew what he was doing... and, just as importantly, the *animals* knew what he was doing. It was all about trust.

The people at the curbs took steps back as he passed. The llama looked at them, chewing its cud calmly as it did. Its large brown eyes seemed to consider everyone there for a moment, and then finally judged them to be uninteresting. The cattle, for their part, never looked at the audience.

"I don't like it," said someone.

Some kids asked Henrietta Pratt about the llama. They thought it looked funny, like something from a book. She whispered llama-secrets to them and they smiled. Helen could not hear what the woman told them.

"I don't like it at all," that same someone said.

Sheriff Sherman again patted his pistol, this time for his own benefit. Secretly he hoped that the animal *would* run amok. Then he would be needed.

Dick Dick saw Scotter Boober passing and he winced, just as he had winced when he first heard the bagpipes.

Midgets, he thought....

"You okay?" his wife asked, touching his arm.

"Of course. Perfect." He leaned down to kiss her, and when he stood tall again he caught sight of Polly Anderson in the crowd. Polly licked her lips seductively and then walked on. "Jesus," Dick Dick muttered. His body didn't know what to do: shiver at the thought of Scooter Boober, or pop a boner at the thought of unlimited executive services.

"What?" Betty Buckthorn said, staring up into his face.

"Nothing. Let's go see my float."

It came more slowly than the rest of the parade, taking its own damn time. There was no arrogance in this, however, only the simple fact that the float was so heavy. It really was the grandest float in the entire parade, as of course Dick Dick had both wanted and planned. Representing Burghville's largest industry, it had to be grand. Anything less would have been disappointing... would almost have been embarrassing.

But before it came down to where Dick Dick was standing, something else happened to draw the crowd's attention, something that sent people scrambling.

Ultimately, it wasn't Scooter Boober's bull that went crazy this day, it was more machinery:

First, three of the Knights of Columbus cars (sans drivers) came flying back down the road, against the grain of parade traffic. Immediately following were the three Knights themselves, screaming and flopping their hands around madly in an apparent attempt to warn people. The cars went amazingly straight for a long time, but finally two of them came too close to each other and hit tires. One of the cars took an immediate left and headed right for the crowd. This was what caused people to scramble.

The car hit the curb, flipped end-over-end, and continued on down the sidewalk, running down the ankles of the slowest people.

The car that sent this one off the road flipped as well and landed on its back like a dead beetle, tires spinning vainly against the sky.

The third car continued down the road, right for the legs of the next horse. This horse reared, whinnied, and nearly tossed its rider. The car, thankfully, veered off at the

116

last moment and slammed into the lame John Deere tractor, where it was engulfed in a plume of smoke.

As if all of this wasn't bad enough, it caused a chain reaction that spread from the parade to the audience and back.

From Helen Keller's position high on the library lawn, it looked like bedlam.

In just a few moments there was a tiny Knights of Columbus car careening madly down the sidewalk, swiping people in the legs, sending some to the ground with little shouts of surprise; there was a horse galloping out of control down Main Street, tossing its rider around like a rag-doll; there was another tire blow-out on yet another of the John Deere tractors; there was yet another float coming down the road sans flowers, just a skeleton of wood on the back of a trailer; the elementary school band freaked out and scattered like frightened chickens, dropping their instruments in the process (the sound produced was not so different from the song they'd been playing); the final convertible carrying the final Memorial Day Queen contestant suddenly stopped and threw itself (the driver would claim) into reverse, tires squawking; this convertible slammed into the pick-up truck behind it, causing the float that truck was pulling to topple sideways onto the street; the Knights of Columbus continued to chase after their runaway car; the clowns tried to calm the audience, but there was nothing calming in the sight of orange-haired men in white-face with big shoes waving big white hands and screaming "stay calm" from candy-apple-red mouths... in fact, this was quite frightening to everyone; up the street the fire-engine's ladder began to raise, against the wishes of the firemen; the ladder snapped the power-lines that were stretched across the street so that there arose a violent protest of loosed electrical current, causing still more people to run screaming for cover; Carol Slugg was trampled by an escaping gang of children (she let out a choked scream of alarm and fell to the ground, breaking her cross in the process); the startled horse had now startled the other horses, and one of the riders was indeed thrown to the pavement... though his feet remained in the stirrups, so when the horse took off he was dragged screaming down Main Street.

117

It was the sight of this latter incident that caused something to stir in Sheriff Sherman. He pulled his pistol out of its holster, pushed past Father Preston (who was trying to calm people, thinking himself to have a better chance than the clowns), and stepped into Main Street.

"He's got a gun!" somebody yelled. It was Candy Cleaver, who, like the rest of the Jaycees in the crowd, was completely dumbfounded by how the parade had turned out.

Hearing this phrase, so familiar from movies, made people scream in terror.

Sheriff Sherman raised that gun and fired four rapid shots into the sky. The sound reverberated throughout Burghville's downtown.

It didn't work: instead of quieting everyone, the sound of the shots only made everyone scream louder and break into confused running. There were people everywhere, in the sidewalks and streets and surrounding yards. Horses ran down the sidewalks, that damn mini-car was headed back up Main, engine whining and trailing five Knights of Columbus. The final Memorial Day Queen contestant, passenger of the ill-fated out-of-control convertible, was lying in the backseat with her legs up to the sky and her dress around her waist (not a position she was unfamiliar with). To an observer of the scene, such as Helen Keller on the library lawn, it looked like a riot, or a mass flight from an approaching terror, such as Godzilla.

Parents grabbed their children and looked for safety while others just ran in any direction they could, colliding with each other and tripping on abandoned strollers and lawn chairs. Sheriff Sherman put his gun away and stood there confused as people ran hither and thither around him. Guns were symbols of authority, were they not? People were supposed to *respect* them.

The whole thing looked ridiculous, the entire population of Burghville scattering like spilled marbles, only it didn't seem anyone was scrambling *to* anywhere: they all seemed to run in circles, either up the sidewalks (and back again) or up the street (and back again). A family unit would head in one direction, only to be confronted with the sight of quickly approaching clowns and horses, then they would turn the other direction and see

118

a tiny car racing toward them. In some places throughout the world people know how to flee. Here in Burghville, this was not a reaction that was instinctual. Apparently.

And then, amidst all of this confusion there rose a strong and loud voice, standing out from the screams and shouts and stopping everyone. It was Dick Dick Buckthorn:

"Look!" he boomed.

There was a collective turning of heads.

It was the Buckthorn Industries' float, slowly coming down Main Street, slaloming around the rest of the motionless floats that were in its way.

The float was being pulled by a gorgeous forest-green truck with brilliantly shining chrome rims and bumpers. As the whole works idled slowly down the street, Sheriff Sherman stepped out in its path.

"What is this idiot doing?" he said. He put his hand on his holstered pistol. Just in case.

Still the truck came, pulling the massive and spectacular float behind it. Both the sight of the slowly approaching truck, and that of the float itself, caused a stir of apprehensive excitement in the crowd, which, scattering madly just moments before, was now watching in silence.

The Buckthorn Industries' float was incredible:

Mounted on a huge trailer, nearly as long as that of an eighteen-wheeler, was an enormous display of craftsmanship and art, an intricate mosaic of carefully positioned flowers dyed every color of the rainbow. The entire float stood a good twenty feet above the trailer it sat on, so that it towered over Main Street and threatened to take out electrical wires like the fire engine ladder had. Every inch of the thing was covered by flowers: roses, tulips, lilies, daffodils, many varieties of unidentifiable things that looked like lace. It was beautiful in its color and style, but even more so because of what it depicted. Dick Dick, not wanting to settle for one scene, had instead instructed his "float engineers" (his term) to make something that incorporated the following ingredients: the raising of the flag on Iwo Jima, the Statue of Liberty, and the Revolutionary War soldiers carrying drums, flute, and flag. On both of its sides was a banner that read

119

BUCKTHORN INDUSTRIES: HELPING AMERICA MARCH ON!

It was, all in all, a spectacular sight.

"What is this idiot doing?" Sheriff Sherman asked again, his hand still twitching over his pistol.

It became increasingly clear, however, that there was no one driving that forest-green truck. It slowly approached the sheriff, coming to a stop just feet from him, and there was no one to be seen in the cab.

Sheriff Sherman looked at the crowd around him. He saw Father Preston, Henrietta Pratt, Candy Cleaver. Carol Slugg made the sign of the cross.

"What is this shit?" Dick Dick Buckthorn said, coming up to the sheriff.

They stared through the windshield of the truck, saw nothing move.

"You wanna pop a few shots into her?" Dick Dick whispered.

Sheriff Sherman looked at him. He was about to open his mouth and say *yes* when there was a sound like crumpling paper from the float itself.

The crowd took steps back. The float began to shake, at first just slightly and then as if it were rocking. The rustling grew louder, and petals began to fall from the frame, floating like Autumn leaves (or psychedelic snow) to the pavement.

"What the..."

Carol Slugg said: "Our Lord Jesus protect us..."

Helen Keller, still standing on the library lawn, shook her head. This was certainly the most interesting thing to ever happen in Burghville, as far as she knew.

The float's petals continued to fall, coating the asphalt below and slowly revealing the wooden frame they once covered. It was like watching a scene of decomposition in time-lapse. The float shook, gently rocking the trailer.

"You got a defective float there, Dick Dick?" asked Sheriff Sherman.

Dick Dick shook his head and said nothing.

The sound of chittering laughter could suddenly be heard from inside the float, growing louder as each layer of petals fell. The good citizens of Burghville frowned.

Mouths were agape, awaiting words to fill them. This, whatever it was, ran counter to everything Burghville believed in, everything Burghville needed. Whatever it was, it just wasn't right.

"What the..." somebody said again.

A few moments later the top half of the Statue of Liberty caved in with a soft sound like the flapping of moth wings, opening a gaping hole in the float that revealed... well, there's no subtle way to say what it revealed.

About twelve tiny people, none more than a foot tall, were sitting there under a spill of candy-colored flower petals. They had sharply angled chins and noses and great beard spotted with colored scraps. Some were insatiably stuffing petals into their mouths, eating them with joyful gluttony, while others had pipes between their lips that sent curly-cues of smoke over their heads. Some were raising their hands to greet the newest fall of flowers, like New Year's revelers greeting confetti, and still others were just lying back and patting their stuffed tummies.

All of them, though, were laughing. It was a chittery sound of delight and abandon. An ancient laugh, wise as well as gleeful.

The laugh of the wee folk.

"Welcome to Burghville," whispered Tracey White, somewhere in the back of the crowd. Her husband shivered beside her.

Part II

"Wherever you come near the human race,
there's layers and layers of nonsense."
--Thornton Wilder
Our Town

6

The woods were full of gentle pattering: the sound of last evening's rain still dripping from the leaves to the forest floor. She woke to it slowly, coming up by degrees from a deep slumber full of dreams, lying there with her eyes closed once she was fully awake, just listening to that soft sound. She remembered the womb. The sounds had been like this: rhythmic, repetitive, soothing. A person could lie for hours listening to such sounds. It was like entering another world, like returning to that womb, held safe and secure in the depths of one's mother, listening to the comforting rush of blood, the steady beat of the heart, the liquid murmur of a living body.

She opened her eyes. This was not like that short journey down the vagina and into light, though, this was like a journey from one womb to another. In this case, from sleep to her temporary nylon foster parent. Her sweet reliable Coleman mother.

She stared at the ceiling of her tent. She could see the shadows of raindrops as they hit the nylon and rolled down the side of the tent, leaving streaks of shadow like snail trails. She sat up and stared out the mesh of the tent's flap. The day out there looked dull, the forest close and compacted, with a low ceiling of gray clouds somewhere up above the drooping wet canopy.

She climbed out of her sleeping bag and unzipped the tent flap, letting in the cooler air. She stuck her head outside, examining this new day. The air smelled clean and there were no sounds save that gentle dripping of water on leaf and dirt. She took a deep breath and then climbed out into the morning, standing there completely naked. Being naked was the only way to ever leave a womb, and the best way to greet a forest in the morning. When you were naked you were open, unguarded, innocent, the way a forest expected its creatures to be.

Helen Keller lifted her arms to the canopy and stretched her back. She took another deep breath of cool fresh air and watched a squirrel scamper up a tree not fifteen feet from her.

"Good morning," she said. The squirrel did not respond, instead continued up until it found a more suitable branch where it could watch her safely.

Helen stood there a long time, naked as a jay-bird, letting the coolness of this post-rain morning settle like mist on her skin, moistening her breasts, settling like drops of dew in the soft jungle of her pubic hair. At last she wandered off into the woods a bit, squatted, and then returned to her tent refreshed. Goose bumps covered her legs and arms and wet leaves clung to her thighs and she decided it was time to dress. She crawled back into the tent, then emerged a few minutes later in jeans and t-shirt and sandals. She walked to her fire-pit and frowned at the gray sludge inside of it. It would be hard to start a fire today. *Possible*, but hard, and she did not want to start off this day with anything even slightly difficult.

She brushed her hair back behind her ears and again looked out over the forest. The rhythm of dripping water was continuous, absolutely filling the woods. The grayness of the cloud cover was full as well, as if this were a painting on which something had been spilled. Beautiful, though. Every day was beautiful, regardless of whatever aesthetic qualities it may or may not have had. A stupid phrase came to her: *Do not search for the days of niceness, but the niceness of days.*

She smiled, remembering Sam, the artist-poet who used to own the house in town, her winter home. He'd been big on Zen crap, and she used to kid him about it: all of his little sayings, which were meant to sound wise, had been to her nothing but idiotic paradoxes and puns:

Do not search for the love of meaning, he would say, but the meaning of love.

126

Ooh! she would say in mock-awe. How wise! That sort of thing might strike some as being *deep*, but to her it sounded like something you would say to a child. She'd seen wiser things written on restroom walls.

Wisdom is simple, he would say. Attaining wisdom may in fact be like going back to a child-state, when truths were easy and uncomplicated.

She told him that truth was anything *but* uncomplicated. Her idea of truth was that found in nature, and of course nature is never easy and always complex.

Nature is part of truth, he would say. We can look there for answers as well.

It is the *only* place to look for answers, she would answer. It is the whole truth, not a part of another.

Her smile widened. God, how she missed those days of arguing and debating. And she missed his ideas, his art. She remembered how he was going to train spiders to spin web artwork. He had said that spider silk was stronger than steel and resistant to bacteria, and that the army wanted to find ways to make bulletproof clothing from it. If they could they would try to make weapons as well, he said, and such a lovely thing should not be associated with man's inhumanity to man. To that end, he wanted to train spiders to form webs in strange and beautiful new shapes. The making of Art, he said, will be the first human use of arachnid silk. A school of art might even grow around the practice: the Charlotte's Web School. They would be renowned the world over.

He had begun studying the world of spiders, and had started to develop a theory that if the temperature of the spider's surroundings could be altered as the spider spun, then a different shape might take place. All that the human Artist would have to do would be to alter the temperature in pre-designated ways, so as to influence the shape he or she wanted. This artwork would be all the more precious because the spider would eat it every day, and make a new one each night.

Helen had thought it an interesting idea, though she also knew that nothing any human could come up with would be able to match the beauty of the original design. Man cannot improve on Nature, much as he can try.

You'll see, the artist had said. He had even begun to order garden spiders for this work when he dropped dead. The beauty of life is in the life of beauty, he told her. They hadn't been his last words, but they'd been close.

Such a guy, she thought now. She remembered once when he was trying to come up with a way to influence the formation of clouds.

Why settle for *thinking* a cloud looks like an elephant? he asked, when it actually *could* look like an elephant?

They had argued about that idea for a long time.

She shook her head at these memories, wishing she could have them back but knowing they were more precious to her as past than they had been as present. That was the trick to life: appreciating each moment as much as you appreciate your memories. The most common thing you hear people say is *If only I'd known*, and *If I could have that to do over again I'd cherish the whole thing*, and *If I were back there now I'd really tell him how I felt*.

Such a shame, this. The present is wasted. A person longs for the future and mourns for the past, and all the while the present is wasted.

She thought a moment, listening to the gentle drumming of the rain drops, then climbed back into her tent. She emerged wearing a blue flannel shirt, then looked down at her wet fire-pit again and decided she would have to catch something to eat in town, if she was going to eat at all. She started to leave her campsite but stopped, raising her head suddenly like an alert dog catching a scent on the breeze, and listened to the woods. At first she heard nothing but the sound of water on wet leaves and grass. Then she heard a fragment of music, a flute sending a cute little trill into the air. It was a strange yet attractive music, as calming in its way as the music of wombs. It sounded old, and being old had had time to perfect itself, to do what it wanted to do, to cause just the right reaction in the ears and minds of its listeners.

Helen Keller was the only human in the Burghville area to think that music was beautiful.

It was the music of the wee folk.

*

128

No one called them wee folk. They called them "those damn little things," or "those god-awful little monsters," or "those freaky little pests," or any number of much harsher labels. Americans have no words for such creatures, since they are simply not part of the landscape of American myth and legend, and so "god-awful little monsters" would have to do for now. They'd been called worse over time.

"Look at them," Sheriff Sherman said to a deputy as they cruised down Main Street. He said it with a stew of disgust and disbelief in his voice. "*Look* at them...."

The deputy was of course already looking. Impossible not to.

They were everywhere, in every yard, smoking pipes, drinking from tiny cups, eating grass and flowers right out of people's gardens. They were lying on sidewalks and patting their fat little stomachs. When they saw the cop car passing they raised their little hands and waived, just as casually as country people waiving at a passing neighbor. Not a care in the world.

"Jesus..." muttered the Sheriff.

"What do you suppose they are?" asked the deputy, a young kid.

Sheriff Sherman could think of only one word to answer that. It was a word a lot of people were using:

"Vermin," he said, then he lost himself in thought.

*

They were doing good work on the grass of Burghville's yards: people had watched them as they ate it, saw them put the blades in tiny wooden bowls and eat them like salad. They had also watched them dig up the roots to make some sort of tea, which they sipped with relish. Afterwards, as they did after almost *everything*, they danced and sang and played music. They were everywhere, too. Those people who had not locked themselves into their homes in fear had trouble getting out of their driveways sometimes, what with the little creatures running everywhere.

"Maybe they're leprechauns," someone said from behind blinds. "If we give them their lucky charms back they'll go away."

"Why don't you go catch one and get your three wishes."

A pause. Then: "I'm fine right here."

Things had changed in Burghville since Memorial Day, you see. Since being seen gorging on the flowers of the Buckthorn Industries' float, and being identified as the source for the turmoil at the parade, the little creatures had ceased hiding in the shadows. They had multiplied and grown lazy. They now sat out in plain site, at first in only a few yards but then, as their populations grew, spreading into nearly every place available. It was sometimes impossible to drive down certain streets at any speeds greater than five miles an hour without the damn things running in front of you, seemingly without care for their own safety. And you'd better keep your windows up, too, unless you wanted to see a bunch of them napping in your backseat.

"This is crazy!" was the first general consensus. The second, quickly following, was this:

"This has to end!"

No one had seen anything like it in all their lives. At least, few in Burghville had....

*

"What do we do?" Tracey White whispered to her husband one night under the covers of their bed.

"We don't do anything," he said.

"We can't do *nothing*."

"We've been pretty good at it so far. Why should we do anything?"

"Because, Timmy, you *know* why...."

"Shhh! No more talking about it. Keep your mouth shut and say nothing!"

"Timmy, we—"

"Shhhhh!"

She rolled over to face away from her husband. Outside, on their front lawn, strange music played on

130

through the night. No, not so strange to Tracey White: she'd indeed heard it before.

"Shhhh!" her husband said again.

Neither of them had slept in days. All of their conversations were just like this one, and their lovemaking had ceased. There was a full box of condoms in the dresser drawer, waiting.

*

It is hard to do justice to the change that Burghville had undergone since that Memorial Day. It was as if a curtain had been lifted on reality, exposing the great and wonderful and incredible world of magic that lay underneath. It was as if everyone had been slipped a mickey of LSD. It was as if the entire town was sharing a single fantastic dream. It was, in a word, unreal. Everywhere you looked, tiny little people were running amok. Absolutely crazy.

Carol Slugg sought out Father Preston on the evening after the parade, finding him at home. He did not answer the door right away, but after she had pounded and pounded for twenty minutes he finally opened it and looked out at her.

"This is serious," she said immediately.

Father Preston nodded. He knew it was serious, all right. Anything that sends Carol Slugg to his house was serious. His phone had been ringing all afternoon and he had not once dared to answer it. He had not wanted to hear that voice. *This* voice.

"This is serious," she said again.

"There are no prayers for this kind of thing," he said to her, looking beyond her at the church across the street. He was thinking of the missing clappers. He was putting two and two together, wee folk and clapper-theft, and not feeling good about the math. "If that's what you want."

"I don't want that," she said, though she sounded disappointed.

"I... please, I have to think about this... I need time." He rubbed at his temples, hoping to massage a threatening headache away. He felt drugged and confused.

131

"We have much work to do!" Carol Slugg said as the door was closed on her. "*Much* work, Father Preston! The Lord expects—"

*

Things that happened in the immediate aftermath of the parade:

*

Only one person spoke. It was an elderly man with a thin and tired voice, one of those voices only the very old possess, the sort that sounds like its owner is speaking through burlap. Few people heard him speak, and no one who did paid any attention. Later he would say the exact same thing, only in a much more public way. With a mouth full of ill-fitting dentures, this is what he said:

"Them's elves."

And then—

*

The crowd broke. Everyone scattered for real this time, none of that mad scrambling in circles. Seeing those *things* on what had been the Buckthorn Industries float was just too much. People ran screaming for their homes and children cried like they'd been slapped by Santa. All of the floats and little cars and musical instruments had been abandoned in the rush. In no time at all the entire street was empty and quiet... except for the wee folk themselves, who climbed off the Buckthorn Industries float and out of other hiding places to stare up and down the street, apparently confused. They were amazed at the sudden commotion they had caused, all that screaming and fleeing for what, *them*? They stood looking around, at the street, the lawns, the abandoned floats, the forsaken lawn-chairs, the spilled candy, a clown-shoe or two. Then they broke out in laughter.

*

132

The sun melted and spread like wax over the horizon, coating everything in pink hues. None of the streets were quiet, though: from nearly every house came the sound of hammering as people fixed two-by-fours over their doors and windows until their homes looked like derelict buildings in reverse, all the boards on the inside. Like the house in *Night of the Living Dead.*

Then entire families huddled together, thinking about what they'd seen and what it all meant.

"This is crazy," they said to each other. It was all they said, over and over. Crazy, crazy, crazy….

*

Carol Slugg left Father Preston's house and crossed over to the St. Michael's Catholic Church. She went inside and knelt before the altar, praying to her God for deliverance from this evil. She knew they were evil, whatever they were. Such things *had* to be evil, because they were strange and she'd never seen anything like them before. She knew with all her heart that they were the spawn of Satan.

One thing she didn't know was that back on Main Street the wee folk had built a good-sized fire using her giant cross. It sent gorgeous swirls of flame into the evening air.

*

Candy Cleaver, like everyone else, ran home and locked her doors. She went to the sink, pulled out a white bottle of anti-bacterial counter-top cleaner, and poured some of it into a rag. Then she walked around the house with the rag over her mouth and nose and stared at her dolls, thinking absurd thoughts that didn't strike her as absurd, that actually frightened her deeply. They were:

Living dolls look like fake dolls;

Real eyes look like glass eyes;

Real mouths look like doll mouths.

And on and on. Until the cleaner kicked in. On and on.

133

And on and on, indeed. For the next few days following the parade Burghville was at a standstill. No one went to work. Few people ventured outside. Few people even let their dogs outside, preferring to pick up piles of poop in livingrooms than witness the senseless slaughter of beloved pets at the tiny hands of "little monsters," even though the week folk never once made threatening moves towards family pets and indeed even seemed to prefer dogs and cats to their owners. Still, everyone chose to barricade themselves inside and stare out windows as the "god-awful little things" ran openly in the yards. People called each other on the phones until someone wondered aloud whether the creatures were listening in, and then most communication between neighbors stopped cold.

Burghville was under siege. Workdays came and went and businesses did not open. The conveyor belts at Buckthorn Industries did not turn. Nothing was made, nothing was sold, nothing was bought. The town was in stasis. The only movement was that of the wee folk themselves, and the people watching them from behind curtains.

And then Henrietta Pratt stepped forth. It was her nature to do so.

She had locked herself inside like everyone else at first, but she had observed the little men and women carefully. She was used to observing nature's creatures, used to watching for subtle variations in movement and behavior in wild animals, like the birds and squirrels that came to her feeders. She began to form a theory about these strange creatures, and gradually came to a conclusion: they were not dangerous. Despite having killed that sparrow in her yard they were not dangerous. The sparrow could have been for food, she figured, and nothing she had seen so far indicated they were a threat to people.

To prove this theory, she ventured out one morning to try and communicate with a small group drinking grass-root tea on a neighbor's yard. She'd been thinking about the word she'd heard that one day, and it was this word she spoke to the creatures as she came up to them:

"Dizzlemuck," she said.

They just stared at her.

*

"Look at that fool," Henrietta Pratt's neighbors said when they saw her leave her house, cross the street, and enter their yard. They too had been watching the small group as they drank their tea on what remained of the grass. The father of the household had been thinking about getting his shotgun out and taking care of those things. His four-year old son was petrified at the thought of the monsters, and his eight-year old daughter was delighted, thinking she'd entered a fairy tale. It was his daughter's response that worried the father: what if she got curious enough to venture out there, just like that fool Pratt woman was doing?

"Look at that fool," he said.

The little things were sitting there around the cooling remains of a little fire, on which they had brewed their tea. The thought of that grass-root tea disgusted the father of this household. He thought that was one of the sickest things he'd ever seen. And top that with the attitude of those monsters: they were lying there like they owned the place, without a care in the world, sipping their tea and laughing and singing and now and then getting up to do little jigs. Once, in anger, the man had knocked on his window, hoping to scare them away, and the little things had looked over and waived. Jesus.

Now Henrietta Pratt was crossing the road and approaching them! She walked with confidence, her hands at her sides and a tentative smile on her mouth. When she entered the yard she brought her hands out, palms forward, and said something. The man didn't know what she said.

Something foolish, no doubt.

*

"Dizzlemuck," she said as clearly and pleasantly as she could. She hoped her smile wasn't too toothy, that it didn't look like a snarl. When the little people just stared at her, she wondered if she'd made a mistake. She wondered what *dizzlemuck* actually meant. She wondered—

"Dizzlemuck to you, too," one of the creatures said, and then they all laughed.

It was the first communication between the wee folk and the citizens of Burghville and, roughly translated, this is what was said:

"Holy shit."

"Holy shit to you, too."

Dizzle meant sacred, or holy, you see. And *muck* meant shit. In wee-folken.

*

After this exchange, something wonderful happened. The wee folk had a sense of humor, of course, as most ancient creatures do, and they recognized the good-hearted attempt by Henrietta Pratt. So, after laughing, they offered her a cup of tea, which she accepted, and which she sipped there on her neighbor's lawn.

And which tasted all right, really, or as good as grass-root tea can get.

"Dizzlemuck," one of the little people said, shaking his head and sighing.

"Dizzlemuck," Henreitta Pratt repeated, again as pleasantly as possible, looking at each of her new friends as she did.

Holy shit, indeed.

*

And so it was in the first few days. But, this attempt at communication notwithstanding, things only got more complicated once the presence of the wee folk was accepted and once the initial shock at the sight of them faded, once people no longer thought they were in a dream or experiencing a mass hallucination brought on by a spiked water supply (and there was indeed a theory like this circulating, the logic behind it being that a terrorist group

136

with less-than-deadly intentions would find it perfectly sensible to taint a country's water supplies with drugs in order to lull the citizenry into numb complacency; one thinks of, say, an international Apple Dumplings Gang, or an hallucinogenic Grand Fenwick).

This was quite the situation for Burghville. It was, as they say, unprecedented.

*

Helen Keller stood there in the forest, listening to the music of the wee folk. She'd never heard anything like it before in her life, yet she understood what was being said in those notes, in that melody, in the playful passion beneath it all. She understood it quite plainly that cool moist morning. It made her want to smile, which she did there in the haze of a new day's sun, with her home sighing and whispering around her and her friends, most of them unseen, slithering and crawling around her feet and circling on thermals above her head.

It was a new day indeed. She thought it may even have been very like a birth after all. Out of the womb and into the world at large. From womb-music to this odd little flute in the distance. From innocence to experience.

Something like that. Anyway, onward. To Burghville.

*

Joe's Joe on Main, besides serving the best coffee in town, was also a pretty good diner. Nothing gourmet, of course, but pretty good all the same. The food could best be compared to an ugly hooker: it would do in a pinch.

Helen Keller was not the only customer this day, but the place was far from packed. The older woman who owned the place (there was in fact no Joe at all) was present, and there was a woman in a power-suit sitting at a table near the window. She looked out of place to Helen, more suited for New York than Burghville.

"Coffee," Helen said to the owner when she came in. And, in anticipation of the next question: "Black."

137

Then she took her own table kitty-corner from the power-suited chick, the best place to observe her.

This woman was the saddest person Helen had seen in a long time. She looked like someone had taken away her reason for living. Maybe her credit cards had been stolen. Maybe someone she loved had ceased loving her. Maybe she was thinking of a childhood pet that had been killed by a car. Maybe she was thinking of all the things she wanted and could not have. Maybe she was thinking of all the people she had stepped on in order to get where she was today. Maybe she had realized the pointlessness of her way of living. Maybe she was thinking about all the suffering in the world. Maybe she had realized that mankind will never ever make anything remotely as beautiful or strong as spider silk. Maybe she was realizing her childhood dream of being an astronaut would never come true. Maybe she was just sad to be sad.

Helen watched the woman for a long time, long past the deliverance of her own coffee and the ordering of her eggs and rye toast.

In time she realized why the woman in the power suit was sad. It was the same reason that made other people in town drink or beat their dogs or punch their wives or shoot up road-signs with shotguns:

She was stuck in Burghville.

Helen couldn't take it anymore. She picked up her coffee and walked over to the woman.

"Are you all right?" she asked.

The woman turned from the window she'd been staring through and looked at Helen with red eyes. She hadn't exactly been *crying*, Helen realized, she'd been doing that slow-leaking thing that comes with a mixture of frustration and worry and depression. The stew of the used and abused.

"I'm stuck here," she said.

Helen nodded. "I know. Why can't you leave?"

The woman looked back out the window and sniffled. "Because of *them*...."

Helen saw three little people sitting in the middle of the street. They looked harmless to her, like all of these little people. She didn't know quite what to call them

138

(fairies? elves? gnomes?), but she knew they were nothing to worry about.

"I can't get in my car because of them," the woman said. "They're living in it... so I'm stuck here."

"Don't you know anyone who can drive you?"

The woman snickered and shook her head. "That's not going to happen."

"Your eggs," the owner of Joe's Joe said at Helen's left side. Helen turned and took the plate from her.

"Can I sit here?" Helen asked.

The woman in the power suit shrugged her shoulder-padded shoulders. "Sure..."

Helen set her breakfast down and sat opposite the woman, tried to radiate an aura of happiness. Which was easy to do, considering she was happy.

"I have places to go," the woman said. She was still staring out the window. The three little creatures in the street were passing a single pipe around and apparently laughing at each other's jokes.

Helen lifted her eyebrows as she ate. "Mmmm?"

The woman continued: "I have appointments to keep. And there my car sits down that stupid little road, useless to me. They've got little beds in there and everything. It looks like a dorm room for midget-midgets. And they have my keys and they keep the doors locked and... I won't go near them, I just *won't*." The woman sighed viciously, an exasperated sigh entirely in keeping with her broad-shouldered power-suit. "Can't someone *do* something about them?" Her tone was angry and spiteful. One imagines the same exact tone, and the same exact sentence, being used to refer to blacks in the good old days.

Helen looked out at the little men as she ate. She considered the question carefully. Then she said:

"Like what?"

The woman's face was a painful mask of disgust. "Kill them..." she said quietly.

Helen could have sworn the three little men on the street tensed. She could have *sworn* it. She watched them for a long time until she was convinced they had heard nothing, that they were focused only on their pipe and their jokes.

"Or something," the woman said.

139

Helen continued to eat her eggs in silence. When she was done the owner of Joe's Joe came and took her plate and asked her if she wanted more coffee.

"No thanks," Helen said. Then she looked at the other woman. "You know," she said, "did you ever think to ask them if they would let you have your car back?"

"*Ask* them? Girl, are you crazy?" She looked at Helen as if she really wanted to know the answer to this question, as if it was truly a possibility, as if she were now for the first time seeing this young and vaguely hippie-ish woman across from her.

"You could try it," Helen said. "I'm sure they could find a better place to live."

The woman just stared at her. "Are you out of your *mind*?"

Helen sighed. She looked back at this woman, held her eyes firmly, and nodded. "I just might be. But when Mankind evolves, it will be the crazies who lead the way."

The woman's stare was cold, unwavering. "What?"

Helen sighed again and stood from the table. "Nothing. Welcome to Burghville." Then she paid for her food and left.

*

In the time that followed the Memorial Day Parade Helen, like Henrietta Pratt, had grown fascinated by the little creatures. She knew they were harmless. Pranksters, maybe, but harmless. It helped, of course, that she was gifted with her unique "sight" but she had also observed them closely... as apparently few others in town had. And, truth be told, they had never struck her as all that odd in the first place. Nature was full of mysteries. Fairies existed? Ho-hum, yawn. Take a close look at your neighborhood park and you'll see a lot stranger things than fairies eating and dying and fucking. These creatures might be different from anything else previously known, but they were as much a part of the Earth as any other living being. There were many more mysteries out there, things no one has even dreamt yet, things unimaginable to the human mind.

140

Things, in fact, that might never be seen by human eyes. Of this she was certain.

When they had first appeared on the Buckthorn Industries' float Helen's eyes had widened and she had found herself smiling... as she did whenever *any* new sight fell before her. She had smiled when she had first seen a snake mating-ball, when she had first seen a Luna moth, when she had first come across skunk cabbage melting snow with its passionate plant-heat, when she had first met Sam the artist, when she had first discovered her little talent.

She stared down at those creatures on the float and her reaction had been unlike anyone else's: she felt a surge of unalloyed joy rising from her ankles to the top of her head. She didn't know why it came, but she had enjoyed it, and she had enjoyed the tingling it left in her nerves. Something was up, she had thought. Something wonderful was afoot.

And then everyone scrambled and she had been caught up in that excitement and she ran too... right into the library behind her, out of breath and letting the heavy door slam shut behind her.

The librarian looked up a moment later, long after the echo of the closing door had faded, as if not willing or able to pull himself from the book he'd been reading. His name was Mr. Lynn and when he saw who she was he smiled. She came to the library often. Gatherings of books were like nature: there was always something more to be learned from them. And what was a library or a bookstore anyway but another sort of forest?

Helen nodded and walked up to him. He was leaning over his big central desk, where a very large book lay open; an old book, ancient, like a collection of Egyptian spells. Its pages were yellowed and stiff-looking, like parchment or mummy skin, and she imagined that it would smell like dust.

He looked at her over his bifocals and smiled. Helen was witness to the birth of wrinkles around his eyes and mouth. He had a handsome face, a bit pale but classically-lined, with a firm chin and kind, warm eyes. "How's the parade?" he asked. His voice echoed throughout the stacks.

Helen frowned and cocked her head back toward the door. The library was a big old building, solidly built and obviously sound-resistant to anything outside of its doors. She had never noticed this fact before.

Mr. Lynn, it appeared, had not heard the commotion. He'd been busy in here with his nose in this ancient tome.

She smiled at him. "Best one ever," she said. "Why are you open today, anyway?"

"Oh, I never close this place. The locks are broken and I can't find my *Gone Fishing* sign."

She nodded.

"What can I help you with?" he asked. "More books on snakes?"

"No... I was thinking more along the lines of cows."

"Cows, huh?"

"Types of cattle."

He stood tall and frowned thoughtfully. He considered the subject as he looked around at the high ceilings and massive bookshelves.

"I think we may have something in..." he said, letting his voice trail off. "Follow me, Helen." He left the desk and crossed the library. She followed, thinking.

"Maybe something on little people, too," she said. What the hell.

"Little people?" he asked, not looking back as he bee-lined for a particular shelf.

"Yeah. Little people."

"What sort of little people? You mean dwarves? Short people?"

"No. Dwarves are dwarves. I mean little people." Then she caught movement out of the corner of her eye and when she turned her head spotted a little man nestled back on a high shelf, his nose buried in a book (*101 Naughty Jokes*). "Elves... or fairies... or gnomes."

"Those aren't all the same, you know."

"What's the difference?"

He stopped and looked back at her.

"Well," he said, as if explaining something obvious, "for starters, some of those things are better than the others."

142

She frowned. "Better how?"

He studied the books in front of him, then pulled down a rather thick thing titled AGRARIAN EQUIPMENT AND ANIMALS. He handed it to her. It was surprisingly light for its size.

"Better," he said, "as in some would be more preferable to have around you than others."

She glanced around to see if there were any other little people in the library but saw none. "Why?"

He gazed at her over his bifocals and she thought for a moment how fatherly he looked, with those glasses, his faint crow's feet, the respectful flecks of gray in his hair. She realized she had no clue about his personal life. Perhaps he *was* a father. Perhaps his children were these books here, stacked with care and tenderness on their shelves, organized and clean.

"Let's get you a book," he said, smiling, and then he led her to the other side of the library.

*

The book was called *Celtic Mythology*, and she checked it out along with the book on farm equipment and animals. By the time she left the quiet of the library Burghville's Main Street was completely empty of people. Only the floats and instruments and cars remained, looking like remnants of a battle. She could hear flute music and that wonderful little chittering laugh, but she could see no sign of the little people themselves.

She left town with a book under each arm, loving the feel of them, their weight and presence. Books are so like flowers: both are wonderful when opened. She thought about those creatures, wondered if they were following her, wondered if they could speak and what they might say. Judging by that laugh they might be good for a few jokes, if nothing else. Perhaps even 101 naughty ones.

Little people. Good grief. And again she smiled, feeling that peculiar and unfounded rush of joy ripple through her body. It was a strange day, suddenly full of mystery. Only one thing was apparent:

Something wonderful was afoot.

143

7

Betty Buckthorn reached out and touched her husband between the legs, making him jump.

"Please," he said, brushing her hand off and walking away. He stood by the window and stared outside, thinking.

"Couldn't we just..." she started to say. But she was talking to his back now, and it was hard to romance a back. He stood there in nothing but his boxers and she laid there on the bed, stomach-down, in her robe. She had nothing on under that robe... just a blush on certain parts of her skin. And he had nothing on under those boxers but certain parts that a woman wanted. Certain parts a woman needed. Certain parts that her own certain parts called out for. Certain parts that—

"You know what this could mean?" he said. He said it in his CEO voice, which was deep and stern, the voice he used at board meetings and when he was lecturing managers. "You know what this could mean?"

She opened her mouth to speak, then closed it. Opened it again. Closed it. She didn't know if he was speaking rhetorically. She stared at the broad expanse of his hairy back and wondered how big he had been as a baby. He could easily have been a twelve-pound newborn. Easily. His poor mother.

"This could be a big problem, is what it could mean," he said. He continued to stare out the window, where the floodlights were blazing over the yard and woods. Those floodlights were part of the property's security system and were meant to go on in the event of a breach, but he kept them on all the time now. Like Father Preston, the Buckthorn's had put two-and-two together, concluding that "the little monsters" had indeed been in their house at some point. That they must have stolen her batteries, for instance, was a conclusion they made easily. "Who knows how big a problem it could be, too? It could be *huge*, and do you know what *that* means?" He turned to look at her.

She smiled up at him, to show she was listening.

"It could mean big problems for Buckthorn Industries," he said. "And the town, let's not forget the town. Buckthorn Industries *is* Burghville. If the Industry goes, Burghville goes. And that means this," and he gestured to what she guessed meant the whole house, or maybe their whole life, "could all be gone." He stared back at her, as if awaiting a response.

She dropped her eyes until she was staring at his crotch. "Why don't you come here," she purred.

He sighed. "Not tonight, Betty. Not now. I have too much on my mind." He crossed the floor and headed out of the room.

"Where's my vibrator, then?" she asked sassily. At least, she meant it to be sassy.

"Aren't you worried about those little *things*?" he said.

"I have *big* things on my mind."

His head popped around the corner to look at her. She turned to look back and held his eyes... licked her lips sensuously, may even have cupped one of her breasts. These were such natural actions for her she rarely knew she was doing them.

Dick Dick sighed. "Not tonight." Then he was gone.

Betty rolled onto her back and stared at the ceiling. There were things stirring in her, where they always stirred. What was this curse she was blessed with? What sort of woman was she?

She was a healthy sexual creature, that's what she was, and what was wrong with that? Why should she worry about those little things running around when there were other, more immediate concerns to be dealt with… concerns that were much more fun to deal with, anyway? With the alarm system activated twenty-four-seven she was no longer worried about breaches. She was worried about britches. She wanted britches off and hands on. God-awful little monsters be damned.

She sniffed, tried to smell pipe smoke and could not. She was alone. *They* were alone, here in this big house with no one around and a fifty-thousand dollar security system protecting them. They were living in a fort. And what else was there to do in a fort but fuck? Valley Forge was said to have been orgy heaven.

"Dick Dick?" she called. She couldn't handle it anymore, she needed him.

"I think we should hire a full-time watchman," he said as he passed by in the hall, bare feet swishing on the carpet.

She sighed and felt those things stirring again. Her secret womanly coils and tubes were humming. Floodgates were opening, dammit. Her skin was hot and sensitive.

"Honey?" she called, trying again.

Swish-swish went his feet on the shag. He was mumbling to himself as he walked. She heard only these words: *problem*, *big*, *security*, *Burghville*.

She decided on a shower, her second that night. In a shower, no one can hear you come.

When she came out he had put music on: themes from World War II movies, filling the house as it poured from secret speakers. It was music he put on when he was getting down to business.

She sighed and went into the bedroom. She wanted a cigarette, but Dick Dick had been around all day and would be around all night. She would have to wait until he went to bed before she could slip out onto the back deck.

"I don't think I can sleep," he said, passing by in the hall again. She realized he was pacing from one end of the house to the other.

146

"Could you take something?" she called after him. "A pill?"

"—goddamn little monsters—" he was saying.

Betty sighed.

*

What was going on in Dick Dick's mind was this: since the Memorial Day parade there had been a marked decrease in worker attendance at Buckthorn Industries. Simply put, people were afraid to go to work. Sure, some had come every day, and they would be rewarded, Dick Dick thought, but they made up only twenty-five percent of the total workforce. People were frightened, was what it came down to. No one wanted to leave their homes.

And it was ridiculous, it really was. Didn't they know that the town must go on, that there was work to be done, that things needed to be made and sold and bought? What if all of America acted like this? What would happen to the country?

It was this thought that disturbed him the most. What if all of America shut down because of those god-awful little monsters? What if Burghville was simply the beginning? What would that mean for the United States?

Didn't they *see*? If workers stopped working, the country would stop, period. It was that simple. And was that the way they wanted the rest of the world to view us, that we quit because of some goddamn little *things*?

He couldn't stand it. He decided right then and there (at the same exact moment his wife was coming to orgasm in the shower) that he would personally write a letter to all of his employees urging... no, *demanding* that they all return to work the following Monday. This nonsense had to end. He went into his study (which had been decorated to resemble a log-cabin, with knotty-pine walls and a great oak desk and chairs made of polished tree branches, a rug made of bear skin his brother had given him, lamps carved to look like wolves, and three big paintings of unrealistically lit outdoor scenes) and sat down at the desk. He began to draft the letter, keeping it simple and to the point, yet trying to be diplomatic in tone. This is what it said:

Dear employee:

Although it is understandable to be confused and worried in times like this, when we are faced with such a strange set of circumstances, when everything we had once accepted is now turned upside down and when we fear for our homes and families, it should also be remembered that we have other duties, chief among them being our duty to our communities. We are all part of not only Buckthorn Industries but also Burghville, our beloved town. We must remember how closely tied these two are to each other, and how dependent on them are those homes and families we cherish. This said, I believe the time has come to put fear and anxiety behind us and move on with the business of our company and our town... indeed, the business of our country. I believe you will agree that we should all return to work, because it is work that turns the wheels of community. It is work that moves a town and a country forward. This said, I implore all employees to return to work this coming Monday. Any missed time will not be counted on your records, and any missed deadlines will not be viewed negatively when evaluation time comes. Of course I understand that this is a very odd situation Burghville is going through right now, but I hope you also under-stand that the time has come for us to get back to work and continue to move not only Buckthorn Industries forward, but also to move forward Burghville and this great country called America.

---D. D. Buckthorn

He smiled when he finished. The letter captured everything he wanted to capture, appealing to his workers' sense of community, family, and patriotism. How could they not be moved by such words?

He left the study and crossed his house again, thinking about how behind in production Buckthorn Industries now was. He knew there were certain product lines that were overdue for shipping. The BUCKTHORN BETTER MOUSE NUKER was one of those, long overdue for shipment to Texas, where it was a good seller. The chains that carried it there would be calling soon, wondering what was going on. And what would he tell them? Would they even believe him?

He wondered, not for the first time, if Burghville was the only town experiencing this... whatever it was. He suspected so, since there was nothing about it on the radio or television. Then it also occurred to him that it must stay this way, that word must not get out about those goddamn little monsters. This absolutely *must* stay a Burghville issue only. It must not leak to outsiders.

"We can handle this ourselves," he said in a whispered version of his CEO voice.

But how...?

*

One thing Dick Dick did was this: the very next morning he went out to his yard, started up his gas-powered chopper, and went crazy on the underbrush and saplings that were growing there. This served three purposes:

One, it got his aggressions out;

Two, it kept down rodents and insects;

Three, it prevented those god-awful little monsters from using the underbrush as a hiding place.

It served another purpose, too, one that Dick Dick was unaware of: it allowed Betty Buckthorn to slip out onto the back deck and smoke a cigarette. The sound of that roaring monstrosity eating away the vegetation allowed her to know exactly where her husband was at any given moment. When he was in the front, she slipped out and got her nicotine fix.

Meanwhile....

149

*

Sheriff Sherman sat behind his desk with thoughts swirling and morphing like amoebas in his head. From the street out in front of the police station he could hear that odd little music, that annoying laughter, and occasionally the sound of tiny feet patting by on the sidewalk. But, as he had been trained to do back in his days as a cadet, he was ignoring those extraneous outside stimuli and concentrating on what needed to be done. The only problem was this: he didn't know what that might be.

Many calls had come in to the station telling him *something* needed to be done, asking him what he was going to do to stop this craziness. He had said the same thing to each of the callers:

"Just relax, we're working on it, everything will be all right."

Perhaps the most common line of bullshit people are given over the course of their lives is that someone somewhere is working on something.

Sheriff Sherman stared over his desk, past the phone (which even now was blinking one red eye to tell him someone was on hold) and out the window. Evening was on and he could barely see anything out there. The Main Street streetlights had been flickering for a while, those that still worked at all. The vermin had done something to them, he believed.

And what will *you* do about the vermin, Sheriff?

His wife had actually asked him this that day. He rarely went home anymore, and it was for the tone of her voice alone that he did not. She sat there in her chair and smiled smugly at him. She thought he was an idiot. She had *always* thought he was an idiot.

"What will you do about the vermin, Sheriff?" she asked as he putted about the kitchen making himself a lunch. She said *sheriff* like it was the most ridiculous word in the world.

He had not answered. A man shouldn't answer his wife when she thinks he's an idiot, it only leads to trouble. Best to say nothing and wait for the divorce lawyers to do the talking.

150

She had laughed at his silence.

He sighed now, and looked out the window again. He could see movement out there, small shadows hopping and bopping.

Jesus, what the hell *was* this? he wondered.

"Sheriff?"

He looked up and found one of his deputies standing there. These deputies were all young guys, fit and trim yet absolutely without ambition. They thought being a cop in a town like Burghville was an ideal beat. They liked the quiet.

"What?" he growled.

"Call on line four."

He sighed and looked at his phone. There was nothing worse, he decided, than a call on line four.

"Who is it?"

The deputy shrugged. "A concerned citizen?"

Sheriff Sherman sighed again and leaned forward. His belly hit the desk and he grimaced, thinking about Chief Wiggum and Buford T. Justice and....

He picked up the phone.

"Sheriff Sherman here," trying to sound busy.

"Sheriff, this is Terrence McKinley over here on Hillside."

Sheriff Sherman sighed once more, a deep and heavy sigh that ended as a ragged gurgle in his throat.

"Yes...?"

"What are you going to do about these vermin?"

"We're working on it," he said.

To which Terrence McKinley over on Hillside replied: "Bullshit."

*

Carol Slugg had always traveled with a crucifix around her neck, but usually it was inside her clothes, dangling between the deflated sacks that were her breasts. Now she held it in her hands wherever she went, like she was warding off vampires.

She spent a good portion of her time at the St. Michael's Catholic Church, praying in front of the altar, sometimes sleeping in a pew so she could wake wrapped in

151

the arms of her Lord. She wanted to feel spooned by God, if you will. She prayed hard, harder than she ever had before. She prayed for strength, for willpower, for the Lord Jesus Christ to see the town through this moment of trial.

One day, though, she came to the church and found the doors locked. She looked at the house across the street, then crossed over there and knocked on the door.

No answer.

She knocked again, harder. Still no answer.

"Father Preston!" she screamed, trying to see through the door's thick window. "Father Preston, are you there?"

No answer.

She turned and looked at his yard, stared at it for a long time before the little form of a tiny man was revealed to her. It was one of *them*: a foot tall, wrinkled and bony of face, with small eyes and a rumpled hat.

She brought her crucifix up and held it before the little man.

"Back off, spawn of Satan," she hissed. "I know where you come from: you're nothing but demons from the bowels of hell!"

The little man shook his head and said: "Bloxmuck." Then he tipped his hat at her and walked on, moving quickly across the street and disappearing around the side of the church. In wee-folken *bloxmuck* meant nothing more, and nothing less, than *bullshit*.

Carol Slugg, not knowing this, made the sign of the cross. "Heaven help us...."

*

The wee folk had discovered a variety of games. One was to remove manhole covers and roll them down the streets, laughing and whooping when they slowed and spun like pennies before collapsing with great clangs. Another was to line the beds of pickup trucks with plastic tarps (stolen from wherever they could find them) and then fill those beds with water to make instant pools. The sight of tiny people diving into the backs of their giant Fords and Chevis frightened people to no end.

152

Still another game was to travel by electrical lines, dangling like circus acrobats. They were good at this, too, never falling. A look around town would reveal any number of little people swinging from wires over the streets, twirling and spinning expertly. This caused a lot of homes to lose their phones and a few to lose electricity, and many more calls were placed to Sheriff Sherman asking him to do something. The sight of those zapping and popping lines, and the little vermin swinging unaffected in the middle of it all, also frightened people to no end.

Still another game was to appear inside of people's homes for fleeting moments, to allow themselves to be seen for only a fraction of a second before disappearing in the blink of an eye. The wee folk loved this game because they knew how hard everyone had worked to secure boards over their windows and doors. Of course, the citizenry of Burghville did not realize that wee folk are magical creatures and that wood and steel and Master locks cannot keep them out. More than one little person was seen sitting inside a fridge, stuffing themselves with pie or leftover chicken. And more than one Frigidaire was closed and never opened again.

The wee folk had also started talking to the Burghvillians, now that Henrietta Pratt had broken the ice. Few of the Burghvillians chose to talk back, other than to say *scram*! or *get*!

"Where ya going?" the wee folk would say when someone left their house and tried to get into their car. "Where ya going? Watch'ya doing?" they would ask, crowding around the person's feet.

"Get away!" the human might shout. He or she might even kick at the wee folk, who always moved easily out of the way. More than one time a shoe had gone flying and the wee folk had started a game of keep-away with it, exasperating the humans. And, as a result, more than one person had shown up at work with only one shoe.

"This has to end," everyone said.

"This is crazy."

Other games the wee folk had taken to playing: they would re-shape hedges, giving them strange shapes that struck the Burghvillians as utterly monstrous; they would let air out of car tires; they would ride bicycles, three steering and one on each pedal... upon crashing (which was almost a certainty) they would simply abandon the bikes; they would ride family dogs, too, which the dogs didn't seem to mind but which struck their owners as the most disturbing thing they'd ever seen; they had stolen spray paint from the hardware store and had started to repaint SUVs to their own artistic satisfaction, preferring SUVs for their large canvases... many people had woken to find that their huge Durangos and Explorers and Tahoes, once forest-green or canary-yellow, had been repainted with swirls of brown and day-glow orange; the little people had also taken to re-writing bumper-stickers, so that they had entirely different (and often absurd) meanings:

WE VOTE PRO-LIFE, for instance, became WE VOLES ARE PRO-KNIFE.

NO GOD, NO PEACE became NO GODFREY, NO PEAS!

IF IT'S TOO LOUD YOU'RE TOO OLD! became IF IT'S ON A CLOUD IT'S TOO COLD!

They were very good with a Sharpie and some white-out, but even they would be the first to admit these weren't terribly clever adages. And though they played all these games with broad smiles on their little faces and much laughter all around, none of the Burghvillians joined in. People remained, for the most part, locked inside, under siege. Even when the wee folk offered them tea or a smoke the humans would not reply, just walk on or run away.

Everyone except Henrietta Pratt, who joined them often. She did not care for the grass-tobacco (it gave her a headache) but she was learning to enjoy the tea. And she was learning to enjoy feeding the little people as well. She made them many meals, sneaking them out into her backyard where the wee folk would gather in groups to relax and talk with her. They had a preference for pies, she noticed. She made them cherry and pumpkin and apple pies. Only the latter went over a tad flatly: some of the wee folk told her it tasted like muck and threw it on the ground. Others seemed to enjoy it immensely. To make up with those who disliked it, she brought out some home-made cinnamon bread. The wee folk loved it, and they seemed to enjoy her as well, she noticed. They treated her with respect.

154

They left her flowers and bushes alone, too. She thought it was because she fed them real food. She was wrong. Later she would put two-and-two together.

"So, what exactly are you guys?" she asked them once.

This question nearly killed the whole relationship.

*

Days went by and little changed. Every moment it seemed there were more of the little people, either dangling precariously from electrical wires or dancing in the middle of the streets. Yards became deserts as the little creatures ate up the grass and used its roots to make their tea. Under the influence of the warm Spring weather people's flower gardens began to bloom, with roses and daisies proudly lifting their heads up to the sky, only to be immediately eaten by the wee folk. The only good thing for the people of Burghville was that after eating such flowers the wee folk appeared sluggish and ill. They would gulp down a handful of roses and then just lie around, moaning a bit... though their moans were melodic and soothing to the human ear, like the humming of a sensitive singer-songwriter from Seventies AM radio.

While they were lying around like this the people of Burghville could easily walk out to their cars without being hassled; the little monsters would just stare silently at them as they passed. Though this was unnerving, most Burghvillians took advantage of the lull in insanity and tried to get on with their lives.

However, things did not change for Buckthorn Industries. The Monday Dick Dick had written about in his inspirational letter came and went without any increase in worker attendance. Dick Dick, in his office, took this affront personally.

"Don't they get it?" he wondered, stewing in his anger, staring out his huge office windows at the empty campus of his company. "Don't they *see*?"

The unpatriotic bastards.

*

155

And so it went once the wee folk revealed themselves. Though the town still felt that it was under siege, by now most had also realized that the little creatures posed no physical threat. They were merely a hassle, little pains in the ass. Most of Burghville at least attempted to get on with their lives, but most of them also knew that there was a greater issue here than being under attack: a look around town revealed, quite plainly, that the way of life in Burghville had changed, that *that* was what was truly being threatened. Look at the yards: once beautiful and full, now they were nothing but dirt. Look at the flower gardens: nothing but cemeteries of bare skeletal stems. Look at the SUVs: covered in dreadful graffiti.

Burghville had once been the epitome of an American small town. It had been quiet, reserved, peaceful, beautiful, a place where you could raise a family the right way, where nothing much happened. A town where conventions were rarely, if ever, challenged. A town of surfaces, where everything was as it seemed, where there was a place for everything and everything was in its place.

Now look at it: a noisy zoo.

It was crazy.

It had to end.

Now.

*

Dick Dick Buckthorn picked up his cell phone and placed a call to Sheriff Sherman. He told the sheriff to get the word out that there was going to be a town meeting the following day, at which suggestions would be made as to how to solve this crisis.

"It's crazy," Dick Dick said, "and it has to end."

Sheriff Sherman agreed wholeheartedly. He had his own Plan, after all. And it was time.

156

8

Father Preston found a letter stapled to the front door of the St. Michael's Catholic Church. At first he thought he was being run out of town by angry Lutherans, then he thought it might be terms of surrender from the little people. He was wrong on both counts, of course, and the truth was worse.

It was from Carol Slugg. This is what it said:

Dear Father Preston:
As a concerned member of your congregation, I speak now on behalf of that entire congregation, and indeed on behalf of the entire town when I say that the time has come for the power and strength of the Lord Jesus Christ to rain down on the Satanic forces that now hold our town captive. As our representative of God, you are looked to by us to lead the charge of goodness. We look to you to guide us into the pit of this darkness as we attempt to cleanse and re-baptize our town. The Lord grants each of us certain gifts and gives to each of us
certain duties. We see your duty, as Father of our beloved and Holy Church, to be a leader in this fight. We ask you to please come to a plan of action, to consult with us on this plan of action, and to lead that action when the time comes. And the time is soon, dear
Father. The dark fog of Satan is on us now! We need you to lead the way for the Heavenly rays of God to shine down! We need you, in short, to now completely fill your role as spiritual adviser and intermediary for God's message and will. We need you to step up into this role, which you have been preparing for since you first heard the voice of God calling

you to the priesthood. We would hate to have to look elsewhere for this guidance, but rest assured we would have no choice should you fail now. Go in peace now, Father, as you begin the search for God's answer.

--Carol Slugg and the
St. Michael's Catholic Church

Father Preston read this letter on the steps of the church and upon finishing it felt a sick heaviness in his stomach. He looked around at the neighborhood in which the church sat. Large elm trees stood in every yard and the houses all had nice roofs and good siding, the pure backdrop of suburbia. It was a comfortable neighborhood... and yet he had never felt comfortable here. Even in his house he had not felt at home. Hard to feel at home, maybe, when the house you lived in was owned by a church's congregation. It made everything he did seem like at best an affront and at worst a sin. He felt horrible whenever he stank up the bathroom. And then there was that thing that happened to him every morning, that stirring that greeted him cheerily as it struggled against his pajama bottoms.

Well, that might not be his fault. A man cannot be held responsible for the reactions of his body to subconscious stimuli. Even the Pope, one assumes, has woken with certain engorgements. It was entirely natural... though imagine the disappointment that awaits the papal penis upon awakening.

No, a man cannot be held responsible for such things... though Father Preston knew quite well that *his* engorgement (which he liked to believe was on an entirely different scale than the Pope's) was the direct result of *tangible* stimuli: namely the girl, Helen Keller.

A man might not be held responsible for subconscious thoughts, but what if those subconscious thoughts were the direct result of *conscious* thoughts? What then?

Holding Carol Slugg's letter there on the steps of the church made him feel suddenly paranoid. Eyes were on

158

him, if only figuratively. People were looking to *him* for leadership. To *him*! To Lee Preston. The same Lee Preston who as a third-grader had once crapped his pants in phy-ed, who had gotten in trouble with three other eighth-graders when they had all tried to sneak into the girl's locker room, who had drifted through high-school like a zombie, who had once finger-fucked a girl in his parent's Buick LaSabre... and who, immediately after this latter episode, had had dreams wherein he had shrunk down to plastic army-man-size and crawled up inside of her, like some bizarre little explorer in a vaginal wonderland.

The same Lee Preston.

The same Lee Preston who dreamt now of Helen Keller, who thought the things he thought in the dark of night, who woke with a penis hard enough to pound nails. Who sometimes thought about the Pope's erections.

The same Lee Preston.

Standing there now, in the sunlight of this new day, looking around at the neighborhood, he thought:

What can I do?

We would hate to look elsewhere for this guidance, the letter had stated.

He knew damn well where she would get her guidance. Only Carol Slugg could lead Carol Slugg.

"Let her, then," he whispered to himself. He crumpled up the letter and turned to the church door. He pulled out a key, a heavy old thing that looked like it belonged to an ancient monastery, and unlocked that door. He pushed it open with a creak of its hinges and let a wash of new sunlight into the dusty interior of the church. He'd been keeping the place locked now, which just seemed a sensible thing to do. Part of the reason for this was keeping the little people out, and part of the reason, maybe the main part, was keeping Carol Slugg out. He knew the woman too well: some day she would lock herself in there and take over the whole thing, appoint herself High Priestess and declare the church its own country.

Maybe I should let her, he thought. He turned back to the door once he was in the church and re-locked it behind him with a clang.

He held the letter in his fist, crumpled and sweaty, and as he turned to walk down to the altar he realized that

159

fist was growing tighter and tighter. Was this unconscious rage? Sexual tension?

He was marching up the center aisle of the church, staring down at the floor in front of him, when he heard a cough. The sound was small and ragged, yet it echoed up to the rafters, off the Stations of the Cross statuary, away from the stained-glass saints on the windows, and around the altar. By the time it returned to his ears he had stopped walking and was standing there completely still. Very un-priest-like shivers stretched over his back.

"Father Preston?" a voice said. It, like the cough, was small and ragged... though pleasantly ragged, as are the voices of tough woodsmen or aging poets and painters. You hear such a voice and you picture wrinkled eyes twinkling warmly, tough mouths set tight in purpose yet quick to smile. You picture a beard like a snow-covered woods.

Father Preston turned his head slowly and immediately lowered his gaze three feet.

"It's good to finally meet you," said the little man standing there. He did indeed have warm wrinkled eyes, a friendly mouth, and a gray-speckled beard. He did indeed seem to radiate wisdom... though of an unassuming and unforced type. He pulled a pipe from a pocket and smiled at the priest. "Mind if I smoke?"

The pipe lit itself with a tiny orange flash. Smoke rose to the air in a single thin column and made its way to the highest point of the church's ceiling, where it congregated politely, away from the lungs of the human. Within seconds the little ball of smoke broke apart and faded, disappeared completely. Father Preston could smell nothing but the familiar odors of the church.

The little man's smile broadened as he pulled the pipe from his lips. "One should avoid second-hand smoke," he said.

*

Burghville's Town Hall was a large white building near the courthouse. There was a large yard around it, which was usually full of plush grass but which was now nothing but dirt and a few dead and dried strands of

160

Creeping Charlie. The Town Hall was mostly one room, a great open space filled with chairs and a podium on a stage. The other rooms were much smaller and were used for administrative duties, and as such were tucked at the rear of the building, like shameful private orifices. On this day that great open hall was filling with people, the sound of their feet on the old hardwood floor like the sound of elephants shuffling nervously. Whispers and murmurs filled the place. There was talk the entire town would show this day, even those who had not dared venture outside since the appearance of the little monsters. It would be a spill-over crowd, was the word: like a scene from a Southern melodrama, with people perched in the open windows or standing for a glimpse through the front door, everyone fanning themselves in the swamp of body-heat. In the crowd outside people would ask: "What'd he say?" and a murmur would go backwards, repeating some grand bit of wisdom. This meeting had been the talk of the town ever since Sheriff Sherman had announced it the day before. It had spread like proverbial wildfire down the streets and sidewalks and alleyways. If nothing else, its very mention suggested to the people of Burghville that their town leaders were actually *doing* something, were finally getting serious. People like to believe their leaders were busy finding solutions. It was a comforting thought, realistic or not. Much more comforting to believe your politicians were actually working than it was to picture them standing around performing, say, a Senatorial circle jerk.

Standing at the front of the Town Hall were Sheriff Sherman and Dick Dick Buckthorn. They were talking quietly to each other as people continued to file into the building. What they were discussing is unknown, but when the figure of Helen Keller entered and took a standing position against the back wall they each fell silent and turned to look at her. They stared at her as men sometimes will at a young woman: blatantly.

She looked, as usual, very pretty, like something you'd find growing in a field, something natural and healthy and full of boundless kinetic energy. She had the grace of a beast and yet the stillness of a plant. She was part squirrel and part trillium, part badger and part spotted

161

coralroot. She was the prairie smoke tickling the ass of a stalking bobcat. She was a sunflower and a whitetail doe, merged somehow into the aesthetically pleasing form of a young Caucasian biped.

Sheriff Sherman and Dick Dick Buckthorn both understood this, even if they could not quite put it into these words. To them, the above flower references would be so much gibberish. What they knew was that she was gorgeous and fresh and natural.

What they didn't know was that she had almost not come to this meeting. What they also didn't know was this:

*

She had slipped through the forest that morning quietly, searching out the source of the flute music wafting like a breeze through the air. She felt it was about time she sought out these new and exciting little creatures. It was about time she tried getting to know them.

It was proving to be a warmer morning than the one before, though when she woke there had been a cool and soft dew lying like crystal beads on her chest, and though when she rose and left the womb of her tent to squat behind the nearest tree her skin had tightened like a drum. Despite this, she could feel in the slowly rising sun a threatening warmth, as if it was going to lay over the land in a manner it hadn't since Memorial Day. She dressed and made a small fire in her pit. She had wood sorted already, each different size given its own pile: tiny twigs for kindling, the next size up to feed the fire, intermediate-sized sticks for forming a good solid base, and then progressively larger sticks for the meat of the whole works. Separating the firewood in such a way was one of the first acts she did upon returning to this place each summer. It made the campsite look neat and orderly. Indeed, Helen kept this area cleaner and neater than a lot of people kept their homes. Her reason for this was simple: she was a tenant here, this being not only her home but also the home of snakes and field mice and squirrels and jays and chickadees and ants and rabbits. A person had to be sensitive when one is a guest, so she kept it as clean and orderly as she could. Besides, this really was her *home*. It

162

was the only home she knew anymore, besides that house she hibernated in during the winter. This was where she lived, and a person must take care of the place they live, especially when that place is as beautiful as this.

"I used to live on a cliff overlooking the Atlantic Ocean," Sam the Artist had once said. "I found it to be the ideal place for meditation... until I realized I was not focusing on my mantra so much as the roar of the breaking waves below me. Nature has never served my purposes as far as enlightenment goes. I find it distracting."

"Nature is enlightenment," Helen had said.

"I want to find the nature of enlightenment, not the enlightenment of nature."

"I thought Zen was about nature."

"Not my Zen."

"Fuck you and your Zen."

"Search not for the Zen of fuck, but the fuck of Zen."

"Jesus..."

"Now *there*," he said, "was a person like you, who went to the wilderness to search for enlightenment. I guess that's been a popular thing to do throughout the ages. All the prophets went to the desert. They talked to snakes. Jesus talked to a snake, I believe. The snake was the devil. The snake tempted Jesus. Jesus told it to go to hell."

Helen snorted her disapproval. "Instead snakes lived on, and Jesus died. There's a lesson there."

Sam had laughed and stared at her.

"What?" she asked. She thought maybe she had something on her lip. They had been making a dinner of pasta and white sauce when this conversation had picked up, while outside a virgin snowfall lost its virginity in a threesome with gravity and ground.

"Snakes," he said with a sigh. "It's always snakes, snakes, snakes. You know, the idea of snakes as evil creatures came very late in Christianity's life. When the Bible was written snakes were held in high regard, seen as symbols of both fertility and reincarnation. Cobras are worshiped in India even today."

"Ridiculous," Helen said. "Snakes don't need our worship. They don't need us at all, period. No animal does."

Sam smiled as he stirred the sauce. "That is why I like my Zen. It's my own personal Zen, my own search for enlightenment and beauty."

"Which makes it selfish."

"Well, it's not for everybody."

"It's pompous. If it's only for you, and only for your enlightenment, then that must mean you think you're better than the rest of us. You hope to be more-enlightened-than-thou."

"You know me better than that. I would love for you to join me in my search for enlightenment, but alas I will not go to the wilderness and you cannot join me where I go. Give me that spoon."

"And where do you go?"

He tapped his head, then his heart, then his belly.

"Jesus…" she said again.

He smiled. "Do you talk to snakes when you're out there in the woods?"

"Yes."

"And what do they tell you?"

"They tell me you need to keep stirring that sauce or it will burn."

He smiled again, a sort of Buddha-smile, and then after a few moments had passed, with the sound of the bubbling sauce and the boiling water for background, he told her a poem:

"Love is an illusion, untouchable, only the pain of its exit tangible and hard/ a man may butt his head into a tree and feel the same/ and never yet know the joys."

"Did you write it for anyone in particular?"

"Yes. For mankind."

Her turn to smile, hers not at all Buddha-like… more like the smile of the lotus flower Buddha sneezed upon.

"Tomorrow," she said, "I'll take you to the woods. It's time you leave those damn paintings and spiders and what-not alone and come out with me. I'll teach you to talk to the snakes."

"Will they *want* to talk with me?"

"If you're respectful."

She stood over her little fire, cooking her breakfast on this hot morning and remembering that conversation.

She remembered most of their conversations nearly in full because each of them had been like little poems, like conversations seen in the shapes of clouds. Sometimes she thought of things she *should* have said, retorts and philosophical rebuttals she wished she'd been able to bounce back at him, such as asking him if Buddha had not found enlightenment while in nature... while sitting under a fig tree, in fact. But she knew what he would have said:

"That was Buddha. I'm not Buddha."

To which she would have told him he was starting to resemble a Buddha anyway, and that he should go easy on the pasta. And to which he would have said:

"Will the snakes talk to a fat man?"

And she would have said: "If he's respectful."

It was for the sake of this latter statement that the memory had come to her this morning. Her mind sometimes worked like that, in a roundabout way. She'd been thinking, as she stirred the coals and flattened the fire enough to accommodate her grill, of how best to approach those little people. She'd been wondering if they would even talk to her, but then she realized:

They would if she was respectful.

The book *Celtic Mythology* had not proven very useful, unfortunately. About all she had gotten out of it was that the town of Burghville was inexplicably dealing with a sudden outbreak of fairies... although don't call them fairies, the book said. Call them the Good People, or Fair Folk, or the Gentry. They apparently get pissed when you call them fairies. Homophobic little wee folk.

The book had not said anything about why they appeared or what they wanted or how to get rid of them. In fact, the only thing the book had truly done was confirm that these were in fact wee folk. Burghville was being overrun by the Gentry. Which in itself was very interesting, if not revealing: the book had not taken sides in the debate about whether or not such creatures actually existed, which hadn't seemed to be much of a debate in today's modern digital world. So, that said, it was interesting that such an ancient myth should be proven real in a place like Burghville. What next? Sasquatch on Main? UFOs landing at the City Park? Werewolves

165

running for city office? Vampires on the night-shift at the Amoco?

"Jesus turning water to coffee at Joe's Joe?" she heard the phantom voice of Sam say. "A short-order Christ?"

She cooked her breakfast this morning quickly, just some sloppy pre-made pancake mix and water, shaken vigorously and poured onto a griddle. They cooked slowly at first, then started to sizzle at the edges. While this happened she spooned coffee into a pot and placed it over the coals. By the time the pancakes were done the coffee was done as well and she was sitting back, letting this new morning fill her with its promise.

In a nearby tree a downy-woodpecker hammered patiently for insects. She watched him and he occasionally watched her, two Earthlings enjoying breakfast. Two living beings doing what living beings do, crossing paths only briefly.

In the fluttery movement of his body around the tree trunk she read the following:

Just do what you do. That's all life requires of us...

She raised her tin coffee cup to him. Amen.

*

"My name," said the little man in the church, "is said to be confusing for humans. A tongue-twister, I guess. You can call me Orson. It's the closest I can get."

"Orson," Father Preston repeated softly, barely above a whisper.

Orson was walking down the aisle, headed towards the altar. He turned after a few steps and smiled at Father Preston.

"Aye," he said. "Orson. Does that work for you?"

"Work... for me?"

Orson placed his pipe in his mouth, sucked in some smoke, and nodded. His eyes were like magical coals. When he exhaled the smoke drifted lazily from his nose, rose up to the rafters, and like the rest of his exhalations faded into nothingness.

166

"I take it I don't offend you," said Orson. His voice had an accent... vaguely Scottish, yet with its own strange inflections.

Father Preston shook his head. "No...."

"Good." The little man turned and continued up to the front of the church. When he came to the first step that led up to the altar he took off his hat. Father Preston thought for a moment that this was an act of respect to the sanctity of the church, but then the little man tossed the hat to his left, where it came to rest on the bowed head of the life-size statue of Mary that hung from the wall there. On the opposite side of the church, like a companion bookend, was Jesus. This latter was one of two life-sized works of statuary depicting Christ: the other sat further to the left and showed him in agony on the cross.

Orson took a look around the church from the vicinity of the altar, surveying all the statues and the intricate woodwork and the play of sunlight through the stained-glass windows.

"Magnificent place you have here," he said.

Father Preston hesitated, then started for the altar. "Thanks."

"The symbol of your religion is an ancient device of torture," the little man said, smiling all the while down at the priest.

"That's one way to look at it."

"Aye... and what's the other way to look at it?"

"It's a symbol of what our Savior went through to save our souls."

Orson inhaled on his pipe calmly, nodding.

Father Preston came to the altar and stood looking at the little man.

"What do you want?" he asked.

The pipe came out of the bearded mouth. "I'd like to talk."

"Why? And what about?"

Orson's eyes twinkled. The pipe went back into his mouth, then was removed. With a slight movement of his lips the little man exhaled a small cloud that hovered for a moment in the air. Then, with a subtle movement the cloud took the shape of a perfect cross, a geometrically

167

precise crucifix. A second later it broke apart into a thousand little clouds which dissipated into nothing.

"About whatever's on your mind, dear Father," Orson said, eyes alight. "For starters."

*

The beauty of nature is this: it does not give a shit about you, and yet it permits you to take from it all the wisdom it has to offer... if, that is, you take the time to notice. Every second she was out in a forest or a field, Helen Keller took notice. She did not always understand the wisdom that was given to her, but she at least understood that it *was* wisdom and that it *was* given to her. Years could go by before she might understand its full meaning. Such was the nature of nature's lessons: not elusive, but patient.

On this morning she finished her breakfast and let her fire die down. When she had cleaned up her campsite, when she had tidied up her tent and the few personal belongings that sat here and there, she noticed there were still some coals left. The worst thing to do, she believed, was douse a fire. It was disrespectful to the energy of the flames... that energy which, of course, was the very reason humanity had persisted so long as a viable species. The energy of fire was what enabled mankind to evolve as much as it had. Without fire where would we be? There ought to be a religion around it like there had been once, a worship of flame.

Why had none of the fire-gods persisted? she wondered as she studied those few remaining coals. Certainly fire was still a valuable and valued thing in today's society, so why had those particular deities allowed themselves to get bastardized and co-opted and drowned during the rise of Christianity and Islam and Hinduism? Perhaps the fire-gods simply weren't as strong as she thought they were. Nevertheless, she believed it was sacrilege to douse a fire. And still, this said, she had no choice this morning: she gathered up handfuls of sand and poured it down to the flames.

Helen Keller: destroyer of unborn religions, terminator of creeds! However, fortunately or unfortunately, she was also a member of humankind and therefore she could make another fire that night, so:

Helen Keller: mother of flame.   And, quite possibly, who knows, if things turned out the right way, sometime in the distant future: Mother of the New Fire Faith!

It was mid-morning now, and the flute music of the Gentry could still be heard off in the distance.

She began to follow it to its source.

*

"We are an ancient race," Orson was saying. He had hopped up onto the altar and was sitting there smoking his pipe and dangling his feet. Those feet, by the way, like the feet of all the wee folk, were covered in soft leather shoes, your basic moccasins. All of the wee folk's clothes resembled the clothes of certain aboriginal peoples: hand-made, rough yet attractive, practical yet not without charm. However, a close look revealed that the buttons were some pure sort of metal, smooth as steel yet lustrous as opals. No bone or shells or rocks for them: even the Good People had room for style.

Father Preston was standing on the floor of the church, two steps below that altar and therefore now looking up at the little man before him. He had not closed his mouth in a long while.

"An ancient people," Orson said, "who have been around since what you will call the Dawn of Time. We are among the very oldest of the races. We are of this earth through and through, as much a part of it as the minerals and plants and animals. That said, you could imagine that some sort of power of observation has developed among us. After all, if you've seen it a million times you sort of know how it will turn out. Life on this world is a lot like syndicated reruns, shall we say. Aye?"

Father Preston said nothing.

Orson nodded.   "Aye.   And yet there remain mysteries.   Of course, always mysteries.   Life itself is maybe not a mystery, not to us, but there are still shadowed spots we haven't fully explored. There are still corners of the world we haven't been to." He sucked on his pipe and

169

looked at the priest out of the corner of his eye. "Are you understandin' me, dear lad?"

Father Preston shook his head.

"No? Well, ye don't need to, not really. Suffice it to say that there are those among us who are curious, some more so than others, and there are those who are adventurous, some more so than others, and... well, let's just say the reason we are here, good Father, is because of that curiosity and that spirit of adventure. The details are rather boring, and actually protocol demands I don't speak of them. Nevertheless, we are here in your neck of the woods, and we are a presence to be dealt with. Oh, not in any threatening way. But..." The little man smiled at the priest. "There are those among you who know what we are. To be sure, you can count on that. There are people here among you who know what we are and why we are here." He sighed. "There are also those who *think* they know what we are and why we are here, but they are mistaken and misled. This old crone, for instance, the one who carried the instrument of torture in your parade..."

"Carol Slugg," Father Preston said.

Orson made a face of disgust... practically winced at the mention of the name. "Aye... Carol Slugg. She is a blithering idiot. Believes we are of the Devil, or some such thing. I'd like to ask her which Devil. Throughout history there have been many that your people believed in."

"Lucifer."

"Beg pardon?"

"Lucifer. She means Lucifer. Satan. The devil of the Bible."

Orson laughed to himself. "Aye... and which Bible, good Father? There have been many of those, too."

"*Our* Bible."

Orson smiled. "I understood what you meant. You'll have to forgive me, I'm one for arguments. I like debates. I like thought. I like to lead others into thought. I was once a teacher of sorts, and I guess I still am. Only... well, you're my only student right now."

Father Preston frowned. "Why me?"

"I told you we were an observant lot, my race. It comes with age, I'm afraid. And I, good friend, am among

170

the oldest of my race still walking this earth. Too old for some things, still much too young for others."

"So... why me?" Father Preston could not shake the ominous feeling that had crept up his back and nested in his spine like a bird. He could not look through the oddness of this encounter, the strangeness of the whole thing. It was as if he had fallen into the pages of a fairy tale, yet it was not like a dream. It was real and vivid.

Orson smiled again and puffed on his pipe. He said: "I've observed some things about you, good Father. I know what's in your heart."

Father Preston swallowed.

Orson laughed again, the pipe bouncing up and down between his teeth.

"Don't be worried, Father. I didn't mean to make it sound so... so gothic. I know how it must look and feel. Let me put it another way: I hate to see an intelligent and sensitive being go off course chasing shadows. If only such a being could open his mind he might see another world, one of wonder and beauty. Perhaps even the world that already lies within himself."

Father Preston said nothing.

Orson nodded pleasantly, the warm smile back under his beard, twinkles in his eyes. His little feet swung playfully back and forth, like those of a delighted child on the end of a dock.

"I just think you and I should talk," he said.

*

The woods were lovely this day. Lovely dark and deep... no, not dark at all, bathed in a golden wash of sunlight. Every living tree, every tangle of undergrowth, every blade of grass, every speck of bare earth, every rabbit scrape, every pellet of deer shit, every stiffening mink corpse, every bright genitalia of every spring-blooming flower, every deadfall trunk, every rotted old fungus-infected stump, every mockingbird hidden deep in every bush, every darting cardinal and every sighing field they darted over, everything in this forest today was absolutely and utterly beautiful. It wasn't just the soft touch of sunlight over it all, either, it was just that every now and then the ever-expanding length of the Universe permitted a blanket of beauty to sneak into the world... into every world. Mars has its gorgeous days. Venus is said to look its finest on Earth's August 24th. Visit Jupiter's moon Io on March 16th and your eyes will water. The Universe permits cracks to form in the blandness of existence. Perhaps it does this more often than not, but it cannot be said that existence necessitates beauty and wonder, nor can it be said that life is beautiful simply because it *is* life: look at any Senator, lawyer, televangelist, and you will struggle to see anything aesthetically pleasing. No, life and existence do not in and of themselves cause beauty. Only the Universe can do that, by opening those cracks in perception. And this was one of those days.

Of course, it may be that this day was beautiful only in the eyes of Helen Keller. Beauty might very well be in the eye of the beholder.... since even on its best days there is little to appreciate in the Saturn moon Titan.

But Helen did indeed find this day beautiful, at least as far as it played out in the forest. She walked calmly among the trees, cutting through underbrush like she was a ghost gliding through walls, jumping onto giant fallen trees and walking their lengths, playing monkey-bars in their branches, then swimming through fields, stopping to smell flowers or observe the work of bees. Once she saw a garter snake lying at the edge of a field and she paused to admire its freshly-dark and vivid colors. It had recently shed, and she reflected on ancient man's reverence for the serpent as a potent symbol of reincarnation. Reincarnation as Helen saw it was bullshit, but it was still a lovely thought. It was poetry, not fact. Sometimes mankind has taken poetry too seriously and made religions out of it. Alas. However, there were better reasons for revering snakes.

She admired the bright and perky little wide-eyed fellow for a while, then moved on.

She hopped over tiny streams, crossed meadows, pondered the twisted trunk of a dead tree at the top of a kettle, then finally came to where the music was loudest.

It was a single flute, sending melodic trills into the air. Had it been a saxophone instead, and had it been coming from the farthest end of a New York tenement alley on some hot and rainy summer night, it would have sounded jazzy, something John Lurie might lay down as an afterthought.

But it was just a flute. *Some* form of flute, anyway. It sounded wooden, homemade. Pretty.

Helen came to a hill and knelt down at the top to look over at the other side. This was a dark part of the forest, and quite close to town. In fact, she heard a car horn at one point, an agitated driver pissed at a member of the Gentry, most likely. Still, it was dark and wet here, nestled in the lowlands. Shadows of night hung on all day in this area, partings in the branches above bringing down only a few curtains of sunlight. Those canopy-producing trees were massive, and the ground below them sparsely vegetated. The ground was quite open, in fact, covered only with a soft blanket of last year's leaves. Yet it was a lovely and joyous place... made more so by the presence of the Good People down below.

Helen had no misconceptions that she could sneak up on them. And indeed, when she looked over that hill the flute music instantly stopped and every little head down there turned her way. Quiet filled this section of the woods. A cardinal may have sung its song, but that was all.

Helen swallowed. There were maybe twenty of the little people down there, some sitting on stumps, some smoking pipes, others paused in mid-dance. All of them were staring at her.

A few seconds went by and then each and every one of them said, in unison:

"Greetings Helen!"

She had been fully expecting that greeting. Had it not come she would have been very disappointed.

*

"What makes you think there's *anything* on my mind?" Preston the Father asked Orson the wee folk. It came out the wrong way, but before he could re-phrase it Orson said:

"It's all over you like a stain."

"There's nothing on my mind, other than...." He stopped and stared at the little man.

173

Orson, for his part, puffed seriously on his pipe, then smiled and exhaled a perfectly spherical cloud that moved past the ducking priest and down the aisle of the church. At the front doors it faded... or so it seemed to Father Preston. In fact, the sphere passed through the heavy wood and out into the sunlight. There it rose up to the steeple and knocked against one of the bells, sending a single lovely tone over the town.

Father Preston barely heard the tone. He was staring intently at the little man on the altar, thinking about Rumpilstiltskin and whether this little fellow knew there would be no first-born young coming from the priest before him.

"Love," Orson said.

Father Preston frowned. "What?"

"Love is on your mind. Or something quite like it."

Father Preston's frown deepened.

"You *are* in love, are you not, even as we speak?"

And deepened.

Orson smiled. "Aye, you are. It too is all over you like a stain. A much lovelier stain."

And deepened still.

Orson took another deep puff on his pipe and settled back a bit to observe Father Preston carefully. The little man's eyes sparkled with intelligence and mischief. His smile was open and friendly.

"Aye," he said softly. "Love...."

*

The first thing Helen had asked the wee folk, once she was given a tiny cup of grass-root tea, was this:

"What's the name of that tune you've been playing?"

The flute-playing little man on the sun-bathed stump was named Puddlefoot. He answered this way:

"Tomfoolery in C major."

And he gave her a little riff that pleased everyone.

*

174

The Town Hall continued to fill with people long after Sheriff Sherman and Dick Dick Buckthorn noticed the appearance of Helen Keller. They came, these people, in groups of no less than four. There was safety in numbers, apparently, or so they thought. These groups marched quickly into the Town Hall, where Sheriff Sherman had positioned three of his six deputies at the front doors as sentries. This use of the deputies served both to reassure the gathering Burghvillians and also to make a point: Sheriff Sherman planned to propose, for the first time, the details of his Plan, and those three deputies would be the first incarnation of what he had in mind. Feel safe with just those nitwits out there? he would ask, in so many words. Then imagine how you would feel with fifty? A hundred? Five hundred? Imagine how a SWAT team would make you feel. Imagine how safe you would feel with a platoon of law enforcement officers continually making the rounds of Burghville's streets, keeping them free of any and all dangers. Just imagine.

He scanned the swelling audience for the face of his wife and could not see her. Good. He didn't need to look out there and see her laughing when he made the suggestion. He didn't need her lack of confidence. He didn't need her, period.

The town gathered together this day with looks of seriousness on their faces. The only people who didn't have this look were Helen Keller (she appeared both amused and worried), Henrietta Pratt (who looked almost absurdly happy, smiling a big contented smile at everyone) and Tracey and Timmy White (who looked guilty). The Town Hall filled to overflow with the standing-room only crowd, and the seriousness pervaded all present. The children, too, much to their credit, had sensed the grimness of this day's tone and were, for the most part, keeping silent. A few teenagers giggled and flipped each other off across the room, a baby screamed three high-pitched demonic screams of the sort only an infant can manage, a six-year old made fart noises, and a ten-year old boy kept asking his dad if they could stop at the Dairy Queen on the way home. In general, though, everyone was solemn and sober.

175

Except, someone else who didn't look serious was Candy Cleaver. Like Henrietta Pratt she looked absurdly happy... but she also looked the way cartoon characters look after someone whacks them with a frying pan. She emitted a faint odor of rubber-cement, and there was a subtle sheen under her nose, a gleaming mustache.

Dick Dick Buckthorn, still standing next to Sheriff Sherman, managed to move his eyes from the form of Helen Keller to that of his wife.

Betty Buckthorn was sitting front and center. For some reason she had worn a low-cut shirt that accentuated her cleavage. She had said it was going to be a hot day and she wasn't going to sit in a stuffy building with three hundred or so other hot people and not be comfortable. But that, Dick Dick thought now, was a hell of a lot of cleavage. And that skirt, was that something a respectable businessman's wife ought to be wearing? If she were to sneeze or have a sudden brilliant idea that skirt would rise up and reveal, to anyone who might be looking, her baby-blue panties. Sweet Lord!

Dick Dick shook his head and looked away from his wife. His eyes fell on the gnarled countenance of Carol Slugg, who looked like a sickly vulture impatiently waiting for the body of modern culture to die so she could feast on her righteousness.

Dick Dick shivered.

In time the crowd swelled to its capacity and no more people came into the building. Everyone who was coming was here, the rest were still barricaded in their homes or, worse, being prevented from coming by the little vermin themselves.

Sheriff Sherman leaned close to Dick Dick and whispered: "The Mayor should be here."

Dick Dick sighed. "Mayor Darrow is no longer a viable part of this community."

Sheriff Sherman sighed. He would have preferred proposing his Plan with the Mayor present, or at least someone who had some pull. But perhaps the people he really needed on his side were these here: the citizens. And Dick Dick Buckthorn, after all, was large enough, in both the physical and influential sense of the term, to have his own gravitational authority.

"Let's get this thing going," Dick Dick said. He stepped away from the sheriff and stood behind the podium, dwarfing it. He leaned down to the microphone and tapped it with one large index finger.

The microphone exploded.

*

"I don't know what you're talking about," Father Preston said. "I love no one. I mean, I love... I love God, and Jesus, and...."

He was still standing two steps below Orson, who remained casually perched on the altar, still swinging his legs like a lazy and contented child. The smell of the little man's pipe was the most wild odor ever to appear in that church... at least since one of the original workers on the structure had fired up a doobie at lunch-time, just prior to dry-walling the basement. This smell, this grass-tobacco odor, was much more untamed than the typical church smells: stale incense, over-sweet fat-woman perfume, morning-breath, the funk of Saturday-night sex and day-after guilt.

The little man took the pipe from his mouth and shook his head. "I believe there's someone else."

Father Preston frowned. He wondered if it was possible that this little man had seen him walk by Helen Keller's house all those times. The thought was more than scary.

"Listen, dear Father. I'm only here to talk with you, pass the time, as they say. I like discussions. I like give and take, learning, teaching, sharing stories, getting to the heart of something. So, that is my only agenda here, not accusing, not corrupting. Just talk." The little man sighed. "And something tells me, just from having observed you, that you are interested in talking with me too."

Father Preston did not reply. He simply stood there, staring up at the little man. His choice seemed obvious: talking in here with this strange little man, or going out *there* and facing the likes of Carol Slugg, who would be asking him, in the face of this "crisis," to make decisions he didn't have it in him to make.

177

Orson was examining his pipe, which had apparently gone out. He was staring into the bowl like he was amazed to find it empty. After a moment or two of this he looked back at Father Preston.

"Tell me," he said, "why did you become a priest?"

*

After the smoke from the little explosion had wafted into the hot and stale air of the Town Hall, and after Dick Dick had carefully checked his finger for burn marks, and after the crowd had settled again, Dick Dick passed on a microphone and let his booming CEO-voice do the amplifying, hoping everyone could look past his singed eyebrows:

"Welcome, everyone. Good afternoon. Most of you know me, Dick Dick Buckthorn, and of course this here's Sheriff Sherman." He looked at the Sheriff, and something passed between them... at the prodding of Sheriff Sherman's raised eyebrows.

Dick Dick sighed. "Sheriff Sherman would like first to express his thanks to his deputies for keeping this meeting safe. Deputy Day, Deputy Dill, and Deputy Dew are out front ensuring the security of all of us here. You've all seen them when you came in. Sheriff Sherman and I would like to express our thanks."

Mild applause for the deputies.

"Now," Dick Dick said, "now let's get down to what this is all about." He gazed out at the crowd like a preacher contemplating a congregation. "We all know what's been going on. This town is under siege, pure and simple. We're experiencing something the likes of which we've never seen before. None of us has seen anything like these little... *vermin* before."

Tracey and Timmy White exchanged glances.

"And there's a good chance no one else in the entire world has ever seen anything like this. There's a good chance, fellow citizens, that Burghville is experiencing something unique, that Burghville alone is under siege, and that, as a result, Burghville alone must find a solution."

178

"Why don't we call in the National Guard?" someone called out. A murmur of approval rose from the crowd.

Dick Dick frowned. He had expected to make a speech, not carry on a conversation. His CEO-voice was not used to taking questions.

"Call in the Army!" someone yelled. Soon many voices were calling out solutions, each person expressing a desire to see a favorite branch of the Armed Service marching down Burghville's Main Street.

Dick Dick held his hand up for silence.

"Listen," he said, "I know that calling in outside forces who are better equipped to handle such things is the first emotional response in times like this. But if you'll all sit back and hear me out, I think I can show you why that would be the worst thing to do." He stepped closer to the crowd, giving them what Betty Buckthorn called his *I can feel your pain* look. "First of all, do we want to be the laughing-stock of the rest of the world? 'Look at poor little Burghville, it can't handle its own problems.' I think not. We've always prided ourselves on our insular attitude, on our self-sufficiency. People, we don't *need* any outsiders trotting in here and feeling superior when they solve our problems. We don't need that and we don't want that, do we?"

A collective "No!" rose into the air.

"Secondly, I believe we *can* solve this problem. We've got brains, we've got will-power, we've got passion. We can solve this problem ourselves as surely as we have solved any other."

"How?" someone called out.

"Bring in the Marines!" someone shouted.

Dick Dick glared at this last person. "Didn't I just go over that?" Then he looked at the rest of the crowd.

They stared back expectantly.

"Before we understand the *how*," he said, "we must make sure we understand the *why*. Why, people, *why* do we even want to solve this problem?"

A murmur spread through the crowd. It was a confused murmur and Helen Keller, back there against the wall, easily read the single thought that accompanied it:

What in the hell is he talking about?

After the murmur had subsided, some individual voices broke out, at first clearly delineated and then overlapping.

"One at a time!" Dick Dick said, again raising a hand.

"Our *yards*," a big-bellied man said. "Take a look around town for Chrissake! Look at our yards! Everything looks like a damn desert out there! Burghville used to be pretty, every summer it was the prettiest little town I've ever seen, and now look at it! Those *things* are destroying everything!"

"Our flowers too!" a woman called out. "They've set up camp in my tulips and daffodils and eat whatever moves! They eat whatever *doesn't* move! And I can't even get in there to weed around the ones they haven't touched. He's right: Burghville used to be pretty, and now...."

"And what about the SUVs?" someone else asked. "This damn graffiti they do! Everything looks terrible! Burghville is starting to look like a ghetto!"

The crowd rumbled in agreement.

"They're hedonists! Ungodly hedonists! Drinking and smoking and eating and doing nothing else!"

Dick Dick just stood there, watching everyone, nodding as they spoke. Sheriff Sherman, just a few feet away, was nearly shaking, itching as he was to disclose his Plan. He just had to wait for the proper moment.

"The only person's yard they haven't attacked is Henrietta Pratt!"

The rumbling rose in volume and heads turned to search out the sun-dress-wearing figure of Henrietta Pratt, who was still smiling contentedly.

"That's because she feeds them!" someone said.

Now the rumbling became the sort of sound that can accompany a mob. Many a lynching has started with such a noise.

"I've seen her! She feeds the damn things!"

"I've seen her too!"

Henrietta Pratt said nothing. She stared back at her accusers defiantly.

Helen Keller knew what the woman was thinking: she was thinking that there was no law against feeding the little people, and she was also thinking *Fuck you!* to each of her fellow townsfolk.

Many people thought that two-word phrase, Helen knew. Many of them wished it at others all the time. It was the single most common thought people had around Christmastime, in fact. And yet Helen had never known anyone to think it with the same pleasant calmness as Henrietta Pratt. She thought it with effortless ease, and with an utter lack of bitterness. Fuck you, like saying good morning.

Dick Dick silenced everyone and looked down at Henrietta Pratt. "Did you want to say something to that?" he asked.

Fuck you! radiated from her like a halo.

"No," she said simply.

Dick Dick sighed, clearly disappointed in her, and looked at the others. "Why else do we even want to solve this problem? What are these little monsters doing?"

"Attacking machinery! Our phone hasn't worked since they've been here!"

"That's right! And yesterday they started up my snowmobile and drove it down the street! The track is shredded now!"

Marty LaBelle the mail-man rose and addressed everyone: "They've taken to ruining my route! I deliver the mail and they catch up to me a few houses down, handing me the letters I just delivered. 'You dropped this,' they say to me." He looked at everyone. "That's why you haven't been getting your mail. I've been *trying* to keep up with my job, but..."

"That's a Federal offense!" someone said in absolute shock.

"They're an affront to everything Burghville stands for!"

Dick Dick jumped on this last comment, it was what he'd been waiting for. "Yes," he said, voice booming over the Town Hall, "yes, what you just said. They're an affront to everything Burghville stands for! But what else?"

Another murmur, this one of contemplation. As it was for most crowds, especially those murmuring like a mob, contemplation was difficult. Minutes passed. Then:

181

"They're an affront to everything that is good and American!"

This was Candy Cleaver, speaking up through a glistening mustache of rubber-cement.

Dick Dick's smile widened. The murmur of the crowd settled into silence. Everyone thought this over.

Helen Keller looked at the back of Candy Cleaver's head and read this message:

Lysol burns but Pledge has the edge.

Dick Dick nodded. "Exactly," he said. "Exactly. These little monsters are not just an affront to our little town, but to the nation as a whole. Imagine if they were to spread! Just imagine: factories shutting down, businesses failing, the government dismantled! Imagine: America under siege. Our great nation hostage to a million little monsters!"

The crowd stayed silent, contemplating the frightening image. Again Dick Dick stood there smiling, letting his point sink into the citizens of Burghville like an arrowhead.

"It's up to us," he said in time, in a softer voice. "It's up to us to stop it. *That* my friends is *why* we have to do something. Now... just what do we do?"

"Kill them!" someone shouted. This was another big-bellied man, around thirty-five, with a PETA cap on his head (People Eating Tasty Animals) and a NASCAR shirt stretched over his gut.

At this, and at the approving sound of the crowd, Henrietta Pratt finally stood to speak:

"Where in the world is your humanity!" she asked. "Where in the world is your compassion for other living beings?"

People booed her. Someone told her to sit down.

"They're not *humans*!" a voice called out, nearly hysterical. "You'd cry over such beasts and let us suffer, you bleeding heart!"

"Not humans?" Henrietta said. "Look at them! Two eyes, a nose, a mouth, beards, walking upright, *talking*... what do you mean? They are absolutely humanoid! They fulfill all the definitions of being human!"

182

People shushed her, booed her, waived their hands in her direction in a gesture of dismissal. A single clear voice could be heard:

"They're not human! They're too little to be human!"

At this, Scooter Boober stood on his chair. Only those around him had known he was present, but now everyone quieted.

"Excuse me?" he asked in a surprisingly forceful voice. He looked toward Dick Dick Buckthorn.

Dick Dick shivered, thinking: *Midgets*....

Scooter Boober said. "Let's find some other qualification, other than size, for not being human, please." Then he sat down.

"Well..." the man in the NASCAR shirt said. "Well... what the hell are they, then? What the hell are these things?"

Suggestions arose. Only three people in town truly knew, and all of them were present at this meeting: Helen Keller, and Tracey and Timmy White. None of them spoke, however, as suggestions were made:

Demons;

Mutations;

Aliens;

And on and on. At last an old man stood. He was the same old man who had spoken at the parade, the same old man no one had listened to. Now, here at this meeting, he said the same thing he had said then:

"Them's elves."

A hush settled on the Burghvillians. Everyone was both struck by the solemnity and authority with which he spoke, and also confused, because the old man had old dentures and his speech was unclear.

"Themselves," someone repeated. This is what they thought he said: Themselves. And something about the normally unthreatening word was morbid and eerie in this context. Themselves.

"Themselves," someone else said. The word made its way among the people like a beach ball at a concert, passing from mouth to mouth, tongue to tongue.

"No," the old man said. "Them's elves, what I said: them's elves! Elves!"

His voice was lost in the rising buzz of conversation. Only Helen Keller heard what he said, and she thought: Well, not too far off.

Dick Dick again hushed everyone. "Listen... listen, I don't think it really matters what they are. As I see it, all that matters is getting rid of them. We're dealing with something un-American here, and we should deal with it like true Americans: quickly and efficiently."

A roar of approval mushroomed from the crowd.

Helen Keller, standing back there against the wall, shook her head. She felt both sad and amused. Like most of modern society, American or otherwise, this struck her as hilarious as well as frightening. These people here had no clue. And, though she knew quite well what was going on, she chose not to speak. Later, maybe. For now she was content to watch them make fools of themselves. The most she did was laugh at the next suggestion:

"We all have guns! Make it open season on the damn things and us boys'll take care of it in one afternoon!"

Sheriff Sherman's turn to speak: "Listen, listen, settle down. Let's leave the gun-play to us law enforcement officers, all right. Speaking of which, as I see it, what we need in this town, not just for this situation but for always, for everyday safety, is one large unified force of—"

"One afternoon!" the same man shouted. He stood and turned to look back at his buddies, who all shouted and whooped and gave him thumbs-up. They roared like frat-boys at a gang-bang while their women beamed proudly.

"A unified force of—" Sheriff Sherman tried again. Dick Dick cut him off:

"Any other suggestions?"

"Yes!" came a ragged and thin little voice. Heads turned, then were turned back again, as if to avoid a bright light.

It was Carol Slugg, rising from the sea of faces like a swamp-thing rising from lily-pads.

"Oh Jesus," Dick Dick whispered to himself.

"Yes," Carol Slugg said, "I do have a suggestion. The answer to all of this seems pretty plain to me, but all of you, clouded as you are by your unholy quest for material

184

pleasures, are blinded to the simple truth: these creatures are spawns of Satan, sent here to test us! This is our hour, our time to prove the worth and conviction of our faith! Can't you see this? These are demons, and demons cannot be destroyed through earthly means. The force of Heaven's goodness is required. Now... it's a pity our dear beloved Father Preston did not see fit to being here today, but a lack of spiritual guidance should not keep us from seeking the Lord's help in ridding us of this evil. The lack of a decent Christian role-model in our day-to-day lives should not keep a true Christian from following the word of Jesus! Priest or no priest, we must face these demons with the light of the Lord and *force* them to leave our town at once! Yes, *force* them, for this is a war, fellow citizens of Burghville, this is surely a war... this is our ultimate war. This is a war for our souls!"

She looked at them all with her squinted eyes.

"And afterwards," she said, "we must forever change the way we've been living, so that nothing like this happens again. We brought this on ourselves, we with our sinning and our hedonism. You know who you are. After this war is won, and with God's help alone it shall be, then we must make significant changes to how we've been living. We must fully embrace the Lord and His Son. We must live as God's children. That, my friends, is what this test is all about."

She stood there for a while, staring at everyone. No one spoke. The hush was nearly religious in its own right. Carol Slugg felt, right then, that her words had finally reached them, that she was finally being reckoned as a force for God's—

"Any other suggestions?" Dick Dick asked.

*

"Can I ask you something?" Father Preston said. He had started to pace in front of the altar, with the eyes of the little man following him. He had not answered the question Orson had posed, had instead been pacing for some time, head down, eyes on the tiled floor.

"You're avoiding my own question, but go ahead," Orson said.

185

"Why are you here? All of you, I mean."

Orson laughed. It was a small, friendly laugh, absolutely without malice. "Why not?"

Father Preston stopped and looked at him. "Well... it's Burghville. I mean, Burghville is...."

"A nice place to live but not to visit?"

"Something like that."

Orson nodded. "It'll do, this town."

Unsatisfied with that answer, Father Preston began to pace again. After a few moments he asked:

"What are you, then? Dwarves?"

"Dwarves?" Orson nearly fell off the altar laughing. "Dwarves? Hi-Ho and all that? Oh my..." He caught himself from slipping backwards and laughed louder. In a flash his pipe re-lit itself, great flames bursting from its bowl, licking at the little man's face and hair. He laughed even more and *puff!* the fire went out.

"I didn't mean to offend you..." Father Preston said softly.

"Dwarves..." Orson shook his head and smiled down at the priest. "I'm afraid we are not dwarves. What we *are* is unimportant, since labels are so restrictive, but suffice it to say we are Good People."

Father Preston did not realize that this was indeed a label, not having much of a background in Celtic myth. He thought the little man was being evasive.

"But just call me Orson, dear Father. We're friends now, are we not? Labels of race or gender or nationality just get in the way. We are friends, Father Preston and Orson the Good Person. And, as friends, maybe you could do me the favor of answering my question. Why did you become a priest?"

"That's a long story."

"Do you have to be somewhere?"

Father Preston, who had heard about the Town Hall meeting, shook his head. "No."

"Then tell me: why a priest?"

Father Preston looked around at the church that surrounded him, at the church that was holding him, at the church that, on another metaphorical level, had swallowed him. The thing about churches was they pervaded everything, they dominated your senses. Step through their

186

doors and you cannot forget where you are. They have a presence and a smell and a sound that fill you, for better or worse. When you are in a church you are nowhere else.

"It started with a desire to help people," he said.

It started with a death, is what he wanted to say.

*

Betty Buckthorn, she of the heaving cleavage and the short-skirt, the eternally engorged clitoris (the bane and be-all of her existence), the one-cigarette-a-day habit, she and she alone knew what her husband's agenda was this day, she and she alone knew what he was thinking as he stood up there like the cock of the walk he was and directed (orchestrated too fine a word) these proceedings. He had told her that morning, though she had suspected it already. She had known him better and longer than most people, and she could read him like a TV guide.

It bothered her, too, though she wasn't entirely sure why. She had known full well what sort of man he was when she agreed to marry him, she had known exactly what his goals and ambitions were, she had known what ideas lurked and gestated inside his brain.

But, most of his goals and ambitions had been overt, as larger-than-life as his personality. This time there was covert action going on, and a sneaky sort of manipulation along with it.

She took in a deep breath, swelled those breasts out like five-star-generals full of pride, and looked at her husband. When he next glanced at her she seductively parted her legs so that he could see her robin's-egg-blue panties. He saw, looked away, and a moment later looked again. In that short moment those panties had seemed to tighten over the crevice that lay underneath them, as tight as a wet-suit over her swollen pudenda, like a scarf held over a partially-gaping mouth. It was all there under that pretty baby-blue: her womanhood, beckoning and moist.

Dick Dick Buckthorn thought:

*

Jesus!

187

Because five rows back sat Polly Anderson. Jesus. And yet, other than these distractions (wife, Polly, Polly, wife) things were going along nicely for Dick Dick. This meeting was turning out exactly as he had wanted. Every emotional response he could have hoped for was present:

Anger!

Fear!

Righteousness!

Patriotism!

Determination!

And, along with it all was something else he had been hoping for:

Insecurity.

Ah yes, public insecurity! The businessman's aphrodisiac. The *good* businessman's aphrodisiac. For if a businessman was worth his mettle he would seize that uncertainty, pounce on it like a lion pouncing on a gazelle. He would recognize in it an opportunity, an opening. An opening like that underneath those baby-blue panties—

Jesus! Dick Dick turned so that he was no longer able to look in his wife's direction. What was she doing, trying to ruin him?

He stood there listening to the complaints and fears and insecurities of Burghville and inside, just under the surface, barely contained, he was smiling. It was a good to have a fearful public, good to have a citizenry in panic, but *only* when one has a solution. And *especially* when you're a businessman and that solution will directly benefit you. Ah yes!

Dick Dick stood there as the people of Burghville expressed their hopes for a solution, their *need* for a solution. They seemed rather pathetic, but a good businessman does not look down on that pathos: he revels in it, he nurtures it whenever possible. It was only the pathetic nature of the citizenry that could keep a businessman in business. He must never be offended by the pitiable and wretched quality of the people around him. He must *love* it.

And, he must take advantage of it whenever possible.

These people here all understood that something had to be done, that Burghville was under siege and that

188

Burghville might be the only hope for the nation. They understood this, they *believed* it, they felt it in their bones. Burghville was a symbol for the nation as a whole. Burghville *was* America! This plague of surreal vermin was not just happening to Burghville, it was happening to the entire blessed United States of America!

Yes, Dick Dick thought, you better believe it.

And now he had them where he wanted them. He had them just exactly where he *needed* them.

Are you ready for the solution? he thought to himself as he stared out at their faces. Are you ready for it? Of course they were, look at them: as expectant as baby birds waiting for a regurgitated worm.

He quieted them all with a raising of both of his huge arms, and then stood in that silence for a single sweet moment, reveling in it, feeling larger than he really was, feeling so larger than life it wasn't even funny, so incredibly *huge* as a man and a figure that he had to struggle mightily to keep from smiling. Everyone was looking at him. Everyone was waiting. Everyone was *needing* him to speak, so he said, slowly:

"This is a plague, my friends, and a plague demands a remedy."

They continued to stare, wanting more. He absolutely loved this. The smell of money and power rippled through his mind, as they had since he was sixteen.

"Many fine solutions were put forth here today, and you should all be commended, but I believe there is only one answer. It will require work, but if we dedicate ourselves to this cause, if we unite in our patriotism and our anger and our resolve, then we can solve this problem. To that end, I propose that we stop fooling around, that Buckthorn Industries kick into high gear and begin production of a super-toxic spray, a pesticide that will finally rid our good town of this plague. We've done it to mice, we've done it to ants, we've done it to bats, we've done it to aphids, and by God we can do it to *these* things! It will be good for this town, and it will be good for this Nation!"

Silence. Then applause. This applause went on for minutes, fever-pitched, full of vigor and determination and tenacity and happiness. When it subsided and Dick

189

Dick was about to speak again, another voice, feminine, rose into the hot air of the Town Hall:

"You people are all insane!" it said.

It was Henrietta Pratt, standing now, facing the glares of her neighbors full-on. She radiated a strength and steadfastness that were new to her... or at least rarely seen publicly. Normally she was a pleasant-faced and happy woman. Now, however....

She said: "I can't believe what I'm hearing. You're planning on poisoning them. Not only will you kill perfectly innocent *humanoid* creatures, creatures just like you and me, but you would poison your own children and grandchildren with some terrible super-spray! This is insane! We're dealing with creatures that deserve to live, that deserve respect, that deserve our protection. For Heaven's sake, people, Scooter Boober was right: you would judge a creature not human because it is shorter than yourself? What is this world coming to? Has anyone here even thought to *ask* them if they would leave? They—"

She was prevented from speaking further by boos and catcalls. The people had a leader now, someone who not only had a plan but the ability to carry out that plan. They had heard Dick Dick's words, felt the emotions he wanted to stir in them, and they, like any such crowd, wouldn't tolerate dissent.

In anger Henrietta Pratt pushed her way through the crowd and out of the Town Hall. A cheer rose up when she was gone.

"Now then," Dick Dick began, "we can finally get down to—"

Another feminine voice, this one creaky and thin: "Heaven help any of you!" It was Carol Slugg, of course, glaring at them all. "You can ignore my words, you can ignore my advice, but you cannot ignore the words of the Lord! His wrath is great, his vengeance powerful, and if you all choose to ignore the only *true* solution you will fail this test and fail it mightily! I don't agree with Miss Pratt: these creatures no more deserve to live than do the serpents of Hell, but I do know that they can only be defeated through God's righteous work. I have long believed in the cause of Buckthorn Industries, but not if it will make

190

people stray from the One True Path. You are all on a course of damnation!"

With that, she too left the Town Hall. There was an immediate lightening of the air as she passed, a cooling, a sighing of molecules big and small. The buzzard had flown and the dying culture could relax.

Heads turned back to Dick Dick Buckthorn. And then:

Somewhere in the Town Hall there was laughter. It was an entirely shameless and disrespectful laughter and it was as grating in Dick Dick's ear as the sound of nails on slate. One thing he hated was disrespect.

Heads turned again, in unison, like the heads of marionettes on a single string, and the collective gaze of the good citizens of Burghville fell on the figure of young Helen Keller standing at the back of the Hall.

She wanted to speak, she really did, but it was impossible. So she laughed.

And laughed.

And right about then there rose the scream of a fire-engine's siren... and since the entire Burghville Fire Department was in the Town Hall there also rose a communal look of confusion. Suddenly the building emptied as everyone rushed to see what was going on.

Only three people stayed behind: Scooter Boober, shaking his head, Betty Buckthorn, standing to smooth out her skirt, and Helen Keller, laughing.

*

She knew it was a serious matter. And still, come on, the absurdity of it would have made even Ralph Nader bust a nut. Even in the face of the Apocalypse there would be room for a dirty joke or two, something about fucking the first thing that moved. As in:

First man: If it was the end of the world I'd fuck the first thing that moved. What would you do?

Second man: Stand right here.

So Helen laughed. She laughed mostly, she believed, because she didn't know what else to do when witnessing the suicide of a society. She laughed because it was just so sad.

191

That morning, when she had visited with the wee folk in the woods, she had learned quite a lot about them. The most important thing was also the most obvious: they were magical creatures, beings of this Earth but also above it, created from its energy. They were as much Earthlings as any other animal, but through that energy, and through the very age of their race, they were also something else. *Magic* did not do them justice. They were science and enchantment and supernatural rolled together in perfect balance.

Wee folk, the library book called them. The Good People. The Fair Folk. The Gentry. All of these were so cold, though, too much like *labels*.

"What do I call you?" she had asked them earlier that day, once a cup of tea was in her hand. An interesting thing about those cups: they felt organic, as if forged right here in the woods, but of what material she couldn't say. Bone, perhaps. Or some magical mixture of bone and leather and rock.

"What do I call you?" she asked.

Which was when she was introduced to Puddlefoot the flutist, and Max Paddledoor, and Aryie, a beautiful little creature who moved like a leaf in a breeze, and Thressa, mother of four, and Jorgana the Elder, who was not old at all but a younger Fair Folk with a charming and pleasant personality, and Tom Tom, who did nothing but laugh and pound out rhythms on a tiny drum. And others, at least fifteen of them, each and every one of them greeting her with a shake of the hand and a tip of the hat.

"How do you know me?" she asked.

"Ahh Helen," said Max Paddledoor. "Even the birds know who the bird-lovers are."

The other wee folk nodded in agreement and tittered amongst themselves. Cups of tea and pipes of grass-tobacco were raised. Tom Tom did a roll on his drum. Puddlefoot trilled again with his flute and was promptly answered by a chickadee.

Helen nodded too, though she was still confused. She might have been blessed with the Sight, but she could read nothing from these creatures, as if her own power was rendered ineffective in the presence of their own. The only

192

thing she could sense, the only thing she *knew*, was that they meant no harm.

Max Paddledoor smiled and looked up at her. "Doesn't feel like you're in Kansas anymore, does it?" Then he winked and did a little jig.

No, Helen Keller thought. No, absolutely not....

*

The wee folk were scattered all over the town and surrounding area: some chose to hang around the woods, others got into trouble in Burghville. Earlier that day Helen had been told that there were more than a hundred of them running around.

"Some have taken to multiplying for multiplying's sake," Thressa said. "That's normally not our way."

Puddlefoot nodded. "Aye. They seem to have gotten that from your culture." He shook his head at the thought.

It was a group of the newest wee folk that started the fire engine that afternoon and drove it down Burghville's streets, lights blazing and siren screaming, the ladder occasionally rising to the sky, a mob of angry humans chasing after them like Keystone Cops. It was a good ride, that one: though they swerved all over the streets and nearly hit trees and cars, though they occasionally drove on lawns, at one point taking out a fire hydrant and sending an arcing geyser into the air, they made it safely back to Main Street and the parking lot of the bank before the angry humans finally caught up to them.

A number of Burghvillian males tried to catch the wee folk as they jumped from the truck, but of course they failed. The wee folk scampered off, disappearing down sewer drains and up light posts, laughing as they went.

"This is too much," someone said.

Dick Dick stood there watching the scene. He shook his head and then turned to the crowd.

"Where are my chemists?" he growled. "It's time to get to work."

*

193

Other people getting to work this day:

Henrietta Pratt was writing a long letter detailing her proposal for asking the little people to leave Burghville. She was planning on asking them herself, but she thought it would not only look better, but also be a nice gesture, if someone with official status in town were to ask as well. She would send this letter to Sheriff Sherman, the Courthouse, and Dick Dick Buckthorn. Hopefully a copy would make its way to Mayor Darrow, wherever he was;

Betty Buckthorn went to work, so to speak, in the women's restroom of the Town Hall. She was done in minutes and then went to find her husband;

Carol Slugg gathered together a close-knit group of like-minded individuals from the St. Michael's Catholic Church congregation, people who tenuously believed the things she did but who needed that little extra prodding that only she herself could provide. They would try one last time to confront Father Preston on this issue, and then, should that prove futile (as Carol knew it would) they would lead the Heavenly Charge themselves;

Candy Cleaver went home and got to work dusting the inside of her nose with Lemon-Scented Pledge;

Tracey and Timmy White barricaded themselves back inside their house. They had an argument about why they had even gone to the meeting in the first place, Timmy thinking it had been a bad idea and Tracey insisting it would have looked suspicious for them not to show up. A lot of people didn't show up, he said. Yes, but a lot of people don't know what *we* know, she countered. In the end this argument petered out. Tracey wanted to make up by making love, but Timmy went to the basement where his model railroad display was set up and there he stayed, sending his steam-powered passenger train around the track over and over again;

Scooter Boober returned to his hobby farm. He had decided to quit his job at Buckthorn Industries sooner than he had planned. He would take cow and llama shit over bullshit any day, he would even take *bull*shit over bullshit any day. He would take literal castration over the figurative castration of factory-life any goddamn day;

Helen Keller returned to the woods to find Puddlefoot and the others. She had promised them she would report on whatever events transpired at the Town Hall. She was also, like Henrietta Pratt, getting used to that tea. Unlike Henrietta Pratt, however, Helen was also enjoying the tobacco;

And good Father Preston was busy getting down to the dirtiest work of all: telling Orson the Wee Folk the story of his life.

9

The first time she knew she had the Sight, Helen Keller had been eight. She was spending a week at her grandparent's farm, which hadn't been a farm so much as an old house in the country with two decrepit barns and an overgrown yard of bushes and trees. Sure, Grandma had kept a garden, but this was mostly a hobby; Grandma and Grandpa Keller had in no way been suppliers of the nation's food. That garden had yielded beans and potatoes and corn and tomatoes, but no one outside of the immediate family had ever eaten them. It was a selfish garden, as all the best gardens are.

For one week every summer little Helen would be sent to her grandparents, and she loved it. Those times were among the very best of her life, full of innocence and adventure and discovery and laziness, that magical laziness that can only come in childhood and that can only happen in the presence of grand folks. She remembered entire afternoons spent watching clouds form and dissipate above her, or tracking bees, or lying on her stomach to trace the daily wanderings of snakes. She remembered dreaming with ladybugs, laughing with butterflies, staring at soaring hawks. And she remembered weeding in Grandma's garden, and helping Grandpa in his shed, and eating big breakfasts every day, and those fires Grandpa would have at night when they'd all sit outside and tell stories. She remembered it all like it was yesterday.

The summer she was eight, though, was the most memorable of all.

The first part of the week had gone along like all the others, with those lazy afternoons and quiet nights, with the philosophies only a child can find in cumulous and clover. On Wednesday there had been a storm, thundering its way over the countryside, grumbling like a giant bull, sending rivers of rain down to the roof of the old house, pushing streams like melted diamonds down the windows as she and her Grandma sat on the porch and looked out at the swirling tempest. Grandpa had said they were crazy watching the storm, but of course he sat there with them and together they marveled at the swirling darkness and the flashes of light that lit the barn and woods and made everything look blue and electric. After a time Grandma left to fetch hot chocolate for them all.

The next day the world had a fresh look, a softer, greener hue. The sides of the house and barn were darker, the leaves and lawn and garden plants rich and vivid. Helen felt as if she had fallen into a painting, that some artist had just finished caressing the canvas with his last brush stroke and everything was still wet. She was careful where she put her hands, lest they come away colored. The sun was parting clouds like theatre curtains and by noon the world would be dry.

It was just before noon when Helen found the snake. Just a fox snake, a common Midwestern species, *Elaphe vulpina*, a mottled but beautiful animal with a perfectly coppery head. That head sometimes got the critter in trouble, when ignorant people thought the snake was a venomous copperhead, *Agkistrodon contortrix phaeogaster,* and killed the poor thing. Helen, who knew quite well that the only venomous species she was likely to encounter in these parts would have rattles on their tails, easily caught the snake and held it lovingly for a while, calming it. When it was soothed she admired it closely, marveling at the auburn eyes with the large inquisitive pupils, at the gorgeous though subdued colors: the background of soft yellow and the blotches of chocolate brown. She felt its dryness in her hands, felt the intelligent flickering of its tail against her forearm, felt the cool lick of its tongue on her fingers. Then she smiled, knowing that this here was something special indeed, and turned to carry it to the farmhouse. Grandma would love to see it.

When she came around the corner of the old barn she nearly ran into Aunt Anne. And Aunt Anne, Grandma's sister, immediately screamed and shouted this:

"Get that goddamn thing away from me!"

Helen did not have time to be hurt or upset. Something strange happened to her, some force like electricity coursed through her body, made its way up her legs and backbone to rest, zapping and popping, at the base of her brain. She stared up into the terrified face of Aunt Anne and immediately realized something. Being a young girl, and being innocent of the repercussions of such things, little Helen Keller opened her mouth and gave voice to this realization:

"Jack used to chase you with snakes," she said. "He would run you down and make them crawl all over you."

Aunt Anne's face went white. Instead of staring at the snake she was staring at Helen.

"It's all right, though," Helen said. "They can't hurt you. They never *could* hurt you. He chased you with garter snakes."

"Okay Helen, okay, go put the snake back," Grandma Keller had said then, coming up behind her sister. She shooed Helen away. As Helen left she heard Aunt Anne say:

"What kind of a monster is that?"

And Helen knew she meant her, not the snake. In the days to come she would find out that Aunt Anne's brother Jack, who used to chase her with garter snakes, had been killed when he was thirteen, drowned in a river one rainy spring. No one ever talked about him anymore because it was rumored that his own father might have done the deed in a drunken rage. The whole situation became one of those family secrets people hide away and pretend never happened. That little Helen Keller might have heard the story was not the issue that troubled Aunt

197

Anne, what troubled her was this: she had never told anyone about Jack chasing her with snakes... in fact, she had nearly forgotten all about it herself. Grandma was seven years younger than Aunt Anne and would have been around one year old when such things had occurred, so *she* couldn't have known. No, Aunt Anne understood right away that something else was going on here, and to that end, she never really talked to Helen ever again. And whenever she looked at her she did so out of the corner of her eye, like she was looking at something that was not to be trusted.

"How did you know about Aunt Anne and Jack?" Grandma asked Helen not long after the incident had occurred.

"I just did," was all Helen could say. What she wanted to say was this:

The same way I know that you fell in love with another man after you and Grandpa were married.

She held her tongue that time. She was learning fast that this new talent would require her to watch what she said.

She was to meet that requirement only half the time, though. That was just her nature.

*

Like this was her nature: living in the forest, sleeping in her tent or under the stars, bathing in cold crystal streams, breathing as one with the trees and dirt and animals. She was a part of Nature, of course, as are all of us, and she embraced her roots with the earth fervently, passionately, with tenderness and love. Every day in the forest was a family reunion for Helen Keller. Every day was like coming home.

She was sitting on a stump in a pool of sun that had spilled through the canopy, smoking a cigarette filled with grass-tobacco. She had gotten the paper for the cigarette from her winter house. Sam the artist had been fond of rolling his own, so to speak.

"How come," she had asked him once, "most people who say they're into Zen also smoke dope? What's the connection there?"

198

Exhaling, he said: "Oh little girl, for some things there are no answers."

"Try."

"Okay: deep down we're all a bunch of fucking hippies."

To which she said: "I thought so."

Now, sitting on this stump and smoking this cigarette, holding each breath for a moment or two before exhaling a sweet cloud into the forest air, she smiled. Sam would have loved this tobacco. He would have loved the wee folk. He would have loved the sheer artistry, the sheer poetry, of their very existence.

"The girl is smiling," Max Paddledoor said.

Puddlefoot held his flute across his little lap like a baby. "I'll say."

Thressa, the mother of four, shook her head. "Oh leave her alone, you two."

The wee folk were lounging about on the forest floor. Thressa's children were off playing with the animals, badgering a badger perhaps, and the others were in town or elsewhere. It was the day after the Town Hall meeting, and everyone was relaxed. There had been a wee folk meeting last night, at which Helen had related everything that had been said at the Town Hall. None of the wee folk were much impressed. In fact, there had been shrugs all around. And then a party. Of course, a party: music and tea and food and laughter.

"You're not worried?" Helen asked. As an answer, she was pulled into a dancing ring of Good People, where she was spun around and around like a luscious top.

"Oh Helen Keller," they said to her this morning. "You too are part of this Earth, as much from the dirt and air as we are, and as much above all of that too, as much something electric and wondrous and supernatural. Are *you* worried?"

The forest had sighed its breath back into her, filling her lungs like never before, the smell of the trees and ground in her nose like perfume. She looked down at the wee folk and smiled again. She said:

"Play it again, Puddlefoot."

Tomfoolery in C Major filled the air.

199

*

"That goddamn impudent little girl," Dick Dick Buckthorn was saying. He was saying it over and over, in fact, as he paced from one end of his large livingroom to the next. Through the hidden speakers came the love theme from *Rambo*. Not a bad song, really: violently emotional, like caveman sex.

Betty Buckthorn was lying on the couch. She was trying to watch television with the sound off, which wasn't all that hard. Television is a lot like politics: it's all about the images, baby. Still, every time the figure of her husband cut in front of her she frowned.

"Can't you relax?" she asked him.

"Relax? As a matter of fact, I *am* relaxed. This is how I relax, Betty. This is my bread and butter, my reason for living, the love of my—"

"I thought I was your reason for living...."

He looked down at her and sighed. "You are. My work is my *way* of living, that's what I meant."

"Your way of living is stressful."

Another deep sigh and he resumed his pacing. After a time he stopped again, near the patio doors, and stared out at the forest. Floodlights lit the trees out there like searchlights in a prison yard.

"Who is that Helen Keller girl anyway?" he asked, mostly to himself. "Laughing at me like that... who does she think she is, little hippie bitch."

"Relax, Dick Dick... no one paid her any attention. She's just a little hippie chick, the town's resident oddball. Every community has to have one."

"Not *this* community. Not *my* community." He looked back at his wife. "One thing I hate is people laughing at me. I hate it with a passion!"

His teeth were clenched, his hands tight fists, his eyes red with anger. Betty looked at him and was shocked: she had never seen him like that before.

"Maybe she wasn't laughing at you," she said. "Maybe she was—"

"No, no, she was laughing at me. I know the type. Little hippies think they know better than the rest of us, think that we, the sort of people who *made* this country, are

200

idiots. They think we're fools. They think the men of industry want to ruin this world, when in fact it's us who make it better." He shook his head and looked over at his wife. "No, she was laughing at me. There's no doubt in my mind...."

"So? Forget about it. Come over here." She licked her lips and kept her mouth parted in expectation.

"No," he said. "No, I have things to get ready. It's a big day tomorrow. I've got my chemists working all night to come up with something and tomorrow we meet to see what we've got. I have to come up with a plan. The chemical is one thing, the dispersal of that chemical is another." His eyes went dreamy with the possibilities. "Spraying by plane, distribution by the private sector... so much to think about. Which way is there more money for me? Selling to the consumer or getting the city to pay us for air diffusion? Hmmmm..."

Betty wasn't listening. She rarely did anymore. Dick Dick tended to ramble anyway, and lately it had gotten worse, so she just ignored him and stared at the silent images on the television screen. After a time Dick Dick left the room and the music was turned off. She smiled and undid the television's *mute*.

After a few moments she muted it again. It was better with the sound off.

Fifteen minutes later the phone rang. She listened to it for a while, through four or five rings, and then she looked over the couch in the direction Dick Dick had gone.

"Honey?" she called.

Nothing.

"Honey, phone!"

No answer.

She sighed and sat up straight. The Buckthorn residence had five phones, one in the kitchen, one in the bedroom, one in the garage, one in the rec-room, and one right here next to the couch. She contemplated this latter one, then sighed on the eighth ring and picked it up.

"Hello?"

"*Betty!*" shouted a familiar voice.

"Hey Willy Billy," she said. "How have you been?"

And Willy Billy Buckthorn, brother of Dick Dick Buckthorn, said: "Finer than a cunt hair, baby, finer than a cunt hair. Where's my big brother? He left a message saying he needed me. Has someone been laughing at him again? Oh Jesus, tell me this isn't about that time in Florida...."

*

Though it would never come out to Betty Buckthorn or anyone else in Burghville, Willy Billy Buckthorn was perhaps the only person in the world who knew just exactly why Dick Dick hated for people to laugh at him. It was a simple story: back in kindergarten little Dick Dick Buckthorn had shit his pants at nap-time and everyone, the teacher included, had laughed at him. Simple as that, baby. Simple as that.

*

Betty went to fetch Dick Dick, and while he and his brother talked she went to the bedroom and got to know her vibrator better. It was during this session, halfway through in fact, that she burnt the damn thing out. It fizzled and hissed and went dead, emitting a tiny cloud of blue smoke and leaving her clitoris in a familiar state of mind: aching for more.

"Dick Dick?" she called, hoping he was done talking to his brother. She heard heavy footsteps coming and she tossed the vibrator to the floor and tried to lie there on the bed as sexily as she could, mouth and legs parted just so, every orifice glistening in welcome to her man.

Dick Dick came into the bedroom and barely noticed her lying there.

"Willy Billy's coming!" he said. "He'll be here tomorrow! Nobody flies a plane like Willy Billy, babe. He's our man, our hero."

"What are you talking about?"

"The pesticide, babe: Willy Billy will fly the plane that sprays it on those little monsters."

202

Betty opened her mouth to say something, but Dick Dick turned and left the room, once again leaving her and her clitoris alone.

Aching for more.

*

"It started with a desire to help people..." Father Preston was saying.

"Help people?" Orson asked. "And how did you think you'd do that?"

"Through teaching them the beauty and wisdom of God and Jesus... show them the holiness of our very existence, the supremacy of our souls and minds, show them what we might become if...." He let that trail off. The little man was looking at him strangely.

"Here's why," Orson finally said, "here's why the human belief in the superiority and moral supremacy of their own species is inherently false: life is fragile, and life is precious, and life is a rare and gentle thing. In the words of shamans and holy men, life is a miracle. If so, and there is no doubt, then it must be said that all life on this planet Earth is precious and fragile and deserving of respect and freedom. When someone says that they believe humans are above the other animals, that they are in some way superior and dominant to the other species we share this planet with, one has only to ask this question: could you please name another planet on which could be found whales and spiders and ducks and ants and bison and eagles and snakes and jellyfish? There will follow a long and dumfounded silence of the sort your kind is adept at. *All* life on this planet, Father, from the lowliest bacteria to the mightiest human mind, is precious and worthwhile. It's *all* holy. No living thing is on this planet by accident. And every living thing is equal in merit... to the objective eye." He smiled. "Are you objective, Father?"

*

Carol Slugg had one thing in common with her savior, that thin little nappy-headed Middle Eastern philosopher who was killed by Romans roughly two thousand years ago for preaching Socialism: she could hold a crowd.

Like this one here, the rag-tag group of followers she had snagged from the congregation of the St. Michaels Church. This group consisted almost exclusively of elderly women, the single exception being a girl who looked like Sally Fields in *Sybil*. This latter woman was very quiet and soft-spoken in conversation, so soft-spoken everyone had to lean in to hear her, but when she prayed it was another matter altogether. She became like a Mississippi Baptist Minister on speed: she would close her eyes and shake her fists and stomp her feet to some unheard rhythm as she recited prayers and gospel. Her face turned red, sweat beaded on her brow, and she took on that same crazed, lustful look in the eyes that NRA members get when oiling their guns. After the second time this happened Carol Slugg had pulled her aside and told her to tone it down.

"Some people," Carol said, "might mistake all that for demonic possession."

The young woman had nodded and said nothing more. When it came time for prayers at the next meeting, Carol herself volunteered.

At this meeting she stood before her apostles and they stared up at her admiringly, taking in whatever she had to offer them. She could hold a crowd, indeed. She would have made a good politician if she hadn't been so righteous and holier-than-thou and weird and crazy, if she hadn't thought her way was the only way and any attempt at compromise was a weakness... actually, she *would* have made a good politician, come to think of it.

It was two days after the Town Hall meeting. Carol Slugg was saying:

"Father Preston has abandoned us. He has abandoned this whole town. Like the moral coward he is, he has run away. No one has seen hide nor hair of him in days. And, if that isn't enough, he locked the church up so none of us can have entry to the house of the Lord."

A murmur passed through the small crowd. Some of the elderly women made signs of the cross, and more than one set of dentures popped out to say hello.

"It's true, people," Carol Slugg said. "It's all true. We are now officially without a priest. We are now without a representative of our church. We have no leader. But this is no surprise. I'm sure I wasn't the only one to notice Father Preston's lack of leadership, his utter lack of interest in any of us. Was I?"

Heads shook, necks creaked.

"I say: Forget him. Forget *any* of them. It is up to us and us alone. It is our duty to rid this town of the satanic plague that has befallen it. It is up to us to return the glory and power of God's light to Burghville!"

Thin, elderly cheers all around. The young woman smiled and nodded, her thick-framed glasses shining in candlelight, the eyes behind them closed.

"This town has been controlled by infidels for too long. It is time God returned to their hearts. It is time for us to go to work."

She went on like this for some time. Her words were, in the general scheme of inspirational mumbo-jumbo, rather cliché: if the references to God and Burghville were removed then her speech would have been no different than one Patton might have given, or what Hannibal might have muttered, or Hitler... or Jim Jones... or Osama bin Laden... or Rush Limbaugh, for that matter. There was probably a book somewhere where such things were laid out. Perhaps there was a college course: Inspiring Fucking Idiots 101.

Carol Slugg's acolytes bought it, like all the fucking idiots before them and all the fucking idiots to come. It was just as she had expected, of course.

So she gets an A.

*

Tracey White crossed the quiet street in front of her home without incident. She saw no little people as she walked... she saw no big people either, for that matter. This was the second day after the Town Hall meeting and Burghville had fallen strangely quiet. Not to suggest that the wee folk had ceased all tomfoolery, but only that the initial hysteria had died down a bit: even wee folk, presumably, get tired. So on this morning when Tracey crossed that street she saw no wee folk but plenty of evidence of their existence: broken phone lines, grass-less

205

yards, graffiti, re-written bumper stickers, remains of campfires. She paid none of it any mind as she went up a walkway and knocked on Candy Cleaver's front door.

Candy Cleaver answered a minute later. Under her nose was a line of white liquid.

"Morning, Tracey," she said merrily.

"Ahh, morning, Candy..." Tracey frowned. "You have something here," and she touched her own nose.

"Really?" Candy brought a finger up and touched the white spot... which did not come away. "Did I get it?"

"No, I think..." Tracey's frown threatened to overtake her eyes. "I think it's dry."

Candy tried again. Again she failed.

"It didn't come," Tracey said. "Lick your finger maybe..."

Candy shook her head. "Forget it. Come on in, sweetie. What a lovely day!"

Tracey entered the house. She was struck immediately by a smell. It was sweet yet chemical. She wondered if Candy had been working on some dolls and turned to ask her.

Candy was still standing in the doorway, taking in great breaths of air through her nose and smiling out at the bright day.

"You okay?" Tracey asked.

Candy turned with a giant smile. "Of course! Never better! Come in!" She shut the door and marched past Tracey. The two women sat on the couch.

"Working on your dolls?" Tracey asked.

Candy cocked her head. "No, why do you ask?"

"I thought I smelled glue or something..."

"No. Not working. Not doing anything. What about you? What brings you over here?"

Quietly: "I have a problem...."

Candy, still smiling, leaned closer. "Problem? Oh goodness, that's not what we want to hear."

"No, I... I don't even know if I should tell you."

"You can tell me anything, Tracey. Anything at all. It will only be heard by me and my little ones."

Tracey's frown again pushed at the fortress of her eyes. "Your little ones?"

"My dolls, silly."

206

"Oh... well, I just don't know if I should even—"

"Oh spill it, honey, and get it off your chest."

Tracey thought for a while... a good long while, sitting there with Candy watching her and nothing around them but silence and doll eyes. Those dolls were really something: they occupied nearly every horizontal surface in this house, from shelves to the television to window frames to the refrigerator. They looked out upon the home like... well, like wee folk. Like *creepier* wee folk, if that was possible. Little eyes stared blindly and little legs dangled and little hands hung palms-out, as if for charity. What sort of charity does one give a doll? Tracey wondered. She decided burning them was the kindest thing to do.

After a time she reached into her shirt pocket and pulled forth a slip of paper.

"I found—"

"Do you know how *hard* it is to fix tiny shoes?" Candy asked suddenly, leaning even closer and touching Tracey's knee. "Do you know how *hard* it is?" Her eyes were even wider than they had been in the doorway, nothing but white orbs with dots of brown in the center. Yes, Candy Cleaver's eyes looked like bird-droppings. Exactly.

This was when Tracey White realized what the smell in this house was. It was also what was under Candy's nose:

White-out.

"I should get going," Tracey said, putting the slip of paper back into her pocket.

Candy pouted her lips like a little kid. "No, stay. I'll make coffee. I got some of that Java Joe coffee. Please stay and have some and tell me your problem." She suddenly put a hand over her mouth. "Oh my god, Tracey... you're not *expecting*, are you?"

Tracey thought: Yes, I'm expecting my life to fall apart any minute now.

"It's about time for you two to hear the pitter-patter of little feet!" Candy said.

Tracey winced at the image. "I should get going...."

207

And right about then there *was* the pitter-patter of little feet: on the roof, doing a jig.

"Maybe I'll stay," Tracey said. And Candy went to make coffee.

*

Henrietta Pratt made calzones for the wee folk in her yard. It must be understood that these wee folk were not the same wee folk that Helen Keller met. *Henrietta's* wee folk had moved into her yard ever since she started cooking for them, and had not left except for brief excursions to the neighbor's yard to get grass-roots for tea and to munch on the occasional tulip. By this time there were well over one hundred wee folk in the Burghville area, most in the town itself but some (the ones Helen knew) choosing to spend the majority of their time in the woods, with only occasional nights in town. All of the wee folk knew each other, of course, but it could not be said that all wee folk were the same, that if you've seen one Good Person you've seen them all. Quite the contrary: the wee folk in Henrietta Pratt's yard were much lazier than the rest, and much coarser of character. These little people were prone to belching and telling dirty jokes, although they showed Henrietta nothing but respect. The wee folk Helen knew were gentler, and more refined... more given to introspection, more open to pondering the passage of time. Other wee folk, such as the ones that now occupied the courthouse, were partiers. Still others were much too fond of the grass-tobacco (the Weed of Weeds, they called it) to be much more than minor nuisances to the human citizens of the town: these Good People did not cause havoc so much as simply lie around in parking lots and driveways, or sleep in cars, or sit on sofas and flip through the televisions, or sleep in satellite dishes and disrupt the flow of boxing and porno. Of course, to the Burghvillians this distinction could not be made, and any wee folk was a bad wee folk.

All of this said, Henrietta's wee folk accepted her calzones graciously and invited her to join them. She agreed. It was during this little feast that she asked them how long they were planning on being in Burghville. Their

208

answer, spoken by the most vocal little man among them, was nearly Brando-esque:

"How long ya got?" he asked.

Henrietta waited until the titters died down, and then she posed her question. *The* question:

"Do you think you could... maybe... head off to somewhere else... soon?"

"You mean leave?"

"Well... yes. I mean, you're a pleasure to have here, but the town has business it needs to get on with."

"Business?" Confused wee folk faces all around.

"Yes, business. I mean, people have work to do and lives to live and of course there's the whole matter of..." She stopped herself and looked at all of them. They were staring at her dumbly, as if not comprehending her at all.

"Is there someone among you I should talk to? Someone in all the others, maybe? A chief, or something?"

Pause.

The mini-Brando said: "Would you like us to take you to our leader? Is that what you be asking us, dear Ms. Pratt?"

She shrugged. "I suppose so..."

"You be standing on her, you be breathing her into your lungs. You be feeling her in every cell of yer body. There's no need to take you anywhere."

That was all he said. Then he bit into his calzone with vigorous relish while the others nodded in agreement.

*

In every town like Burghville there arise two types of mentalities: one is insular, the belief that the town is the be-all and end-all of existence, that life and reality end at the city limit. The second mentality is the opposite: the belief that the town is nothing, that being there is a living death, that everything that is good and exciting and worthwhile lies outside of its borders. Both mentalities are false, of course, the truth being somewhere in between. However, the point to make here is that Burghville itself held only the former mentality in abundance, Helen Keller and Father Preston being among the very few truly aware

209

that there was indeed a rest of the world out there and that it did, indeed, offer its own wonders. Everyone else regarded Burghville with awe and love. They believed they had all that they needed right there on Main Street, even the Whites, who had glimpsed a bit of the marvels the rest of the world offered on their matrimonial trip through Scotland.

Newspapers were not read with any devotion in Burghville. Television news was viewed only as a curiosity. International relations were regarded as freak shows. If it wasn't happening in Burghville, it wasn't happening, period. And if it didn't affect the town in any direct way, it was best not to bring it up down at the local bar.

Or, Heaven forbid, the local church.

*

On this second day following the Town Hall meeting, Carol Slugg went back to the church to try once again to gain entry. She of course found every door locked as tight as a right-wing ass. However, something about those doors was secretly begging to be opened. She stood back and looked at the big church. It *wanted* her inside of it, she knew. It *needed* her inside of it. Good lord, the sexual metaphors were thick and intense: this building needed her to penetrate its depths so she could impregnate it with her holiness. Ahhhh!

Father Preston was not fulfilling its needs, she thought. So I must take over. This building *demands* satisfaction!

Although she regarded it as the presence of her Lord filling her soul with love, what Carol Slugg was feeling at that moment actually *was* sexual passion, all those sexual metaphors causing a chain reaction in her subconscious, resulting in the flowing of blood to her creaky and dusty private parts. Things grew engorged *down there*. Skin flushed. Juices slowly began to flow.

Let Jesus fill me! her soul might have clamored.

Her private parts (as she would call them if she ever thought of them at all) thought: We'll just take whatever's handy... please... for the love of god...

210

*

It was late afternoon on this second day after the Town Hall meeting that Dick Dick Buckthorn had a realization... or a suspicion, rather. He gave it voice while Betty was flipping through the television, the Buckthorn mansion being one of the few homes in town still able to get channels via their satellite dish. So far the TV had revealed nothing useful, except to make clear that the wee folk were a uniquely Burghvillian problem. As she flipped past a talking head rambling on about terrorism ("... we're uncertain what means could be used in the future...") Dick Dick said, in a soft voice:

"Those little fuckers might be some sort of biological terrorism...."

To which Betty replied: "I need a new vibrator."

*

On this same afternoon Tracey White and Candy Cleaver finished a second pot of coffee and then sat for a while under the watchful eyes of Candy's dolls. They fell silent, tongues uncertain what train of thought to follow: their caffeinated brains were galloping at hyper speed and changing topics madly. At one point Tracey said:

"Blubba blubba..." She may even have said "Poopie" once or twice.

Candy looked at her. "You said you had some trouble?"

Tracey shook her head. "No, I can't talk about it... I really can't..."

Five minutes later Candy had pulled forth a can of air freshener and a plastic bag. These items had been sitting, apparently, on the floor next to the couch.

"Most of the yellow is like the purple-blue," she said.

Tracey frowned. "What?"

Candy sprayed the contents of the can (*Wildflower Fresh!*) into the bag, humming to herself as she worked. The song she hummed was vaguely Barry Manilowesque, though it could have been something from the country genre.

Tracey didn't know how it happened, but soon she was lifting the plastic bag to her own face and inhaling deeply. She felt guilty with all those glass eyes on her.

But they'd seen it before a million times.

*

"I've seen it before a million times," Orson said. He was walking up and down the middle aisle of the church, where a thousand blushing brides had walked with thighs atremble, where a thousand caskets had been wheeled, where a thousand young kids had stood in line to receive First Brainwashing.

"A people capable of great and grand and wonderful things ends up losing all potential through arrogant belief in their own uniqueness, their own supremacy. History both written and unwritten is littered with such stories. It's a shame, really. A terrible, terrible shame. And it's a shame mostly because the solution to avoiding it is quite simple: objectivity, Dear Father. Objectivity spiked with empathy. Quite simple. Quite easy."

"I think I'm objective, yes...."

Orson looked at him out of the corner of his eye. "Separate from everything around you?"

"Well..."

"Observing, noticing, yet, being a priest, staying above the fray?"

Father Preston nodded. "I try to be, yes. That's my job as a minister of the church."

"Hmm...." Orson paced a little, then looked up. "Is it also your job to fall in love with a member of your congregation?"

"She's not..." Father Preston began, then stopped himself.

Orson smiled. "Of course. Now, back when you were deciding to become a priest, did you ever...." He stopped and examined Father Preston closely as the priest stared down at the floor with deep and distant eyes. A look full of empathy filled Orson's face, made it as warm as

212

freshly baked bread, as kind as the eyes of a saint. Which Saint? Nicholas, of course.

Orson sighed. "Are you hungry, Father?"

Father Preston nodded. They'd been in the church for two days and had already finished the communion wine and whatever food had been in the office fridge. It was actually amazing what you could find in a church refrigerator: a person could live in a church for weeks without ever having to leave, subsisting on leftovers from various church functions, casseroles and muffins and donuts and bread and cheese.

"What would you like?"

As soon as Father Preston opened his mouth to answer there wafted through the church the smell of pizza. Pepperoni pizza.

Just what he'd been thinking about.

"Special delivery," said Orson. In a flash another wee folk came walking up the aisle, a large pizza box in his hands. In another flash he was gone and Father Preston and Orson were alone again.

Orson carried the box up to the altar and lifted its lid, on which was printed the words PIZZERIA CELTONIA, a restaurant Father Preston had never heard of before. Inside the box lay a very fine pepperoni pizza steaming its lush odor into the air.

Father Preston stood there, watching.

"Please," Orson said. "Eat. Enjoy."

"I'm a priest," Father Preston said. "I don't….."

Orson smiled. "You don't believe in magic? Why don't you fetch some water and I'll turn it to wine?"

"How did you know I wanted—"

"Please, Father. I'm an old soul. Like I said, I've seen it all a million times."

Father Preston didn't know what that meant, but he finally walked over and lifted a slice of pizza from the box. He ate it in silence, though he was thinking quite loudly. And what was he thinking about? Magic? Religion? Pepperoni? Water and wine?

No.

Her.

*

Helen Keller. Here she was lying on the West side of a grassy hill somewhere in the middle of the forest, an afternoon sun caressing her body like a lover. She was nearly naked, as she always was in the woods: cut-off shorts, no shoes, a small T-shirt short enough to reveal her tanned tummy and the delicate hairs leading deliciously southward. Her hair, though not long, lay fanned out around her head. Butterflies landed on that hair, rustled their wings, and took flight again. Other insects crawled through the grass and, upon coming to the warm skin of Helen's legs, crawled onto her in joy: here was a new world to explore! Their little legs tickled the fine hairs on her skin, causing her to toss tiny smiles to the sky. She kept her eyes closed all this time, her strangely elfin eyes, those Asiatic orbs set like lost jewels on her slight and delicate face. She could lay like this for hours, eyes closed, heart open, letting the forest fill her as it may. It was like being at the center of an orgy of Nature.

Again, another conversation with Sam the artist:

He had said: "Don't you think the point of being human is to rise above the natural world? Isn't that what separates us from the other animals, the ability to willfully transcend our environment? I mean, fine, take from Nature what Nature has to offer you, but to deny the inherent and definitive ability of Man to overcome such things, to be separate from Nature, seems backwards. Denial cannot be good, in any form."

She had laughed. "Remember that the next time you refuse meat."

He brooded for a while. "I see wisdom in Nature, too, but there is wisdom in Poetry as well. There is wisdom in Art."

"A poem that doesn't deal with Nature is a poem that lies. Art that doesn't represent wilderness represents what? Concrete and steel? Give me a fucking break."

"Nature is given significance *by* Mankind," Sam said. At the time he was working on a clay sculpture that resembled, to Helen, the Eiffel Tower. "To you a ladybug's movements are wise, they reveal Truth. But without you to give it that meaning the ladybug's movements are simply locomotion. Without you to assign

214

it worth, the ladybug is simply on its way to eat or screw or whatever it is ladybugs do."

Helen had laughed. "And who's to say eating and screwing are not worthy? Who's to say they don't reveal Truth? Or, rather, that they don't contain Truths which would exist without the observation of Man?"

He had blushed, which was quite a sight on his middle-aged face of wrinkles and crinkles.

"Do Zen Buddhists fuck?" Helen asked, deliberately taunting him.

"Let me work," he said. "And I'm not a Zen Buddhist. I'm a *Sam* Buddhist."

"Do you close your eyes and try to fuck the Cosmic Pussy?" She imitated, quite badly, a mantra she had heard him recite.

"Let me work, sassy girl."

"Is there a mantra one performs when on the eight-fold path to orgasm? Can you perform cunnilingus on the Universe? Is there such a thing as Cosmolingus?"

Still blushing, he turned away. "You are a bad girl, Helen Keller. A very bad girl."

She pretended to spread an imaginary vulva with her fingers and went *Ommmm* to an imaginary clitoris. Her lips vibrated beautifully, giving pleasure to the air, to the Universe, to the Essence of Everything.

"A very bad girl," he said.

"You are a bad girl, Helen Keller," said another voice, here, now, in this world, this time.

She opened her eyes there on the hill and saw, first, a cloud in the shape of a slightly pudgy middle-aged man (Sam!) and then, turning her head, the figure of Puddlefoot the Flutist. He was smiling at her and shaking his head.

She sat up. "Why?"

"As much for the things you *want* to know as the things you *do* know." That was all he said before turning and waddling off through the grass. He played a few notes on his flute as he went. She thought the song might have been "Waltzing Matilda."

From the top of this hill one could see out over most of the forest. The tree-line was moving like seaweed in a current. The afternoon sun was somehow muted.

215

Crows flew along the horizon, silent as ghosts. The clouds moved lazily past, including the one that looked like Sam. Somewhere inside of it all, contained like a breath held in check, was something that made her smile.

Sometimes life, and the simple act of living, was like that.

Smile-worthy.

*

It was not that she didn't respect religious beliefs, and not that she didn't think people who were into such spiritual pursuits were serious and intelligent. It was just that she knew the truth, and the truth was this:

There was more to be learned from the bird called cardinal than the man called Cardinal. There was more to be learned from homing instincts than *Omming* mantras. There was more to be gained from quiet objective observation of plant and animal life than there was to be gained from self-conscious meditation. There was more to be learned in the prick of a thorn than from the prick at the front of a church.

There was no guilt in Nature: what happens, happens, and it is the fault of nothing but biology and instinct. Why do animals seem to possess the very same sense of calm and peace that religious folks search all their lives for?

Because they simply *are*, and have no need to ever *be*, Helen knew. They do what they do and they never needlessly hurt another living creature. Unlike humanity, which... well, that's an old story. Read the papers. Read your history. Look at the nearest freeway system. It's all there.

Face it: Man's search for a God has in no way led him to peace, has in no way helped lead to understanding, has in no way benefited any single living thing, plant or animal. And what, then, is the point? This Judea-Christian God (not to mention every Hindu God, every Bushman Deity, every Egyptian Lord, every Indian Spirit) has failed in everything it was created to achieve. Time to kick Him/Them/It out of office.

Vote Mother Nature. She won't let you down.

216

"Honey?" Betty Buckthorn said.

"Yes, Angel?"

"Do you want to make love?"

"I'm working."

"Can't you stop for a while?"

He looked over from his mahogany desk to where Betty was seductively standing in the doorway.

He sighed. "I really need to finish this. Mark Lackey just faxed over some ideas for the spray."

"The spray?"

"The new pesticide."

"Oh." She thought a while. "What about later, then?"

"Later I'm going to go in to the factory, I think. I want to get as much done as I can before Willy Billy gets here." He looked back at his work.

"My vibrator's broke," she said.

"We'll get a new one."

She started to say more, then closed her mouth. Her husband sat behind his desk looking nearly Presidential. She wondered how many President's wives were sexually unsatisfied. Did Martha Washington have a wooden dildo?

Dick Dick looked up at her after a few minutes. "Do you think you could put some music on for me? Something suited for work? That *Dirty Harry* soundtrack, maybe?"

"Sure." She waited a moment longer, watching him sitting there behind his Ross Perot desk. She wondered if something about such desks leads to impotency. Or homosexuality, perhaps.

Outside the sun was a deflated balloon.

*

Burghville *was* a pretty town, at least at certain moments and in certain light: like now, with this deflated sun floating ever lower on the horizon, with this purple light spreading out over the streets and yards, with all that

217

color in the western sky running and bleeding over the clouds, with that single eastern star looking down like a silver eye. During such a time Burghville seemed quaint, pleasant, a town out of another time. A place where the American Dream comes to be dreamt, where the American Wet Dream (three cars and a giant SUV with backseat television and DVD player, a large-screened television for the livingroom, eight kids to watch those televisions, and a massive house with a massive yard of smoothly-cut grass) was spurted every single night onto the sheets of Hope. Yes, Burghville was, at certain moments, the quintessential American small town. At certain moments in a day's progression, Burghville was everything it wanted to be.

However, as Emerson once said: Even a corpse is beautiful if you shine enough light on it.

*

Now, about Tracey White's train problem:

The day after the Town Hall meeting, when Father Preston was firmly ensconced in the St. Michael's Catholic Church with Orson the Wee Folk, when Carol Slugg was already busy with the first meeting of her like-minded Acolytes, when work was already under way at Buckthorn Industries to make the most toxic and effective pesticide ever, when Helen Keller was (as usual) resting in the woods with the wee folk, when Betty Buckthorn was (as usual) weak in the knees, when Scooter Boober was busying himself with the pleasant and comforting chores of his hobby farm, when Sheriff Sherman was working overtime to finish the details of his Plan, when the whole town was hunkered down and waiting for its liberation, Tracey White was doing laundry. Timmy was in the basement watching his toy trains go round and round... and to be fair his set-up *was* amazing: so life-like that to watch a train go down the track past Astroturf fields and Styrofoam mountains, be it a steam-engine or a Japanese bullet-train, was to feel like a god looking down on a pathetic world (this really is the hobby of the insecure). The White's washer and dryer had their own room upstairs, next to the bathroom. As Tracey pulled clothes from the hamper and placed them in the washer she came across a

218

pair of Timmy's pants, and per habit she immediately went through the pockets. In the past this act had revealed coins and cash and movie-tickets and receipts from restaurants and business cards and a few hard-candies. On this morning, with the sound of wee-folk singing and dancing outside, Tracey White's simple wifely act revealed the following:

A train ticket to the East Coast. Just one.

And it was one-way.

*

Prior to this event Tracey White had never huffed a single house-hold product. And of course she wouldn't huff her first until the very next day, with her introduction to Candy Cleaver's *Wildflower Fresh* air-freshener. But perhaps she *should* have grabbed her own can of fake-flower aerosol at that moment: it would have tempered her reaction to finding that train ticket.

And her reaction?

Pure almighty rage.

*

But that was the day after the Town Hall meeting. Now it is the second day... or, rather, the end of the second day. The sun falls below the horizon and Burghville goes from the prettiness of muted light to the dullness of shadow. Underneath the brief stillness that falls over the town at this hour (it is wee folk suppertime) there is a hum of covert activity.

And then a moon rises ghost-like and graceful into the evening sky.

10

"I hate the goddamn moon!" said Polly Anderson. Dick Dick had seen her on Main Street's sidewalk as he roared to Buckthorn Industries in his giant SUV. She'd been trying to put aside her fear of the little people long enough to move from one building to another, from Joe's Joe to the post-office to the bakery to the video rental store. Dick Dick saw her as she was moving from the video place to the Pet Korner, which was fortunate for her: that pet store had been closed for a full year by this time. People in Burghville preferred to get their pets the same way they got their psychological problems: from family and friends.

"I hate the goddamn moon!" Polly was saying as she rode with Dick Dick to Buckthorn Industries. "I fucking hate it!"

"Just relax, babe, just relax."

She sulked there on the passenger side... which was approximately fifteen feet away from the driver's side of the massive vehicle. She stared out at the evening. Normally she did *not* hate the moon, but normally she wasn't in a town overrun by evil little creatures.

"And I hate those goddamn *things*!" she said as a little person ran scampering through a yard.

"You and me both, babe," Dick Dick said, and he pulled hard on the wheel and drove his truck right up over the curb and onto that dirt lawn, attempting to run that wee folk over. Failing this, and succeeding in only taking out some lawn-jockeys and a now-vestigial sprinkler, he pulled back onto the street. "You and me both. Look at this town. Look what they've done to it." He said this with the same tone he had used in the past while talking about environmentalists and "candy-asses" (his term).

"Oh Dick Dick," Polly Anderson said. "What's going on here?"

He reached over the mighty expanse of the vehicle and patted her leg. "Nothing I can't handle, Sugar. Nothing I can't handle at all."

She sighed and continued to sulk in her seat. "Look at me," she said, struggling to smooth out her dress, to fluff up her breasts with a quick and well-practiced lift, to moisten her lips with her tongue. "I look dreadful..."

"You look fine."

"I need a shower."

"There's a shower near my office."

"I want to go home."

He paused, then looked at her there on the far side of the Canyonero. This rugged monster of a truck, it should be said, had never, not one single time in its life, been off-road, unless you counted that brief escapade on the lawn back there. It was strictly a creature of concrete and asphalt.

"Where *is* your home?" he asked.

She was close to sniffles. "Connecticut."

"Connecticut, huh? You learn your kind of trade in Connecticut?"

"Connecticut... Maine... Texas... wherever. You learn as you go."

"Hmmm...." He thought hard as he drove through Burghville. "You ever meet Ross Perot?"

"Before my time, baby."

"What about....?"

She leaned over and touched his closest arm with the tips of her fingers. "Dick Dick," she purred, "you know you're my favorite."

He looked at her, smiled, and then looked back at the road. "Shit!" he shouted.

Seven wee folk were standing there, dancing in a little circle.

"Fucking bastards!" Dick Dick screamed, and then he floored the accelerator and roared toward them, the truck's massive engine screaming madly. Six of the wee folk scattered, the seventh just stood there and let the truck barrel down on himself.

There was a *thump* on the SUV's belly and Dick Dick looked at Polly. "I think I got him!" he shouted gleefully. "I think I—"

221

Polly screamed when the wee folk appeared upside down on the windshield, smiling broadly from under a big beard, little eyes sparkling.

Dick Dick hit the wipers but the little man took hold of them and went for a ride, laughing joyously as he was taken back and forth across the windshield.

"Son of a bitch!" Dick Dick said. He turned the wipers on full-speed and the little man only laughed harder, staring in at the two humans with a crazy look of delight on his face.

Dick Dick slammed his big foot down on the brakes and his truck screeched to a smoking halt. The little man was flung from the truck and landed on the street. He stood and shook himself off, like a cartoon character shaking off birds and whistles. With a graceful, elegant rhythm he folded one arm over his belly and bowed in the headlights.

Dick Dick floored the gas again.

This time the little man jumped gracefully out of the way, somersaulting into the air and onto the closest yard.

The giant SUV, engine growling, took out Buckthorn Industries' front gate, sending fencing and chain flying everywhere. When Dick Dick finally brought it to a stop with most of the front gate on its hood, he looked over at Polly Anderson (who was hunched down in her seat with her legs up on the dash and her dress at her waist).

"Those little fuckers are going down," he said softly. This tone was a low variation of his CEO voice, the one he used when he was beyond angry, when he was pissed at the world and he felt it would be prudent for the world to get out of his way.

"Oh Dick Dick..." Polly said, close to tears.

Back in the shadows there was wee folk laughter.

*

Also seeing the moon this evening was Father Preston. He was standing under a stained-glass window that had been opened a sliver via its top hinges. Framed perfectly in the center of that sliver was the moon, a fat glowing pumpkin skull caressed by the branches of an oak.

Around the moon was an ever-thickening wall of shadow, the sort of night that usually comes only in the Fall. It was a witch's night, heavy and still.

"She's beautiful," Father Preston said. He wasn't sure himself who he was referring to. It could have been the moon. It could have been Helen Keller. It could have been someone from a long time ago.

Orson, back at the front of the church, was studying the statue of Mary that hung from the wall there... and which still held his hat on its head, cocked jauntily askew, *Cabaret*-style. He did not look over at Father Preston when the priest spoke. The stone-skin of Mary's body fascinated him, and he lit his pipe as he studied it. The smoke formed a question mark above his head, then faded into the still air of the church.

Father Preston was reflecting on all the moons he had known. It seemed to him that a good fat moon had always accompanied the major events of his life. There had been a full moon the night he decided to become a priest. There had been a pretty quarter-moon the evening his father had died, he had seen it through the foggy glass of the hospital window. There had been many moons. Had there been one *that* night all those years ago, shining on the broken glass, the tortured metal...?

He and Orson had just finished a long talk, one of their longest so far, on the nature of worship. Specifically, Orson had wondered why, if one believes in a god, one would find it necessary to *prove* that one believes in that god. If such belief is an accepted part of one's life, why not simply live a life of justice and peace, why this need to actually *worship* in an official setting: in other words, why this need to go to a church or synagogue or mosque? Surely, Orson had said, to live a life in accordance with a god's wishes was to worship? So why all this pomp and circumstance and pageantry? Could it be that gods are vain and egotistical? Perhaps they were insecure?

Father Preston didn't know. He had always believed it was because people felt closer to their god at a sanctioned and holy place where they could feel his presence. In that way, then, it wasn't for the deity at all, it was for the person himself.

"But why," Orson wondered, "does a god's presence only seem to make itself known in a designated place? Didn't your God create the entire world? The swamps? The fields? The forests? The mountains? The deserts? Why not go *there*, like the prophets of old, instead of to cold buildings?"

Father Preston didn't know.

Now they were both standing by themselves, Father Preston watching the moon and Orson watching Mary. The Virgin, for her part, looked quite sexy in her hat. She could have been a pricey exotic dancer. She even had the snake to go with it, though she was apparently standing on hers: a bit of coil and a head were all that were visible underneath her robe.

Father Preston's mind was a swirl of thoughts. He felt odd, being in here for three days now with this strange little man, discussing the things they discussed. He felt that Orson was leading him to something, that the little man had an objective in all this. And, though this disturbed him, Father Preston did not want to leave. The questions he was being asked and the questions he was asking had been swarming inside of him for some time now. Walking had always been his way of putting them out of mind, but now that swarm of thoughts was out front and center... not angry, like bees, but fluttering and seductive, like the gathering of monarch butterflies.

Plus, being locked in the Saint Michael's Catholic Church kept him away from the people outside, some of whom would be looking to him in this time of "crisis."

He turned his eyes from the moon and looked at the little man. What did he know? Father Preston wondered. What does he know about me?

"I know you're in love," Orson said, his back to Father Preston.

Father Preston swallowed. "You've said that before. It's not true."

"No?"

"No. And stop smiling at me like that. It's creepy. And for the love of God stop reading my mind, if that's what you're doing. Just stop it."

"I don't read minds. I read souls."

224

Father Preston walked over to where the little man was standing. Together they stared up at Mary.

"You believe in souls, then?"

"Aye. But understand that a soul is nothing more than the energy created by the simple act of living. *All* living things have souls: plants, trees, ants, squirrels, cats, snakes, men. A soul is the warmth that comes from living tissue. The soul of skunk cabbage burns so warmly that it can melt snow and ice. Some people are warmer than others, too. *Love* makes a soul burn warmer. It is such heat that I am attuned to. I'm sensitive to warmth, you could say."

Father Preston nodded.

"Now why," Orson said softly, "does your culture like to make their religious figures Caucasian? Look at this woman here… she looks like a model."

"She's beautiful."

"Aye. But is she accurate? Why do these people all look like American Midwesterners in your paintings and sculptures?"

"I don't know."

Orson looked up at him. "Apparently people only feel connected to things that are like them. A falsity is easier to connect with than the truth."

Father Preston considered the figure of Mary: long hair pulled back under a headscarf, thin lips, high-cheekbones, thin waist, very petite form. He wondered if the figure had been created during the height of Audrey Hepburn's fame. He imagined a lonely sculptor in a workshop somewhere circa 1961, pining for a Hollywood star he loved and would never know.

"Maybe she was modeled on someone the sculptor loved," he said. "A girl he knew once long ago… a girl he maybe lost.…"

Orson smiled warmly. "Are you thinking of someone yourself, Father?"

Father Preston said the name without thinking: "Tina Johnson." It was a name he hadn't spoken in years. The sound of it hung heavily in the air.

"Do you want to talk about it?"

"No."

225

"Is this Tina Johnson maybe the *real* reason you became a priest?"

"I said I don't want to talk about it."

"Well you'd *better* talk about it, maybe. The name sits like a shadow on your tongue. It *means* something." He sighed, exasperated. "A life wasted chasing a delusion is a life not worth living in the first place, Father." The little man spoke in a different tone than before, more stern, more direct, without patience.

Father Preston looked at him. The butterfly-thoughts were swarming like temptresses. And with those butterflies, something else fluttered... something beyond thought, beyond feeling. Something much more elemental than either.

Orson sighed, and when he spoke again his tone was much softer, much warmer, much more paternal and calm:

"A soul cannot and should not deny an elemental truth. Denial may seem all right for priests and monks, but it kills them as surely as it seems to bring them peace. This girl, Tina Johnson, she loved you?"

Quietly: "Yes."

"Would she have wanted you to deny yourself love and happiness? Would she have wanted you to wander here in these cold impersonal walls, surrounded by wailing sinners and crazy Carol Slugg? Would she have wanted *any* of this for you?"

Father Preston was close to tears: they bubbled at the corners of his eyes.

"These are the questions you need to ask yourself," Orson said, "before everything you need passes you by."

One eye spilled over and a tear snaked down Father Preston's left cheek, pooling finally at the corner of his mouth where he could taste its saltiness and warmth. It was a taste he hadn't known in years.

"All of this," Orson said, indicating the church and everything in it, "is trappings. It's all for *show*. It has no depth, because it means nothing. Meaning is attached to it all by the observer. This statue of Jesus on the cross is all wood and plaster and paint. To some it has a sacred quality, but it *cannot* be sacred. Only that which is truly sacred can be sacred, see? Only that which is real and true can be sacred. And what is more sacred than love? What is truly more holy and worthwhile than the deep and pure love of one being for another?"

Father Preston turned away and started down the center aisle of the church. "I need to be alone," he said.

Orson just nodded, a smoke-sphere like a cat's eye marble floating over his head, golden and blue in the dim light of the church.

*

Tina Johnson... one of those names that means nothing to most but which reverberates with tones both dark and lovely to a select few. Or, in this case, to the select *one*, for Father Lee Preston was the only soul in Burghville who knew what that name signified.

Tina Johnson....

Orson had asked him why he had become a priest, and Father Preston had said it was because he wanted to help people. A half-truth. The person he wanted to help was himself, to escape from that name as much as humanly possible. And it had worked, to a degree. Late at night, when he was half-asleep, it might come to him cloud-like, vaporous, but never like this, out front, in block-letters, demanding his attention.

Tina Johnson.

And he, back then, had been simply Lee Preston. For a time their names had been tied together closely, one never mentioned without the other... for a sweet and gentle time. It was there on the side of an ancient elm on the outskirts of that old and distant town:

TJ + LP.

A million years ago.

*

This same evening, the second night after the Town Hall meeting, Carol Slugg saw her acolytes to the door, wished them a good evening, told them to be careful, admonished them to hold their crucifixes aloft as they walked to frighten away the demons that haunted this town, and told them she'd see them tomorrow. Then she closed

227

and locked that door and turned to her empty house. Actually, that house was decidedly *not* empty: it was a clutter of religious books (the *Joy of Sects*, perhaps) and crosses and candles. Carol Slugg was big on crosses and candles. There were also pictures of Jesus and Mary on nearly every wall... those very same Aryan visages that Orson and Father Preston had been talking about. Carol Slugg, for one, did not buy the idea that her beloved holy figures were dark of skin or black of hair... she did not believe that they looked like anything other than how they appeared in the movies. She believed they were zit-free, clean-smelling, clear of eyes, sharp of cheekbones, and white of teeth. She believed that their hair was soft and Pantene-fresh. She believed that they were healthy and young, with clean minty breath. She believed halos of heavenly light followed them wherever they went. She believed that they were able to hover over any mule and cow shit that happened to get in their way. She believed they might even have spoken English. She may even have believed that they never once, any of them, squatted behind a bush or boulder to relieve themselves. Perhaps she believed Mary never menstruated. She may have believed that the Apostles, though they were coarse workingmen, never once passed a vulgar word amongst themselves. She may also have believed there wasn't a gay man, a lesbian, or an anarchist among them. She may have believed that all of the Apostles believed inherently in the divinity of Jesus. She may have believed that Jesus never said "No one can come to me without hating his own father, mother, sister, brother," though he did, right there in Luke, chapter fourteen, verse twenty-six. She may have believed that Jesus was a Christian... though of course he was a Jew. She may have believed, if we go further back in time, that the Judeao-Christian God is the only god mentioned in the Bible, though He is not. She may have believed, to jump forward to the present, that the Pope was pure and never stank up the Vatican bathrooms... or that he never woke, like Father Preston, with happy erections. She may have believed any number of things about her own religion, and she would have been wrong. In fact, she knew very little about the Bible itself, though she read it often. Like most people who read the Bible, she took from it what she *wanted* to take from it, and she only read the parts that *everyone* read. The Bible was like a Greek restaurant: everyone got a gyro.

Now, after seeing her own acolytes to the door and turning to her quiet house, she took down her most cherished Bible (it was the thickest, with lovely paintings of dying and suffering men, just beautiful) and sat down to read the high-lighted parts. Reading was never enough for Carol Slugg, though, and soon the Bible was closed and she was praying aloud. She prayed like no other living soul, save for a few Death Row inmates and the occasional stock-broker. She prayed with passion and vigor, with an athletic energy that made sweat pour from her pores. She closed her eyes and prayed like it was the last prayer she would ever have the chance to utter:

"Oh Dear Father we ask you to…"

And so on.

Fists clenched, jaw firm, eyes closed, ass tight, back straight. Only her womanly parts stirred, just as they had at the church. And so it was that Carol Slugg's womanly parts also prayed, but for a god of a different sort. It had been ages since they had received the attention they craved, and so they prayed now for communion, for absolution, for deliverance, for sanctuary, for the staff of life, for *anything*. They prayed in vain, though, as the rest of Carol Slugg paid those parts no mind. If the soul is said to be the warmth created by living matter, then the most soul-full part of Carol Slugg sat nestled (uncomfortably) between her legs, heated and moist and ready to play… but, alas, denied its needs and desires once again.

An infrared image of Carol Slugg would have revealed a creature of the saddest kind:

Cold of heart, hot of groin.

After nearly twenty minutes of praying she fell into a trance. During this trance she was quiet and calm and every muscle in her body was relaxed. She sat there with her eyes closed and her head down, her hands open, her fingers unclenched, her mouth open just slightly. She felt tranquil and fulfilled.

It was the closest to orgasm she would ever get.

And it lasted three hours.

229

Dick Dick Buckthorn sat listening to his chemists. They were in the conference room near his office, and from that office could be plainly heard the sound of a shower hissing hotly. Everyone present tried to ignore the sound of that shower. They knew who was in there, and they had long suspected what her purpose was... and, of course, three of the four chemists were men and men cannot keep from imagining a young woman like Polly Anderson in a shower. They imagined soap frothing on thighs and breasts, foaming like sea-water on the shores of her horizon. They imagined feminine fingers exploring a feminine landscape.

Three erections sat across the table from Dick Dick Buckthorn. Three erections and one absolutely uninterested vulva.

Dick Dick asked: "So, what do you guys have for me?"

Three pairs of legs were crossed.

"We think we have it," said the female chemist.

Dick Dick leaned forward. "And...?"

One of the men opened his mouth to speak but the woman beat him to it:

"And we believe it's everything you wanted. Maybe even more."

Dick Dick smiled. "Show me."

She began to unfold a thick sheath of papers, but Dick Dick shook his head.

"No, *show* me. I don't want to see the *math*, I want to see the *product* itself!"

The four chemists looked at each other.

"Okay," the woman said. "Let's go to the lab."

Somewhere in another room, close by, a shower stopped running... and for a moment, brief but sweet, four men (yes, Dick Dick included) imagined a beautiful young woman stepping wet and hot from a shower to dry herself on soft white towels. Aside from mountaintops and cloud formations and inheritances of large sums of money and the deaths of their enemies, there is no more beautiful image that a man can ponder.

"Okay," Dick Dick said at last. "Let's go."

For the interested, the ingredients of this product can be found, in various forms, on any typical household product one can find under the sink or in the medicine cabinet, most such products sharing ingredients the way the British monarchy shares genes. There was nothing new in this new pesticide, only new combinations. It should be said, though, even if it should be obvious, that this product would in no way ever be passed by the FDA or any other government agency... even the CIA or the army would have shied away from it, perhaps, although one wonders about the Army Corps of Engineers. It should also be taken as a given that these four chemists, Buckthorn Industries' best and brightest, had followed not one single regulation during the testing and making of this product. It should also be stated that, since it was a pesticide, there had been tests on living animals, rats chief among these. And, lastly, it should be stated that on this late evening, with Dick Dick Buckthorn in attendance, the four chemists were going to demonstrate another test of this product on yet another animal.

*

The lab at Buckthorn Industries contained many test animals. One entire large room was dedicated to housing cages and cages of rats and mice and insects. There was, in fact, a full-time biologist whose job was to breed and raise and keep these animals healthy so that one day, if all went well, they could be subjected to any number of atrocities. So far in the many years of Buckthorn Industries' existence no animal-rights warriors had ever broken in and tried to liberate these creatures. Perhaps even animal-rights workers would be overwhelmed by the sheer number of roaches and ants and mice and mosquitoes and spiders and rats and raccoons that made their homes here. The volume of animals was awesome, and indeed that full-time biologist had an entire staff underneath him, people whose job was to oversee the various needs of the insects and rodents until, as stated previously, it came their

231

time to submit to the genocidal practices of the Buckthorn Industries Department of Product Development. So, one could imagine what chaos would occur should these creatures be let loose... we're talking five-hundred thousand roaches alone. Now, add in the security measures that Dick Dick had paid mightily for and you had a nearly impenetrable fortress, with a dungeon filled with the winged and wriggling.

On this evening a single fat rat was placed in a fifteen-gallon tub while one of the chemists (wearing thick protective clothing, like that of an astronaut) took a small vial of this new product and held it up for Dick Dick to see. Dick Dick and the others were in another room, looking in on the scene from behind six-inch thick glass.

The liquid inside the vial was a deep and brilliant green that caught the stark light of the lab and cast psychedelic designs on the walls and ceiling.

"Wow," Dick Dick said.

The other chemists nodded.

And then, just like that, the chemist in the other room turned that vial over and dumped its contents, less than a tablespoon's worth, into the tub and on top of the rat.

Almost even before the liquid came in contact with it, the rodent went into mighty death-throes of agony, writhing and squealing and shaking violently. Blood foamed at its mouth, poured from its nose. It ran in circles, head-butted the side of the tub a few dozen times, and then was still. Where the liquid had touched its back the fur was gone and the skin was bubbling, revealing the smoldering bone and muscle beneath.

Dick Dick Buckthorn smiled. "Perfect," he said.

The chemist in the other room closed the vial, threw it in with the rat, and then carried the whole tub over to a slot in the wall labeled INCINERATOR. Once the contents of that tub were dumped down the chute he turned and immediately left the room. When he came out by the others he was sweating and there was a look of fear on his face.

"We'll have to evacuate the entire town," he said to Dick Dick.

"Yeah," Dick Dick said.

"The *entire* town."

"Yeah...."

"The whole thing. Everyone. The whole kit and caboodle."

"Yeah... yeah...."

*

A word about mushrooms: once, back when the yards of Burghville were full of green and lush grass and tightly-clipped evergreen hedges as square as a Marine's jaw, back in the days before Burghville's lawns were nothing but bare earth pocked with the tiny feet-print of little people, back in the days when the sound of ratcheting sprinklers filled every summer evening, the good people (as opposed to the Good People) of Burghville, the caring and concerned and loving lawn-tenders of Burghville, had been familiar with one species of mushroom that seemed to be the bane of their existence... their only bane, back in those days of more simple worries. This species of mushroom was *Psathyrella foenisecii*, commonly called the Haymaker's Mushroom, and was one member of the trilogy of lawn-terrors, along with dandelions and Creeping Charley. While Creeping Charley was truly an enemy of Burghville's lawns, dandelions and Haymaker's Mushrooms did little but altar the aesthetic vision of narrow-minded individuals, and, in the case of dandelions, were actually beneficial, having deeper roots that pulled nutrients towards the surface, where the shallower-rooted grass could partake of them. In fact, all of these plants are rather beautiful, certainly more so than plain old *grass*. Creeping Charley's flowers, so delicate and tiny, are such a pure purple-blue that they are a sheer joy to look upon, and dandelions signify innocence and beauty in one proud package. Dandelions are one of the symbols of spring and summer, in fact, and their sun-bright yellow looks absolutely stunning against the deep green of even the most pesticide-ridden lawn. One wonders why the good folks of Wisconsin have not embraced them, in tandem with the lowly grass, as being natural symbols of Green Bay Packer pride.

Once upon a time there were few people in Burghville who did not enjoy the simple (-minded) pleasure

233

of running over Haymaker's Mushrooms with the mower and spewing out chunks of *Psathyrella* viscera. And why? To have that nice uncluttered lawn that someone, somewhere, once upon a time deemed *normal*. Who was this person and what was their motive? Perhaps Henrietta Pratt knew for sure, but one can guess that it was a Puritan who thought that a wild and natural lawn was the mark of an uncultivated soul in the lawn-owner, that to let things grow free and natural without any attempt to make them conform to human standards of geometry and color was to befriend the Devil himself. In this way, it became engrained in the minds of millions of Americans that the only good and decent lawn was one that was free of mushrooms and dandelions, one that was cut down like a jarhead's skull, that was free of animal burrows, that was watered more often than a public urinal. In the process, of course, millions of Americans made more work for themselves: all that watering of thirsty non-native grasses, all that mowing, all that spraying of herbicides and pesticides... all that asthma, all those mutated frogs....

It was not the Haymaker's Mushroom that sprouted fat and healthy in Henrietta Pratt's yard, however... she had actually not seen one of those 'shrooms in years, not since she had torn out the old non-native grass and replaced it with bluestem. Not that the Haymaker was non-native (it wasn't), but her yard became less wet and therefore less hospitable to plants of the mushroom persuasion. Henrietta Pratt rarely watered her grass. There wasn't need to, the grasses native to the area being hardier and able to accommodate the natural swing of the weather, dry as well as wet.

No, it was not the much-disliked Haymaker's Mushroom that grew in Henrietta's small patch of grass. It was something else indeed, something that appeared different each time you looked at it. Sometimes this mushroom looked like any familiar capped 'shroom, sometimes it looked like a morel, sometimes it had the wet, clammy look of a Velvet Foot, sometimes it did not look like a mushroom at all but rather like the skunk cabbage. Most of the time, however, it looked simply like a fat, wet, thick-stalked Fairy Ring Mushroom, the cliché mushroom of fairy tales and folklore. Which was fitting, of course: it

234

grew as the result of wee folk activity, and wee folk themselves *invented* fairy tales and folklore... just don't call them fairies.

Like the Haymaker's Mushroom, however, *this* 'shroom had psychotropic qualities. The National Audubon Society Field Guide describes such mushrooms as having the ability to "induce altered states of consciousness," but the Wee Folk 'Shroom is slightly different. It induces altered states of *perception*. The difference is subtle, but that difference is everything.

You don't "trip" on these Wee Folk 'Shrooms. "Trip" implies going somewhere else.

On *these* mushrooms you stay where you are, and you see your world like never before.

*

Henrietta Pratt knew better than to go mucking around with mushrooms she was unfamiliar with, knowing as she did that some of them can kill, but she supposed some kids, somewhere, were eating them by the handful, hoping for a cheap high. She hoped no one got sick or, god forbid, died because of them. The town already viewed the wee folk as enemies, so she could only imagine what the outcry would be if they were linked to a death.

They're killing us off! someone would shout. And then it really would be open season, more so than it already was.

"Don't touch those!" she shouted to a middle-aged man who was examining the 'shrooms that speckled his front yard.

He looked at her for a moment, then shook his head and kicked at the mushrooms, sending gray bits of moist viscera into the air.

"I suppose you think they're *endangered* or something," he said, saying the word like it had a terrible taste. "It's people like you that...."

She didn't catch the rest of what he said. She turned and walked away, back to her own yard. Go ahead, she thought. Go ahead, then, eat all you want. Maybe I'll fetch you a little Deadly Galerina for an appetizer....

235

Helen Keller was also thinking about those mushrooms, though at first she thought about them only in passing. Sam the Artist had been fond of 'shrooming in his time. He received no visions from these experiments, though, only a heightened sense of color. Helen had said she thought you were supposed to receive grand god-inspired Universe-expanding visions.

"No," he had said. "It's enough to see such colors. Such salmons!"

So, having noticed the mushrooms that sprouted wherever the wee folk spat or shat or pissed or made love, she had pondered them only long enough to wonder what Sam would have made of them and to wonder what colors such as fuchsia and patterns such as plaid would look like with 'shroom juice coursing through your veins. Then, knowing like Henrietta Pratt that mushrooms were the last thing you wanted to mess with if you didn't know what you were doing, she put them out of her mind.

She did, however, partake liberally of the wee folk tea and the wee folk tobacco. She had never known you could make such tobacco from the roots of lowly suburb-grass. And, interestingly enough, none of the wee folk even gave the mushrooms more than a passing glance. In fact, they seemed rather perturbed by them, some even kicking the fat 'shrooms as they passed, as if they were thick wet footballs or the asses of congressmen.

On this evening, with a moon in the heavens like a bruise of light in the skin of the sky, Helen was seated near about thirty of those mushrooms and she herself was paying them no attention. She was sitting at the edge of a forest field and in the middle of that field, roaring right in front of her, was a gigantic bonfire throwing flames to Orion. The glow from the flames threw colored shadows and fiery flickers over her face.

In one hand she held a pipe, one of Sam's from the house. In that pipe, of course, was grass-tobacco.

In her other hand rested the cool dry head of a snake. It was her friend the hog nosed snake. An Eastern hog nosed snake, to be exact, *Heterodon platirhinos*.

Maybe not the very same one she had shared her house with over the winter, but a gorgeous one either way.

The significance of the snake demands a flashback to that afternoon, when the sun was slipping to the horizon like a prom dress to the floor of a Chevy. It was around the same time that Orson the Good Person was telling Father Preston that there were no such things as angels. Helen would have been the first to dispute that claim, however.

Webster's describes an angel as being first, a messenger of God, and secondly as an "immortal spirit." Well, there were *plenty* of immortal spirits in the world, Helen knew.

And that afternoon one of them slithered out of the grass and tickled her ankle with its tongue.

*

She'd been alone for a while, off doing her forest duties. These duties included but were in no way limited to observing and noticing. Observing and noticing do not mean the same thing, of course. One can observe plenty but notice little. One can observe a twig moving gently in the wind, or one can notice that that twig is in fact an insect, a member of the walkingstick family. Some things, however, demanded to be observed and *not* noticed, and one of Helen's duties was to tell what required which.

She was standing on the side of a small hill, staring ahead to a particularly dark patch of forest. A few minutes before five turkey vultures had soared overhead, wings in rigid V's, bald red heads looking this way and that.

"Don't even think about it," she told them.

They soared on.

And just a few minutes after they were gone she heard the hooting of a barred owl, the classic call of "Who cooks for you?" She had always thought there was something accusatory in that call, or if not accusatory at least condescending. Or maybe just sad. After all, *no one* cooked for her. She was, in some ways, alone in the world. An orphan, as Father Preston had wondered? Suffice it to say that the people Helen Keller came from were far away, and suffice it to say that she had yet to find a place she truly belonged. Suffice it to say, also, that Burghville was only a

237

temporary stopover for her... albeit one that had been her home for nearly eight years. But eternity is a long time and "temporary" can mean a thousand years, in the larger scheme of things. She had no intentions of staying in Burghville the rest of her life... but nor did she have any clue where she would end up next. Wherever it was she would go there alone, and most likely she would live on the fringe, as she did here. That was the way she liked it.

So, who cooks for her? Well Jesus, did someone *have* to cook for her?

She had a right to think it a sad call. But, in truth, and in fairness to the beautiful barred owl, it was also not a sad call at all. It was just a call, the owl version of "whassup" and "is anyone out there?"

When the immortal spirit, which was the Eastern hog nosed snake, came out of the grass at that moment and licked her bare ankle, Helen smiled. That first definition of Webster's is correct, too, after all: an angel such as this *is* a messenger of god.

It just never mentioned *which* god.

*

And what did this messenger, representing so much to so many, symbolizing to some rebirth and fertility and to others death and sin and temptation, what did this serpent have to say?

She knew the little hog nosed snake had something to tell her, she could sense it in its eyes and in the flicker of its tongue against her skin. She could sense it in the way it coiled over itself and gave her a classic snake-pose, its tail curled up cutely. She stared down for a while, into its lidless eyes, and smiled. Though it could not hear her voice, she spoke to the serpent:

"What is it, little fellow?"

The snake's tongue came forth again and tenderly touched her ankle. Such a small tongue, that forked thing. Miraculous. The whole design of the snake, from tongue to tail, was an engineering miracle, a near-perfect model of efficiency. Indeed, most of the animals people dislike are among the very best that nature has to offer in terms of design and art: consider the perfectly-made shark, or the superb adaptations inherent in the spider family, or the bat, the only mammal that has truly mastered the art of flying (when was the last time you heard about a bat going down over the Atlantic and killing sixty people?). It is a pathetic soul who would think these animals are in any way *less* than what they could be. Quite the contrary, they are the very face of the phrase "Be all you can be," and more than that, they are what they are, nothing more. Popeye was wrong when he said "I am what I am," for the very nature of being a human was to always struggle to be what you are not. Had Popeye truly been what he was, he would have been a snake.

Anyway, after this last flicking of the tongue against her ankle, Helen reached down and picked the fellow up. She held him to her face and looked into his round eyes. His slightly upturned nose was so cute she wanted to kiss it, but she did not, of course, allowing the animal to keep its dignity. All she did was stare into those eyes and wonder what it was this little guy had to tell her.

And what *was* it he had to say? The same things her other winter guests had told her:

"Follow the course of natural things." But there was one other little message she gained from this Eastern hog nosed snake, one final important point:

"If you have the power to do something good, *do* it."

Somehow, though, Helen had always known that.

*

So here she was at this big bonfire in the woods. Around that bonfire the wee folk were dancing and partying, which meant they were laughing and singing and kicking each other and shouting out jokes and calling each other names. Some of the wee folk who were staying in town had come out as well to mingle and dance, rekindling ties and forming new friendships. The music that swelled around those lifting flames was primal and wild, yet full of melody too, an ancient disco rhythm for which the disco-ball was always the moon. Helen had been pulled into the counter-clockwise dance around the fire twice but was resting now, not having the energy level of the Good

239

People. She was content, for the moment, to smoke her tobacco and watch the others.

Occasionally the snake would stir and she would look down at him. In the light of the fire his brown and black scales gleamed as if wet. He felt warm, but continued to stay where he was, taking it all in. Did he like what he saw?

She was not the sort of "pagan" to believe that everything, plants and animal, had the same feelings and beliefs. She was not a fan of anthropomorphism, even as she understood, and was obviously sensitive to, the "language" of such creatures as this. She had been given many messages from Mother Nature's creatures which she had not been able to assign meaning to, they had simply been too cryptic, or too complex, or too completely different from her own way of thinking for her to understand. Other people might have interpreted this as the animal having nothing to say at all, but she knew the truth: just because we humans don't understand something doesn't imply there is nothing to understand. There is, indeed, meaning in everything.

Helen loved nature enough to know there was meaning and significance in the falling of a single autumn leaf, the pulsing of a single star, or the shining of the moon, regardless of whether she understood it or not. The beauty of nature is that it cares not one bit for our perspective.

And although there *was* meaning in everything, in some way or form, sometimes Man is not meant to know what it is. Sometimes it's enough to believe a falling leaf is just a falling leaf.

Nonetheless, all that said, she believed that the hog nosed snake was enjoying the sight of the little people dancing and singing around the fire. She believed he could feel the pulse of the music and that, in his own way, he was smiling. He may have been assigning his own meaning to the scene, the likes of which he most likely had never seen before.

He may even have been assigning the whole thing a snake-significance, meaningful only to serpents.

Anthropomorphism in reverse. Well, slither me timbers, why not?

So the bonfire continued, throwing liquid hieroglyphics against the nearby forest trees and sending a thin gray cloud of smoke to the moonlit sky. Puddlefoot the Flutist was playing like he never had before, and of course Tom Tom the drummer was keeping a frantic, frenetic, friendly pace. Other wee folk were pounding out counter-beats on old stumps or, when the mood took them, each other, and many of them were singing songs... though it could not be said that there was *one* song being sung, each of them offering up a spontaneous verse or two pulled from air or arse.

Helen smiled. She'd been smiling a lot at this little get-together. The vibe that rose from the scene was friendly and warm, unlike that of any other party she'd attended over the course of her young life... of course, this party was different from any other in almost *all* ways. Never had she been with folks who lived so completely in the here and now, and yet who were also so much a part of the past and future. Being with these creatures, and watching them party and sing and dance as if this was the last bonfire there would ever be, was like being in the presence of a pure animal spirit, a force it was nearly impossible to describe. It wasn't a force like Dick Dick Buckthorn's, which demanded to be reckoned with, which did not fill the air so much as suck it away like a vacuum. No, the force of the wee folk was an overall *good* feeling, a presence that seemed to *fill* the air around you with lightness and joy. The presence of the wee folk produced the same feeling people get when they learn they have a day off, when they hear the first robins of spring, when they discover they are about to have sex, when they have had a second glass of wine, when they see a baby smile up at them.... only it was magnified intensely, felt in mind body and spirit.

The wee folk had much to offer simply through their very presence, and through the very acts of mischief the Burghvillians hated them for, so Helen mostly watched them as they partied. There was great camaraderie among them, and it was a pleasure to observe. Even the petty fights that momentarily broke out had a friendly tone: someone would push someone else as they danced, then the two would face off, mutter words Helen could not

241

understand, dance opposing jigs, puff angry and intricate designs of smoke, and then clap each other on the shoulders and continue on, moving once more around the bonfire. It seemed to Helen that in this little society (ragged though it was, with no apparent leader... and no apparent *need* for a leader) anger was accepted, not frowned upon. It was seen as just another emotion, one to be expressed and transcended. In other words, the Good People did not hold things in. They did not let emotions stew inside of themselves like humans did. You would not find therapists in the Wee Folk world. You would not find classes on "Anger Management." You would not find people talking about "overcoming," and you would certainly not hear one of them discussing his or her "issues."

The wee folk recognized all of their emotions as natural and healthy, and they did not forbid free expression of them. As a result, theirs was a much more open society than any Helen had ever known or heard of, and she found it a sheer pleasure to simply observe them. Occasionally one of the wee folk would wander over with an outstretched hand to pull her back into the dance, and she would smile and shake her head. They seemed to understand her need to remain an observer, taking no offense at it and recognizing that it was just her nature. And a few of them would see the snake at her side and nod in understanding, realizing she was sensitive to things other members of her kind were blind to.

However, her "sight" did not manifest itself in regards to the wee folk, and they seemed to notice this, for they were not afraid of what she might read in them. But Helen thought she understood now, sitting here at the fire, why she had received no messages from their movements or minds. It was simple:

Being so open with their emotions, there was nothing to read. Any messages they had to give were given freely, out in the open. This should not be misinterpreted as their lacking depth. Quite the contrary, they were a very deep and wise people. It was just that they kept nothing hidden.

They, like the snakes, were what they were. Period.

*

The bonfire continued to roar and wee folk continued to dance around it, always counter-clockwise. The music lifted, swelled, changed tempo, changed melody. One hundred different verses rose to the smoky night sky on tiny joyful inebriated voices. Tobacco smoke joined bonfire smoke in a magnificent column of gray that gave the stars a muted, soft hue. Only the moon remained untouched by that opaque and spicy cloud, with the wind working in its favor, blowing East. It shone down clear and bright on the scene, like a chaperone. But it was a busy chaperone this evening.

There were many sights demanding its attention....

*

To some, the moon is nothing. To others, it is everything. On this evening the moon touched all of these people, as it touches *everyone*, regardless of how they feel about it. We are all the sons and daughters of Luna, she pulls at both our tides and our emotions. When Man needed his first god she was it, sacred and, for all intents and purposes, eternal.

She is also an aphrodisiac.

Betty Buckthorn wandered her large and empty home this evening, not paying much attention to the moon as it sent bright rays of light through the windows of the back deck. The house was quiet. Dick Dick had left two hours earlier and for a good hour and fifteen minutes of that time Betty had run around trying to find the hidden stereo so she could kill the "Love theme from *Rocky*." She finally found the stereo in a secret cabinet in the wall behind his office door. Now the house was quiet... maybe too quiet, not one single sound filling its spaces, save for the soft hush of her bare feet on the carpet.

She thought nothing as she wandered the house, other than fleeting realizations of just exactly how large the house really was. Did two people really need this much space? Had she been in a thinking mood she may have reflected on the old days, back when she had first lived on her own, away from her parents. She would have

243

remembered tiny apartments shared by three people, or larger flats occupied by six. She would have remembered sleeping four to a room in that huge old decrepit house near the university, men and women both, clothes everywhere, dishes piling up, a fridge full of beer and pizza. And, had she thought about those pre-Dick Dick days, she may even have smiled, recalling a time when she would have been unable to comprehend the life she lived now, when the thought of being a *wife* would have struck her as absurd, a cop-out.

But no, she was not thinking as she walked around the Buckthorn residence, crossing the livingroom with its giant TV and entering the rec-room with the pool table, returning through the livingroom to stand on the back deck for a while, then sliding ghost-like back through the house and into the kitchen and then up to the bedroom and back again, over and over, the entire route taking her twenty minutes to complete.

No thinking. Just wandering. And feeling, plenty of feeling. And what was Betty Buckthorn feeling on this evening, while a bonfire surrounded by wee folk blazed somewhere off in the woods, while Carol Slugg sat deep in some sort of Holy trance, while Tracey White slept off a Pledge-hangover, while Dick Dick was watching a rat die a grotesque and painful death in a cold white room on the other side of Burghville?

She was feeling horny, of course.

Horny and vibrator-less. Horny and sick of her own fingers, horny and nearly on the verge of turning on the damn dryer so she could get some pleasure courtesy of Kenmore. Horny and....

Just horny, period, with a capital H.

So, tender of nipple, aching of clitoris, she wandered her house, not knowing what to do with herself. She didn't place blame on the moon, though its soft light came through the windows of the house and set her blood to flowing. She didn't blame the moon because she gave it no notice.

After a long time of wandering the giant house (and looking carefully at every object she owned, searching for something to screw... thinking about how so many objects in the average home look phallic) Betty at last

244

crashed on the couch in front of the massive TV. She reached for the remote but stopped, choosing instead to sit there and stare at the ghostly reflection of herself in the giant screen. For the first time all night she had a thought:

Is this what I am now? A lonely woman sitting on a couch in an empty house?

She stared at herself for a time, then slowly parted her legs. She was wearing a white terry-cloth robe and nothing else, and as she parted her legs the ghost in the television screen imitated her. Soon they were both sitting slouched and spread-legged, admiring the silkiness of their legs, the muscle-tone, the inviting gape of their vulvas.

Betty sent a hand down her leg and the ghost did likewise. Two sets of fingers pushed through soft, sweet, perfumed pubic hair. Another set of hands softly fondled a breast.

Only one sigh was heard.

She closed her eyes for a time, opening them only slightly to see the gray ghost in the TV screen gently caressing the inside of its thighs. The house seemed less quiet now, filled with a rush that may have been a breeze in the eaves or blood in her ears. When her fingers slipped into silky wetness she knew it was the blood, flowing hot and vibrant through her veins.

"Ohhh...." she moaned softly.

And when the next thing happened it happened quickly and it happened without fanfare, just as if it was meant to be. And maybe it was. Maybe it was right and maybe it was beautiful. Perhaps it was inevitable, too, in some way. Maybe in the overall scheme of things everything is meant to happen... not in a fatalistic sense, but in a context of *chance*. Everything in the Universe comes down to numbers, the mathematicians tell us, and perhaps that means that given enough time anything that *can* happen, will. Therefore, perhaps everything the mind, human or otherwise, can think of may, somewhere, someday, come true. Maybe fate isn't so different from chance, then. Maybe fate is, in the end, just another roll of the dice. If so, on this night Betty Buckthorn rolled a four.

Four wee folk, that is.

They gleefully went to work on Burghville's most challenging job:

245

Satisfying the wife of Dick Dick Buckthorn....

*

The Gentry. The Fair Folk. The Good People. Those damn vermin. Those monsters.... on this night Betty Buckthorn just chose to refer to them as "God" and "Jesus" and "Yes, oh Yes, oh God oh Jesus *Yes!*"

Just don't call them Fairies.

*

Dick Dick Buckthorn was smiling. This smile had nothing to do with the lips of Polly Anderson, which were at this moment sweetly engulfing his penis and which had never felt so good. This smile of his had nothing to do with the delicate tips of her sensitive fingers, which were tickling his testicles with a gentle and practiced skill. This smile had nothing to do with the great mahogany desk he was sitting on. No, Dick Dick Buckthorn was smiling because of a rat. And not the rat so much as the way it had died, squealing there in that closed-off room as the ultimate Buckthorn Industries chemical ate away its flesh. It was that image, and all that it signified, that was making Dick Dick smile.

"Mhmmm..." Polly Anderson moaned between his legs. He looked down at her. She loved her job, she really did. So the feeling was mutual: he loved her job as well.

"Mhmmmm..." he moaned, imitating her. She was so good at what she did that he could stay erect even with an image of a burning screaming writhing rodent in his brain. What a girl.

She looked up at him. All of her earlier anxiety and fear had dissipated, it seemed. Which made sense: she was safe now, in familiar surroundings, doing familiar work. She was offering her services at this particular moment for free, in return for nothing but sanctuary from the little monsters. What she really wanted was to leave Burghville, but Dick Dick had told her to relax, wait a day or two and everything will be taken care of. No more monsters. Just wait. Trust me.

246

Trust me, he had said. Ahh yes, right there, that's it…

"Mhmmm…" he said again.

Another smile made its squirmy way over his mouth. Despite those monsters, despite what was happening to the town and his company, Dick Dick had plenty of reason to smile. Tomorrow Willy Billy would arrive and the plan would be set in motion. The monsters would be exterminated. And he, Dick Dick, would be a hero. Again. He would save the town. Again.

Most powerful man in Burghville? You bet your ass.

"Mhmmm…"

Those tickling hands, the soft warm tongue, the lips like a constrictor….

Still another smile played over his face. Dick Dick's face, it should be said, was not an ideal place for a smile. Sure, he looked all right smiling that big Teddy Roosevelt smile, the sort meant to fill up a room with charm and pomposity, but for smaller, more intimate smiles, Dick Dick's facial features were ill-suited. Most such expressions came off looking rather strained or… *peculiar* on him. Despite being a big, healthy, robust man, when Dick Dick Buckthorn smiled a certain way, like now, he resembled the sort of blithering idiot one might find in an insane asylum, smiling at private thoughts that would greatly disturb the rest of us.

This last smile was the product of further images, ones yet to come but imagined quite intensely:

The new spray being sent over the town, the little monsters screaming in terror and pain, Burghville's residents at last coming out and celebrating the return of their way of life. Another parade, this one honoring Dick Dick Buckthorn….

Ahh, glory.

"Mhmmm…" moaned Polly Anderson.

Dick Dick stared down at her. How many such women are there in the world? he wondered. What would he do if Polly Anderson were to decide to move on with her life?

Her lips tightened and loosened, tightened and loosened.

247

"Mhmmmm…"

He closed his eyes and rested his head back. The smile on his face was now a shadow of its former self, small and faint and without substance. He stayed like that, feeling the young woman at work on him and thinking nothing… until another thought worthy of thinking came to him, that is. This thought was the memory of what that chemist had said:

We'll have to evacuate the entire town.

And that thought of course produced other thoughts, and that shadowy little smile soon left Dick Dick's face. His penis stayed hard, of course, but he ceased thinking about what the woman was doing to him. She was an expert, anyway, she didn't need his help in any of this.

Evacuate the town, Dick Dick thought. Hmmm…

Now, he was no genius but he knew quite well that it was impossible to evacuate the entire town. Well, it could be done, but was it something he *wanted* to do? Wouldn't it create further fear in the townsfolk? Wouldn't he rather save Burghville from the monsters *without* further inconveniencing the Burghvillians?

Did he really, in short, want to let the whole town know how dangerous this new spray was?

No. No. Again, no.

And yet, he had seen what that stuff had done to the rat. He could well imagine what it would do to people, and the image of citizens burning and screaming on Main Street was not something he wanted to contemplate for too long.

So what, then, was the answer? What was the grand solution? To spray or not to spray?

Well, of course they would spray, there was no way around it. The real question was what to do with the fucking *people*. Of course they would spray, it was in the end the only real answer… of course they would spray… of course they would… they would….

Dick Dick Buckthorn sprayed.

"Mhmmmm…"

And at that moment….

*

248

Betty   Buckthorn   was   moaning,   sighing, writhing....

*

Carol Slugg was praying....

*

Father Preston was remembering....

*

Helen Keller was partying....

*

...and the moon was waxing over it all, a beautiful smirk on her pocked face.

Part III

"Follow the course of natural things."
--Heterodon
platyrhinos

11

Come morning, the moon was nothing but a figment of dream. Some moons linger into the day, but not this one. The light of this new morning, peaking through the cracks in the forest, frightened dear Luna into darkness. Well, the moon is good, the moon is wonderful, the moon is the goddess... but to every celestial body its time, and this morning, like every morning, belonged to the Sun.

Helen Keller was the first person to see that sun, stirring as she did in her soft shadowy patch of ferns as the heat from its rays pressed on her face. She turned her head and saw the remains of last night's bonfire, a great gray pile of ash under a slowly rising haze of smoke. She looked the other way and saw the wee folk scattered around her, passed out from the party, sleeping away the dawn.

Helen stood, stretched, and walked off into the woods. She came to where the wee folk children were sleeping, the sound of their gentle snoring like the chorus of distant frogs. These children had been put here by tender and caring parents, far enough from the fire so that they could sleep in peace but not far enough to be out of parental range of the wee folk moms and dads.

Helen smiled down at them all, perhaps fifteen total. Happy little faces smiled back from dreams, tiny little hands folded prayer-like over tiny chests.

She smiled there for a while, loving the warm, comforting feeling that emanated from them, and then she frowned and leaned down to one little wee folk girl. There was an odd object under this girl's head, serving as a pillow.

Helen's smile returned. It was a tampon, of the sort that Sheriff Sherman had found on Main. This tampon, like all that the wee folk had stolen, had been embroidered with the name of the child who owned it:

Lynera, in this case.

Others had Millen. Or Tumbledown. Or Thimblehead.

They made excellent pillows, they really did, and the embroidery was perfect, done in pastel-colored thread. The string from one of those tampons was tied loosely to the wrist of one little boy, and Helen realized how nicely that would serve to keep the pillow close, should it be pushed away during the night.

Ingenious, she thought. The world and its creatures never ceased to amaze her.

She wandered off still further into the forest, at last making her way back to her campsite. She climbed into her tent and emerged with a new set of clothes and a little bag filled with toiletries. She again walked into the woods, headed for a secluded little stream she had found once while berry picking. The water of this stream was cold and clear and, she liked to believe, pure, though that could not of course be proven. So far, in all the time she had spent bathing in it and using it to brush her teeth, she had not developed oozing blisters or a third arm or any sort of irritating rash. So she thought she was safe. For now. Perhaps she would never be able to have children because the chemicals in the water were making her infertile, but so be it. She had never seen herself as the mothering kind. Oh, she liked to mother things, indeed, but to actually *be* a mother, to have that responsibility, was something she had never wanted for herself. In many ways she was too selfish. In many ways she was too wild. In many ways her life was too transitory. In many ways she was just too young.

She stripped naked this fine moonless morning and walked into the stream, sitting down in the middle where it was only two feet deep. The water lapped against her breasts and made her nipples perk up like antennae. She opened the bag of toiletries and pulled out a bar of soap. She began to wash herself, and after a time, with the sun climbing ever higher into the sky and the whole forest beginning to wake around her, she began to sing. Like the wee folk the night before, she made up the words as they came to her.

And what sort of song was it that young Helen Keller sang on this sunny morning? What sort of melody came to her mind as she sat naked and fresh in a forest stream with the animals stirring around her and the sky clear and eternal above her?

It was a song the forest birds did not shiver to hear. It was a song that made the whitetails perk up but which did not send them scattering through the woods. It was a song that complimented the celestial song of the sun itself. It was a song that celebrated the morning and did not challenge it.

It was a love song.

And finally, standing from that stream with her buttocks pocked by the streambed pebbles and her skin glowing pink and healthy, Helen returned to dry land and dressed slowly. Above her she heard crows squawking, and to her left she heard a squirrel gossiping. When she was fully dressed, in cut-off shorts and a T-shirt, of course, she headed back to her tent. When she got there she found three wee folk, Puddlefoot, Thressa, and Tom Tom, mucking about a small fire.

"Good morning," she sang to them.

Thressa smiled at her. Puddlefoot brought his pipe to his mouth and played her a quick note or two. Tom Tom beat a gentle rhythm on the ground.

"Sit down," Thressa said. "Relax, dear girl. We're making you breakfast."

Helen smiled and sat down cross-legged, watching them. "But why?" she asked.

"Silly girl," Puddlefoot said, smiling and shaking his beard.

Thressa patted Helen's leg tenderly. "Why not?" she asked in that beautiful melodic voice of hers.

"Aye," said Tom Tom as he fed the fire more wood. "Why not?"

Helen nodded and settled back to watch the wee folk work.

To some questions, she knew, there just aren't any answers.

255

*

It may not need to be said that Sheriff Sherman was going crazy. First of all, he had lost his opportunity to display power and authority at the Town Hall meeting, those roles having been occupied nicely by Dick Dick Buckthorn. Secondly, he had seen his chance to implement his grand Plan slip away, overshadowed once again by Dick Dick's control of the situation. Instead of the Plan, Burghville would get some sort of pesticide. Sheriff Sherman was growing to believe that his only chance to establish an Ultra Safe Community had been lost. Would there ever again be another crises like this plague in Burghville? He doubted it. He was just not that lucky.

Thirdly, he was beginning to believe that the entire town looked at him the way his wife did: as a loon with pipe dreams. A laughingstock. And come re-election time, guess where he would be? During this time of crises, when the town had needed someone to lead it, where had their sheriff been? Standing behind Dick Dick Buckthorn, that's where. He had lost all credibility.

The Sheriff had not been seen in days for this very reason. Even his deputies had been unable to find him, until at last they discovered him in a storeroom at the Station, going over and over the Plan and wondering aloud if it wasn't by chance a masterpiece of law enforcement, if it wasn't by chance worthy of a Nobel Prize. When the Sheriff was thus discovered, he bolted from the office in his squad car, racing through town and headed towards....

He had nowhere to go, of course. Anywhere he went people would look at him and whisper "there sits the useless sheriff, overshadowed by Dick Dick Buckthorn."

What good is he anyway? they would wonder. Damn fool is just taking up space.

He's a human appendix.

The Vestigial Policeman.

Yeah, well I for one am sick of supporting him.

Dick Dick Buckthorn for Sheriff!

Dick Dick Buckthorn for Mayor!

Dick Dick Buckthorn for President!

256

Sheriff Sherman had felt actual pain at these thoughts. And whenever he passed another car he looked away so that he wouldn't have to see its driver laughing at him.

So it happened that Sheriff Sherman ended up returning to his home for the first time in nearly a month. He had known he was returning to a woman who thought he was completely stupid, but she had *always* thought that. He was well used to her mockery. Facing her was easier than facing the rest of Burghville.

When he got there, though, he found that she had left him.

Sorry honey, her goodbye-note read. *I can't take this anymore. Have a good life.*

And it was then that he went *truly* crazy. He had never wanted his wife to leave him, he had wanted to leave *her*. So what Sheriff Sherman found himself facing, head-on, was nothing but a gigantic symbol. And even to a man who had no use for symbols, who wouldn't have understood one if it bit him on his fat ass, this particular symbol was just too blatant, too much a slap in the face, and its sheer force caused something to snap in him.

She had left him. She had no need for him anymore. Just like the rest of the town. Just like Burghville. He was no longer needed. He was *unimportant*.

And Sheriff Sherman, alone in his empty house, thought: We'll see about that, we'll just see about that....

*

It took her a while, but Henrietta Pratt finally realized that the reason the wee folk were leaving her yard alone, why they weren't eating her flowers and shrubs and grass, was because the plants were native to the area. The wee folk, she realized, were drawn to exotic and invasive species. When she asked one of them why this would be so, the answer she received was the same one Helen had received this morning:

"Why not?"

257

Only, Henrietta's answer was accompanied by a belch. The Good People in her yard were slobs, they really were.

And why not?

On this morning Henrietta Pratt slipped three letters into three envelopes and set out down the sidewalk to drop them into a mailbox. These were the letters she had written to the sheriff, the City Council, and Dick Dick Buckthorn, asking them to please first consider diplomacy when dealing with the wee folk. It was her lifelong belief that diplomacy should always be the first course of action, that diplomacy is the surest path to civility and peace. She knew that the people she was dealing with did *not* have this belief. To them, violence and force were perfectly acceptable ways of solving a problem. She was used to such people, though, and she knew what got them motivated. She had hinted in her letter that should violence backfire they would have to face the public as failures, and that if anything happened to the citizens of Burghville themselves they might face dire repercussions. Of course, she privately knew that she was the lone dissenting voice in this matter, but a good threat of public retribution always came in handy when dealing with public figures.

After depositing the envelopes in the box she returned to her house, went around to the back, and met seven of the little people. She had attempted to ask them to leave herself and they had shrugged the suggestion off. Now she decided to be blunt with them. She marched right up and said:

"You're in danger. Some of the people in this town are planning to get rid of you with violent means. Your lives, and the lives of your children, are threatened."

And to which they replied, in unison:

"Bloxmuck."

*

Tracey White had not seen her husband in hours. He had slept on the couch that night and, when she woke in the morning, she had found him gone. Well, not really gone, since she knew damn well where he was: he was down in the basement with his goddamn trains.

258

What is it about toy trains that attract some men? she wondered. She decided it was a lack of imagination and a love of predictability, those trains not being able to take off on spontaneous side-trips, and having no ability to go anywhere but the same damn place they've always been, just around and around the track, over and over again. Mindless. Joyless. Dull.

She stood by the basement door and could hear him talking to himself down there. She didn't know what he was saying, but she was certain it had something to do with that train ticket she had found.

Leave me, will you? she thought as she made breakfast for herself. She sprayed a pan with Pam... then sprayed a bit on a towel and held that towel to her face, as if she were about to run through a smoky room in a burning building. Pam didn't quite have the power of Pledge, as Candy Cleaver could have told her, but just the act alone helped. She began to relax.

From the basement came the very faint sound of a train whistle. She listened to it with a bitterness growing in her heart.

And then, in no time, her eggs were done frying and she had an idea.

She went to the basement stairs and called down, in a sweet and lovely voice:

"Honey? Would you like some breakfast?"

Whoooowhooo! went the tiny train whistle. A few moments later there were footsteps on the stairs.

Tracey White met her husband with a pretty smile.

"Good morning," she sang.

*

"Wake up, Father," Orson was saying. "Wake up."

Father Preston opened his eyes. He had been sleeping on the altar, like a sacrifice. Only he was no virgin.

He sat up and looked around the church.

"Someone was knocking on the front doors," Orson said, smiling. "Guess who it was?"

259

Father Preston groaned and rubbed his eyes. "Slugg...."

"Exactly! You win a prize!"

"Did she go away?"

"Aye."

Father Preston groaned again. "I feel hung over."

"That's right. That's the feeling you get when you talk about things the way we've been doing. When you've got things to think over, you should feel exhausted and worn-out. Entirely natural, good Father."

Father Preston sat with his legs dangling from the altar, just as Orson had done that first day. He looked out the one open stained-glass window. The morning was a bright one, the sort of morning that usually makes people wake happy and optimistic.

"What's going on out there?"

Orson shrugged. "Oh, they're plotting our death. No big deal."

"How?"

"Poison, I think. Now, are you hungry?"

Father Preston frowned. "Sure. Yes. I mean, no... I should..."

"You should what? Get back to work?"

"No... no. I..."

"You should eat. I'll get us something." And the little man disappeared in a flash to the back of the church.

What am I doing here? Father Preston wondered. No shower in days, and all this talk. All this talk and where was it getting me?

He considered the church around him.

There was something to be said for churches. They could be beautiful when they wanted to, like plain women. But they could be boxy and awkward and over-large too, like those plain women after a bad breakup. Some temples approached the realm of beauty, but it was a garish beauty, over-decorated and rather shallow, like aging hookers. One had to wonder if the people who made and decorated such churches and temples actually thought there was anything of value in the *ideas of that church*. Certainly it didn't seem so: all those statues, all that stained-glass, all the marble, all the polished wood... was any of it needed? Was any of it necessary in order to worship a god?

Certainly the god wouldn't have cared. Orson was right, most gods are vain, they wouldn't give a fuck where you worshiped them so long as you worshiped them, period. So what, then, was the purpose? To show that god how much he was loved?   Again, unnecessary... and sort of sycophantic, really. And what kind of a god would care about stained-glass and marble? A shallow god. Ahh, then, perhaps the perfect god for modern society.

But no, Father Preston was buying none of it. He thought he knew the truth. The truth behind the marble and the statues and the glass, and the realization of this truth made an electrical spark of excitement race through him:

Most people suspect, deep inside, that their beliefs might be full of shit, and having a garish and proud house of worship is their way to compensate for this suspicion. It made them feel justified in their beliefs. It made them feel, too, better than others; the same reason they had gigantic homes and exotic cars. Which might be why such people are so deeply offended by atheists: they feel that everyone should want what they have, and when they meet someone who doesn't want and doesn't need what they have, it bothers them to no end.

Father Preston sat there on the altar, studying the church around him.   St. Michael's Catholic Church. Amazing how insular the place was, how sheltered from the outside world. It seemed a sort of war was brewing out there, the old war of US against THEM. Seems people were plotting the death of these little people. With poison, Orson had said. But you would never know it, being in here.

A church, then, could be said to be either sanctuary from daily life, or a temporary denial of daily life. Father Preston thought he knew which: if this place was indeed a sanctuary from daily life, people would be there more often. But as it stood they only came once a week, and most of them dozed through the service anyway. Church to them was both a duty and an escape, serving the same purpose as a Friday Night Fish Fry, or bowling, or the movies. Some place you took the family to in order to get away from the daily grind. But no one took anything substantial away from it, of this he was sure.

He'd seen their faces every Sunday, half-awake, dark-eyed, hung-over, treating each Mass like a shot in the arm: just waiting for it to be over. Most people got more out of watching the little kids climb around the pews in front of them than they did from his sermons, and he thought there was nothing wrong with that. Such things as the playing of a child are worth more than any stuffy words he might give groggy voice to. Such things make the world go around. It is for the joy of small little details that we are here on this earth in the first place.

What was he giving them in his sermons? Old parables. Dusty riddles. Ancient words of wisdom that have very little to do with today's world.

He'd seen their faces, he knew. To look into a church was to look into the face of boredom, to look into the face of vestigial thoughts.

It was, really, a look into the past.

The wave of the future, he knew, must be to *exit* the churches, to get out into the world that God made! The natural world was made first, why worship in a man-made structure of cold brick and steel? The prophets of old went to the wilderness, so going to the wilderness must be good enough for us!

These thoughts, these realizations, caused in Father Preston no distress and no worry. They excited him. That spark of excitement raced through him again. He hadn't felt such a thing since...

Since seeing that girl, Helen Keller, dancing naked in her window all those weeks ago.

He jumped off the altar and looked around. He was very aware of how much he needed a shower.

"Scrambled eggs?"

He turned and saw Orson approaching, balancing a plate in each hand. On each plate rose steam from eggs and bacon.

Father Preston clapped his hands together and turned back to the altar. "Up here, my good man," he said.

Orson complied. "Why Father... you're in a good mood today."

"Time for a change, maybe."

262

Orson climbed up onto the altar and started into his breakfast. "All is right with the world and God is in his Heaven?"

"Sure, why not?" Father Preston dug in as well.

Orson waited a few minutes, then he asked: "Do you know that in the old days, before there was Christianity in Europe, people worshiped a variety of gods? And did you know that one of those gods resembled what the Christians came to consider the Devil?"

"Yeah?" Still eating.

"Aye. Interesting coincidence, that. Seems as if Christianity did its hardest to discredit those ancient religions because they saw them, quite rightly, as threats, as competition. They began to tell people that the devil had cloven feet, and horns, and what-not... just like that old god had. Isn't that interesting? Politicians work that way, too. It's called co-opting an issue. What do you make of that?"

Father Preston was eating with glutton-like relish. "Hmmmm..."

"Easter bunny, too," Orson continued. "He was the sidekick to a pagan god, Eastre. Of course, it was hard to transform a bunny into the image of a devil, and so they just sort of co-opted him as well."

"Mmmmm..."

"My point is there have been many gods. Mankind has changed gods the way he changes underwear. Interesting, isn't it? What makes the latest god any better than the old ones? What makes Him more true, more real, more important?"

Father Preston kept eating.

"Good eggs?" Orson asked.

Father Preston nodded but did not look up.

Orson thought a while, carefully, studying the priest before him. A tiny little finger scratched a tiny wizened chin. Finally he said, slowly, softly:

"All this sort of talk is fine and good. Philosophy is healthy, it questions the answers and tries to answer the questions. It gets us through, it allows us to see every angle. It is by its nature logical and sane, cool and reasoned." He paused, watching as Father Preston ate. A moment later he said: "But fuck it, aye?"

263

Father Preston frowned and looked up, some eggs hanging on his chin, like flags without a breeze.

"Aye," Orson said, "fuck it for now. It matters not to me what you choose to believe. Belief does no harm unless forced on others. Religions, as practiced by the individual, as undertaken in small insular communities, are harmless. Nothing wrong with having beliefs, with worshiping. Either what you believe is true or it is not, and in the end," he said, shrugging, "what does it matter either way?"

Father Preston blinked, and Orson leaned to him and stared into his face, gazing there deeply, looking not at the eyes, not *into* the eyes, but *beyond* the eyes, to whatever lies there in the dark depths, to whatever secrets rest hidden in the shadows.

"But love," the little man whispered, a soft smile on his face, "*love* is important. It matters indeed whether a man believes in love or not. Love is undeniable. It is real. No amount of philosophical wrangling can argue its existence, try as some might. But even more than this, dear Father... even more than this, what matters is what lies deep down in your own heart."

Father Preston blinked again, silent.

"Dear Father... this religion around you, good or bad... is it what you need?"

"Need...?"

Orson leaned even closer, smelling of woodsmoke and spice. "Does it make you complete?"

The egg-flags jiggled. "I...."

"Or do you need love?"

Father Preston shook his head. "I don't know...."

Orson leaned back, the soft smile still there, warm and friendly. "When you do know, it is then you must make a choice." He gestured at the church. "This, as I've said, is all fine and good, and there may indeed be love here... but is it the sort of love that you, Father Lee Preston, desire? Or is there something else out there? Better still: is it the sort of love your God wants for you? Or does He have other plans?"

"I...."

"If you're not feeling complete now... maybe you should ponder another path. Maybe that's what your God

264

really wants. Why else this feeling in your heart? Why else these questions? Why else the long lonely walks at night, through this town, past her house. Maybe He's trying to tell you something."

"*Her* house...?"

Orson's eyebrows raised. "You think I wouldn't know about the girl?"

Lee Preston thought a moment, then looked up.

"But what's God trying to tell me, then?" he asked.

"That this life here," again indicating the church, "is not for you. That deep down, you are a man full of love, waiting for the opportunity to give it away, to hold another human being, to touch them, to feel their warmth in the darkness of the coldest night, to smile when they're around and cry when they're gone. Think about it, now. How does it make you feel?"

Father Preston thought about it. His mind filled with images of young couples holding hands, old couples huddled on park benches, babies caressed and kissed, tears shed, widows and widowers and newlyweds and families. He thought of a million vows exchanged on a million moonlit nights, a million declarations of fidelity, a million promises, hearts broken and mended. He thought of his own hand holding another's long ago, the feel of skin on skin, minds and souls trying to merge, prophecies whispered in the silence of backseats and beds, meaningless bits of poetry breathlessly sung into the ticklish recesses of a tender ear. He thought of the passion of youth, the sadness of age. Old men wrecked by the passing of a wife, young men shaken by the sight of their newborn son. He thought of love, all forms of it, all shapes, swirling around each and every one of us, blind and all-seeing, eternal and momentary. Love, pure and simple. Love, complex and harsh. Love. Touching all, keeping us together, separate, awake and dreaming. He thought of love lost, love found, love rediscovered. He'd seen it all. He had looked into its eyes and seen its soul.

He began to cry.

*

Candy Cleaver woke to the brilliant morning sun hesitantly, like a car engine slowly turning over in the middle of winter. First she was aware of silence, then she was aware of the strong odor of Lemon-Scented furniture polish. She opened one eye a sliver, then the other. She lay there on her couch, staring at the water stains on the ceiling. After a few moments she opened her mouth and took in a deep breath, feeling the sun on her face. It was morning.

She rose from the couch and went to the picture window that overlooked her front yard. The day out there was more than brilliant, it was glowing like a cliché painting from some artless hack. A real Thomas Kincaid kind of morning.

"What a beautiful town," Candy Cleaver said aloud to the dolls in her house. Raggedy Anne said nothing. Raggedy Andy was also silent. Tracey White's old doll, Little Sarah, was mum. Likewise the myriad other little beings stuffed with fiber and cotton and sewed like ICU patients.

The living doll on top of the television, though, who had been studiously watching Candy wake all morning, like a Good Person version of Jane Goodall, said:

"Aye, 'tis my lassy."

Candy didn't scream. She turned and looked at the little man and said nothing, not even when he offered a tip of his hat in greeting. Such a thing did not surprise her anymore, did not shock her. It was all par for the course these days.

And besides, it was a lemon-scented sort of day. Which meant that anything, absolutely anything, could happen.

*

Betty Buckthorn woke naked, warm, and ravished on her couch. She opened her eyes, saw the new day swelling around her, and smiled. No dizzlemuck here: Betty Buckthorn actually felt *satisfied*. For the first time since that writer fellow she once knew, in fact.

She sat up, ran her fingers through her hair and looked around the livingroom. She saw no sign of those strange little men.

It was odd: her womanly parts did not ache today, did not long for attention. Indeed, it felt to her as if they were sleeping. Resting. What does a vagina dream of, what does a clitoris sound like when it snores?

Before she could fully contemplate those questions there rose through the Buckthorn house a melodic tone, electric and impersonal, causing an instinctual tightening of all her muscles, causing her to likewise instinctually close her robe.

It was the doorbell.

She walked through the house, pausing before a mirror to quickly appraise herself. She looked terrible but quite rested. Then she went to the front door, peered out the peep-hole, and sighed.

Upon opening the door she was greeted by the over-bright smile of Willy Billy Buckthorn, her brother-in-law. That smile, so much like Dick Dick's, made her feel guilty, made last night feel like some horrible drug-induced bit of debauchery.

"Woo lordy," he said with entirely too much energy for morning. "Don't you look just as pretty as ever!"

And Betty Buckthorn had a thought: Why should I feel guilty? If those little people aren't people at all, how could what I did be cheating? And Dick Dick himself had said they were not people, she was just following his logic.

"Good morning, Willy Billy!" she said perkily. "Come on in!"

She stepped aside to let him pass.

*

Like Betty Buckthorn and Candy Cleaver, Carol Slugg woke on her couch. The last thing she remembered of the night before was slipping into her prayer-trance. After that she did not recall lying down or falling off to sleep. This realization frightened her, at first, since she was not the sort of person who enjoyed a loss of control. In fact, she was starting to worry that perhaps Satan had temporarily gotten hold of her when she realized that she had woken with a wonderful idea.

She sat there on her couch, suddenly breathless with excitement. In a flash she was up and dressing and getting ready to hit the morning. She had to find her acolytes, there was work to be done. The Lord's work.

Amen.

*

Many people in Burghville were having ideas. Perhaps it was something in the water. Maybe the presence of the wee folk was making the citizens of Burghville more creative. Maybe it was that Carol Slugg, and Tracey White, and Sheriff Sherman, and even, soon, Father Preston, were being influenced by the strange events of this summer to pull things from somewhere deep down in the storage space of their minds. Maybe. Certainly Henrietta Pratt, who like Father Preston was also yet to have her idea, would be influenced directly by the presence of the Gentry.

But the one other person who was soon, very soon, to arrive at a sudden course of action was not influenced by the wee folk at all. No, Helen Keller was going to find her initial inspiration from the one source where good ideas are virtually guaranteed to arise from:

A library.

Of course, at some point her other inspirations would be a large hairy beast and a substance that the United States government considers a dangerous drug, but first and foremost, it was a library.

12

Not just any library, the Burghville Public Library, of course.

On this morning, full from her wee folk-made breakfast, Helen left the woods and wandered into town. She wanted to see what she could find out about the plan for the wee folk's removal, wanted to see what new developments may have sprung up. She found Burghville calm and rather pretty: the morning light was layering everything with two-tone color, touching it all with a gorgeous yet restrained hand, from giant oak trees looming over houses to the plastic flowers some people had placed out by their front doors to give their yards at least the appearance of vegetation. The sky over the town was fresh and blue and quite conducive to joy. Helen found her steps light and happy as she walked under that sky, and at one point she even skipped a bit down a sidewalk.

She saw few people as she walked. Even Main Street seemed rather empty. Now and then a car would pass her, the drivers looking at her nervously, suspiciously, but she could read nothing from them. Once a little Honda had passed her and she had laughed when she saw a group of wee folk driving it. She also smiled at the few wee folk she saw scattered about on barren lawns. Most of them seemed to know her, or at least to recognize that she was a friend, and they smiled or nodded as she went by.

She thought, as she walked through the town, of how things had changed in so little a time. Burghville had always struck her as being arrogant, in the way that only a meaningless and insecure American small town can be. Such towns suffer from inferiority complexes, of course, and always struggle to pump themselves up, to appear bigger and more important than they are. It is the nature of

269

such towns to covet city-hood, which is what gives birth to sprawl. A town of four-thousand must feel like a town of four million in order to avoid feeling like a town of no one.

The arrogance of Burghville was gone now, though, the town seemed sort of... Helen searched for the right word. Not frightened, no, just... *intimidated?* Yes, that will work. Burghville was intimidated. There was definitely a feeling of cowardice to the streets now, a hunched-shoulder, lowered-gaze mood. It was as if the town was afraid to pump itself up or stick out its neck for fear of having it cut off. And, truth be told, it was a rather good look for the place. Intimidation suited Burghville, it made the town feel the way a small town would have felt one hundred or more years ago. Along with intimidation comes quaintness and character. Arrogance lacks any of these. Arrogance is ugly, graceless, utterly without style. It takes a touch of humility to breed charm.

Helen liked the way the town felt this morning. She liked the shyness. Despite wearing next to nothing, she felt like a young maiden in the olden days, an innocent little girl wandering down the streets of her quiet little hometown.

"Helen Keller!" a voice cried out to her.

She was passing the Burghville Public Library and when she looked over saw Mr. Lynn in the open doorway, waving at her.

She waved back and skipped up the steps to stand next to him.

"Good morning, Mr. Lynn!" she sang.

"Good morning. You look happy today."

"Why shouldn't I be?"

He looked around at the quiet street. He was cleaning his bifocals with his shirt and had to squint out at the town, which made the wrinkles around his eyes deeper. "No one else seems happy. No one else seems to be *anything*. I haven't seen anyone in weeks. Have they given up reading?"

He still doesn't know what's going on, Helen thought. And it was a beautiful thought: the library as a place for quiet contemplation of eternal subjects, not as a place for current issues. Leave the current events for the bars and bowling alleys.

"I don't know," Helen said. She looked at Main Street. "Maybe they've forgotten the joys of it. Maybe they're making babies."

He smiled and slipped his glasses back on his nose. "Future readers, I hope…"

"Of course."

"Listen, Helen, I just popped my head out to breathe some of this clear morning air and there you are, skipping merrily down the sidewalk. Quite a sight for sore eyes, believe me."

"Thank you, that's sweet."

"But I'm afraid I do have some news."

She frowned at him. It was hard to read anything from him, and she thought she knew why: he had read so much throughout his life, had taken in so many ideas and subjects, that his mind was like a library itself, absolutely stuffed with *things*.

"You have two over-due books," he said.

She opened her mouth, then nodded. "Oh yeah…."

"A book on little people, and a book on cattle."

"Oh yeah…" She had forgotten about them.

"I wouldn't want you to run up too great a fine," he said, sweetly.

She smiled back and touched his arm. "Of course, and thank you very much."

"No problem." He looked out at the town again, took in a deep breath. "Sometimes I'm blown away by my good fortune. Sometimes I'm amazed that I get to live in such a pretty town, such a *quiet* little town. Nothing ever happens here, so there is nothing to occupy my mind, nothing to take my thoughts from whatever it is I'm reading. You know, I can sit in the library all day and never know if it's raining or snowing outside. I can sit in there and finish a big old book in two days. Sure, someone might come in and I'll talk with them and help them, but for the most part I get to sit in there and absorb all those great minds, those great ideas. For all I know the world could be ending and I'll be in there hunched over some book and not have a single clue. Wouldn't that be something?"

"It would," she agreed.

271

He smiled at her. "The trick to life, I believe, is finding what you love to do and getting someone to pay you to do it. Life's too short to do something you don't absolutely love, wouldn't you agree?"

"Yes."

"Priorities," he said. "It all comes down to priorities. We're given what, seventy-something years on this beautiful planet? Barely a scratch in the larger context of Time. A person has to decide if they want to work themselves to death for three cars, a huge house, a giant entertainment center, and whatever else they desire... or work less and *live* more, less money and yet more happiness. Simplification, is the word, there's a wonderful book on the subject inside. Simplification. Voluntary poverty, others might call it. I call it finding what you love and being willing to pursue it." He continued to stare out over the town, his eyes distant, soulful, and then he smiled down at Helen. "Well, I suppose I should get back in. It was nice seeing you."

"Nice seeing you," she said.

The door to the library closed tightly behind him, and she was alone again. Standing as she was in a patch of sunlight, she lifted her shirt to warm her stomach. The soft skin of her tummy was warm and tight, covered with faint downy hairs. And of course there were her legs, trim and tan and equally warm. Had Mr. Lynn noticed? She couldn't be sure, though she suspected so. She knew that she was seen as an object of desire to most men, it was impossible for her not to. And, honestly, she didn't mind.

Just that morning, during breakfast, Thressa had told her she was pretty. And Puddlefoot had said "Aye" and winked at her.

But, Thressa had said, has your beauty ever gotten you love?

And she had to admit that it had not, exactly. There had been love, of course, but it was always, in the end, illusory or transient. There had been boys and there had been men but never could she say that there had been that great life-affirming *love* of the sort all the poems and songs talk about. Was she unusual in this? No. Life is made up of moments, and most of those moments are filled with feelings, and so most of her feelings, whether love or displeasure, were therefore *of* the moment... which meant that they were bound to be transcended, as is the fate of every second and every minute and every day.

Never had that great love of your life? Tom Tom had asked.

She could not say that she had. Nothing, anyway, that someone would ever write a book or poem about.

"It would be hard to share myself," she told them, "I mean truly share myself, as a person in love must, with another person *and* with this planet I call my home."

"Nature could encompass you both," Thressa had said.

Puddlefoot agreed: "Love is a quality, not a quantity, anyway: there is enough room under its umbrella for all."

But Helen could not be sure. Her love of nature, of everything wild and free and dangerous, was total and complete. She supposed some would consider her obsessed, or a fanatic... and indeed she had occasionally read such judgments in people. But if she was obsessed it was only because she too was wild and free and dangerous. She *was* wilderness. She *was* nature. She was of the earth as surely as she was a woman. She was a pagan, remember. A *true* pagan, not the sort described by Webster's Dictionary.

Standing there on the steps of the Burghville Public Library, feeling the warmth of a new sun on her delicate tummy, Helen thought about love. She came to no conclusions, and no conclusions came to her.

*

Helen came to Burghville this morning in order to see what could be learned about the town's plan for wee folk eradication. Unfortunately, the one person she could have learned it from was on the opposite side of town, waking on the floor of his office, stirring and stretching his great arms until he felt, next to him, the warm body of Polly Anderson.

She was staring at him.

"You were talking in your sleep," she said, smiling. "I think you were talking about your penis."

273

"What was I saying?"

"Something about Willy Billy has come...."

And Dick Dick Buckthorn sat up suddenly, every nerve in his body awake, his eyes scanning the office, trying to register what time it was.

"Where are my clothes?" he asked, standing.

Polly Anderson shook her head and sighed. "You never took them off."

And so he hadn't.

"I have to go," he said, starting for the door.

"Where?"

"Home."

"And what am I supposed to do?"

He stopped and regarded her. "Ummm... stay here, if you like."

"If I like? What does that mean? You said you were going to get rid of those goddamn things so I can get out of here!"

"I am, I will. But you'll have to be patient. I'm still working out the details."

"Dick Dick! I want to get the hell out of this town!"

"And you will, you will. I promise. But not yet. Just wait. Stay here, take another shower, find something to eat in the lunch room. The fridge is usually stocked. Just wait, I'll be back."

She frowned, pouted, stuck her tongue out at him.

"You'll be safe here," he said.

"And what am I supposed to do while I'm waiting?"

He looked around his office, thinking. Then he smiled down at her.

"Tidy up?"

She opened her mouth to protest this, to say she was offended, to say how dare he suggest such a thing, but he was gone, just like that. Gone. She stared at the empty doorway for a while, then she sighed.

What sort of life is this I have? she wondered, not for the first time.

*

274

So Helen Keller, having come to Burghville to see what the latest developments were, found no one from whom to read anything. There was a strong buzz, like wild electrical currents, hovering around every house, and that buzz suggested that something was indeed up... or that the people who lived in those houses had *hopes* that something was up. But she could not gather any details.

Except... except just as she decided to head back to the woods to retrieve those library books, just as she was turning around on Main Street's eastern sidewalk, she looked at the town and saw, briefly, on that very same Main Street, visible to her clearly but without definition, ghost-like, a giant swarm of animals marching down the road, reflected in the windows of the surrounding buildings.

This was the same "vision" she'd had at the Memorial Day Parade.

There had been a few visions throughout her life and they were always like this: faint but very real. Normally, however, they never repeated themselves. Could it mean something?

Most often she had no clue what they meant. Were they things that were *going* to take place? Things that had *already* taken place? Things that *might* take place? She had no clue. And maybe she didn't need to have a clue, maybe it was enough just to be the one to see them, to be the one who was sensitive to such things.

Whatever it was, there they were, a great marching swarm of animals, insects and mammals and reptiles, coming down Main Street. There was something sharply angry about these critters, as if they had just been turned away from Noah's Ark. She saw the outlines of spiders and cockroaches and squirrels and snakes and raccoons, all coming right down Burghville's Main Street, just as if they belonged there, as if it was their town, their natural habitat.

And then, just as quickly as the image appeared, it was gone. Main Street was empty again.

Just like that.

"Hmmm..." was all Helen Keller said, and then she continued on her way.

*

As she was walking through town, in the direction of the forest, she happened to see Henrietta Pratt standing in her blooming healthy yard. The two women smiled at each other and exchanged simple little waves, but Helen Keller took something more away from the brief encounter. What she took was this:

The realization that had she lived, her own mother might have been someone very much like Henrietta Pratt.

"Hmmmm..."

*

As she was leaving Burghville Helen also happened to see Dick Dick Buckthorn's giant vehicle go roaring past. She watched it go with interest, knowing that behind the wheel was the person who was responsible for the threat that hovered over the wee folk. She could read nothing from the vehicle, though: it was going too fast, and perhaps her "sight" was somehow weakened by the stream of noxious fumes that flowed invisibly from its metal anus, and to which she was particularly sensitive. The stench of unleaded fuel fogged her mind and all she was able to take from the sight of that hellish automobile was this:

"Hmmm...."

Which meant, really, nothing at all.

*

And so Helen Keller left Burghville this morning, headed back to her home in the forest. She was not sad to leave the town. She had gone there to see what could be learned and had found nothing, so be it. She gladly entered the woods once more, causing deer to dance and birds to sing and squirrels to smile.

Which meant everything.

*

Tracey White had watched her husband devouring his eggs this morning and had smelled the odor of ozone from the toy trains in the basement. She had watched as he over-stuffed his mouth, as bits of food fell hither and

276

thither, as his tongue swirled the growing mush of egg and bacon and toast inside his mouth. She had watched all of this and she had known what she was going to do. She was going to seduce him.

"Everything good?" she asked as she sat across from him.

He nodded. "Very good," he answered through a full mouth. He didn't seem to notice that she was not eating. When at last he was done he sat back, belched, and smiled at her.

"What are your plans today?" she asked.

He shrugged. "There's a little project in the basement... nothing important."

"Oh."

Pause. "Why? What were *your* plans?"

"Oh... nothing, really." And she stood, took his plate, set it in the sink, and left the kitchen, leaving him frowning after her.

A moment later he rose from the table and wandered down to the bedroom. There, on the bed, stark raving naked, was his wife. His rather pretty wife, actually. His very sexy wife.

"Uh..." was all he could manage.

Her fingers traced a delicate path between her breasts, down around her navel, and still further, tickling over-sensitive areas.

"Uh..."

She smiled a wicked little smile, may even have licked her lips, as is a woman's prerogative.

"Still hungry?" she said, legs spreading just slightly.

"Uh...."

The springs of the bed, at the behest of the two maestros, played a lovely song.

*

Now, imagine you're a sperm. Just a single sperm, one among millions, awaiting deployment inside the coils of a man's body. Heads and tails jostle around you. The sound of whooshing fluids fills the air like muzak. The heartbeat, so prominent, suddenly grows in intensity,

277

speeding and growing stronger. This is it, the time has come. The excitement builds, everyone mans their battle stations. You get in line. You wag your tail like a happy little puppy. You notice that two places ahead of you there is a two-headed sperm, and you decide you simply must beat *that* bastard to the goal line. You look back and see millions of healthy and strong competitors. You tighten your spermatozoan equivalent of a lip and gear yourself up for a fight. You will need your strength for the uphill swim, you will need your resolve for the spermicidal agents that await you in the alien land of your destination. You get ready. You get set. You put on your game face. You await the moment. And then, like *that*, you're off, rushing away in a burst of joy and determination, flooding out with all those others in the frenzy of the hunt, in the exhilaration of the quest, in the violent and glorious race for—

But no, you and the others run headlong into the Wall. *The* Wall. You and the others, competitors moments before, are now in this together, brothers in pathetic arms, soul mates in this disappointment.

The Condom. You've heard of the Condom. Rumors abound in the seminal vesicles about the Condom (and the Shower, and the Hanky, and the Hand, and the Mouth).

But wait. What's this? Could it be? Could it... *yes*! You have stumbled upon an opening, and like a football player charging through a front line you take it without hesitation, pushing through fiercely, knowing others are following you but determined to win in the end. You push forward, racing against the undertow, plowing forward with determination, vowing to be the One. The *One*!

Eggs, anyone?

*

Henrietta Pratt was watching television. It was a show about life on the African plains, and she watched until she was certain that a young and weak baby gazelle was going to be taken out by a pack of lions. When it looked like such a thing was inevitable she flicked off the TV, shook her head, and walked through her house. Her

278

cat, Mr. Stinkels, sat watching her with curiosity. With a vague and unconcerned curiosity, really, of the sort only a cat can conjure. Perhaps he was wondering what the human had against lions eating gazelles. Maybe he was wondering what she had against the natural order of things. Quite possibly he was wondering how a person who expressed such a love of nature and its denizens could be repulsed by the very natural (and beautiful, if he might say so himself) act of predation. He might even have remembered the time when he had gotten outside against her wishes and had brought her the headless body of a vole. The look on her face had been one of horror, even though he had meant it as an honor and a gift. Oh well, everyone has their idiosyncrasies... except me, he thought, watching her pass before licking a paw and yawning.

The truth actually was just as simple as that: Henrietta Pratt had never cared for the grit and reality of the natural world. She wanted the beauty, that was all. She saw the gazelle as a beautiful animal, which it of course was, and could not help but see the lion as vicious. She never saw or thought about the hungry baby lions back at the den, never contemplated the even larger issue of the dance between predator and prey.

As a contrast, just briefly consider Helen Keller, who was at this moment re-entering the forest and who had stumbled across what remained of a rabbit that had fallen victim to a hawk or owl. There was very little left of the rabbit, just a scattering of fur, some glistening entrails, and some blood on nearby grass. When Helen saw this mess she smiled. She understood the order of things. She understood the beauty that dwelled within such acts. She understood that this was the way it had to be.

Henrietta Pratt, however, crossed her house and tried not to think about that baby gazelle. She moved through her kitchen, past all the potted plants that sat on every horizontal surface or hung from the ceiling, and looked out the back window. Her yard was lush and green and mid-summer flowers were starting to bloom. Fat bees flew here and there, searching for pollen. Birds of every stripe twittered and flittered in bushes and trees. Her native patch of bluestem grass was a deep and thick green.

And not one ounce of pesticide or herbicide had been used, she thought... as she often thought, of course, since this was a source of pride for her.

Not one ounce.

She saw three wee folk sitting out there, lazily sucking on pipes. She thought about the danger they were in, thought about the letters she had written. She wondered why those creatures did not seem to care about the threat to their lives. She wondered if they knew something she did not.

Look at them, she thought. So without care, so without worry. It was almost as if they knew how this situation was going to turn out. It was almost as if they could see into the future.

And maybe they could. How would she know? And it made sense, in a way. Maybe they could read the future.

Or maybe....

She frowned.

Maybe they had faith that someone somewhere in this little town was going to help them. Maybe they had the child-like belief that someone would protect them in the end.

But who?

She watched as they lay there on the grass, surrounded by the native jungle that was her yard, covered by a canopy of tree and sky.

Who could protect them when the assholes of the town sprayed whatever it was they were going to spray over the houses and yards of Burghville? Who could do anything to protect that particular mindless juggernaut?

She watched the wee folk for a while, amazed at the looks of calm and peace that lay on their faces, by the gentleness that filled everything they did. Poor little children, waiting for a savior, and absolutely convinced one would come.

But who? And what could a savior do?

If your letters fail at their objective, Henrietta, she asked herself, what will you do then?

Is it ever too late to be an activist, to get off one's ass and *do something*?

One of the little men out there saw her and offered up a smile and a wave. She smiled back but did not raise her hand in return.

That hand, you see, was gripping a pencil and jotting down some ideas.

*

Now, a quick recap of where everyone is at this moment:

Helen Keller is marching through the woods back to her camp, where two over-due library books await her;

Carol Slugg is rounding up her acolytes, getting them motivated for the work that sat ahead of them;

Tracey and Timmy White are lying in bed, contemplating the meaning of a broken condom;

Henrietta Pratt is brainstorming ideas about how to stop the coming wee folk slaughter;

Sheriff Sherman is going over the details of his own plan to sabotage said slaughter;

Father Preston is pondering love;

Candy Cleaver is inhaling a super-strong household cleaner she had bought the summer before to support some Little League fund-raising drive;

Betty Buckthorn is making coffee for her brother-in-law, Willy Billy Buckthorn;

Dick Dick Buckthorn is speeding through Burghville on his way to his massive home in the forest;

And the others? Scooter Boober and Polly Anderson? They weren't doing much of anything at the moment... but later they would play very significant roles in how this whole affair played out.

First, though, consider this:

When summer hesitates in its mid-life, when light and air combine in perfect rhythmic poetry, when all that is alive (the hawk, the snake, the turtle, the frog, the deer, the bear, the human) is Art and the sun is a gem in the deep blue velvet of the sky, how can there be such a thing as hatred, pain, sorrow?

Now:

281

13

A blazingly red cardinal sat on a thin branch just outside the open church window. He'd been singing earlier but had stopped now, having effectively stated that this was his territory, and was now simply looking around, eyes alert and tail twitching.

"Beautiful bird," Orson said, sucking on his pipe.

Father Preston, sitting on the pew closest to this window, said nothing.

Orson looked back at the priest, sighed, and then wandered over to him. He jumped up on the pew and touched the priest's shoulder.

"Are you all right, Father?"

Father Preston looked up at the church around him. The high-vaulted ceiling loomed over the building like an avalanche in pause, the elaborate designs of wood and marble as still and impassive as rock cliffs, the statues of Jesus and Mary and the Stations of the Cross unable to hug, unable to give comfort, unable to hold conversations.

"What am I doing here?" he said, softly, so that Orson could barely hear.

The front of the church, like a stage, sat awaiting an entertainer.

"Father…" Orson began.

"No," Father Preston said. "No. My name is Lee…."

*

Just as it had been Lee all those years ago, and just as her name had been Tina.

282

"Tina, come here!" he had called to her. She had run over to the old elm and he had showed her what he had carved into the bark: TJ.

"And...?" she had said.

And so he had written TJ+LP.

"That's mean to the tree," she said.

"He'll get over it. Now come here."

And, laughing, she had fallen into his arms and then all laughing had ended and they were kissing and the canopy over them, soft and sighing and full of shifting shadows, had held them safely. And anyone watching would have smiled and thought: Ah yes, Tina Johnson and Lee Preston, Lee and Tina, always together, always laughing, always smiling, so much in love, ah yes and of course they would be married, it will be sooner rather than later and they will grow old together and raise a family if they choose and live happily ever after. Because that is what this sort of love is about, and that is what it is here for, and that is the way it must be. To see this young couple was to see the face of innocence and love and freedom. Your eyes are opened by the presence of such happiness. And, though open, there is so much you cannot see: hatred and ugliness and pain. Such love is a philosophy whose logic is limitless and irrational. Ah, a paradox, yes such love is a paradox, it must be, it lives and breathes with a soul of its own. And that which has a soul has no bounds.

TJ+LP.

"Tina, I love you."

"I love you."

"Say my name...."

"Oh Lee, I love you, I love you, I love you."

Such was how it was, all those years ago. And they knew it, these two, they knew exactly what they were in, they knew precisely what had them in its grip, but they did not know enough to realize how fragile it could be. Like all such lovers, those that have been and all those that will be, they did not know enough to stop and let it hold them, to stop and feel each moment as it passed. It was enough for them to be in the moment, to feel only each other, to know only each other, to see no past and no future but only a present... a present of illusion, masquerading as the future. A deceitful present? Perhaps. But a lovely and beautiful present nonetheless.

Tina and Lee. Lee and Tina. To say one name only was to speak a partial truth, to leave a sentence unfinished, to write a poem without an ending.

That was how it was, for so short a time so long ago....

*

And, as fate will often have it, it was when he began finally to think of the future, to think of a moment beyond the one he was in, when it happened, when that moment was paused in the worst way, when he was brought back to the present and rudely, painfully, reminded that the past was all there was, that the future too is an illusion.

He was not there to hear the scream of anguished metal, to smell the burning oil and the spilled gas, but he felt it all. In his heart.

*

"Lee? Lee?"

For so long they tried to speak to him, to say his name, to leave those unfinished thoughts, to write those poems without an ending, to ask questions with his name.

"Lee?"

And for so long he had no answer to give.

*

"Father Preston?" they asked, later.

And his answer became: "Yes, my son." Because he was looking for his own answer, an answer to the question everyone must ask. That question was: Why?

And the only answer he could find was: Why not?

Which did not satisfy, which could not satisfy, which was, too, a poem without an ending. But which was, ultimately, the only poem any of us are ever given.

Why not.

"My name is Lee," he said now, without sadness, without bitterness.

The cardinal flew off, a blur of brilliant crimson. He watched it go with a smile on his face.

"Hello, Lee," said Orson, holding out his hand. "Nice to finally meet you."

*

"Well I'll be dipped in shit!" bellowed Willy Billy Buckthorn. He rose from the couch to shake the hand of his brother.

Dick Dick jumped right into business:

"I need you to fly a plane."

Willy Billy frowned and winked at Betty Buckthorn, who was sitting on the chair opposite the couch, still dressed in her robe, her legs pulled to her chest defensively.

"This is the greeting I get!" he said to her, still frowning but flashing a big Buckthorn-style grin. "From the big brother I haven't seen in—"

"We got work to do," Dick Dick said. "No time for small talk."

"Wow. Sounds serious. Wanna tell me what it is?"

"Not really," said Dick Dick.

But he did anyway.

*

Dick Dick chose to tell his sad tale in his office, perhaps feeling more comfortable behind the great mahogany desk. Willy Billy sat in the leather chair opposite the desk, listening intently, turning his eyes from his brother to the few taxidermied heads on the walls around him, the blank-gazed whitetail, pronghorn, and bear. When the story was finished he looked at his older brother and raised his eyebrows.

"Wow," he said.

"Wow, what?"

"Quite a story you got there. You and the old lady been doing some herb, Dick Dick?"

"Dagnabbit Willy, don't make me prove the goddamn thing."

Willy Billy's eyebrows were further raised and he toyed with the heel of one of his cowboy boots.

Willy Billy Buckthorn, born William William Buckthorn, was not as physically imposing a man as Dick Dick, was not the sort to suck the air from a room, to dominate a conversation, to carry around with him his own little atmosphere. He did, however, possess the same admiration for those Texas oil types... and, in fact, he even resembled JR Ewing, a resemblance made even greater by his penchant for white suits and hats. Now, had he been a fat man this would have made him look like Boss Hogg, but instead, being tall but leaning to the thin-side, the look actually fit him quite well. Add the cowboy boots and you had a sort of funhouse-mirror image of Dick Dick Buckthorn. It was this fact, his smaller physicality, which drove Willy Billy's desire for success, which made him pursue objects and passions like a collector. He wanted to have more, and be able to *do* more, than Dick Dick. Which was why he alone among the Buckthorn brothers could fly a plane.

"Little people?" he asked now, looking at his brother.

Dick Dick sighed. "Yes, goddamnit. I don't have time for this sort of shit, this explaining everything, this proving of everything. I need you to fly a plane. You'll see soon enough how real this fucking thing is! I just need you to follow orders."

Willy Billy's turn to sigh. "Now, Dick Dick... don't order me around."

"I'm not ordering you around."

"Sounds like you're ordering me around."

"I'm not..." Another patented Dick Dick sigh. "Will you just fly the plane for me?"

Pause. A long pause. A scary pause. A businessman's sort of pause. A *dealer's* pause. Then Willy Billy said:

"What's in it for me?"

"Jesus fucking Christ."

286

Willy Billy smiled. "I have to get something for my trouble, big brother."

"Jesus fucking Christ. You can't do me one favor?"

"I guess not."

"Jesus fucking Christ."

"Well, let's look at it this way: you're asking me to fly a plane over your town here, which is in itself a very dangerous and tricky thing to do. Plus, you want me to spray some sort of pesticide over it as well, which could have who knows what sort of effects? Who's responsible should anything go wrong? You? Me? Seems like it might be me. Now, why would I wanna put my ass on the line like that?"

Dick Dick sighed again. These were great, rib-heaving sighs that seemed to rumble forth like muted thunder from the center of his chest. He looked across the great expanse of his beloved desk and studied his younger brother. His baby brother. His goddamn brother.

"What do you want?"

Willy Billy threw his head back and stared at the ceiling, stretching his arms in the process.

"Oh... it'll come to me."

"Well, decide quickly. I want to do this thing today, if I can." Pause. "Money? Name your price."

Willy Billy smiled. "Money is money... you can get that anywhere."

"You want an interest in Buckthorn Industries?"

"No. Not quite."

"Well, what then?"

"You're really desperate, aren't you?"

"Name your demand."

Willy Billy looked at Dick Dick and there was no disguising the smile on his thin lips: it was trending to evil, full of mischief and trouble. Some might describe such a smile as reptilian, but we know better: reptiles don't smile, and reptiles are not evil. No, this smile here was fully and completely and utterly human in its guile.

"I want to sleep with your wife," Willy Billy Buckthorn said.

Dick Dick just nodded and sat there motionless for a long while, no expression in his eyes, not one single

287

quiver to brow or cheek. Then he simply opened his mouth and called out: "Honey!" His voice roared through the Buckthorn residence. "Honey!"

There was no answer.

"Where is she?" Dick Dick said, rising to find his wife. "Honey?" Still no answer. "Where is that woman?"

In a word, gone.

*

"Holy water," Carol Slugg said. She had gathered her acolytes and now they were in her house, her dark sunless house with the shades drawn and the heat growing like a moist culture in the stale air. "Whatever they plan, we substitute Holy water for their ineffective poison."

"Holy water..." the acolytes repeated, like a mantra.

Carol's eyes were wide and wild with the Fury: "Holy water...."

The youngest woman, the one who resembled Sally Fields in *Sybil*, was the only one in this group who looked concerned. She leaned forward and glanced at the others. Her voice, when it came, was thin and shy and hesitant.

"But... how?" she asked.

To which Carol Slugg replied: "Let us pray for guidance."

And they prayed.

*

"We'll find her later, Dick Dick," said Willy Billy Buckthorn. "I'll fly your plane for you, if you can guarantee Betty will be... obliging."

Dick Dick thought of the vibrator, the masturbation, the horniness that his wife radiated like an aura.

"Not a problem," he said.

"Okay, then," Willy Billy said, smiling. "Let's get cracking."

*

288

What Willy Billy was thinking was this: a night with the alluring and sexy Betty Buckthorn, just for crop-dusting a town? Bring it on.

But what he didn't know was this:

*

Sheriff Sherman sat in his parked cruiser, right near the large shed that held the plane Dick Dick was planning on using. The plane had been generously donated by a former farmer who now owned a candy store on Main Street, his farm long since sold to meet the bills. It was a good plane, and had seen its share of dusting duty in years gone by. For most of its time it was kept here in this hanger at the tiny Burghville airport, which was really just a very large field with a few strips of asphalt running through it. Someday, the farmer always told his wife, someday I'll sell her. And he'd been meaning to, until recently approached by Dick Dick. If this works, Dick Dick told him, you'll see her in a museum. Hot damn, thought the confectioner-farmer. Hot damn.

Sheriff Sherman was staring at the hanger. He was thinking. And what he was thinking was one single thought, repeating itself over and over in his head, buzzing like a mosquito:

Wouldn't it be wonderful if Dick Dick Buckthorn was to fail? Wouldn't it be wonderful....

*

And what Willy Billy also didn't know was this: that Henrietta Pratt was at that moment wondering how she might substitute native plant seeds for the pesticide the little plane was to carry....

*

And he didn't know that Carol Slugg was brainstorming with her acolytes to find a way to steal a supply of holy water from the St. Michael's Catholic Church. They decided there wasn't enough there, that they

289

needed gallons and gallons of the stuff. Carol declared they would use Burghville tap water.

"It needs to be blessed by a priest," the youngest woman said. The Dissenter, as she was secretly coming to be known by the others.

"I'll do the blessing," Carol said. "We don't need the *priest*...."

*

And what Willy Billy also didn't know, what he couldn't possibly know, was that at that precise moment Helen Keller was returning to her camp in the woods, that she was about to go through her tent in search of those library books, and that once she found those books she would go on a journey that would, directly or indirectly (depending on how you looked at it) change Willy Billy's little life forever.

Ah, and here they are, she found them:

Agrarian Equipment and Animals, and *Celtic Mythology.*

Just for shits and grins, and just to give it equal time, she opened the first, which she had not perused at all, and opened, miraculously (or coincidentally, depending on how you looked at it) to the reason she had gotten the book in the first place. It was a picture of Scooter Boober's weird long-haired red cow. The caption read:

SCOTTISH HIGHLAND CATTLE.

"Hmmmm...." said Helen Keller.

She read that the average weight of bulls of this species was two thousand eighty pounds, with cows averaging eleven hundred pounds. She read that it was used for beef and draft work. She read that it hailed from northwest Scotland, and she read—

Wait a minute. It was this last bit that caught her. So the beast actually *came* from Scotland and wasn't just called Scottish Highland for the hell of it. She sat staring at the animal for a long time, at the long shaggy fur, the impressive horns, the incredibly calm presence it radiated even from a photograph. She did not move, just stared at the picture, thinking.

290

After a while she reached over and picked up the other book, staring at its cover.

CELTIC MYTHOLOGY stared back at her in solid letters. And underneath those letters was an oil painting depicting a deep forest scene. In that forest, sprinkled here and there amidst the trees and bushes and mushrooms and rays of sunlight, were four little people. These little people were smoking pipes. And laughing. And apparently singing.

Helen looked up at the canopy above her. She was sitting just outside her tent, with the forest resting comfortably around her. The forest on the cover of the book was darker, but it wasn't really so different from this one. Certainly the sunlight was the same, dusty and solid as it slipped through the branches to the ground, where it pooled like melted gold.

She looked back at the books, looked from the cow to the forest scene and back again. She thought:

Scooter Boober had a Highland cow. Highland cows are from Scotland.

Burghville had wee folk. Wee folk are from Scotland, among other places.

And then she thought:

I wonder what that cow could tell me about them wee folk....

And then she thought: But how....

Which was when it occurred to her, and which is when she again thought of Sam the Artist. In life, you never know how one person will affect the lives of others. You never know how one statement, offhand or otherwise, could change the course of history... or, if not *history*, at least a history, such as this little tale.

It was Sam the Artist, you see, who once said to her:

*

"I've been on two Vision Quests in my life. One was in New Mexico, a little peyote experiment that yielded nothing but a few singing leopard lizards. The other was out in Washington State. That was a mushroom trip. I had a conversation with a deer. The deer told me I was a

291

beautiful person with a wonderful soul who did not need to do drugs to see truth and beauty. And then she too sang a song: she sang 'Danny Boy' and I cried."

*

And now, all these years later, Helen Keller sat up straight and stared into the forest with a huge smile on her mouth and a bright and excited look in her eyes.

"Hmmm...." she said.

Off in the distance could be heard music, gentle and rhythmic. It was not "Danny Boy," but it was wonderful nonetheless.

*

Candy Cleaver was shaking a can of cleaner at this moment, feeling its emptiness. Frowning, she tossed it across the room, where it clanged against the wall and rolled to a stop a good fifteen feet from the garbage. Her head was spinning. Her mind was swimming. Her emotions were coiled at the surface of her being like agitated rattlesnakes, defensive and angry.

"Komblaffit," she said, trying to say *goddamnit* and failing. She stared at the empty can of cleaner for a long while, as if waiting for it to do something, as if waiting for it to get up and dance or come flying back to her. The can did nothing, though, and so she repeated the word again:

"Komblaffit."

Her eyes were half-closed, she reeked of synthetic orange and pine, her body was swaying. What was going on inside of her brain was no mystery: her brain cells had been cleaned and polished, were now new and improved, could now cut grease and clean windows, could eliminate pet odors, were industrial strength, could be used to get out blood and mud and asphalt, could be used in hospital settings. Some of those brain cells had fresh potpourri odors, or smelled like gardens, or yards, or mountain air, or autumn forests. Her brain cells should not be concentrated and inhaled... doing so could lead to nervous system damage or death.

292

She'd woken up sad this morning. It was the sort of inexplicable sadness which people prone to melancholy were familiar with, heavy and all-encompassing and absolutely without rhyme or reason. She had opened her eyes and seen the dolls around her, every one of them with their own eyes wide and expectant, waiting for her, *needing* her, wanting to have loose strands cut, or stuffing replaced, a hand or arm reattached. She had walked around her house and all she could feel were those eyes on her, calling for her attention. And all she wanted to do was help them, but....

But she couldn't, because they made her sad. She was nearly thirty-six and here she was, living alone with a bunch of dolls. She felt she had all this love to give, all this motherly attention awaiting dispersal, and all she had to direct it to were these inanimate dolls. But glass eyes cannot reflect love. Nylon arms cannot return hugs. Legs with stuffing for muscles cannot walk to greet you when you come home.

"Pillows," she had said. "That's all you are: pillows with faces."

And so it had begun: she grabbed one or two of them and started tearing them apart, shredding them violently... violently at first, but soon she went slower, more deliberately, ripping arms loose and tearing off heads and sending stuffing into the air like snow and eyes across the floor like marbles. She did this until she had gotten to all the dolls, until they were lying around like disaster victims. She had stopped and looked at the mess she had made and *wanted* to feel guilty, wanted to regret this act, but she could not. It wasn't as if the dolls were staring up at her with frightened eyes, it wasn't as if they could ask her why she was doing it, why she was hurting them. It wasn't like Raggedy Ann could cry. In fact, those dolls that still had complete faces (though they may be missing torsos, though their cotton viscera may be spilled across the carpet) were staring up at the ceiling with the same happy or blank looks they always had.

She turned away from the empty can and looked at her house. Stuffing everywhere. Arms and legs lying strewn across the floor. A doll Auschwitz. A Mattel massacre.

293

And she felt good. She felt that she had done something, for the first time in a long while she had truly done something. Picasso knew this truth as well: to destroy could be as satisfying as to create.

And she felt it was about time. A woman like her needed something other than dolls. She had love to give, and love to give needs love to receive.

The only trouble was, she could not talk now.

"Komblaffit," she tried again. Her mouth was mush, her tongue swollen like a bee sting. She left the kitchen and walked down the hallway to the bedroom, stepping through doll stuffing as if it was cottonwood seed, some of it still settling to the floor, some of it being kicked up by her feet to find the dark and still corners of the house. Later mice would find this stuffing and use it to line their nests, but for now it was tossed randomly by the current of her passing. She went to the bedroom and looked into the mirror above her dresser.

She was a mess. Dark eyes, puffy lips, exceedingly pale complexion.

"Dore a bess," she said. And, hearing herself, hearing the alien tongue she was speaking in, she thought she might cry. Instead, she smiled. The odor of lemon and orange and pine and potpourri surrounded her like a full body halo. She looked into the mirror and through her swimming head she thought she could see two of herself, one this dark-eyed wreck, the other the girl she had been, the young woman she had been only ten years earlier. The woman with the life ahead of her. The woman without the industrial strength brain cells.

She saw both these women, side by side in the mirror. She remembered that the younger woman had always wanted a husband, had been absolutely convinced that she would have a husband by thirty, and a child, maybe, by thirty-one. It wasn't that that woman had *needed* a husband. Far from it: that woman had started a good life for herself, all by herself. She didn't need a man to guide or protect her. It was nothing of the sort, it was just… she had so much love to give. And a love not given goes to waste.

That woman had always seen herself tending to another, giving them support and care. But time flew and she found herself here, this ragged mess in the mirror, giving her support and care to dolls. And dolls were worse than cats: they gave absolutely nothing in return. Cats at least give you a scent-marking now and then.

Well, she was young, she was….

She stared into the mirror, at that puffy dark-eyed soul. Was she really so young? And with a brain that could now get out even the toughest stains, did she really have that much time left here in this life?

She saw a tiny figure behind her, sitting on the bed. Tiny eyes looking at her, tiny face expressionless, tiny arms and legs still.

"I dot eye got doo all of do," she said. She stared at the doll in the mirror, where he was reflected right through that younger version of herself, and then she turned and glared at it.

"I dot eye got doo all of do, komblaffit," she said again. She walked to the bed and reached down to take hold of the doll, to rip his arms from their sewed sockets, to tear him apart and let another snowfall of stuffing fill the air.

But as she reached down the doll suddenly lifted his arms and hugged her. He hugged her so tightly, so warmly, that she felt nothing but a new calmness, a strange peace. It had been so long since she had been hugged. A lifetime.

She hugged the doll back, at first hesitantly and then strongly, pulling herself to his tiny comforting chest, feeling his little arms around her, holding her securely, safely.

"There, there," the doll said.

Candy Cleaver began to cry. They were lemon-scented tears.

*

"Mushrooms?" Puddlefoot said, taking the flute from his mouth and looking at Helen. "*These* things?" He looked behind the stump he was perched on and regarded, with distaste, the four fat wet 'shrooms that grew there. "What do you want to know?"

295

Helen shuffled her feet on the forest floor. She looked from Puddlefoot to Thressa, who was off a ways with a small child in her arms, swaying him gently back and forth, cooing soft words into his ears.

"Well..." Helen began. "I was wondering, has anyone ever... eaten them?"

"Eaten them, eh?" Puddlefoot brought the flute back to this mouth and played three notes, bright and quirky in the noontime light. This done, he again looked at Helen, considering her for a while.

"I suppose some people might find such a thing appealing," he said in time.

"What would happen?"

"Are you asking if they're poison, Helen Keller? No, they're not poison, but they *are* disgusting wet fat little monstrosities. Some among us believe we'd be perfectly clean and neat if it wasn't for those damn things."

The way he said this made her realize he counted himself among such folks.

"Certain mushrooms can make people see things," Helen said.

"Aye."

"Can these mushrooms make people see things?"

He looked at her, a small smile on his mouth, the flute held in pause halfway to his lips, the chubby little fingers placed expectantly on the instrument's holes. The air around him trembled, awaiting the music that was sure to come.

"They can't make you see things," Puddlefoot said. "They're not drugs, if that's what you be asking." Now he sighed and shook his head. "Why would you ask me for? Oh sure, ask the musician about mind-altering substances. Why of all the cliché's..." And he began to play the flute, more quick notes that sounded like a familiar melody in reverse.

"I'm sorry," Helen said, "I never meant to—"

"Don't worry about him," came a voice behind her. She turned to see the drummer, Tom Tom. "Sometimes the wind could insult Puddlefoot."

Puddlefoot played louder.

Tom Tom jumped up on a fallen branch so that he was only a foot below eye-level with Helen.

296

"I know what it is you're asking, girlie," he said respectfully, "girlie" not sounding offensive at all coming from him. "And maybe I can explain it better than Mr. Pissy-foot here."

"Hey!" said Puddlefoot, stopping his music.

Tom Tom ignored him: "No, these mushrooms we leave behind do not make a person see. They do not create hallucinations. Instead, they—"

"You'd best apologize," Puddlefoot said.

"Toss off," Tom Tom answered, then continued to Helen: "Instead they *allow* a person to see. And though what a person might see is not necessarily real, it *will* be true. It will not be an illusion."

"Oh…"

"Now, us Good People would never think of eating them, but certain humans have indeed partaken of them, and what happens is… well, for a moment the line between truth and mystery vanishes, and answers can be revealed. It's sort of like having a vision."

Helen smiled. This was close enough to Sam's "vision quests" to further strengthen her conviction for the course of action to follow.

"But fortunately or unfortunately, one has only a single chance to have such a vision. After the first time, the mushrooms fail to do much of anything. A person becomes sort of immune, it seems." He smiled wistfully. "Of course, it also seems that one vision is all that is necessary per lifetime."

Helen nodded. "Thank you," she said.

Tom Tom leaned in to her and whispered: "Thinking of partaking a little?"

She shrugged and tried not to blush. "I don't know…."

"Well, have fun!" Pause. "And be careful: sometimes the revealed truth and perception are not what one wishes them to be."

"You'd better apologize!" Puddlefoot said again. "I won't be called names."

"Oh—" Tom Tom began.

"I mean it! I—"

Helen left them there as they made amends the old-fashioned way, by playing a song together, Puddlefoot sending a joyful melody into the air, Tom Tom keeping time on a nearby log. The music followed her for a time as she walked through the forest.

When she thought she was alone, she picked two fat wee folk mushrooms and carried them with her. As stated previously, these wee folk 'shrooms looked different depending on what angle you perceived them from, what your emotional state was, what the light was like around you.

These ones here looked a bit like morels, but in her hands morels had never felt like this: these mushrooms vibrated against her skin, a subtle hum that was barely noticeable.

Helen thought they might be singing. This image, and all it implied (the soul of nature, the joy of every organic thing, the music found in all life forms) made her smile.

It was early afternoon.

*

Due to the presence of the wee folk Burghville was at a moderate standstill, though life surely continued and people were growing slowly more and more accustomed to the strange little people on their lawns and sidewalks. It wasn't as if the citizens of Burghville were going to *accept* the wee folk, or even get used to them, but people are resilient and adaptive creatures and life, anywhere, goes on. However, there was something else happening under all of this resilience: every citizen of Burghville went about their lives knowing that something was going to happen soon, that the powers that be were hard at work fixing this problem. If the Burghvillians had one core belief, it was this: that someone, somewhere, was going to fix all their problems. This might be a uniquely American belief. It was certainly a uniquely childish belief.

Here in Burghville, the good citizenry was looking to their industry leader to solve this problem. Had they looked to their government they would have found a bunch of frightened idiots on the city board and one persona non gratis mayor. Those frightened idiots had no idea how to do anything, certainly not something requiring real solutions and real foresight. And that mayor, Mayor Darrow, was off at some "mayor's convention" in Florida... which meant he was baking himself on a beach and basting himself with cocktails. He was not to be looked to here.

No, it was Buckthorn Industries all the way. And looking to Buckthorn Industries was, for the citizens of Burghville, the equivalent of holding their breath and waiting. For something. Anything.

Someone *was* looking more closely at Buckthorn Industries, however. This was someone who really had no choice, who was essentially stuck in Burghville (or so they thought), someone who was, quite literally, stuck *in* Buckthorn Industries. Someone who suddenly found themselves with a bit of free time on their hands and a bit of information available to their eyes.

This person was Polly Anderson, and to pass the time she was doing some reading. What she was reading was not in any way labeled THE SECRET FILES AND EVIL TRUTHS ABOUT BUCKTHORN INDUSTRIES.

But it might as well have been.

*

It didn't take any snooping to find these files. In fact, there was nothing secret about them, because no one considered them to be worth hiding. They were just files and reports, all routine, all documenting the daily monotonous routines of the company. They were nothing but simple archives of the way things were at Buckthorn Industries.

Polly Anderson found them by simply opening some file cabinets. At first she had only glanced at them, not seeing anything immediately interesting. And then something had caught her eye. And then something else had caught her eye. And then another thing. And another. And another. Soon she was sitting on Dick Dick's office floor with paperwork scattered all around her, reading everything with absolute interest.

Suffice it to say that anything horrible you could imagine a company doing, Buckthorn Industries did it in spades. It was allowed to do most of this, legally speaking, because it was "grandfathered" past the majority of current regulations… "grandfathered" with punctuation marks because Dick Dick made sure the date of his company's founding was much older than it really was; he did this by merging his *real* grandfather's cough-medicine company, which employed all of five workers, into his own, insisting (through slippery lawyer work and slippery lawyer words) that that early twentieth-century company had evolved naturally into Buckthorn Industries. It was all rather clever mumbo-jumbo, designed for the single purpose of allowing Buckthorn Industries to avoid certain regulations. Dick Dick thought those regulations, and indeed, *most* regulations, were a) pointless and b) too restrictive to his company's future success. So Buckthorn Industries was "grandfathered" past many environmental and safety rules. It had happened quite easily.

When you consider that Buckthorn Industries was a manufacturer of dangerous chemicals, all of them designed to kill things quickly and easily, then you can well imagine what horrible and evil things they could have been up to. Consider the forest that surrounded Burghville, consider the streams and rivers that ran through that forest, consider what damage could be done to the water table the Burghvillians relied upon. Consider, too, air quality. And then consider, and shiver, and shiver again, as you consider where a company like Buckthorn Industries, a company run by a man such as Dick Dick, would deem it prudent to dump the waste left over from their manufacturing processes. Where would Dick Dick think was the cheapest, most convenient place? Well…

In the woods behind Buckthorn Industries there is a dip in the land, and in the spring, after heavy rains, that dip fills with water and becomes a vernal pool. And in that vernal pool, as yet undiscovered by any biologist or child, there is a salamander, and on that salamander grow eight legs. And at the end of each of those legs there are claws. Those claws are not found on any other known amphibian, but they help this species here fight off the raccoons and snakes that see them as a food source. And those raccoons and snakes have no chance against these salamanders.

Those claws are razor sharp, you see. All thirty-two of them.

300

Now sleep well, children of the new environment.

*

Poor Polly Anderson. It is always hard when a person is confronted by the way they have chosen to live, by the path they have decided to take. In most lives there are rarely great moments of epiphany. There may be smaller ones, but not those great life-changing eye-opening moments where a person suddenly realizes a deeper truth about the way they have been living. When such an epiphany *does* come, it can shake the foundation that that person stands on, or it can whisper into their ear. It was the latter sort that came to Polly Anderson this afternoon in Buckthorn Industries. The details, complex and deep, of how she came to this realization, the complex mental and emotional processes that were covertly working inside of her all her life, will not be gone into here. This is not the story of Polly Anderson's epiphany… but keep in mind that she was mighty pissed at the way Dick Dick had left her there in his office.

No, all that needs to be said is that she had chosen to live her life a certain way, had chosen years ago to place her mind and heart and lips upon a certain course, and that on this day all of that changed. She saw something clearly for the first time, and seeing something clearly is a rare thing in this muddled day and age. Seeing clearly is more precious than gold.

Let's just say that Polly Anderson had once held successful businessmen on pedestals (how this is a manifestation of certain daughter-father issues will not be looked into here); and let's just say that she saw them as the be-all and end-all of humanity, that she saw in them what some people see in royalty, namely, the penultimate expression of being human; and let's just say that this view of hers had led her all over the country, from little Burghville to big Houston, from Michigan to Florida, from the offices of R.J. Reynolds to offices in Washington; and let's just say that prior to her adventure in Burghville Miss Anderson had harbored dreams of going overseas, ambitions of international "relations," shall we say; and now, let's just say that on this afternoon in Burghville Polly

301

Anderson suddenly realized something about those businessmen, something that may have been stirring deep down in her subconscious for a long time. Perhaps she summed it up best when she looked up from her reading this day and said:

"Those fucking assholes."

With those words, a life was changed forever.

*

Okay, one brief bit of detail, one little clue, about Polly Anderson's mind-set at this moment:

When she was twelve she had been allowed to fire someone from her father's business. The poor sap had been brought into Mr. Anderson's office and was met by the pretty and smiling face of young Polly, who was sitting behind her father's big oak desk.

"You're fired," she sang in her perky little-girl voice.

"Is this a joke?" the man had asked.

"Be out of here by two."

It was everything her father (who was hiding in the closet) had told her to say.

"You did it perfectly," he told her afterwards, after the poor fellow had left the room in tears.

It was the first time she had ever felt proud... and the first time she had ever felt *powerful*.

That memory came back to her there in Dick Dick's office, with the company's papers strewn around her like sheets of shaved ice. Whatever she felt at this moment, it was most certainly the opposite of *proud*.

"Those fucking assholes," she said.

*

"So...?" Tracey White said.

Her husband, sitting in his chair, was silent.

"What are you thinking about?" Tracey asked him.

"I'm thinking... I can't believe it broke."

"Those things happen. They're not one hundred percent reliable."

"That's the first one that's ever broken on me."

She watched him, saw the way his thoughts played over his face, twisting his forehead grotesquely, causing great crevasses to form above his eyes. The poor sap, he looked so *wounded*, so frightened, like a man who has seen a ghost.

"Is it all that bad?" she asked, timidly, bracing herself for his response.

He shook his head and appeared to consider answering, but stayed silent.

"So this is all we're going to do today?" she asked. "Sit here and dwell on it? It happened and that's that…"

"We should talk about it more."

"Talk about it how?"

He started to turn his head towards her, then kept it where it was, staring straight at the wall.

Tracey, on the couch perpendicular to him, sighed.

"Talk about it how?" she prodded.

"We should talk about… what could happen."

She could tell it took effort for him to say this, as if he were pronouncing a judgment he did not want to make.

"You mean…" she said.

"You know what I mean."

She nodded. Waited a respectable few moments. Said: "And how would you view that?"

Now he did look at her, and she was unable to read what was in his eyes… except to decide that he would view it badly. And of *course* he would view it badly: what he was thinking about here was not in any way compatible with that train ticket she had found in his pocket.

A deep part of her stirred at this thought. She couldn't tell if it was a pleasant stirring, one of joy and excitement, or one of fear. It was like there was a snake inside of her, shedding its skin.

What he said next surprised her:

"I am full of guilt."

She frowned. "At what?"

"At this town. At what's happened here. At what's *happening* here. At all this trouble we've caused."

She stared at him.

"You know we caused it," he said. "We have to confront the fact: *we* and we alone are responsible for this mess."

"It's not a mess…"

"It's a horrible mess. We've ruined this town. It was always so pretty, it was what we always wanted, a pretty little town where we could have good jobs and live our lives in peace and quiet. And now…"

She smiled, that smile obscured by a very faint odor of window cleaner.

"And now *nothing*," she said. "It's still pretty. Nothing is ruined."

He slunk back and down into the couch, like Ruth Buzzy being eaten by a giant Muppet. "Everything is ruined. We've caused so much trouble."

She smiled again, shook her head, started to laugh a little. "I don't know what you're—"

"You know what I'm saying." He glared at her. "Goddamn it, Tracey, you know what I'm saying."

And of course she did… or at least that part of her that was not squeaky clean and without streaks did.

Against her wishes, her mind filled with hazy images of sweet Scotland, of lovely Scotland, of beautiful romantic gray-skied Scotland….

*

It had been a charming and private affair, just the two of them, no family, a sort of well-planned elopement.

Afterwards they had driven further north, to beautiful Grantown-on-Spey. This was in late August, so it was just before the winter came and the ski season began in that part of the country. In fact, summer was enjoying a great last fling up there in the highlands, with clear skies and warm temperatures. There had been dinner and love-making that first night, during which the condom had not broken. There had been a quaint breakfast the following morning at the Inn, as well as more love-making.

After a week and a half of enjoying the town and hiking in the nearby forest they drove off, headed south via an old and nearly single-lane highway, making their way slowly to Edinburgh, the source of their eventual departure home. They had both wanted to see the rural side of this country, which was almost all there was, really, and they had both wanted to take their time, to enjoy sightseeing when it struck their fancy, to avoid keeping to any schedules or routines. It had been a pleasant, wonderful time, with the country alternately spread open before them and folded against itself, as if it were keeping secrets. The old road curved its way deep into forests, down into the depths of shadow before curving back out into the bright and fresh skies of open, sloping farmland. They had not seen one other car during the entire seven-hour drive, just pastures of sheep. It had been wonderful.

And then....

*

And then they had broken down in *that* forest, the one that reeked of myth and legend, the one that surrounded them like a living breathing creature. It was a beautiful forest, like a painting, a complex landscape of light and shadow, its open under-story spread out invitingly, speckled with stumps and deadfall branches, its canopy flecked at the very top with golden sunlight and darkened below with thick green shade. They had each seen forests like this before, in the illustrations of fairy tales.

This was the sort of forest where Hansel and Gretel had met the witch.

And there they sat, the new White family, the car ticking underneath them, teasingly. Timmy turned the key in the ignition over and over, but the engine would not turn. And, knowing nothing about cars, and having no tools anyway, Timmy had decided it would be best if he were to walk down the road and try to find a farm. There had been one not too far back, he thought... though it may have just been a decrepit shed at the edge of an endless field. He gave his new wife a kiss, and started walking.

"If you find any cows," she called to his receding back, "bring them back and we'll ride 'em out of here."

He had waved goodbye.

Once she was alone she had stared into the forest. It seemed to stare back.

After a time the need to pee came to her. She continued to stare into the forest, considering all those shadows, thinking about how alone she was.

305

After some deliberation, and not having much of a choice, she climbed out of the car and stood there, looking up and down the quiet old road. The road was more than old, she decided, it was ancient: gray and cracked, with weeds sprouting up through the pavement. It had probably not seen new blacktop in decades, and this was a major highway, according to the maps.

She listened. Heard nothing. She looked the way her new husband had gone, and of course did not see hide or hair of him.

She was alone.

Her bladder protesting now, she turned and entered those woods, finding the going easy, the ground so open that she had not needed to step over one single bush or root. A chattering little squirrel scampered off at her presence.

"Sorry buddy," she said.

She went quite a ways into the forest, trying to get as far as possible from the road, just in case the one time a farmer happened to come by she would not be found squatting there in his woods. And she loved these woods: that fairy-tale mood enveloped her, made her feel as if she had stepped right into a children's book. The trees in this forest were not like any she had ever seen before, were more *solid*, somehow stronger, and of course they radiated an age that was nearly palpable. Their bark was coarse and tough and she thought it was possible to see faces in its texture, a mouth here, two eyes there. This must be how some of the old tales came about, she thought. She imagined what it would have been like to have wandered such forests a thousand years ago, in the darkness, all alone, seeing these faces looming out at you. She thought there might even have been a fairy tale or two about a witch turning someone into a tree, but her memory of such things was vague.

She made her way quite deeply into the woods, finding that the further she went the wetter the air became. She expected to wander into a swamp at any moment, but it never happened. Instead, she came to where the canopy opened and sunlight spilled down like a curtain. That sunlight was so thick she thought she could reach out and touch it. Pollen and insects hovered there in the dusty light, making a haze that swirled and danced in a gentle breeze.

She looked around. Nothing here but trees and stumps and mushrooms. She looked back the way she had come and could not see the rental car.

Good enough, she decided. She lowered her pants, squatted against one of those trees, and soothed her bladder.

While pissing, she thought she saw movement out of the corner of her eye, but when she looked there was nothing.

Birds. Or squirrels. Maybe a roebuck.

She finished, stood, and pulled her pants back up. Then she—

There was movement again, behind a fallen tree. She stared there for a long time, waiting for something to appear. Nothing did.

She thought she had seen a flash of color with this last movement, and the thought made her shiver. What if someone was there? What if she had stumbled upon a farmer taking his lunch break? What if these woods were not so deep as she thought, what if there was a subdivision right over there....

She stared at the fallen tree for a while, made a few hesitant steps in that direction, saw nothing. From somewhere came the sound of birdsong and the sound of squirrel claws on the side of a tree.

She frowned, then turned and started back. When she had walked for five minutes she suddenly stopped again. Nothing here looked right. Nothing looked familiar. No, *everything* looked familiar: there were no unusual landforms, no peculiar deadfall trees, no tell-tale sign of her entrance into the woods, nothing to mark her way. There wasn't even traffic on the road for her to hear and follow.

"Shit," she hissed.

She walked on again for a ways, then stopped.

"Shit," she hissed again.

A bird of some sort chirped, then was silent. Another sent a cute little trill into the forest air before also falling silent.

The new Mrs. Timothy White was lost.

"Shit."

Movement behind her made her turn, but again she saw nothing. She did not, however, feel so alone anymore.

And part of her wanted to call out to whoever might be there, but she couldn't bring herself to do that. To call out like that would have made her feel more frightened.

Maybe, she thought, if I wait long enough Timmy will lay on the horn for me. Then I can follow the sound back.

And in the meantime?

She took a few steps and then stopped again. There had been a faint noise, almost musical, like a brief trill of a flute. Some strange bird?

She swallowed and started walking again, looking towards the hint of sun she could see through the canopy. It was noon, she thought, so it was impossible to tell which way was east or west... east being the direction she needed to go.

She walked a bit, then stopped. Something was different here, in this part of the woods. If it was possible, these trees here seemed even older than the others, the faces in their bark wise and judgmental.

"Shit," she said one more time.

"Lost, are ye, lassy?"

She spun around violently, fists clenched, not sure what sort of a person this was... friend or foe, old farmer or Scottish hillbilly. She imagined herself in a Celtic *Deliverance*, and she wanted to be prepared. If threatened, she would attack scrotums first and ask questions later.

She had not expected *this* sort of person, however. It was a tiny man, no more than three feet tall, smoking a pipe and sitting on a nearby tree stump.

He smiled at her.

"Oh Jesus," she said, eyes wide in disbelief.

The pipe came out of his mouth and the little man's smile grew wider. "Not quite," he said. "But I'll take that as a compliment."

There was odd laughter all around, as if the forest was filled with disembodied humor.

Tracey spun around again, looking for whoever (whatever) else was here, but saw nothing. She felt like Dorothy in Munchkin City.

"Relax," the odd little man said. "We'll get you back. We don't want you here anymore than you want to be here, you see."

308

"Where's the road?" she asked, voice trembling.

The pipe went back into his mouth. "First things first," he said. "First things first."

*

In stories the little man always requests, in return for services rendered, the human's first born child. But what use could the Good People have for a human baby?

No, the request here was quite different:

Safe passage to America.

Some of the wee folk, it seems, had a desire to travel.

*

And of course she refused at first. The very idea of these little people was ludicrous enough, but to actually allow them to stow away in her luggage and get taken back to the States? Absurd. And she said so.

"Well..." said the first little man, who had been joined by five others. "We hope you like it here in this forest...."

"I'll find my way," she said, feeling angry, feeling as if she were being blackmailed. Blackmailed by mythical creatures. Wonderful.

She started off again.

"You won't get out that way," the little man said.

Tracey stopped and looked back at him. Frowning, she started off in another direction.

"Nor that way."

The little people gave a chittering laugh. They were enjoying this.

Tracey sighed.

"You can't get out of *these* woods in *any* direction," the little man said. He had pulled the pipe from his mouth and was tapping the unlit contents of its bowl to the forest floor.

Tracey stared at him.

He looked back at her, smiling. "A human may blunder into them, but a human cannot leave without our

309

permission." He saw the look on her face. "We don't make the rules, lassy. They're as old as time."

She sighed, feeling quite angry indeed now, quite furious.

"But of course we'll gladly show you the way out... if you take us with you. That's all we ask. Take us with you. We believe you owe us that much, seeing as how you desecrated our home with your... with your *functions*, shall we say."

She had no choice. She said sure, she'd take them with her, thinking that she would renege on the promise at the first chance.

"'Tis a deal," he said.

He and the five others led the way out of the woods... which was a magical way, really, in a direction she had never thought of, a direction she had never *heard* of: the wee folk called it South-North.

Within ten minutes she was at the road. The hood of the rental car was up and Timmy was hunched over the engine, with an old farmer at his side. The farmer's truck was resting half-off the road, its own ancient engine ticking softly.

Timmy looked up to see his wife come out of the woods.

"Honey?" he said. "Did you take a walk."

She did not answer, just walked up to him and hugged him.

"What's wrong?"

"I..." She was nearly in tears.

The farmer stood tall from the engine compartment and regarded Mrs. White with suspicion. He studied her closely, searching for something, and when she turned her head to look back at the woods he looked there as well, a deep frown on his weathered forehead.

"See something, Ma'am?" he asked. He stared carefully into her eyes, as if waiting to study the complexity of her answer.

Tracey looked back at the woods, saw nothing.

"I..." she began, then looked at the farmer and smiled. "No. Just took a walk. Saw some squirrels."

"Squirrels, hey?" He nodded and looked into the forest. For a good minute he stared into the trees, then he looked at her and smiled. "Lots of squirrels. Birds and squirrels. Not much else."

She nodded.

The farmer wiped his hands on his overalls and gestured at the engine. "Should be working now, my good man. Whyn't you try her?"

Timmy went into the car and turned the key. The engine kicked on like new, purring with the solid and comforting sound of a healthy, dependable motor.

Timmy killed the engine, then came out and shook the farmer's hand. "What do I owe you?" he asked.

The old farmer waved the suggestion away. "Ah, forget it. A man was meant to help other men. If I come to America and break down, I'll look you up."

They laughed and shook hands. As the farmer turned to walk back to his truck he again looked closely into Tracey's eyes.

"Beautiful woods," he said.

She agreed.

He nodded, glanced once more into the forest, and then walked to his truck. A few moments later he was rumbling down the road, disappearing around the corner just like Timmy had done earlier.

"Nice guy," Timmy said.

"Let's just go." She jumped into the car... locked the door.

"What's wrong?" he asked, looking through the window.

"Just get in here. I want to go."

He climbed in and sighed. "Vacation's getting to you," he said, smiling. Then he reached for the key.

The engine was silent.

"Son of a bitch," he said.

Tracey White had harsher words.

Timmy tried the key again and still the engine made no sound save for a weak and pathetic little gurgle, like a drain emptying.

"Now what the hell is—" Timmy began, and then he looked at his wife and started to scream.

There was a tiny little man hanging off of Tracey's window.

311

*

She explained everything to him, and at first he could do nothing but shake his head. Americans are not brought up to regard the presence of such creatures rationally. In fact, to see such things was, for Americans, to see signs of one's own insanity, or to believe one had been drugged.

But these creatures here were real. Timmy could smell smoke on his clothes, see the sparkle in his eyes.

"They won't let this car work until we take them with us," Tracey said with resignation.

Timmy nodded. Of course... of course.... as if that was the most logical request in the world.

The first little man came to Timmy's window, where he hung on with amazing dexterity.

"We didn't invite the lady to our woods, she blundered in there of her own accord. First she soiled our home, and then she got lost. And now she owes us for getting her out. We have a deal here."

"I have no deal," Timmy said, trying to sound in control of himself.

The man smiled patiently. "You have a deal whether you know you have a deal or not. The deal was with the lady, and you go with the lady, correct?"

He had to admit he did.

"We few have always wanted to see your homeland," the little man said. "All we ask is to be allowed to stow-away in your things. We'll cause no trouble. You won't know we're there. And once we arrive, we shall part. You'll have nothing else to do with us."

"Aye, aye," agreed the others.

"You owe us," the little man said. "For desecrating our home." He looked at Tracey, who blushed. "And we'll get this vehicle rolling, once you agree. And we'll guarantee it doesn't malfunction again, in all the time you have it." There was a mischievous glint in his eyes as he said this, of course.

Timmy White looked at his new wife, who slumped guiltily in her seat.

"What did you do?" he asked. "Good god, what did you do?"

312

For the price of a piss, a plague was born.

*

Things went smoothly, and the Whites never knew the wee folk were with them at all. In fact, until things started to go haywire in Burghville they had thought that the wee folk had *not* come with them, or that if they had they had done as they promised and parted company. Once things started turning strange in Burghville, the Whites knew what was happening... though they would not voice their suspicions to each other for fear of actually having to put into words something so insane. You see, once they agreed to take the wee folk with them (which in itself was an easy feat, the creatures hiding themselves magically inside the tiniest of places), once husband and wife had acknowledged that yes, they were going to be taking *fairies* with them, they had not spoken of the incident at all. Perhaps they both thought they were crazy... maybe they thought they'd imagined the whole thing, as if it had been the side effect of some bizarre form of jet-lag. And so they had come back to Burghville, married and already harboring a secret, which they did not speak of to themselves, much less to each other. The Whites were going insane trying to prevent their own minds from contemplating the topic, believing, as some do, that to deny the existence of something was to prevent that something from actually existing. But you can't keep secrets from yourself... you run the risk of exploding. And a thing that exists will exist whether or not there is a human mind there to contemplate it at all.

And so, anyway, this was how the wee folk came to Burghville: on a wing and a lie.

*

One other aside: imagine the look on the face of the airport baggage examiner when he x-rayed the first of the White's luggage and saw inside the silhouette of a pointy-hatted little man smoking a pipe, knees to his chest, resting comfortably amidst the blouses and pants.

313

He, too, had said nothing of what he saw. Everyone, it seems, has a fear of insanity.

*

So, there it is, the reason Timmy White was thinking not about the broken condom but about his own guilt. He felt more guilty than the guiltiest Catholic. He looked over at his wife, knowing she knew what he was talking about. *They*, the Whites, had brought this plague to Burghville. They and they alone were responsible.

Tracey White, for her part, was thinking about other things. First of all she *was* thinking about that broken condom. Second of all she was thinking about that train ticket she found in her husband's pocket... that *secret* train ticket. And, more than either of these, she was thinking about the fact that those two things, broken condom and secret train ticket, were related. They went together, so to speak. Like a horse and carriage.

"I sabotaged the condom," she said after many minutes of silence had fallen between them. "It was me."

He frowned at her. It was not an angry frown but an honestly confused frown.

"What do you mean?"

She sighed. "I put a hole in it."

His frown pushed down on his eyes, wrinkled his nose, gave birth to all sorts of new wrinkles in his thirty-something face. He looked suddenly much older than he was. The revelation of lies and trickery is the greatest aging catalyst of all.

"Why would you do something like that?" he asked her.

She sighed again, gathered her strength. This was the way she always gathered her strength, by taking in a deep lungful of air, holding it, and then releasing it as she spoke: "I found your train ticket," she said.

He said nothing for a moment, just nodded thoughtfully, looking down at the floor, his feet.

"Oh," he finally said. Just: "Oh...."

*

314

Outside of the rather stuffy and close atmosphere of the White household the afternoon was aging well, becoming one of those fully mature afternoons that lie particularly nicely on a town such as Burghville, the sort of afternoon that coats it in full and rich colors, that makes it look just that much more like a cliché American small town. *Our* town. It was the sort of afternoon that made you want to get out and walk the sidewalks, do a little window shopping, maybe go to the park and watch the squirrels. All of this was enhanced by the fact that there were few cars on the streets. Later there would be plenty of reason for there to be no cars on the streets of Burghville, later there would be an official statement forbidding anyone to be outside at all, in any way shape or form, and if Sheriff Sherman had been around he would have enforced it like it was the law. As it happens, however, there were few cars on the streets this afternoon just *because*, and Sheriff Sherman was just starting to pull away from his former life, just starting his descent into the shadows.

So, the town was quiet and cliché. The town was lazy and idyllic. The town was glowing under sunlight and clear sky. The town was pretty and all-American.

Like Tracey White, the town was sighing, gathering strength.

14

A church is no place to talk about love.

Nevertheless, Orson the Good Person and the former Father Preston were standing in the vestibule of St. Michael's Catholic Church, and they were both indeed talking about love. In front of them the great heavy wooden front doors were closed, as they had been for a

long time now. Closed and locked against outside forces...
namely, Carol Slugg and anyone else who wanted the
Father's ear. Now Orson and Lee stood looking at those
doors...looking *up* at those doors, in the case of Orson.

"Well, you can't get Tina anymore," Orson said.
"And that's a pity. But maybe, just maybe, you could get
this other. No?"

The former Father Preston shrugged.

"'Tis at least worth a shot, as they say," said
Orson.

Lee Preston shrugged. The twin doors of the
church loomed before him like the walls that kept out King
Kong.

"You wouldn't want to go through the rest of your
life thinking *what if*, would you now?"

Another shrug.

Orson sighed. "It might at least be good to get
some—"

Lee Preston reached out and shoved open those
front doors. Without hearing another word from Orson the
Wee Folk he was out of the stuffy church and into the
smooth fresh light of the afternoon.

Orson's final word there, by the way, spoken to the
dust and pews and whatever bats lived in the belfry, was:

"--air."

And then he just smiled and lit his pipe.

*

Helen Keller held a fat cool mushroom in one hand
like it was an apple, and without further ado or debate she
brought that mushroom to her mouth and took a bite.

The taste was like this:

Musky, nearly sexual, as if she were fellating the
Earth itself, but not in any vulgar sort of way, no, as the
rightful lover of the planet, performing a service in the
name of love. It was a wet flavor, heavy and strong and
strange to the tongue, like the taste of a private magical
moment between lovers. Taking that mushroom over her
tongue and teeth and down her throat made her feel
connected to the world beneath her, the only world she had,
the only world she would ever know. And it was more than

sexual, though that feeling was overpowering: it was also very maternal, that bonding between the giver of life (the earth) and the one being nurtured (herself). It was also communion-like, with the earth as priest and the mushroom as wafer, and she herself the willing yet nervous acceptor of the faith. Plants are the body of the earth, take and eat. The waters are the blood, take and drink. The wee folk 'shroom broke apart tenderly as it passed through her mouth, as if it were made of nothing at all but magic and memory and mystery and wonder... as perhaps it was, just like the wee folk themselves. She took another bite, not sure how much she really needed to have and trying to be careful, and again felt that explosion of sexuality on her tongue and taste buds, again felt a tender mother-child connection, again felt as if she were embracing a spirituality she had never known before.

She took another bite. It was immediately following this third bite that she felt something else stirring inside of her. It built up, quivering and fragile, like an orgasm of the soul.

The forest around her, afternoon shadows fighting with afternoon's slanted sunlight, quivered as well... quivered and grew fragile. Quivered and grew larger. Quivered and became more vibrant, more fresh, more *real*. Her head began to swim a bit, as if she'd been drinking. The half-eaten wee folk 'shroom in her hand vibrated like a captured toad, perhaps even sang again, that silent song of the mushroom she nevertheless somehow heard, the way a deaf person hears Mozart: through her feet, legs, skin, the ends of her hair. She looked down at the mushroom and the others she had gathered. She stared at the half-eaten mushroom and thought she saw it moving, as if something was inside of it struggling to be free. She stared at this struggle for what seemed like a long time, but the slanted light of the sun never moved, never fell further on its course westward. The mushroom moved beneath her fingers, all gray gills and cap and tender wet flesh. She suddenly felt like she was holding Womanhood in her hand. No, like she was holding Manhood. No, some sort of vaginal-penis. No, a child. No, the essence of the planet. Of all planets. Of the earth. Of herself. Of....

A phrase came to her, vaguely familiar:

317

Follow the course of natural things.

And then another:

Always search out the bounds of your enclosures, and always dream of what's beyond.

Yes, she thought. Absolutely. Words to live by. Screw Constitutions and laws and Commandments. All we need are these, to follow the course of natural things and search out the bounds of our enclosures and dream of what's beyond and do unto others as you would have them do unto you and touch me there yes and take me to the ...

She closed her eyes for a second and then looked down at the mushroom. She had dropped it, and it lay with the others she had gathered. She looked up at the woods around her and swayed drunkenly, just as the world seemed to sway and lose its balance. And then everything cleared. Cleared not in the sense of *sobriety*, but in the true sense: she was suddenly able to see everything in focus, from the furthest tree to the birch she was leaning on. Every leaf and twig and flittering insect was in focus, sharply etched in brilliant and vivid clarity. The bark of a distant poplar was thick and as obvious and clear as her own hand, and the magnetic and luminous eyes of a passing horsefly were as dramatic and bright as a screen door three inches from her face. And more, everything that was not clear before, that *could* not be clear, was presented to her in a clarity that was crazy and magical. Things like the sky itself, normally a rather vague ethereal blue, like a smear of air, was now sharp with texture, like blue cement. She felt that if she could reach out far enough she could touch it with a fingernail, maybe scratch her name there for all the world to see.

All of it, so vivid it was like she had fallen into a painting by a master of detail. And it was comforting to her eyes, too: no need for those muscles to stretch and relax as they continually focused on distant and far objects, not with *everything* in such deep-focus... like she was in some lost Orson Welles movie.

The last thing to clear, of course, was her own mind. And when *that* happened, when she was suddenly opened to all possibilities (and it was a physical feeling, like the dilating of her mind, like the lubrication of her brain, the blossoming of a vaginal Third-Eye, the preparation for a mind-fuck perhaps), when she could take in a deep breath and welcome the world around her as a child does, when she knew she could take in anything that was presented to her without worry or judgment, when she knew she would accept whatever came next, that was when Helen Keller left these woods.

That was when she entered the pasture of Scooter Boober's farm.

*

Scooter Boober was not to be seen. At the far end of that pasture, the end furthest from the forest, sat his house and barns, and around that house and those barns ran fencing, and within that fencing could be see the shapes of llamas, and around those llamas flew swallows, and above those swallows sprouted that cement sky. Helen stared over there for a while, once more amazed at the clarity and brilliance of the world, and then she looked to the center of the pasture. Actually, her eyes were *drawn* to the center of that pasture, as if they were being pulled by a magnetic force.

And in the middle of the pasture was the Highland cow. Jennifer, if she remembered correctly. The huge animal was just lying there, shaking its shaggy head at the occasional annoying deerfly or mosquito. The red of the cow's fur was clown-like, bright and in stark contrast to the sparse green of the pasture. Helen found herself trying to think of other things that were that same shade... and failed. She had never seen a beast like this before.

She started towards it.

The animal noticed her coming and it watched her impassively. She was just a little woman, wide-eyed and fragile-looking, tripping on 'shrooms.

When she was ten feet from the animal she stopped and smiled. Her new clarity of vision made every single strand of the cow's fur stand out, made the dark depths between each hair look like a place she could crawl into, lose herself, find herself. Its eyes, a pleasing light-amber, stared at her and she saw herself reflected in the lenses. She saw herself reflected in the great wet red-brown nose, too.

319

She opened her mouth to speak, and that was when the cow said:

"I know what you want. It's about time you came to me. Now shut up and listen."

She knelt there silently by the great animal and listened to what it had to say.

*

The Buckthorn Industries' chemists were ill-fitted for this sort of work: they were loading three great barrels of their new product onto the back of a flat-bed semi. Of course, they had a fork-lift to help them, but none of them had much experience with a fork-lift, either, so that a good twenty minutes were spent as one of them tried to maneuver it around with any sort of grace.

The Buckthorn brothers drove up to this scene and Dick Dick leaned out the window.

"Let's get moving!" he roared at them. They all nodded as they worked. The first barrel was placed on the fork-lift easily, but promptly fell off the tines when the forks were lifted by the driver. The barrel rolled to Dick Dick's SUV and clunked against its side, denting the door.

"Sorry," the chemists said in unison, and they rolled it back to the fork-lift.

Dick Dick sighed.

Willy Billy smiled in the passenger seat. "You've all gone mad," he said.

Dick Dick glared at him. "Yeah? What do you care, look what you're getting for this."

Willy Billy stared out over the Buckthorn Industries grounds. They were idling at the rear of the compound, back near the first of the Industries' large garages. Willy Billy looked around admiringly.

"Is that a new out-building?" he asked. When Dick Dick did not answer (he was too busy watching his chemists) Willy Billy said: "You're making this place grow, that's for sure, big brother." Then he saw Dick Dick's office, where a light was glowing in the afternoon's shadows. "Is someone up there?"

Dick Dick looked there as well. "That's Polly Anderson."

320

Willy Billy's smile grew wider. "Oh... dear sweet Polly. I'd like to say hello to her."

"Later. We've got work to do."

Outside, the chemists had the first barrel on the back of the truck and were working, Stooge-style, on the second. When this second barrel threatened to topple from the fork-lift it was saved by the ankle of one of the chemists, who winced in pain and then hopped around holding his foot.

"You've all gone mad," Willy Billy said again. "Absolutely mad. Haven't any of them ever heard of a pallet?"

Dick Dick told his chemists to hurry, then roared off in the Canyonero, steering it away from his company and back through town. As he drove he continually looked this way and that, eyes wide and excited.

"See her?" Willy Billy asked.

"See who?"

"Your wife."

"I'm not looking for my wife. I'm looking for *them*. I want you to see them. I want you to believe."

"Ah yes. *Them*." Willy Billy smiled and turned his face to the window. "You know what you should do, big brother. You should hire them on as cheap labor, like Oompa-Loompas or something. That's what the prudent businessman would do."

Dick Dick shook his head. "No. You can't control them, they'd do what they wanted. They have to die. We have to be rid of them."

He came to the sheriff's station and pulled up onto the sidewalk in front of it. He laid on the horn and waited a few moments. When no one appeared he jumped out and went inside. A few minutes later he came back looking pissed.

"What do we need the sheriff for?" Willy Billy asked.

"We have to make an announcement."

"What sort of announcement?"

"We have to tell people to stay inside tonight."

"Why?"

"Because of the spray, goddamnit!"

321

Willy Billy shifted himself in his seat so that he faced Dick Dick. "What sort of spray is this, exactly, big brother?"

"It's the spray that's going to save this goddamn town."

"Save it or kill it?"

"Save it, goddamnit." Dick Dick said. Then he threw the SUV into gear and tore off down Main Street.

*

Sheriff Sherman, of course, was off trying to come up with a plan that would effectively sabotage Dick Dick's own. He was sitting in his car in the bushes across the road from the Burghville Airport. As the afternoon sun gave way to evening's pre-natal light he saw movement at the hanger where Dick Dick's fated plane sat, and he ducked down behind his dash... as well as he could, anyway, with his gut hitting the wheel.

Many figures moved in the shrubs, creeping up and then hiding by the hangar. All but one of them carried heavy-looking objects.

Sheriff Sherman frowned and fingered his pistol. Maybe he should just take them all out....

But no, he decided to watch for a while. They might be security hired by Dick Dick. They might be his own deputies, out looking for him. They might be lawyers representing his wife, looking to serve him papers.

He decided to wait before making any moves, just to see what they did. If the time came to use his weapon, he knew he'd be ready. Deputies, security, or lawyers... any way you looked at it, not a bad way to spend some bullets.

He would just have to wait and see....

*

Not seeing the sheriff anywhere, Dick Dick finally stopped one of the deputies and told him to start spreading the word: everyone was to stay inside tonight. Come tomorrow, the evil vermin that were plaguing the town would be gone forever.

322

His voice cracking, the deputy said: "But what's going to happen—"

"Just do it!" Dick Dick roared, silencing the kid. Then, tires squawking, he roared off again.

*

Back at Buckthorn Industries, the chemists were still struggling to get the last of the three fifty-gallon barrels on the flat-bed. It kept rolling off, clanking and banging as it went, once making it all the way to the front gate. When they rolled it back they spent the next thirty-minutes trying to position it on the forks of the lift, but the barrel was so bent now it wouldn't stay. The driver of the forklift had to climb out and help, but of course before he could he hit the controls with his knee and sent the forklift zooming backwards, tossing himself around like a rag doll. This sort of thing went on and on, not so much Stooges-style now as Keatonesque. Possibly Harold Lloydish.

The fetal darkness in the west was growing lungs, moving its eyes, clenching and unclenching its fists. Some time soon, the night would be born.

*

Polly Anderson looked up from the spill of papers that surrounded and nearly engulfed her in Dick Dick's office. She sat thinking for a long time after she was finished reading what there was to read … or after she had read enough and her aching head could not take any more. She thought and then frowned and stood up. Not quite knowing what to do with herself, she started to pace the hallways of Buckthorn Industries' main office building. Her bare-feet made no sound on the beige carpet of the place. Only her breathing made any noise, since she was sighing as she walked. She passed all the office doors, wondering what took place behind them, what sort of evil hid its face there. She stared up at the lights above her, those cold office lights that cast absolutely no shadows. Why, she wondered, have I always felt so comfortable in these places? She shivered as an answer and continued to pace the hallways, looking into Dick Dick's office when

323

she came back that way, frowning at the papers strewn everywhere. She felt sick, nauseous. Only, what can a person throw up to relieve this sort of nausea? When one is sick to one's heart and soul, what does one regurgitate? She just kept walking, listening to the silence of the building, then finally came at last to the large windows that overlooked the front walk and a good chunk of town. Afternoon was settling in slowly, just beginning to send out that diffuse light that signals the end of a day. Burghville was a pretty town, she thought. Sometimes. At least it was now, but what about when Buckthorn Industries got done with it?

She thought about what Dick Dick had told her he was going to do to rid the town of those creatures. The thought of it made her sickened heart and soul quiver. The son of a bitch was going to spray poison over the whole place, over every single house and yard. And why? For the bottom line, for the continuation of capitalism. To make himself look good. The standard reasons.

She opened her mouth to say something, a curse perhaps, then closed it firmly. She looked around again. What could she do here to punish Dick Dick for past and future wickedness?

There had to be something....

*

The former Father, Lee Preston, was racing down Burghville's Main Street, looking everywhere, into every yard, on every porch, down every sidewalk, into every alleyway he came across, looking... looking...

Looking for you-know-who.

*

Candy Cleaver stepped out of her house. She'd been crying for hours and her eyes were red and puffy. She'd cried so much she'd pushed the toxins right out of her body, or so it seemed to her. She felt lighter, as if every new and improved cell in her body, every pine-scented atom, had exited her tear ducts to stain the shoulder of the little person who had held her. She stepped out into the afternoon and looked at the day ending around her. It was either an ending day or a beginning night, but either way she looked at it she felt happy. Something positive coursed through her veins, cleaning up in its own way after those super-clean cells. She felt absolutely washed and pressed, sparkling with brightness. Unscented and without perfumes or dyes. She felt as if she'd just emerged from under her old skin, as if she'd just been made... or born. The opaque light of the western sky seemed to cover her with softness, like a baby's blanket. Like a veil.

She turned back to her house to see if the little person had exited with her, but he was nowhere to be seen. He had told her he would stay behind and "organize things" for her. She wondered what exactly he was going to do, but she knew she could not go back inside. She'd been directed to take a walk. Go out, the little man had said. Go out and take a walk, see your town, enjoy the coming evening. I'll organize things around here for you. She had no idea what he meant but she took in a deep breath and started to walk, taking the sidewalk to the right, glancing to the White household just long enough to wonder why it was so quiet over there. She walked and walked and did as the little man had said: she took in her town, she enjoyed the coming evening. She did not think about the little man once she turned the corner, she had far too many other things to reflect on, far too many other topics for her recently washed mind and soul to contemplate... except, for just a second as she made her way through her quiet neighborhood, that rinsed and pressed mind thought:

I wonder if he'll do the windows....

*

Carol Slugg made the sign of the cross. She was always making the sign of the cross. She did it out of habit, out of routine. It had become more like a nervous tic for her, the way some people's eyebrows quiver when they're tense, or the way others will click their tongues. She did it so much she was not aware she was doing it, just a quick flick of her right hand over forehead, stomach, heart, and right breast. When she was *really*, consciously, making the sign of the cross, as she was doing at this moment, she did

325

it with a pomp and style more befitting a military salute, with a crisp Nazi-efficiency: that hand would flip up with purpose, the bones inside of it cracking audibly, and go on its course without hesitation. And her eyes would deepen, as steely and determined as the eyes of the SS. She would make the sign of the cross and gaze into the horizon (or at the brick wall of an airplane hangar, as she was doing now) like a Christian zombie.

"I'm worried," said a little voice, interrupting this particular signing of the cross just as Carol touched her heart. It was the voice of the "dissenter," looking now not so much like Sally Fields in *Sybil* as the pissed off Sally Fields of *Norma Rae*.

The others looked at her but said nothing, waiting for Carol to answer.

When Carol did it was to say: "Worry is good. Don't you think the Lord Jesus was worried when he was on the cross? Of course he was, but he had a duty to fulfill, a job to do. He had to toughen up and get on with business. And what business was *He* doing? Oh, just saving Mankind! What are *you* doing? And what in the devil are you worried about?"

The young woman said: "I'm worried we'll get caught."

"The Lord will protect us."

"I'm worried it won't work."

Now, from the shadows, Carol Slugg glared at this woman. "It will work because the Lord *told* me it would work! He showed me in a vision!"

The dissenter just nodded and stepped back a bit, behind the others… perhaps to bolt when the time came.

They were standing behind the hangar that held Dick Dick's plane. Each of the women, except Carol, carried with her a five-gallon jug of holy water. Or, rather, it was Burghville tap water that had been "blessed" by Carol Slugg. Which meant she had made the sign of the cross over it while staring into space like a zombie.

They stood listening now. The fading day around them was quiet, that quiet broken only by the occasional mournful bird song.

"It will work," Carol Slugg said, for no reason.

326

The others looked at each other. Standing here in the process of actually carrying out this scheme, hiding in the picky bushes in the dimming light of day, they all felt less like acolytes or disciples and more like common crooks. Or worse, like stupid gullible women.

"It will work," Carol Slugg said again. Perhaps she wanted to say something much more poetic, something Biblical, something grand and touching and deep, but she was not that sort of person. Lyricism did not come easy for her.

"It will work," she pronounced one more time, and then started to move around the side of the hanger. There were three doors on the building, two regular doors on opposite sides and the large garage door on the front, where the plane exited and entered. Carol was moving toward the latter.

The dissenter opened her mouth to speak as the other women shuffled past her, each of them struggling with their respective jugs of water. The dissenter looked into each of their eyes as they passed, as if searching for the sign of a lie. And in a way she was: she was looking into their eyes to judge the depth of their commitment.

At last, once the line of women was past her, she said: "It won't work." She said it with strength and backbone.

The others stopped. They were motionless for a moment, then they stepped aside as Carol Slugg went to the back of the line and stood before the dissenter. The two women stared into each other's eyes, neither of them blinking. It was one sort of strength meeting another.

"It will work," Carol said, barely able to hide the anger she was feeling, "because the Lord *told* me it would work." She seemed to dare the younger woman to question this statement.

Which she did: "Well, He never told *me* it would work."

A murmur ran through the women. It was exactly the same sort of murmur heard on schoolyard playgrounds when someone dares to stand up to the bully.

Carol Slugg's face turned red. Her cold eyes glared at the other woman... actually *glared*, as if they were aflame.

327

"You expect the Lord to speak to you?" she asked. "What makes *you* so special, young lady?"

"What makes *you* so special?" the dissenter asked.

The murmur came again, stronger.

Carol Slugg glanced quickly at the other women, as if to gauge her standing with them, and then said: "God has *always* spoken to me. God and Jesus have always spoken to me, they have always guided my hand."

"Prove it."

"Why should I prove anything to you? If you have such little faith as to not believe a good Christian woman, you don't belong in this work."

"Prove it," the dissenter said again, in a voice so calm it had to absolutely piss off Carol Slugg. "Prove it was God speaking to you and not the devil."

Carol Slugg's face went from red to a deep purple. She looked like she was going to explode. She raised one arm as if she was going to strike the young woman, then she stilled it. She smiled.

"Satan is speaking through you," she said. "We will all pray for you, that Lucifer's power over you be broken by Jesus Christ." She bowed her head and folded her palms together.

The other women did not know what to do. A few of them set down their jugs and did as Carol was doing. The others looked at each other.

And then something amazing happened.

The dissenter said, quite calmly: "You are fucking insane."

And without lifting her head, seemingly without disrupting her prayer, Carol Slugg removed one hand from its folded position and brought it out like a professional pugilist.

She hit the young woman square in the jaw.

The dissenter fell backwards, tripping on the tangled bushes in which they all stood, and fell to the ground with a groan. She shook her head and looked up at Carol Slugg, who had apparently finished praying and was now just looming over the young woman, both fists clenched.

"Oh my God," said one of the other women, but was silenced by a glare from Carol.

328

"You hit me," the dissenter mumbled as she rubbed her face.

"And if you keep spreading your Satanic lies you'll be hit again. You'll be hit until the demon inside of you is cast away."

"I mean..." said the young woman, checking her hand to see if there was blood. "I mean, you really hit me."

Carol smiled. "I suggest you leave us in our work. I suggest you find some place quiet to pray. I recommend the church, if that Priest has it opened yet. If not the church, the little nave behind it, back in the garden. You need to reflect on Jesus, you need to pray to the Lord to have your soul cleansed. You need—"

The young woman jumped to her feet and tackled Carol Slugg. They both went flying back into the other women before falling the other way, into the bushes. Fists were clenched. Punches were thrown. For a while there was no sound except the grunting and groaning of a good old-fashioned cat-fight.

The other women, watching this scene in awe, looked at each other, confused as all hell. It really was quite a sight, these two women beating on each other in the tight little space between the hanger and the bushes. Indeed, for quite a bit of the fight they were entangled *in* those bushes, which held them suspended above the ground like a hammock.

At last, not knowing what else to do, one of the other women said: "Let us pray."

And so they prayed.

*

And still the evening came on quietly, like a radio slowly tuning to silence.

Sheriff Sherman, watching from his hiding place, saw the bushes where the figures had entered start to shake and thrash about. He frowned and fingered his pistol. What in the hell is going on in there? he wondered. Again he debated getting out and performing his duties as an officer of the peace, but in the end stayed where he was. He continued to have faith that they would leave and he could go on plotting Dick Dick Buckthorn's fall.

329

He thought he had an idea, but he didn't know if he had enough time. And even if he had had all the time in the world, there were still *those* people in the bushes. Perhaps they were airport personnel. He thought this might be it until he realized that the airport *had* no personnel, just the two men who worked in the tower. Both of those men did double duty in maintenance and cleaning, but they were not around, judging by the lack of cars anywhere. And why should they be around? It was late in the day and no air traffic could be expected.

So who in the hell *are* they? he wondered.

It was around this time that the naked woman appeared, although at this point Sheriff Sherman did not yet see her.

*

The naked woman was *not* Henrietta Pratt, though she too was close to Sheriff Sherman. She was driving her little pickup down the road to the airport. In the back of that pickup sat a very large plastic tub, the sort people use for either garbage or lawn-debris. In that tub were fifty gallons of wildflower seed. She had cleaned out the garden store.

"Whatchya gonna do with all that seed?" the old man behind the counter had asked.

"Plant it," she replied.

She suspected her plan would not work. Most things that are this crazy do not work, but she also knew it would be a wonderful statement, as most crazy things are, and native wildflower seeds were a hell of a lot better than whatever Dick Dick Buckthorn was planning on spreading. If a person has a chance to make a statement, then that person had a duty to do so. This Henrietta Pratt believed with all her heart.

So let them chase her out of town if they wanted, the fools. It was in their own best interest what she was going to try. And though she knew the people of Burghville well enough to know they would not be able to see the sanity and logic of her actions, that they would not get what she was trying to say, she nonetheless felt a moral obligation to step up and make this statement. To not do so would be... well, unnatural.

So here she came, driving up the old road towards the glorified field that was the Burghville Community Airport.

She, too, did not yet see the naked woman.

*

The announcement was made the only way it could be, over cell-phones. And those who did not have cell-phones were made aware of the announcement by others, so in a sense the announcement was part of a great American tradition. Think of Paul Revere riding to warn of the coming red-coats, then picture the good people of Burghville whispering over shrubbery and deflated children's pools.

It wasn't red-coats that were coming now, though. It was... well, no one really knew what it was. When the initial announcement came from Dick Dick Buckthorn, who called all the sheriff deputies he could, there was no mention of what exactly was going to happen. All that was stated was the following:

"The plague that has held our town hostage for all these weeks will come to an end tonight. Buckthorn Industries, in cooperation with the good citizens of Burghville, will lead the effort to eradicate the pestilence that has fallen over us. For your own safety, and for the effectiveness of the cure, please stay inside your house tonight. Do not leave for any reason, unless it is an absolute emergency. By tomorrow this nightmare will be over. Thanks for your cooperation and your continued support."

That last bit about *your continued support* was pure Dick Dick, always thinking about the future of his company.

"Come tomorrow," he told his brother, "Buckthorn Industries will be seen as the ultimate hero, and I will own this town."

To which Willy Billy responded: "Where's your wife...?"

331

The message was spread quite effectively throughout Burghville. Everyone resolved to stay inside and let the people in charge do their jobs. Old family photo albums and videotapes were brought out. Popcorn was made. Younger couples decided to spend the evening making love. Board games long forgotten in the backs of closets were pulled out, and everyone had to relearn the rules of *Monopoly*. Elderly folks played cards or listened to old tunes and talked about all the other times like this they'd been through: the situation reminded some of post-war bomb scares. Long-delayed projects were completed. Children invented new games to play. Some brought out books to finish. Some listened to old family tales, tall and otherwise.

And at every house on every street, curtains were parted and eyes peered out, searching for whatever it was that was coming.

*

The opaque late-afternoon sun was like a pastel smear over an otherwise perfectly realistic painting. The clouds were like fluffy candy. The tops of trees were lit with cartoon fire.

And that fire, reflected in the eyes of the Scottish Highland cow, was the prettiest thing Helen Keller had ever seen. She stared at it as the cow talked, and continued to stare at it long after the cow had finished. She heard everything the animal said, but she had also *seen* everything it had said. Very odd.

Now it was looking at her, a strange expression on its face.

"That is what you must do," it said.

She frowned. "But will that rid the town of the wee folk?"

The animal looked away, out over the surrounding pasture and the weak shadows that were just starting to spread over it like pools of spilled ink.

"No questions," it said. "Just action."

"But... is the way you told me the course of natural things?"

The cow sighed, shook away a fly, and looked back at her impatiently.

"When you're dealing with wee folk, little girl, what is natural is a matter for debate."

"Then—"

"But not right now. Now is action."

She nodded and started to rise, but stopped in a half-kneel and looked at the cow.

"And everything else you told me?" she asked. "Is it all true or is it also all a matter for debate?" The cow had indeed told her many great and wonderful things about the world and the wee folk and everything, and it was this question she needed answering most of all.

But the highland cow was picking at grass and chewing it lazily. The fire in its eyes was dull, the expression on its face bored, the aura around her not one of Wise Woman but simply Cattle. She was suddenly just a cow, shaking off deerflies in the fading light of a late afternoon.

The mushroom had worn off. Helen herself was no longer what *she* had been just moments before. She was just a girl.

But, of course, that would do. That would do just fine. She stood and gave the cow one last look filled with awe and thankfulness and sympathy. A look like that was a mushy stew of meaning, the look a young girl gives her father when she realizes he is human and loves him anyway. One last mushroom-induced blur, like heat ripple on an August highway, crossed Helen's vision and through wavering lines of color and light she watched the cow look up at her and wink. She was about to say something again and then, just like that, it was a cow again, nothing more. A highland cow. Chewing cud, shaking off flies. That was all right, she thought. That was all perfectly fine.

She smiled down at the beast, then looked up across its pasture. A tiny figure was coming toward her, moving deliberately but slowly, confidently, like it had been watching her all along and simply waiting for her to finish her conference with the cow.

It was Scooter Boober. Around him the farm was quiet and still.

*

Burghville was quiet and still, too. The message had been received. The good citizens were inside, waiting patiently. They had no suspicions, no doubts. People in authority had told them that by morning everything would be taken care of, and by Christ they had no reason to disbelieve them. Oh, sure, a few people were cocky and daring and refused to go inside, namely the town's older teenagers and a few macho men of the buzz-cut-and-beer variety, but mostly the citizens of Burghville stayed inside. They had been told to stay inside until morning, but of course they would come out earlier and find themselves engulfed by....

But no, first things first.

*

Yes, Burghville's streets were quiet and still, but there was still much bustling activity over at the airport. The bushes near the hanger were still shaking as Carol Slugg and the other woman beat the hell out of each other (this was actually the exact image Carol had as she fought her much younger foe: she felt she was actually *beating the hell out of her*), and Sheriff Sherman was fidgeting in his cruiser, unsure what to do. His hand alternately moved to open the door and then returned to its place in his lap. He stared at those shaking bushes and wondered again if he should return now to his policeman duties. The war between action and inaction was tearing at his face, at the very fabric of his being. His mouth twitched, his fingers shook, his lips trembled. To be a cop or not to be a cop, that was his question. Whether 'twas nobler to go over there and keep the peace or sit here on his fat ass and continue to plot the downfall of Dick Dick Buckthorn.

Oh Jesus... he just didn't know. He really had no plan at all, but he could, at the very least, sabotage the plane. Pop its tires, drain its fuel. Something. Spray-paint DICK DICK SUCKS DICK on its side, or something more

334

clever. BUCKTHORN IS A FAG. BUCKTHORN IS A COMMIE. Whatever. He may have had no grand idea but he did have a very strong feeling that he needed to do *something*. It was Dick Dick and Dick Dick alone who was standing in his way. If there had been no Dick Dick then he, Sheriff Sherman, would be the hero in all of this. And, once he was a hero, there would have been no stopping the implementation of *the* Plan.

It did not occur to the sheriff that he had no idea just how he would have been the hero in all this, he just *knew* he would have been. So there he sat, burning and seething on the inside while on the outside his body kept making cop-like movements to exit the patrol car and break up whatever sort of debauchery was going on over at the hangar.

He might have stayed like that forever, torn between his own duties as a lawman and his lust for covert acts of vengeance. He *might* have, if it hadn't been for the naked woman, who finally got him moving, who finally got his fat ass out of the car.

*

Scooter Boober came up to Helen and nodded in greeting. She nodded back and said: "Beautiful evening coming on."

"Yep," he said, looking down at the Highland cow. He seemed to study the animal for a moment, looking for something, and then he looked back up at Helen. "Have an interesting conversation, you two?"

The cow glanced at the two humans, then slowly looked away, chewing its cud in the fading light.

"I just..." Helen began, but didn't know quite what to say. Mention she just tripped on mushrooms so she could converse with the beast? Say she just came out here to look at the animal?

Scooter watched her expectantly. His handsome eyes flashed under his rumpled and dusty little cowboy hat.

"She's a beautiful creature," Helen said at last.

Scooter Boober nodded.

"And I just...." She stopped herself, frowned, looked at him closely. There was something different

335

about him this day, he was radiating something she could barely register, something warm, happy. Something that had been hidden deep inside of him, dormant for years, but which had been brought forth recently, like a long lost memory suddenly conjured by a photograph.

And then it hit her.

"I'll be," she said, smiling down at him. "You *talked* to her! You talked to that woman you once loved."

He lifted one eyebrow, then shrugged, turned his head, spat to the ground, scratched his chin.

"You *did*," Helen said. "You talked to her. When? What did she say? Who called who...."

"You're a strange girl," he said.

"Hey, you have to answer me. What did you talk about?"

"What all old friends talk about: the old days."

"Did you call her?"

"No. She called me. She called me to say..." He looked up at Helen timidly, unsure he should continue, unsure this was something he should say out loud. At last he gazed off over the pasture again, that warm and distant look still in his eyes, making him seem lovelorn, lost, sad, happy, all at once. He said:

"She'd been thinking, about her life and everything. About choices. About choosing the path you want to take and the path you need to take. About pleasing other people or pleasing yourself. She'd been wondering about me, where I was, what I was doing. All her life, she said, she'd been doing things and choosing paths because they were what her family wanted her to do and take. And she realized she wasn't happy, that she'd never been happy, that she was living someone else's life. That she was just going through the motions. Seems she found a letter I wrote her way back when and... well, I guess I said some things that made her think I was one of the paths she should have taken. It was a good letter, apparently. A love letter, all mushy and full of bad poetry, the kind I maybe wrote too much of once upon a time, and it got her thinking about how happy we'd been. She started to realize that because her family didn't approve of me she'd thrown away what might have been the best thing she'd ever had. And...."

He looked embarrassed, and kicked at a rock on the ground. "Well, it was a nice talk."

Helen frowned. "No, there's more. What is it?"

He shrugged his little shoulders and looked to the horizon, which was sharp against the blue-black curve of the sky. "She said she wished I'd been what her family considered normal. She wished I could have been taller, a normal man. Then, she said, we could have been together forever. The way I was... was just too much for her family. A little man, after all, in love with their beautiful full-grown daughter. It was too strange for them. Too bizarre. So she went with their hearts and not her own. She cried, telling me she wished I could have been just a regular guy..."

"And what do you think?" Helen asked carefully. "Is that what you wish?"

He shook his head and gave her a wry little smile, pushing wrinkles to life at the corners of his mouth. "No. I wish she could have been shorter."

Helen thought a moment. "You should go to her, you should see her. She should say screw you to her family. You love her, you should be with her."

His smile became warm and genuine as he looked up at her. "But I am. In my heart, where we're both as perfect as we want to be." And with that he tipped his hat to her, bade her goodnight, and walked back across the darkening pasture to his silhouetted home.

Helen watched the little man for a few moments, then looked over to the cow, which was gazing blandly back at her. She smiled at the beast and gave it a nod. With that, she returned to the woods. There was work to be done this night, she knew. Talk was over, now was a time for action.

*

Tracey White looked at her husband. Timmy White, for his part, was looking at the floor.

"I don't think it worked," she said.

"Huh?" They had been sitting in silence for a while. He had no clue what she was referring to.

337

"My little act of sabotage," she said. "I don't think it worked. I don't think I'm pregnant."

"Oh." He shrugged and continued to examine the floor. "It's too early to know that."

"True. But I don't think I am." She paused. "What if I am, though?"

He looked at her. "What do you mean? We'll love it and raise it up good and strong, what else?"

"I mean..."

His face was serious and stern. "I'm not going anywhere, Tracey," he said.

"And if..." She was on the verge of tears. "And if I'm *not*...."

He slid over next to her and put his hand firmly on her knee, looking deep into her eyes in a way he hadn't done in quite a while.

"I'm not going anywhere," he said again.

"But what about... what about *this*," and she made a gesture that was meant to indicate the wee folk but very well might have represented the world, or life in general.

"Maybe it doesn't matter. Maybe it will work its way out," he said. "I don't know. But I know I love you."

She could no longer contain her tears. "But you were... you were going to leave...."

He pulled her close to him. "I didn't know *what* I was going to do. I was confused. I was crazy. This whole thing has been insane, and I felt guilty. We brought these damn things here, you and I. But they broke their promise, they said they'd disappear, that they'd leave us alone. It's our fault but they *lied*." He saw the look in her face. "Tracey, listen to me," and he pulled her still closer, holding her tightly. "No matter what happens, no matter if Dick Dick Buckthorn fixes this insanity or not, no matter if... no matter if you're going to have a child or not, I am not going anywhere. I love you."

She smiled at him through her tears, then leaned in for a kiss. It had been a long time since they'd kissed. It felt as electric and brilliant as their very first.

"Let's go for a walk," he said, smiling at her.

Tracey and Timmy White had not heard about the order to stay indoors, so they left their house in the dull

338

light of early evening, walking close, holding hands, saying very little, just feeling the warmth of each other's presence.

*

As the night darkened, Helen Keller walked through the forest with a blanket in her arms. She stopped now and then to pluck something from the ground and place it in that blanket. In time she looked as though she was cradling a baby. She was singing as she worked, filling the forest with a lovely melody, making all the birds jealous. And she even rocked back and forth now and then, just as if she was trying to lull a baby to sleep. But it was no child in that blanket, no sir. They were wee folk 'shrooms.

You'd better get a field guide for this: those 'shrooms looked like collared earthstars.

15

Dick Dick roared up to the front gate of his house and came to a violent stop, dust rising around him in a gray cloud. He idled there for a moment with the constant rough twitching of the engine rocking him like a baby. He stared up the long drive to the big house in the woods, his eyes distant, his mouth open just a sliver, completely silent.

Willy Billy watched his brother for those few moments, patiently biding his time, letting this little scene play out. After five minutes, though, he had to speak:

"Are you rethinking this madness?" he asked.

Dick Dick looked at him as if he had forgotten he was there. "What? No, no, of course not."

"You looked like you were spacing out on me."

"I was just thinking…" He stared up to his big house again.

"Rethinking the Betty thing...?"

"No... no, I was wondering if it would be better to buy a bigger house or add on to this one. You know, after all this." He shifted in his seat and played with his chin thoughtfully. "Do you think this place looks like the sort of home the savior of a town should have? Or does it look too... average?"

Willy Billy frowned, then his mouth stretched into an ugly grin and he laughed. "Oh Dick Dick, you never stop, do you?"

Dick Dick looked at his brother. "Stop? What do you mean, stop? A person stops and a person doesn't get anywhere."

Willy Billy reached across the massive seat and slapped Dick Dick on the leg. "Goddamnit, that's right! That is exactly right! Now let's go find that woman of yours."

"Uh-huh," Dick Dick said, shaking his head. "First things first."

Willy Billy nodded pleasantly. He was enjoying this, he really was. Perhaps too much.

"That's right," he said. "First things first. Show me this plane of yours, big brother."

Dick Dick threw the SUV into gear and pulled away from his house, big tires smoking and screaming across the smooth black asphalt.

*

So it was officially evening in Burghville, although there was still plenty of light left in the sky to coat the town a soft purple.

Actually, to be truthful, there was more than just purple in this smoggy soft-focus light, there was orange and yellow and even an odd and subtle form of green that seemed to ricochet off of each leaf on every tree. Had there been grass on the Burghville lawns it would have ricocheted off of each blade as well, but alas the yards were still mostly dirt.

So afternoon was over, evening was upon the town. There was enough light left for backyard baseball games, swims in the community pool, or roller-skating on

340

the side streets, but of course there was no one out to do such things. Aside from the oblivious or the rebels, everyone else was safe inside. Among the oblivious were Tracey and Timmy White and, lost in her own world of thought, a solitary Candy Cleaver.

And a few wee folk, of course. Most of the wee folk were nowhere to be seen, but there were a few out and about. Even in a town suddenly quiet and empty, there was mischief to be found.

Poor Burghville. Every town looks pathetic and sad when its life is suddenly suspended. Even our big cities would look childlike and fragile should their citizens suddenly hole themselves up inside apartments and condos. But Burghville seemed sad to a greater degree, as if it had just become a ghost-town through no fault of its own.

And what made Burghville seem sadder was the feeling, nearly palpable, that something, somewhere, was brewing. Plans and schemes give towns and cities a cheerless aura. Look at occupied Paris. Consider Washington, D.C.

"Something is afoot," one wee folk said to another as they both stood sniffing the air in that hazy twilight.

"Aye," was the response.

"And do we know what we're going to do about it?"

A pause while a pipe was lit and its fresh smoke inhaled and relished. Then: "Aye, we do. We do indeed. Nothing."

"Nothing?"

"Aye. Except maybe have a party." An exhalation of sweet smoke joined the night air.

"What sort of party?"

"A good party."

"A *good* party?"

"Aye. Is there any other kind?"

*

Another of the oblivious: Lee Preston, formerly the Father of the St. Michael's Catholic Church. He was jogging up the streets, looking everywhere for the girl, Helen Keller. He found nothing but the abandoned town.

341

He barely noticed the quiet. It registered on him, he being a sensitive soul, but he had other concerns on his mind. He looked up and down every street, finally made his way over to the house where he had seen her dancing naked. The house was dark and lonely, looking a bit too haunted for his taste. He stood there for a time staring up to that second-story window where she had once been framed. He wasn't thinking much by this time, he was going on intuition and emotion, a man charged up on the electricity of feeling, the thrill of an epiphany, the rush of a turning point. And there was no need to think: what good was thinking anyway? Lee Preston was looking for somebody that had, for whatever reason, touched his heart, and as any cardiologist could tell you, the brain only gets in the way of the heart's business.

But still, finding this house quiet, as he had known he would, he felt disheartened. The girl was not often seen around town in the summers. Maybe she left until Autumn came. Maybe she was gone for good this time. Maybe he would never see her again.

He sighed, and was turning from the house when a voice called out:

"Looking for somebody?"

He turned and saw a Good Person on the sidewalk. This little man was staring up at him with a friendly, crooked smile peeking out from behind a little gray beard.

"No," Lee said, then he frowned. "Actually, yes. I mean, this is a long shot, but... I'm looking for—"

"Aye," the little man said, nodding pleasantly. "Aye, I know, I know. You be looking for Helen Keller, I reckon."

Lee began to frown, then stopped himself. Was it really so odd, given the strangeness of this summer, that this little man should know who he was looking for?

"Yes," he said. "Do you know where she is?"

The little man's eyes were barely slits as he smiled. "Ah," he said, "she is a lovely sight, that girl."

"Do you know—"

"And so gentle a soul, so pure a heart."

"Do you know—"

"So fair of mind and—"

Another voice called out from some hidden place in the shadows: "Tell him where she is, you old fool!"

Much giggling accompanied this voice, but Lee could see no one else. He thought fleetingly, as Helen had earlier, of Dorothy's first moments in Munchkin Land.

The little man laughed himself and pointed off behind the house. Lee looked there and saw the woods, turning darker by the minute in the fading light.

"She's a ten-minute walk that way," the little man said. "Three if you run."

Lee thanked the little man and then started to run for those woods, following the direction laid out by that tiny little finger... following, as well, the growing swell of emotion that was enveloping his heart.

"Now who called me an old fool!" the little man said once Lee was gone, turning to stare into the shadows.

More giggles floated musically into the evening air.

*

By now it should be understood that Sheriff Sherman was quite mad... if not ragingly insane, at least further beyond the line that separates sanity from craziness than most of us will ever get. This madness had a direct cause, too: his inability to further the Plan, his inability to lead the Burghville Police Department into the realm of complete security. His inability to make an Ultra Safe Community. And, of course, behind all such enterprises there is an ego trip underway. Sheriff Sherman was mad because he knew he would never be recognized for what he truly was, for what he knew he had it in him to be: he would never be a hero. He would forever be a second-class citizen, standing in line with everyone behind the likes of Dick Dick Buckthorn.

Staring over to the violently shaking bushes next to the hanger he thought: if only there was a way to topple that son of a bitch. If only....

He was biting his lower lip, his left hand trembling over the door-latch of his cruiser, his legs itching to step from the car and walk over to the scene that was playing out in those bushes, when something caught his eye. He

343

turned his head, expecting to see a deer or some other animal. Instead, his eyes fell on the figure of a perfectly naked woman.

She was coming down the old road that ran in front of the airport, buck naked save for a pair of white tennis-shoes. Longish hair fell to her shoulders and made rippling waves around her face as she walked. Her walk was bouncy, jubilant, full of energy.

"I'll be damned," Sheriff Sherman said.

He recognized her right away: it was Betty Buckthorn. And, like a lot of men in town who had undressed her with their eyes, he was not surprised to see that body of hers. It was exactly as he had pictured it, firm breasts with nipples up front like the hood ornaments of some beautiful foreign car, tight yet soft stomach, legs muscular but not manly. And yes, standing out quite clearly from the lightly-tanned skin of her body like a finely designed architectural detail, the dark patch of her pubic hair.

Sheriff Sherman had thought there would be less hair there. For some reason he had always pictured one of those little Hitler-mustache things all the strippers had. But no, that bush was as thick and healthy as anything found in Henrietta Pratt's yard. No invasive species. No pests. Wild and natural.

"I'll be damned," he said again.

She came down the street defiantly, as if oblivious of her nudity. Her head was up, her eyes wide in the weak evening light. She walked like one of those power-walkers, quick and focused and unconcerned with the world around her.

The sheriff's mouth was open, gaping like the mouth of an idiot. He watched her come and wondered when she would see the grill of his car. He wondered if she would freak out when she did.

She didn't. When she finally turned her head and saw his car, partially hidden by bushes and trees, she only smiled. Smiled, just like she wasn't naked as a jay-bird! He didn't know if she could see him or not, but he returned that smile. He even lifted a hand and waived.

And then, just as she was passing not fifty yards away, giving him a great view of first her smooth round

344

muscular thighs and then the even smoother rounder landscape of her flexing rear, he suddenly reached for the door handle and quickly tried to scramble out of the car. He managed to get one foot out and onto the ground before he realized he was tangled in the seat belt. He swore, fell back into his seat, fumbled with the belt, and then climbed out again.

He ran out to the road and looked to where she had gone.

There she was, walking just as proudly and defiantly and energetically as before, headed for the path that led to the hanger. Her ass moved hypnotically, an upside-down heart beating out a gentle rhythm. He stood there in the street and stared after it. There is nothing like the sight of an ass in the hazy light of early evening.

He opened his mouth to call out to her, and then he saw headlights. They were approaching Betty Buckthorn, throwing her body into silhouette, only the very edges of her curves lit with yellow light, as if she were a drawing outlined in gold.

Sheriff Sherman frowned. Betty Buckthorn was leaving the road for that walkway and he saw her silhouette from the side, all quick-stepping legs and bouncy breasts.

He opened his mouth and again nothing came out. She was headed for the hanger, where all that action was taking place.

Once more he tried to call out, but what came forth was a weak gurgle. He watched her as she disappeared around the front corner of the hanger and even when she was gone from view continued to stare in that direction, as if waiting for the corner to move. His head swam with buzzing, meaningless thoughts.

Then he remembered the approaching headlights and looked back at the road.

But it was too late.

*

Dick Dick roared back through Burghville, saying nothing as he steered his massive hulk of an auto down the little streets of town. He smiled as he saw how quiet and empty the place looked. The message had gotten through.

Willy Billy had his seat all the way back and was lying there with a peaceful, content look on his face. His hands were folded over his stomach. He stared at Burghville and sighed.

"Nice town," he said, mostly to himself. "A nice place to live. Pure America. Really, this is the way all of America should be." He looked over at his brother. "You must agree, big brother. Right?"

Dick Dick looked back. "What?"

Willy Billy smiled. "Nothing. How about some music?" He reached over and flicked on the stereo. Quasi-classical melodies blared out at him, vaguely Wagnerian. He winced and turned the volume down. "Jesus H. Christ, Dick Dick! What happened to you? Where's the country?"

Silently, Dick Dick reached over and hit a button. A CD was pooped out of a little slit, and then modern country came purring out of the speakers, lifeless and without soul.

Willy Billy pulled out the CD and examined the title.

"*Selected Music from Movies Where Good Guys Kill Evildoers,*" he read aloud. "That's a hell of a title."

And Dick Dick said: "Pure American music. That stuff should be pumped into every school. The kids should hum it each morning after the Pledge of Allegiance."

Willy Billy didn't hear this: he was singing along to the country crap, pledging his own allegiance to Texas and Alabama and Tennessee, states he had never been to.

Dick Dick steered towards the Burghville airport.

*

Buckthorn Industries: and here a very agitated and disillusioned Polly Anderson was walking up and down the various carpeted hallways, her mind a maelstrom of thought and emotion. The things she had read about in those papers in Dick Dick's office made her feel sick, literally nauseous. She wandered about inside the compound that was Buckthorn Industries and wondered about the choices she had made and the way she had been living her life. Again, this is not the story of Polly Anderson's life-changing epiphany, and it is certainly not

346

the story of how from that day on she began to live her life in complete contradiction to the way she had been living it previously, and this is most definitely not the story of how she went on to form one of the strongest and most relevant radical political groups in history, and nor is it the tale of how she first went around the world on what she called a "tour of awakening" and ended up saving a rare and mysterious species of marsupial from extinction. No, this is a much simpler story, and all that we need to concern ourselves with is how this Polly Anderson was suddenly awake to the reality that the men she had previously objectified and worshiped were really just fucking assholes who would gladly sell this world (the only one we've got) in exchange for a quick buck. And, actually, all we *really* need to concern ourselves with is the fact that she was walking around Buckthorn Industries feeling angry and abused and violated, that she was searching for something to *do* to make up for those feelings. She was searching for revenge, or something like it.

It wasn't after too much of this ambling around in anger that she left the main office building and entered, via a glass-enclosed skyway, the next building over. This building had a strong chemical smell, but it was pleasant and fruity and reminded her of certain household cleaners. The walls were different than in the office building, without decoration or even, it seemed, decent paint: these walls looked as if they had been coated only with gray primer. And there were more hallways, a seemingly endless labyrinth of hallways in which most of the doors were closed and locked. The whole place lacked aesthetics or frills, nothing even minutely fancy to brighten the atmosphere.

This, she thought as she walked briskly down these halls, was where they did all their dirty deeds. This was where they created the poisons that were killing the world.

Fucking assholes.

She went down a flight of stairs and then down another hallway. Her fists were clenched and she was wondering how to get out of this town.

"Burghville," she said through clenched teeth. "I hope I never see it again ...." She was already dreaming of Africa.

347

She rounded a corner and entered a wider hallway, and there she saw three little men standing by an open door. When they saw her they gasped and slipped through that door, as quick and nervous as startled rabbits.

"What the hell—?" she said. She stopped and thought a moment. The wee folk gave her the creeps, but not as much as Dick Dick and all those other men. And maybe, she thought, maybe there was a way to use them to mess with the evil that was Buckthorn Industries. In fact, maybe there was *also* a way to use them to get out of town. It was the little people, after all, who were living in her car and preventing her from leaving. Maybe that strange girl in the café had been right, maybe she only had to ask them to leave the car and they would.

She ran down the hall to the room they had entered. To her surprise, they were still there, all three of them standing and gazing up into yet another room, this one enclosed within the main room but having walls made of glass. They were staring with awe at the contents of this glass room, and they never looked at her as she came up next to them.

She too was staring with awe at what stood before her.

It was what certain Buckthorn Industry staffers liked to call the Farm.

*

Five-hundred thousand roaches, a million ants, hundreds of mice and rats and mosquitoes and raccoons and assorted other critters all resting in shelf-like cages and tanks.

Frightening to witness? Maybe. Ready to be used against those who had once tyrannized and mistreated them?

Absolutely.

*

Polly Anderson had hung out with enough CEOs to know how to make a deal: in exchange for helping the wee folk with their newly-hatched plan, which they said

348

would put a damper on the town's own plan of wee folk eradication (as well as teach Dick Dick a lesson and, besides, what the hell, be a lot of fun), she would get her car back from the slacking little fuckers who occupied it. Then she could leave Burghville and never look back. Was it a deal?

"Aye," said the wee folk. They even shook hands on it.

And then they got down to work.

*

The woods had their own light, separate from the fading light of evening. This woodsy light was opaque yet expansive, filling all the forest nooks and crannies with its gray-orange glow. There wasn't a crotch in any tree that wasn't touched by this light, and not an owl or deer remained out of its reach.

And still, the former Father, Lee Preston, was having a devil of a time walking. He had always, of course, been a good walker, but he had never done much hiking, which was too bad, since he had had a love of the woods and all things natural since he was a child.

He inhaled the spice of the forest, that smell of earth and leaves and dead sticks and mammals stirring in burrows. He took that smell into his lungs and held it as one holds in pot smoke, then released it with a sigh.

He did not, however, stop walking. He continued as quickly as he could through the trees, headed in the direction the little man had pointed towards. Headed, he hoped, for the girl.

Fallen branches and unexpected drops in the ground stood in his way. After only a few minutes inside the woods he was short of breath and his legs were aching. He walked until he couldn't take it anymore and then he stopped and looked up to the canopy. Through the branches he could see a faint sky, pale blue with a bright star in its center. He stood staring up at the sight, remembering the old poem: Star-light, star-bright, first star I see tonight, I wish I may, I wish I might, have the wish I wish—

"It's not a star."

349

He jumped and looked to his right, suddenly defensive, fists clenched.

It was Helen Keller.

He opened his mouth to speak but added only silence to the quiet woods.

"It's not a star," she said again, with a tone of patience and peacefulness, as if she were teaching a lesson to a small child. "It's a planet."

He nodded, then frowned. "How do you know?" His voice felt and sounded as dry as an old man's.

She simply smiled and shifted her head in such a way as to make her hair slip back from her temples and fall like lace over her ear. In this strange forest light she seemed eerily radiant, like either a fairy or a specter. At that moment he didn't care which, he would take them both. Just please don't let her be a glowing figment of his imagination, a Fatima Virgin, a bit of underdone potato. Just let her be real.

"Planets don't twinkle," she said. Then she smiled again and turned to walk off.

He watched her for a moment, saw she was carrying a blanket in which was wrapped either one large object or many smaller ones. Whatever it was, it wasn't heavy: she did not seem to be having any trouble at all as she carried the thing, sidestepping branches and bushes effortlessly. In fact, she moved with the grace of a whitetail, something that was meant to live in the forest, something that was at home here. Something that was *natural*.

"Wait!" he called out to her, too loudly. A barred owl answered him with a *Who cooks for you*? He looked around sheepishly, then walked to the girl.

She turned and watched him approach. She said nothing and he could not read anything in her face.

He came up to her and smiled. "I..." he began, then could think of nothing else to say. What did he have to say to her, anyway? What in the world could he possibly say that would make any sense amidst all this craziness?

"I'm no longer a priest," he said.

She was silent.

He reached up and removed his collar, tossed it to the ground. It seemed, at that moment, to be a crude

350

symbolic gesture, but he had actually been meaning to remove the thing for a while now.

"I'm no longer a priest," he said again. "One of those little men helped me... helped me change." It sounded lame to him, but he couldn't stop his mouth from forming the words.

She nodded a little, then looked at the ground where the collar lay.

"Pick that up," she said. "I don't tolerate litterbugs."

He bent and retrieved the collar, stuffing it into a pocket.

She stared into his face for a long while, what seemed like minutes, and at first he didn't mind keeping eye contact with her. It had been a while, but he thought that that was how you showed interest in someone... though what did he know, he'd been eighteen the last time he dated. Still, he enjoyed the way her eyes made him shiver and tremble... but then he began to feel naked and exposed, as if she were seeing parts of himself that he wanted to keep hidden. Secret parts. Private parts, though not *those* private parts. He felt like she was *reading* him.

And of course, she was.

"It's way too soon," she said at last, straightening herself so she was standing tall and shifting the load in her arms.

He frowned. "Too soon for what?"

"Too soon for me to love anyone again. Too soon for you to know what you really want."

He swallowed. Could she know?

"And besides," she said, "I don't even know you. How do I even know you're worthy of being loved? Good lord, how do I even know you're worthy of loving, of having such a beautiful feeling?"

He shook his head. "I... I don't know."

"That's right. You don't know. And you know what else you don't know?" Her words might seem cold but she spoke with such a warm voice that he felt like a child being spoken to by his mother, that he was five again and had cut his knee in the backyard. Her voice cooed and sang delightfully. It was a quiet voice and yet there was resonance to it as well. It was, in fact, just exactly like the voice of that barred owl.

She moved closer to him, never moving her eyes from his.

"There's so much you don't know," she said. "This world is full of mysteries and secrets and answers and truths. Like this truth: there are many gods, Mr. I'm-No-Longer-A-Priest. And maybe some of them are all around you right at this very moment."

He looked around, saw nothing but trees and forest floor.

"Oh, you'll see them soon enough," she said, as if reading his mind. "You'll see them in time. *If*, that is, you allow yourself to see them. Then, and only then, will they allow themselves to be seen. Interesting how that works."

He nodded, feeling light-headed, almost drunk. Her voice was intoxicating, mesmerizing, beautiful.

"But you've got so much work to do first," she said. "You've got to open yourself to the possibilities this world offers. You've got to become wide-eyed. You've got to become innocent again. You've got to lose cynicism and see things like a child once more, as if everything was fresh and new. And you've got to clean up. A person should always start a new journey, whether to a new land or a new plane of existence, by bathing."

"Bathing?"

She smiled. The smile lit up the forest like a brilliant half moon lost below the trees.

"Cleanliness is next to godliness, you know," she said.

He just nodded.

*

She led him to the little clear stream where she had herself taken a bath just that morning. She told him to strip naked and climb into it and lie there, no matter how cold the water was, just lie there, do nothing but think and hear and feel.

"You do that," she said, "and maybe some good will come of you." Then she lifted the blanket and its load and moved off into the dark woods, leaving him there in the

352

quiet that was settling between the trees like a fog. The stream was a gray strip before him, and for a time he did nothing but stand there staring at it. Then that barred owl called again. Who cooks for you, who cooks for you all?

Not knowing what else to do but heed the girl's advice, he took his clothes off and headed for the water.

*

Tits and ass, thought Henrietta Pratt. It was a bland thought, at first. A sort of ho-hum thought, the type one has when one looks at one's pinkie finger and thinks *oh, a pinkie finger*. Such a bland attitude to the sight in front of her was the product of her overly-occupied mind. She had been thinking of how exactly a crop-dusting plane's payload mechanism worked, and wondering how her little prank would be viewed come the next morning, and had truthfully not been paying much attention to the unwinding road in front of her when those headlights suddenly washed over the smooth and round form of a naked woman. Of course she knew who the woman was, but before that name popped into her head there was only one phrase:

Tits and ass.

Yawn. The sight before her may as well have been a deer off in the ditch, or a raccoon scampering across the road. At that moment the sight of a naked woman in her headlights was as prosaic as the sight of her own face in a bathroom mirror. And then, of course, just a split second later there was another thought, this one in the form of a question:

What the hell....?

It was then that she realized who the woman was. Mrs. Betty Buckthorn, naked as the day she was born.

"Well I'll be..." she started to say as Mrs. Buckthorn stepped off the road and onto one of the airports walkways. Henrietta's eyes followed her for a moment and then, dumb-struck and open-mouthed, she looked back at the road just in time to see the rather more expansive (and thankfully clothed) form of Sheriff Sherman standing there.

Sheriff Sherman, whose own thought, at that moment, was just a nice and simple little:

353

Fuck!

And then Henrietta Pratt was hitting the brakes... but, as stated earlier, it was really too late.

*

"This would really make an interesting paper for a psychology class," Willy Billy Buckthorn observed as he sat there in his brother's SUV and stared out at the quiet streets of Burghville. He had just mentioned how amazed he was that Dick Dick's decree for everyone to stay inside had actually been followed. They saw no one as they cruised through town.

Dick Dick said nothing, just drove.

"You know," Willy Billy continued, "like a study of abnormal behavior on a mass level. Maybe something about mass delusions, shared hallucinations, mob insanity." He thought a moment. "Maybe something's in the water, that's all." He thought about this as he stared out his window. In time he started to look at his reflection, as such men will. There was nothing remarkable in that reflection, it was really the same face as his brother's, only on a much smaller scale... perhaps containing a bit more of their mother than Dick Dick's, but only a bit. The nose, perhaps. The softness of the cheeks.

"Mhmmmm..." Dick Dick moaned. It was the sort of moan one gives when one agrees with a statement.

Willy Billy looked over at his brother.

"Say something, bro?"

Dick Dick just stared ahead at the coming streets.

Willy Billy sighed again and slouched in his seat. It was a massive seat and there was an enormous amount of legroom but he was uncomfortable. There were just too many possibilities for positioning, and to those with a less creative mind, like Willy Billy, the choices were overwhelming to the point of discomfort. And either way, on a highway everything's a death trap. A suicide rap. We gotta get out while we're young.

"You know, maybe this has gone far enough," Willy Billy said, bringing his knees up to his chest. "All this talk of little people and crop-dusting the town... come on, Dick Dick. Enough's enough."

354

"Look!" Dick Dick said suddenly, pointing off to the right.

Willy Billy looked there but saw nothing.

"Yeah?"

Dick Dick slumped back in his seat. "Missed it. For fuck's sake, Will, keep your eyes open. They're hard enough to see as it is sometimes, but at night...."

"That's the other thing: isn't it a little unsafe to fly a plane that low at night, over a town nonetheless? What about wires, and trees, and tall houses?"

"Isn't Betty worth it?"

"I..." Willy Billy decided not to answer that question. He was thinking the answer was no, that no woman was worth dying for, that he didn't think it was a good thing to risk his life for a piece of tail, but, and this is a big but, he was also quite aware of something else: that for years, ever since he had first met her, a good two years before she had married Dick Dick, he had been in love with Betty. It was a secret only he himself knew, and he thought he had done a good job of hiding it so far, even in the light of this odd deal he and his brother had made. After all, Dick Dick thought this was all about sex, and it was, of course, but Willy Billy had more than just a sexual interest in Betty Buckthorn. He knew they would never have a relationship, that she would never love him back, that he would never get to hold her on cold nights, that he would never get to confide in her as they lay in bed and talked in whispers, that he would never wake each morning and look into her beautiful face... and knowing this he also knew that sex, even the cheap sort this was bound to be, was the closest he would ever get. It was a chance of a lifetime. They would never be in love, but they could be, for this precious moment, together.

It was also a chance to possess, if only for a brief moment, a bit of his brother's life. Dick Dick had it all, and Willy Billy wouldn't have minded seeing what that was like....

"Another one!" Dick Dick screamed, pointing off to another dark yard.

Willy Billy looked, but again saw nothing.

"Dagnabbit, keep your eyes open," Dick Dick said. "You're missing them."

"I'll try," Willy said. "I'll try."

Dick Dick stepped on the gas and prodded the giant car forward.

*

Another automobile, not a giant, came slamming into Sheriff Sherman. Or at least that was how it seemed to him, there in the ever-darkening evening. In reality he was only thwacked by the back bumper as the little truck went into a screeching tailspin. Granted, it was no love-pat he felt on his thigh, but nor was it in any way a fatal blow. Still, the impact sent him tumbling across the road and knocked the wind out of him, so that when he finally came to a stop he simply lay there motionless, a fat lump on country blacktop.

The little truck came to a stop at about the same moment, amidst a cloud of blue smoke and the smell of burnt rubber. The sound of the accident resonated for a while in the quiet, and then there really was silence... eerie and complete, not a creature stirring, insect or mammal or bird.

In time, though, Henrietta Pratt climbed out of the truck. She stood there a moment before walking, somewhat casually, over to the lump that was Sheriff Sherman.

She prodded him with one foot. He moaned and stirred a little.

"Oh my Lord!" a voice said behind her.

Henrietta turned and saw Carol Slugg approaching. She was being followed by several other figures, all apparently women and all apparently rising from the darkness like visions or ghosts.

"Where did *you* come from?" Henrietta asked.

Carol glared at her. "This man's hurt!"

Sheriff Sherman moaned again and started to sit up.

"I barely touched him," Henrietta Pratt said.

Carol bent down to prevent the sheriff from moving, placing her hands on his shoulders. "You shouldn't move," she said. "If it's your back you could injure yourself further, and if, heaven forbid, these are your

356

last moments, then you should just relax and rest and try to pray. I'll pray with you: Heavenly Father, please bless us at this—"

"Oh shut the fuck up, already," said another, younger voice. It was the Dissenter, who was coming up behind the other women.

"Where are you people coming from?" Henrietta asked.

The Dissenter looked at her. "We're out here doing the same thing you're doing."

"What are you talking about?"

"I saw the back of your truck. Planning a little Johnny Appleseed thing for Burghville?"

"I don't know what—"

The sheriff moaned again.

"You need to pray," Carol said to him, and then she looked up at the Dissenter. "And you need to watch your language. When the angels come to take this man they'll hear you and you'll be shamed."

"Whatever."

Henrietta's eyes had adjusted to the evening now and she could see that both of these women had dirt and bruises all over their faces. A thin line of blood ran from the younger woman's nose, and Carol Slugg's eyes were black and puffy. From their hair hung branches and leaves, and their clothes were torn.

"Oh my god," she said, "did I hit you too?" She felt sick.

"No," Carol said, annoyed. "Mind your own business."

"This woman saved you," the Dissenter said. "I was about to take you out."

"Unlikely. Your ass was about to receive a righteous whipping."

"You wanna finish it?" The younger woman clenched her fists and stood rigid, battle-ready.

Carol Slugg started to stand. The other women, so far quiet, all emitted a group gasp and took steps backward.

Sheriff Sherman moaned again and managed to sit up. Carol tried to reach out to push him back down and he grabbed her wrist and twisted it until she screeched.

"Ow!"

Still holding her wrist like this, Sheriff Sherman slowly got to his feet. He looked tired and beat-up, but there were no apparent major mechanical injuries to his body. He took in a few deep breaths, still restraining Carol, until his breathing was fluid and rhythmic.

"Everyone settle down," he finally said, looking at the women around him. "Just relax and be calm. And please, for the love of Christ, tell me what the fuck is going on here."

No one spoke.

"Ahh," he said, "silence is always the giveaway. That means *something* is going on here, and it's probably not legal. No one wants to talk?"

No one did.

He looked at Carol Slugg. "I take it that was you over in those bushes. What are you up to?"

She thought a moment, then looked at him, holding her chin high with pride. "The old fight," she said.

"Yeah?"

"Between good and evil."

The Dissenter laughed.

Sheriff Sherman turned his attention to her. "Anything to add?"

"Yes: you should lock that woman up, she's a threat to society. She's insane and delusional and we'd all be better off if she was away."

"Yes, you'd like that," Carol said. "Then you and your Satan-worshiping heathen friends can rule the world. Well, I don't think so."

"All right," Sheriff Sherman said. "You're all giving me a headache." He closed his eyes and swayed a moment, holding himself up by leaning on Carol Slugg. After a time he looked at the crowd of women. He stared at each of them, taking his time to gaze into their faces. Everyone was silent, a few even averted their eyes guiltily when he looked at them. When his eyes fell at last on Carol Slugg he stepped slowly away from her, his hand poised over his holstered pistol.

"You," he said to her. "Twenty paces."

She frowned. "What?"

"Twenty paces," he said again.

"What on Earth are you—"

He turned and started to walk slowly down the road, counting off each step.

The women all looked at each other, eyes confused, mouths in perfect O's.

"—seven, eight, nine, ten—" the sheriff counted, his back to them.

More confused looks among the women. What he was doing was not something they thought they'd ever see, and although they had each indeed heard and seen worse things in this life, they also never expected to see such a simple little display of absurdity. Wee folk are one thing, but a Sheriff counting off paces as a prologue to a duel? This was the twenty-first century, lawmen no longer acted like Old West barbarians. Right?

"—thirteen, fourteen, fifteen—"

Everyone looked at Carol Slugg. Carol Slugg looked at everyone.

"—seventeen, eighteen—"

Like frightened gazelles, the women scattered.

*

Helen knelt at the edge of the woods, hidden in the thick shadows that dwelled there. Her eyes had long since adjusted to this lack of light, and indeed she had always seemed uniquely adapted to nocturnal wanderings. It made sense, really: she had her other "sight" to rely on, and could afford to be without the full capacity of her eyes. Ever since she was a young girl she had loved to wander about in the darkness. While other children were afraid of the dark she embraced it. There was nothing there at night, she knew, that was not there during the day.

However, she had never seen anything like *this* during the day: Sheriff Sherman pacing off for a duel while women scattered around him, the wacko Carol Slugg among them. It was a comical scene, but she knew better than to laugh and give herself away. If her Sight was giving her anything right now it was the realization that Sheriff Sherman had gone mad. She could read his mind but the only thoughts she was getting were a jumble of buzzing and humming sounds, like cicadas and crickets and live electrical wires. Occasionally the odd name or two

359

would surface, but the only one she recognized was that of Dick Dick Buckthorn. No matter. The sheriff was nuts. Crazy. Loco. Off his rocker. Bananas. And when a person was crazy, and when that person was also *armed*, such details as names are rendered meaningless.

She sat there in the darkness, nearly buried in a bush, watching as the women flew into the woods. They were mostly older women, but even the younger ones did not seem to have the grace that such nightly forest-dwelling demanded. They lacked the proper refinement of action, and so when they entered the woods they made such a racket that Helen heard other creatures, those who made the forest their home, flittering off in a panic. Jesus, even deer did not make such noise. Breaking twigs, snapping branches, running into trees, entangling themselves in undergrowth. It was a mess.

Only a few of the women, Helen noticed, had made a break for the airport. She watched them with great concern, lest they interfere with her plans. She had been, after all, greatly concerned to find these people here, mucking about in the street near Dick Dick's plane. She had come late to the scene, so had missed the fight between Carol and the Dissenter and only heard the accident with Henrietta's truck, that screeching of tires on blacktop. When she first saw them she thought maybe she would have to revise her idea, that maybe her plan would not be carried out after all, that nothing the Highland bull had told her would come to pass. And then, of course, the Sheriff had started to pace off for his duel and now she was seeing a new opening, and she knew one had to take such openings when they were presented. So she lay low, watching as everyone ran off and keeping an eye on the women who had gone towards the airport. She was happy to see that the latter were running away from the hangar, out over the little landing strip and towards the wide open field that lay on the other side. They would not get in her way.

She looked back at the Sheriff just in time to see him finish his pacing and spin around, his gun out and aimed at the darkness. Amidst the humming drone of his mind flittered one word (*HERO*) and then the buzzing took over again, like cicadas gone mad by circumstance, as if they had hatched in the middle of a February snowstorm.

Buzzzzz!

The sheriff said something. Helen could not hear what it was. She stayed motionless, perhaps seventy yards from him, and watched as he looked around. After a few seconds had passed he heard the breaking of sticks and twigs echoing in the woods and he cocked his head in that direction.

More loud noise in the forest, the obvious sound of city folk moving through underbrush, tripping and stumbling and crashing as they went.

"Yippee!" the Sheriff shouted, jumping up and down, and then he turned and ran into the woods himself, gun at the ready.

He's going to kill someone, Helen thought, but then she realized that what he was most likely going to do was kill himself.

Should she do something? She thought about that for a moment, then decided that no, she should not. She had other concerns at the moment.

She waited until she was sure he was gone, enveloped by the dark forest, and then she hefted her blanket of goodies, left the woods, and crossed the old street, headed for the hangar.

*

It occurred to her, of course, that these people had also been meaning to sabotage Dick Dick's plane, for their own respective reasons (that evil little Carol Slugg was always up to something, none of it any good). And it also occurred to her that they may have already finished the job. But she suspected not. Helen thought that whatever had happened out here had gone like this: Carol Slugg and her followers had come here to carry out a plan and the Sheriff, crazy as an insomniac bed-bug, had interrupted them. Perhaps the sheriff had been stationed near the hangar on the orders of Dick Dick himself. Perhaps it was just that he *suspected* someone might try something and decided to station himself there in order to save the day. This would

361

explain the word (*HERO*) that had flashed through his mind. No matter. Either way, they were gone now.

And she could commence her work.

*

She found the water Carol Slugg and her acolytes had left on the outside of the hangar, in five-gallon jugs. She was quite surprised to find them there, needless to say, and yet she was never one to let things go to waste. She decided she would use it to make her mushroom-stew, which could then be easily poured into the ag-plane's reservoir. This was more than convenient, this was serendipity, since she had not realized until she found the water that she had had no plan of how she was going to get the mushrooms to disperse over the town. Some sort of god was watching over this operation, it seemed. So, happy and relieved, she brought the jugs into the hangar and began to mix her concoction. She never had the slightest inkling that the water had been blessed by Carol Slugg.

And she wouldn't have cared anyway.

*

A quiet summer evening in Burghville finds Helen Keller sabotaging Dick Dick Buckthorn's plane, an armed and insane Sheriff Sherman chasing after Henrietta Pratt and Carol Slugg, Polly Anderson hatching a plan with some wee folk back at Buckthorn Industries, a mysteriously naked Betty Buckthorn wandering the darkness, a former priest bathing in a cold stream in the middle of the woods, Tracey and Timmy White walking through Burghville's silent streets, a newly detoxed Candy Cleaver out there as well, bumbling chemists trying to load a truck with Wee Folk-icide at Buckthorn Industries, the good citizens of the town waiting in their homes for whatever was to come, and Dick Dick Buckthorn and his younger brother Willy Billy headed to the airport to commence what Dick Dick was calling the "liberation of Burghville."

It was a night, as they say, to remember.

362

16

Helen was finishing up her work when she heard the sound of an approaching engine. It was a loud engine, big and powerful, and she waited there in the shadowy hangar, hoping it would pass. When the vehicle it belonged to began to slow she swallowed and tried to think. Where to hide? She found a pile of old burlap tarps in a far corner, partially hidden behind three fifty-gallon barrels stinking of oil, and hid herself underneath them. The sound of the engine grew louder, then was quieted. She heard car doors and footsteps. She heard a laugh. Then came the booming voice of Dick Dick Buckthorn:

"—been building to this, goddamnit. This is serious!"

Someone else laughed.

Helen took a deep breath as the door to the hangar was opened and the lights were flicked on.

"There she is!" said Dick Dick. "What do you think?"

"Not too bad," the other person answered. "Should work. A two-cockpitter, huh? I could tell you stories about a Polynesian girl and a rear cockpit that would make your head spin, big brother." Pause. "You're sure you want to do this?"

"Of course, goddamnit, stop asking me. Are you in or not?"

Another pause. Then: "Of course, bro, of course. Let's have a look at this beast."

No speaking for a long time, nearly twenty minutes, just the sound of mechanical parts moving, flaps and rutters tested, perhaps a tire kicked, and then Dick Dick's voice: "Can you handle her?"

"Of course. She's old but everything seems to be in working order. Gas. Oil. Everything that's supposed to move does, everything that's not supposed to move doesn't." He laughed. "I could say the same thing about Betty."

"Look at this," Dick Dick said, ignoring him, "already filled and everything. God, I have some good workers, I tell you. Say jump and they jump. Absolutely wonderful. Might be some raises in this. No, no, stay back, this stuff is bad. Real bad."

"Jesus, are you sure you want to spread this shit around?"

"Just keep it away from you and everything will be all right. Come tomorrow you'll be part of the winning team, my brother. We'll be heroes. They'll build a statue of you in the park."

"If anyone lives...."

"They'll live, goddamnit. They'll live... and they'll be better off. Thanks to the innovative American spirit as personified by good old Buckthorn Industries."

"I'm worried...."

"Don't be. Have I ever failed you?"

The other person said something which Helen could not hear. There were a few moments of metallic-sounding noises, the sounds of someone fidgeting with equipment, of feet shuffling on the cement floor.

"You ready?"

Pause. "All right. Let's get this crap over with."

"Relax, Will. Just imagine you and Betty and your one night of love, and let that fill your mind when you're up there. Just don't forget to pull those levers."

"Maybe I should have said *two* nights. A weekend."

"Whatever you want, just get going."

"Ten-four, Bro."

Helen flinched at the sudden violent sound of the hangar's big door being opened. She pulled close to herself under the tarps and rubbed at her mouth. She tried to read the thoughts of these two men and could not. She had never been able to understand the mind's of such people. All she ever got from them was a squishy sound and a rotten feeling, as if the only thing they ever thought about was the movie *The Blob*. This was true for corporate executives and most politicians.

A few minutes later the plane started up, its propeller cutting at the night air with an increasing *Thwack-thwack* sound, until there was just a steady roar, the mating call of some prehistoric beast.

Over the noise she could hear Dick Dick booming out orders, but she could not tell what he was saying.

Then the plane was out of the hangar and she could hear it speeding off for the runway.

She stifled a smile. This wasn't funny, really... yet she could not help but recognize the absurdity of it all. Wee Folk Mushrooms on the Wing!

And a town about to be sprayed with Magic!

She stepped out from underneath the tarps and saw Dick Dick Buckthorn in the open doorway, his back to her, the lights of the plane shrinking off into the distance beyond him. If she could stay quiet she could slip over to the small side door and head back to town to watch everything unfold. That was her plan.

She took a few steps and Dick Dick turned around.

"What the—" he started to say. Then puzzlement (open mouth, raised eyes) turned to anger (furrowed brow, tight lips) and twisted his face into a familiar pissed-off-businessman look, the look on a lumber-baron's face when he's told of the damn hippies blocking his logging roads, the look on an Exxon captain's face when he spots the Greenpeace boat, the look on a President's face when he sees the polls or the pistol.

"What's up?" she asked politely.

"You," he said, and for a time that was all he said. They just stared at each other as somewhere out in the darkness the little plane caught air and took flight. There was the familiar sound of a roaring engine rising in pitch and leveling off as it left the earth.

365

Then Dick Dick said:

"What have you done?"

Helen Keller bit her bottom lip and shrugged cutely. She could be a smart-assed, sassy little coquette when she wanted to be, she really could, and right now she wanted to be.

"What have you done?" Dick Dick said again, his voice lower, rougher, more ominous, like the engine of his truck.

Helen Keller shrugged and smirked once more.

And then, right at that moment came the sound of gunfire.

*

When you're caught in an absurd situation you can react in one of two ways: with wide-eyed insanity or with defiant determination to remain logical and make the best of it. Here is how various people reacted to the insanity of being chased through the forest by their suddenly psycho Sheriff:

Henrietta Pratt decided it would be best to make a circular course back to the airport, in order to retrieve her truck, which she saw as her best chance to get to safety. There was nothing safe, she reasoned, in running through the woods in the middle of the night. This said, she had already run a good two hundred yards into the shadows and trees before deciding on this course of action. As a result, when she finally started to make that circular turn, doing it as wide as she could and stopping every now and then to listen for the Sheriff, she was way off course, and so her return route to the airport was in reality no such thing: she didn't know it, but she was headed ever further into the woods, away from both the airport and the town, moving in a roughly straight line for the rural outskirts of the Burghville Township, towards a lonely country road surrounded by great expanses of ripe cornfields. There would be a farm sitting only one-half of a mile from where she would come out, and she would go there and knock on their door and ask for a ride back to her truck. All around her would be an incredible blossoming of stars and planets, and she would look up at them as she walked to the farmhouse, she would look up and smile and ponder how small Man was, sitting here on his fragile little planet and mucking about with his tiny little problems. She would smile and feel both infinitesimal and rare, and it is there, on Route 9, that she will pass out of this story.

*

The Dissenter was a smart girl, everyone had always said so, and though she sometimes lacked focus, though she was sometimes too quick to make the acquaintance of people like Carol Slugg, she was in possession of a quick and alert mind. So it was she and she alone who knew what the best course of action would be in this situation: she crawled under the first deadfall tree she could find and waited, breath held, while the Sheriff, blinded by the dark woods like the rest of them, passed by, huffing and puffing and mumbling under his breath. When he was gone, the Dissenter simply stood and walked back to the road. She stood there for only a few minutes before she went to Henrietta Pratt's pickup and found the keys in the ignition. It was only a few seconds after *that* that she was driving back to Burghville, shaking her head the whole while.

*

One shouldn't assume that the Dissenter was the *only* person who hid and waited while Sheriff Sherman passed by... but unlike the Dissenter, the other six who did this had no conscious say in the matter. Being older women, not so nimble, not so agile, they simply tripped and fell as soon as they entered the woods, and so were lying down quite by accident when the Sheriff jogged past.

One of these women actually said: "For all this shit, I could have been a Holy Roller."

And another one, close by, had answered: "For all this shit, I could have been a Lutheran."

And a third said: "I can't find my teeth..."

Another simply spat out old leaves and dirt and calmly shook her head.

Carol Slugg actually took the proper direction and made her way straight for Burghville, coming out not too far from the house where Helen Keller made her winter home. She stood for a moment on the sidewalk, gathering her strength and recapturing her breath, and then she started to walk, head up defiantly, chin at a forty-five degree angle to the ground, mouth tight and set. All of this craziness was going to end, she decided. All of this evil was finally going to be destroyed. She would march up to the powers that be and demand to be taken seriously. It was time, she would say, that this town buckled up and marched straight, and she knew just the drummer to follow. He was called Jesus Christ, and his tune was the only tune there was. His song was the only song in town.

"Call *me* crazy," she said to herself, "when all I'm doing is speaking for the Lord..."

It was late, she knew, but there had to be *someone* around. She made a beeline for Burghville's heart:

Main Street.

*

Sheriff Sherman was also invoking the name of Carol Slugg's lord... sort of:

"Jesus Fucking Christ!"

See, he had just tripped on some fallen branches and shot himself in the foot. Not just once. Not just twice. No, a good and Biblical three times.

"Jesus Fucking Christ!" he screamed into the dark forest.

Like Lee Preston earlier, he was answered by the lonely and resonant call of an owl.

*

The streetlights of Burghville came on like winking eyes, seductive and mysterious, sending muddled yellow light to the sidewalks of town, tenderly waltzing the shadows away, spreading like a picnic blanket for moths.

*

Willy Billy Buckthorn saw those lights come on, one by one. He thought fleetingly of the birth of stars, and then his mind turned to more pressing concerns, like not flying into telephone wires or trees. It had been a little more than a week since he had last flown, but he had never flown a plane this old, and though all the parts seemed to be in order it was still a little intimidating to be sitting in this beast. He was kept on his toes, feeling a little bit like a novice as he fumbled with the controls. In some sense, he thought, this made planes like women: all the parts might be in the same place, but an older one is a little less forgiving. He directed the plane straight for town, using those lights for guides while at the same time studying the release-mechanism of the reservoir for defects and idiosyncrasies.

Part of him couldn't believe what he was doing.

Part of him was thinking of Betty Buckthorn.

Yet another part was thinking about his life and his brother and how things have a tendency to turn out crazier than you'd first imagined, crazier, in fact, than you could ever have envisioned.

He had no idea.

*

Dick Dick stared at Helen, both of them wide-eyed as the gunshots faded into distant echoes.

"What's going on out there?" he asked.

Helen assumed this was a rhetorical question and said nothing.

Dick Dick turned his head and gazed out at the night as the plane flew into the black sky. Then he looked back at her.

"What have you done?" he asked, angrily. "What did you do to my plane?"

She was silent.

Dick Dick glared at her. "I had a plan, dammit, and that plan was going to *save* this town."

Helen cocked her head and regarded him as she would a curious bit of goo found on the bottom of a boot.

369

She said nothing, just stared at him there in the harsh light of the hangar's bare bulbs. Around one of those bulbs a large insect was tapping against the ceiling, apparently trying to bash its head in. Out of frustration, anger? She couldn't tell.

"It's people like you who do all the harm," Dick Dick said. "You're always trying to get in the way of progress, always trying to stop the natural course of things, always trying to stop the inevitable. Can't you see you'll always fail?"

She kept staring at him.

"Stop looking at me like that!"

She didn't.

"Stop it, goddamnit! I demand your respect."

"You don't demand my respect, dickhead, you *earn* it."

"What a horrible mouth you have on you. Were you raised by animals?"

She frowned, then smiled. "As a matter of fact, yes. Something like that."

"It shows. You're a little beast. But you've failed here, girlie. Come tomorrow this plague will be over and everyone will know who the real heroes are, the real true Americans."

Helen smiled. Her smile was so much more radiant than his, almost drawing that insect away from its bulb.

"Come tomorrow," she said, "I think something much bigger than that will have happened."

He frowned, giving his face a hard, stony look, like the side of a bank or mortuary. "What does that mean?"

"That's for me to know," she said sassily, "and you to find out."

*

"What's that sound?" Tracey White asked. She and her husband had been walking arm in arm down one of Burghville's quiet and shadow-filled streets when they heard a distant buzzing, like that of a fly trapped in a garbage bag.

They stopped and listened.

370

"I don't know," Timmy White said. "A plane?"

They stood listening as the buzz became a steady roar.

"Definitely a plane," Timmy White said. They could see its lights between the trees and houses.

"Kind of low, isn't it?" Tracey asked.

Timmy nodded.

"I mean really," Tracey said, "isn't it kind of low?"

Timmy nodded again. "Yes... I'd say it is."

The plane was making a straight line towards the town, so low it looked as if it might collide with the top of an oak or elm.

"Do you think he's in trouble?" Tracey asked.

"I don't know. I don't know *what* the hell he's doing." A thoughtful pause. "Maybe it's those damn fairies...."

Tracey shook her head. "Jesus, I just hope no one gets hurt."

Timmy White nodded.

Within seconds the plane passed over them, roaring past the rooftops, cutting the night air with a violent growl. The Whites ducked instinctively.

"Jeepers!" Tracey said.

The plane's lights left streaks in the sky as it passed.

*

Carol Slugg, moving quickly down Burghville's streets, heard the approaching plane but gave it no real thought. She was thinking only of Main Street, the lights of which she could see just a few blocks ahead of her. She had no idea what time it was but she figured close to nine, nine-thirty. Late, but not too late. If she had to she would leave a note on the door of the Town Hall. *Seek ye the Lord*, she would write. *His path is the only true path.* And maybe: *Listen to those who speak His words, for they shall lead you into His light.* Maybe. Why beat around the bush? If this town had listened to her in the first place they wouldn't be in this mess. And what a mess it was: an insane Sheriff chasing decent Christian women through the woods. For crying out loud.

Only when the plane passed over her, so low she could feel the vibrations of its engine in her chest, did she think that this was it, that Dick Dick Buckthorn was about to spray the town with whatever it was he had invented. She frowned and bit her lip so hard she tasted blood.

It could have been Holy Water in that plane, she thought. If it hadn't been for that little bitch and her Satanic anger. If it hadn't been for Henrietta Pratt hitting Sheriff Sherman. If it hadn't been for the sheriff pulling a gun on them.

Just thinking of it all made her mad. She thought she could actually detect the presence of the Devil: there was a heaviness to the air, a dark and thick feeling, the viscous fog of Satan. Everyone was certainly acting as if they were possessed. The Lord works in mysterious ways, but so does the Devil. And she was certain that Satan was there that night, stronger than he had ever been. He was walking the streets of Burghville. He was almost in control.

But not for much longer. The righteous wrath of God would be on him soon.

She set that bloody lip firm and continued marching toward Main Street.

*

Someone else who at first gave the plane only passing attention was Candy Cleaver, who was still walking the sidewalks of town, thinking sad and beautiful thoughts. She was on the verge of a life-change, she felt certain of it. She felt the way she imagined a baby bird must feel just before it begins to peck itself free of its egg. She felt as if she was standing on the edge of a vast precipice, an enormous and beautiful abyss stretching before her for eternity... or if not eternity, at least for the rest of her life. She was at the beginning of something grand. She was about to put her past behind her. She was going to start anew.

When the plane approached and she saw its blinking lights over a chimney she only briefly thought that

372

maybe it had something to do with Buckthorn Industries. Then, as the plane gurgled past, she forgot about it and continued on. She was completely enveloped in this strange feeling of re-birth that was about her, this odd freshness that was starting to form.

She felt like a totally different Candy Cleaver, and yet she did not know how this Candy Cleaver would live the rest of her life, who she would be, what she might become.

All she would need was a push in the right direction, a little guidance to show her the way....

*

"You're in a lot of trouble," Dick Dick Buckthorn was saying.

Helen Keller half-frowned and half-smiled. "For what?"

"For whatever it is you've done here."

Now she fully smiled. "Oh. That. Relax, Dickie. Life is short. Laugh once in a while. Dance. Smile. Be free."

He started to speak, then shook his head and left the hangar. Helen waited a moment, then followed him.

He was walking back to his SUV. She wanted to call something else out to him, something pithy, something sassy, something clever, but she could think of nothing. Which was probably for the best, she knew. Anything she said would be sort of anti-climactic. Better to let him go back to town and face whatever was coming.

She wondered how he would be under the influence of the Wee Folk 'shrooms. Some people you just can't imagine intoxicated, either by various sundry substances or by life and love. She had meant it when she told him to smile once in a while. She knew very little about Dick Dick Buckthorn, but she certainly knew the type, and that type never seemed to enjoy life. Oh sure, they *said* they did, and they may have enjoyed the little slice of existence they'd set up for themselves, but what they had was not really life and what they were doing was not in any way actually joyous. Such men (the men of power, of course) seemed on the surface to be happier, to be satisfied, but life could never be found in big garish houses, or giant SUVs, or summer homes on once-pure lakes. That wasn't life, it was just living. Joy could never be found in such a lifestyle. A CEO could never be joyful. Nor a Pope. Or a President. Or a Senator. Or a manager. Anybody who could in any way be considered a *boss* could never be joyful. Joy demands three things: happiness, freedom, and an open mind.

No, they just *seemed* happy, and that was how they wanted it, really, that was how they wanted the common man to view them. The CEO, the President, the Senator, all the rich men everywhere, they all want people to view them as happy, they want to be *envied*, for that is how they keep the common man down. The common man, misled to believe that the rich man has what everyone should want, is therefore kept in that never-land between desire and powerlessness, unable to fulfill that desire. This is how the men of power want it. They *need* everyone to envy them. After all, once envy is out the door there is nothing left but hate.

And then there is revolution.

Anyway, Helen Keller spent a few moments reflecting on these old thoughts, and then she shrugged, smiled, and as Dick Dick started up his vehicle and tore off for town, she entered the woods and made her own way back to Burghville.

*

The old women in the woods, still in hiding from the Sheriff, saw Helen pass by and more than a few thought that she looked like some sort of forest goddess, a creature from those ancient myths that had been replaced by Christianity thousands of years ago. She moved through the forest like she belonged there, like it was her home, like she had been born and raised within the trees, cradled in deadfall branches and kept warm within hollow trunks, a pagan spirit moving with ease in the forest night, at one with the secrets it hid.

They all thought she looked beautiful.

*

374

From the plane Burghville looked rather innocent and naïve, a small town wishing it were larger, dreaming of progress and growth. Another sort of people would have made the town an entirely different entity. Rather than a little town wishing it were a city, Burghville could have been quaint and charming. Rather than always dreaming of expanding outward, it could have been focused on improving its interior. It could have been focused on improving the quality of life of its citizens, and not the quantity of their possessions.

But, this was how Burghville was, after all, this was the deck it had been dealt. Who could second guess the way things happen?

Certainly not Willy Billy Buckthorn, who was trying to focus on the job at hand. However, thoughts of the hand-job that might come continually flashed before his mind, threatening his focus. He rubbed at his eyes and tried to clear his brain. There was work to do here, he'd promised his brother.

The plane swooped low over Burghville and then arced around to the east and made another pass. Willy Billy was trying to decide on the best course, factoring in any wind that might be present. He thought it was blowing from the south, but he wasn't sure. To that end, the best thing to do would be to fly low and not give the stuff in the reservoir, whatever the hell it was, the chance to ineffectively disperse through the air.

It sounded like a plan. However, what the hell did he know, he was no farmer, he'd never done this sort of work before. Oh sure, once there had been a low fly-over at a company picnic in Florida, wherein Willy Billy had dropped pamphlets filled with dirty jokes onto his fellow workers, but that was not quite the same thing. Nor was it quite the same thing to fly past and pour the contents of a champagne bottle onto their heads (this was actually at an entirely different picnic in an entirely different state). No, he was the last person one would think suitable for this sort of thing, but he had taken it on. He had taken it on in order to *get* it on with Betty Buckthorn, his brother's wife. Good god, what is the world coming to?

He stared down at Burghville and wondered, not for the first time, what sort of madness had fallen over the place, what sort of insanity had led to this moment. He didn't think it was common for small towns to willfully dust themselves with dangerous chemicals, to hire pilots to crop-dust their streets with pesticides. What were these people drinking? Or smoking? Or sniffing? Maybe it was the result of Buckthorn Industries and its pollutants. That sort of made sense, Willy Billy thought. Chemicals had seeped into the ground, contaminated the water, and hence contaminated the minds of the Burghville public. These people were mad. Yes, it made sense, and actually it was quite funny. Insanity is like that, of course: funny as hell. These people had gone crazy because Dick Dick had polluted them. Polluted their minds, one could say, to borrow a favored phrase of the moral majority crowd. Yet, rather than porn or rock music, it was nice straight-talking conservative businessman Dick Dick Buckthorn who had done it. They had all gone mad at the hands of Progress and Industry. And now they were going to stop all of this with yet *more* poison, fire with fire, madness with madness.

"Little people," Willy Billy muttered to himself up there in his airplane. He shook his head and smiled. It wasn't a pleasant smile, more a sort of *Yeah, they're screwed* smile, a favorite of his lips. He took in a deep breath and gathered his thoughts.

He was reaching for the reservoir release-lever when it happened.

*

As she walked through the woods, Helen did not pass by the stream where the former Father, Lee Preston, sat naked and cold and happy.

In fact, she had forgotten all about him.

*

For his part, the former Father was not thinking of Helen Keller either. His thoughts were in the process of simplifying and uniting into three words that were innocent and universal and deep and full of meaning. These three words explained everything to him, and yet were full of mystery. They answered all his questions and opened the possibility for more, made him feel alive and in the moment and yet a part of all that had been and all that there ever would be. He would never tell anyone what those words were, but he would follow what they suggested to him for the rest of his life.

*

It wasn't the release-lever that Willy Billy Buckthorn's hand fell on: it was on something warm and soft and vaguely familiar. He frowned and looked down to his side, where the lever sat. There was enough light from the plane's dash to give a cool and adequate glow to that space, so that he could see what was sitting there.

It was a little man, bearded and smiling.

Willy Billy Buckthorn screamed.

*

The few people who were out on the streets of Burghville at that moment (among them Carol Slugg, Tracey and Timmy White, and Candy Cleaver) heard that plane suddenly down-shift into a high-pitched roar, and when they looked up they could see by its blinking wing lights that it had tilted to the right, as if the pilot had suddenly needed to avoid some obstacle. The plane's engine stayed at that high-roar for a moment, then the pitch dove in that dying-plane sound (familiar from all those World War II movies) as the plane veered earthward.

Tracey White covered her mouth with one hand, clutching at her husband with the other.

Candy Cleaver stared wide-eyed at the sight, visible to her over the Courthouse cupola.

Carol Slugg frowned, annoyed at the disturbance.

Above them, the plane continued its nose dive.

*

Willy Billy continued to scream as the plane knifed straight for the ground. He was frozen, completely

377

unable to move, completely unable to take his eyes from the little man on the floor beside him. That little man, for his part, never stopped smiling, even as he had to hold onto the seat to steady himself against the plane's drop. His long beard flew out from his face like a scarf.

"Ahhh!" Willy Billy screamed, his voice like a woman's.

The little man lost his balance and fell against the lever which Willy Billy had been reaching for just a few seconds earlier.

There was a screechy, grating sound and then, unseen by Willy Billy or the Good Person, a gray cloud came from the back of the plane, a misty thin strip like a falling Milky Way.

The little man looked at Willy Billy, all puckishly apologetic in his tiny little face.

And right at that moment the machine straightened out, roaring just twenty feet from Burghville as it pulled out of its fall and once again rose to the sky.

Willy Billy looked in amazement at the controls between his legs as the plane leveled and banked gently to the north, returning to pass over the town again. He was not touching those controls, was doing nothing whatsoever to maneuver the plane, had in fact been gripping his legs as the plane was falling, screaming all the time like a girl.

"What the—"

He looked over at the little man again, who winked and said:

"You believe in magic, don't ya?"

I'm going crazy, Willy Billy thought. Whatever's happened to these people has finally happened to me. I've gone insane. I've been poisoned by Dick Dick's pollution. I am now certifiably nutso. Well, if you can't beat 'em, might as well—

Which was when he heard the laughter behind him.

*

Helen returned to town just in time to see the gray cloud coming from the plane, hazy and nearly luminescent against the starry sky. She smiled to herself at the sight.

378

You really are a wicked little girl, she thought. Yes, yes, and oh yes. Wicked wicked wicked.

Which was probably true, and which was probably why she couldn't stop smiling.

Oh Sam, she thought, if only you could be here to see this. I never was one for art, but this here might be my greatest work, a piece of performance art, a bit of theatre, a living sculpture....

She started down the nearest street, headed for Main. After a little while she felt a cool wet mist settling on her face.

It just made her smile all the more.

*

Dick Dick came roaring into town and made immediately for Main Street. He kept poking his head out the window and squinting to the sky but could not see the plane. He wondered if his brother had broken his promise and made off for Canada. Willy Billy was impulsive like that sometimes, it wouldn't surprise him.

Then he caught sight of it, just as it pulled out of its fall.

"Holy shit!" Dick Dick screamed, not believing the sight. He stared open-mouthed as the plane rose to the sky and turned back towards town.

"What the hell has that little girl done?" he asked himself, idling in the middle of the street for a moment before slamming one giant foot down on the gas and squealing off for the center of town.

"What the hell has she *done*!"

He tried not to lose sight of the little plane as he sped towards Main Street.

*

Madness is an interesting thing. One could liken it to the shock of, say, a sudden and violent amputation. Once there was a young farm kid who lost both of his arms in a tractor accident. This kid managed to walk to his empty home, dial for help with a pencil held in his teeth, and then went and sat down in the bathtub so that he

379

wouldn't get the house too bloody. Even as massive amounts of blood spurted from his gnarled, nubby shoulders he was concerned that he not make too great a mess for his mother to clean up. During such a state of shock the human mind will accept just about anything as normal, even losing both arms. Madness is exactly the same. The crazy accept their craziness, since it is all they have, and all they know.

Which is just by way of saying that when Willy Billy Buckthorn heard that laughter behind him he first looked to the little man (the first insanity), then at the plane which was apparently flying itself (the second insanity) and then, quite casually, turned and looked to the plane's rear cockpit. There is no saying what his mind expected to see, no saying what that mind would have accepted as normal at that moment when all the craziness Dick Dick had been talking about was revealed to be true. There is no saying, either, what sight would have sent Willy Billy to the madhouse. Once the little man had been seen, and once that initial shock was over, Willy Billy easily fell into that realm of acceptance where nothing is shocking anymore. He might not have lost his arms, but he had lost whatever it is that separates reality from fantasy. In other words, he had become just like Burghville itself.

So when he turned to look into the rear cockpit he was not expecting anything, he was simply looking to see who, or what, was laughing.

It was Betty Buckthorn. Butt-naked and in complete hysterics.

*

The plane continued to spew its contents over the town below, that brew falling heavily through the air to coat windows and walls and cars and streets and trees, settling into chimneys and vents and lungs. It had a sweet, musky smell, that mist, sexual of course but also all-natural and pollen-like, fresh as dew and clear as rain. It shimmered like an ethereal sheet of ghostly fallen stars, just heavy enough to set the leaves of the town's elms and oaks and maples to shivering, making a soft and pleasing rustle like that of quaking aspen in a tiny breeze. Children stood at windows and screen doors and watched in amazement as it fell, mesmerized by its simple beauty, the flickering iridescence of it, transfixed by the pleasures inherent in such gentle movement. People sit and watch rivers for much the same reason, that unadulterated movement of pure force. The parents of those children watched as well, wondering what exactly this new sort of rain was bringing, and awed by its beauty. Shimmering, iridescent, shining, sparkling, crystal dew... these were words that did little to convey the loveliness and power of this particular mist, all-natural and therefore full of secret, ancient power, the power that lies mostly dormant in the Earth and yet which can be harnessed by those who care and know of it. This was an organic power, mighty and eternal.

And when it seeped into their chimneys and vents and into their nostrils, when all those watching took deep breaths and felt their lungs expand with possibility, when their eyes followed suit, when their minds blossomed like a nighttime sky, that was when the small little insular world that was Burghville opened and revealed, for however short a time, the magnificence and power and immensity of all that the Universe had to offer.

*

In other words, it didn't take long for the town to get high.

*

The plane trailed its misty contents until the last few drops fell over the fountain at the center of Main Street, and still it continued on, circling around and around the town, buzzing low one moment and then rising vulture-like the next. Willy Billy Buckthorn was facing forward now, mouth and eyes wide as the dark world of night raced towards him.

"I heard everything you guys said!" Betty Buckthorn was shouting, her fit of laughter over. "What sort of person do you think I am? You think I can be bought and sold? You think I'm some sort of possession?" Her voice was full of righteous anger, and it carried well

381

over the plane's engine. She continued to berate Willy
Billy, saying he was perverted, that people like he and his
brother ought to be locked up, and as she did he was
tortured physically by the plane dipping at the Courthouse
one moment and then shooting up to the moon the next.

"Oh god *no*!" he was screaming.

The little man next to him was listening intently to
Betty, and every now and then he'd look at Willy Billy and
give him a *tsk tsk*.

"I am nobody's property!" Betty Buckthorn
shouted to the black sky, defiant and daring. "I am my own
person! I am me!"

Willy Billy looked at the plane's suddenly
independent controls. He took hold of them but was unable
to make them do what he wanted, so, hating that feeling of
complete impotence, he let go again. It was crazy. It was
insane. It was—

"Magic," said the little man, who winked again
and made a subtle gesture with his right index finger,
sending the plane roaring earthward.

"Oh Jesus," Willy Billy said. He put his hands
over his face as the lights of Burghville once more came
rushing up to him.

*

Tracey and Timmy White stood watching the
plane as it continued to circle the air above the town. Soon
they felt the mist settling on their face.

"Fog?" Tracey asked.

Timmy White did not answer. Not at first. And
when he *did* answer, it was in response to an entirely
different question, one that may not even have been posed.

"Sure," he said. "I could see myself leaving this
place."

"What?"

He looked at her. "With you. I could see us
starting over in a new place, starting a family maybe…."

"Are you all right?" she asked.

"I will be," he said, smiling at her. "I will be. I'm
sure we *both* will be. I am absolutely positive that we will
be all right."

382

"What are..." she started to say, and then there was music. Yes, real and true music, rising around them. They looked into each other's eyes as they had once looked into each other's eyes all those years ago, back when all they had was youth and the future and possibility. Standing near the dusty light of a Burghville streetlight they drew close, slipped easily into each other's arms, and began to sway to that music, that music playing around them as if from a distance, gentle melodies and soft rhythms, music out of time and place, at once ancient and brand new, the way all music had been to them when they were younger, when the world revolved around them and all rules were broken by the new thing being born in their hearts.

"I will always be in love with you," he whispered to her.

"My heart will never let you go..." she answered.

They danced there in that light, with the evening and that strange shimmering mist settling around them like swaddling clothes, keeping them close, together, isolated, and the town forgotten in the shadows.

They danced to that music. That music was all they had.

*

As she made her way to Main Street, Helen Keller thought:

This place is going to shed its skin. Just like a snake.

It was a wonderful vision, and it made her smile more than she already was. Her eyes lit up as it came to her.

Burghville is going through a shed.

Indeed, it almost made her cry, it was such a beautiful image. But, not wishing to muddy her vision at this moment, all she allowed herself was one solitary tear.

*

Candy Cleaver took that misty air deep into her lungs, and, holding it there, she thought that she had never felt anything quite so clean and pure, so full of possibility.

383

Yes, there was that word again, possibility. And Candy thought that it had been so long since she had taken anything quite so wholesome into her body, something that had no preservatives or additives or imitation flavors or colors, something unadulterated and unmodified, something without artificial *anything*. This here, she thought, this strange misty air, might well meet strict Federal organic guidelines. At least, it sure felt that way to her, it was so clean and invigorating.

She stood for a time near the big open yard of the courthouse, that expanse of grass and elms where the children played football and the ice cream social was held on Labor Day. She stood there watching the intricate play of shadow and light in that space. There were lights alongside the courthouse, but they were of a weaker variety than the streetlights, so their glow was opaque and dull, like early morning sunlight seen through gauze. She stared in fascination at the way the shadows formed by the big elms met the dull light, like old friends who gather once a week for chess or tea. She had never realized it before, but there was such depth to the interplay of shadow and light. There was intricacy, complexity, sophistication. She imagined the conversations that might take place between those old friends would be likewise deep and sophisticated, full of philosophy and imagination.

Thinking this thought, which struck her as insanely beautiful, she realized also that she had wasted a good portion of her life, that too many days had been spent in pine-scented bliss, lemon-tainted intoxication. She had done nothing, had not lived but simply *existed*. This did not strike her as sad, though. To be sad about such a thing was to waste one's time. The past is just that, the past. It has *passed*. The thing to do was to learn from it. She knew she had taken something from that life and she knew that the thing to do was to *use* what she had taken, not only to better herself but also, yes she knew it now, also to better others, to maybe better this town, to perhaps if she could maybe, yes, why not, better the *world*. She knew now that—

And something deep inside of her tingled, as if her soul had fallen asleep as an arm or leg will. She thought it had something to do with this odd mist, and she was only partially right.

It was the mixing of that mist, and its all-natural wee-folken ingredient, with the tiniest, most minute trace elements of her past, some nearly infinitesimal drop of cleaner or polish, some microscopic touch of glue or white-out, of marker or paint that happened to be clinging to her molecules, or sticking to her DNA like gum on a shoe.

She felt the tingle and she placed a hand over her heart. Someone watching her would have thought she was saying the Pledge of Allegiance to the flag that floated from the courthouse flagpole. She kept her hand over her heart, rubbing ever so slightly, until the tingling moved on... not away, but on, slipping to the center of her chest and then spreading out over her whole body. She had another realization, this one quite strong:

Some day I will do this and it will *mean something*.

Mean what, she did not know. But she could picture herself, hand over her heart, thoughts of her past mixing with thoughts of her future into one delicious, delightful stew....

With pine-scented molecule meeting musky wee folk 'shroom, something was born in the heart and soul of Candice Anne Cleaver.

*

One by one the little punk teens who had stayed outside in defiance of the curfew, those little suburban hooligans who thought it was cool to hang out on street corners and yell things at passing cars (not the sign of potential greatness, of course, but everyone has a hobby), one by one they inhaled this odd misty air and took it deep into their lungs. Only instead of a tingling, for them there was a *heaviness*, like that of a heart attack. This heaviness swelled in their chests and then, when it was close to unbearable, it spread outward, not just *over* their entire bodies but away, moving from one person to another, so that one little punk felt as if he were holding up the other, as if that second punk would fall to the ground if the first punk should let go. And of course they could not let go,

385

could only stand there looking at each other, cigarettes dropping from slack lips, previously indifferent eyes widening in surprise and fear.

"Dude, I feel like... I don't know..." they said.

They stood in groups of five or six, staring at each other, arms out for balance, feeling as if they were tethered together on a sinking ship, as if they were the only things keeping each other from flying off the earth.

And when the powers of that mist finally took hold of their minds they looked at each other again, as if seeing each other for the first time.

Their eyes began to tear. They felt a sudden warmth in their chests and stomachs. Images of childhood came to them, forgotten things like lost toys and puppies and bruises kissed by mom. More than one of them remembered the first time they had laughed, others recalled feeling helpless as their parents fought behind a locked bedroom door. Still more remembered first days of school, first times in front of a blackboard, first fumbling attempts at riding a bike, grammas pulling the first loose teeth. All of these things had been forgotten to make room for rap lyrics and phone numbers and all the lies that must be tended in order to get through the teenage years alive. But these memories came now, rising against the misty air, clear as the images of a film, sending hearts pounding and eyes watering and lips quivering. They closed their eyes so they did not have to look at each other.

And then, quite suddenly, there came a new clarity of sight, a new understanding of who they were and where they had come from and where they were right now.

The mushrooms do not make one see things, remember, they *allow* one to see the truth, and the truth that these youths saw this evening was this:

That they mattered, that each and every one of them had a reason and a purpose, that every last one of them was *necessary*.

It was the first time they had ever been told that, by a parent or a priest or a teacher or a cop.

And a little mushroom shall lead them.

*

386

It was happening to their parents, too. And their younger siblings. It was happening to babies in cribs. It was happening to dogs and cats.

As the mist found its way into homes and lungs and minds it cleared away the *other* mist, the smoggier one that clouds most people's thoughts, the one they themselves hang to veil what they know to be true. They began to look at everything around them in a different way. They looked at a stereo and thought:

I worked over-time to buy that system, and I missed my daughter's play....

Suddenly relationships made more sense. Suddenly a husband understood that the reason he had married his wife was because she reminded him of his beloved aunt Martha. Suddenly a wife realized she had married her husband because she had feared she would never meet anyone else.

Suddenly a man thinks: I stay with her because I'm afraid I'll fail without her.

A woman thinks: I can't stay with him anymore, I just can't.

Another woman thinks: I know he cheats but it means nothing.

A man thinks: I will never hurt her again.

A child thinks: My parents did not want to have me.

Another: I am the reason my mother is not a professional singer.

A baby wakes from sleep to realize: I am the most fragile thing in the world.

Another thinks: Everybody loves me now but it will not always be so.

A husky-shepherd mix looks at its owners and thinks: There but for the grace of Dog go I....

Henrietta Pratt's cat Mr. Stinkels cocks his head skyward: Maybe I'm *not* the most important thing here....

*

It goes on and on:

I need to clean up my act and focus on my family. I will never see that man again, he is not going to leave his

387

wife. No one knows I am the most insecure person in the world. I go to work and try to do as little as possible all day. I have it in me to stalk and rape a woman. I will murder her father if he touches her again. I want so badly to love myself, but there is nothing there to love. I have to think I am the best person in the world because if I don't I'll remember all those things my father used to tell me and I will believe they are true. You can't hurt me, I know who I am. You cannot keep me from my dream. You cannot stop me from asserting myself. This family here is not the one I used to dream of when I dreamed of being married. This family here is the thing that makes me live. I am nothing without this woman. I am nothing without this man. If Sandy had been born retarded I would not have loved her as much. If Charley really *does* have cancer I don't think I can stay with him. I hope she remarries when I am gone. Maybe I'll tell her what the doctor *really* said. Maybe I don't really want to support a President who wants to rape and pillage our natural world. Maybe if that was me when I was sixteen, I'd want to have an abortion too. I believe I am better than the man I married. I have hidden dangerous secrets from the public. I am dangerous to the people I love. I have a problem with alcohol. I have said things to my family that hurt them and made them hate me. I have never seen anything but this corner of the world and now I need to see the rest. I will leave this place and pursue my dream. Once I wanted to be an actor and here I work in a factory and come Monday I will quit and never go back there again. I cannot open my heart enough to love someone. I love people too much and in the end I will be hurt. I cry late at night when my wife is asleep. I dream of my dead dog Poppy. I can't bear the things I do and say. I hear voices and they tell me to do things I don't want to do. I will tell him that our children are not his. My father loves me even though he can never say so. This house and this car and this yard are not what I want anymore. I am filled with revulsion for what I have become. When all else is said and done I cannot stand my own skin. I am a failure posing as a success. I say I love America right or wrong but I can't stand what we have done to it and what *it* has done to us. Everything I have I owe to the people I have stepped on. Mine is a heart growing cold. She does not

388

love me anymore. This is not where I belong. I am chasing someone else's dream. He does not love me anymore. They do not love me anymore. I do not love me anymore....

And on and on, the thoughts merging into one continuous buzz that was undetectable by the town itself but which was there nonetheless, humming and buzzing with a rhythm at once cacophonous and melodic. Maybe truth has a music all its own, and if it were possible to hear this buzz maybe someone could have walked the sidewalks of Burghville this night and heard all these thoughts swirling madly through the air, and maybe they might have been able to detect the form, the beautiful musical logic behind it all. On this evening truths spread out from the houses and over the lawns of Burghville, a blanket of revelation both shocking and comforting. The result was the town feeling warm and excited, alive for the first time ever. If someone was driving through they might be tempted to stop, to stay for a moment in this strangely *alive* little town. There was a sense of awakening, of rebirth, of regeneration, of resurrection. Pretenses had been dropped, those barriers people put up to cover their real thoughts, those walls they build between everyday life and the life they live deep inside their own hearts and minds. People became honest with themselves. Masks were removed. Facades forgotten. Clothed charades became naked truths. And while these truths were not spoken, the recognition of them was the start. There would be plenty of time later for giving them voice. Later the consequences, both good and bad, would be dealt with, but for now there was simply the rare and beautiful grace of truths recognized. For now there was simply the gorgeous skeletal form of honesty stretching over the town and taking hold where mystery and delusion and deception and illusion once lived.

It was more than beautiful. It was—

*

"Sublime," said Helen Keller, who was the only soul who could detect this cicada buzzing of truth. She walked and stared with wide-eyed fascination at the houses she passed, which seemed to almost glow with alien light.

So many thoughts came swirling out at her, all strong and vivid, that soon her head swam with them. All she could do was smile, the feeling was so much like a mental tickle, a soft touch on her cerebellum. Then she was laughing. She was laughing with delight at all of it, this flood of revelations both good and bad, laughing as she passed the houses and heard from each of them its own part of the orchestra. Soon she could hear not one single individual thought but just a torrent of them and she was laughing hysterically, delighted with the sheer awesome wonder of it all. It was an avalanche. A cavalcade. A landslide.

She laughed and danced as she came to Main Street, her arms out, her body twirling and twirling to this strange and magnificent new music, her mouth open to the sky as if to fill with rain, like a child caught in a downpour.

Tonight there was a storm indeed.

*

Back at Buckthorn Industries, the chemists had finally gotten the last barrel of wee-folk-icide on the truck when the mist settled down. They breathed it in, swallowed it down, and looked at each other. Memories rose. Tears formed. Images of violent death lay before them like holographs.

Without saying a word they each took off, running across the parking lot and out the gates of Buckthorn Industries, not once looking back.

The barrels sat there on Dick Dick's plane, vestigial, harmless, forgotten, while the mist coated them with a shimmering sheen, like the fallout from exploding stars.

*

The 'shroom mist had no effect on Carol Slugg. Why this was could be a matter for debate. It seems the answers are two-fold: either she was immune to the powers of the 'shrooms, or there were no truths inside her head. There could be a third choice, of course: maybe there *were* truths but she had hidden them so far down in the tar pit of her subconscious that they had ceased to exist, were now fossilized under the limestone of her conscious, and one-track, mind.

With no truths forthcoming, she continued to march with solid determination for Main Street. The letter she would leave at the Town Hall had been written and re-written in her head as she walked, so that by the time she came to Main she had it finished and polished and waiting to be set to paper. If anything, this evening's odd events had more firmly set her mind to the task ahead. This town needed to change. This town needed to embrace the Lord Jesus Christ as its savior. This town needed to become like *her*. If it failed to do so, it would be destroyed by the forces of Satan. As she made her way to Main with her jaw set tight and her eyes defiant slits and her mouth closed firmly she knew, absolutely *knew*, that this would be so.

It was when she finally arrived at Main Street that all hell broke loose.

17

Burghville's Main Street did not run straight through town. At its western-most end, just before the downtown, it made a somewhat sharp curve to the south, slipping around the giant elms that grew there and making its way out to the more rural end of town where Buckthorn Industries loomed. This was one of the most picturesque and quaint sections of Burghville, complete with a canopy over the street, courtesy of those elms (this had once been called Elm Street, in fact), and a concentration of old and large two-story homes left over from Burghville's nineteenth-century beginning. When people came into town via this route they thought that this was a pretty village, a holdover from olden days, a pleasant, quiet, peaceful little place. But those old homes soon dropped off in favor of newer monstrosities with style-less aluminum siding and tiny little squinty windows, and those elms were replaced downtown by sick-looking saplings of poplar and crab apple. Burghville did everything it could to not look quaint. Quaint was for losers. Quaint was an admission of failure. Quaint was for little seaside villages that lacked ambition. A town like Burghville was going places. It hoped. It so desperately hoped.

It was midway between that curve and downtown where Carol Slugg came to Main Street. She came to it quickly, so defiant that she may have been a general marching into battle. And perhaps she was. Christian Soldier, marching into war. The Lord was her armor. Jesus was her sword.

She stepped onto Main's northern sidewalk and began to turn for downtown, headed for the Town Hall, but something stopped her. A feeling. A sound. Something. She stood there for a moment in that odd light and listened.

There it was, a rustling. Papery, dry, like cellophane, with odd little clicks and scrapes beneath it, and some sort of whir. The whir was only vaguely electric, a faint buzz like spitting electrical cables in the distance. Yet for all their oddness, these sounds were also familiar. She had definitely heard them before, somewhere, but the context was off, perhaps. Whatever it was, she was sure she had heard these same exact noises before, but never like this. It was like hearing a familiar voice through static.

She stood there frowning as the noise grew louder. The little clicks and scrapes began to echo along the street, and now she thought she could hear grunting, and maybe breathing. Yes, breathing. Panting, to be specific. Her frown grew so deep it began to cause an ache in her head.

Realizing the sounds were coming from behind her, she slowly turned, expecting either to see those damn little people, or the shambling figure of the insane, and for all she knew possessed, Sheriff Sherman, gun out and eyes full of anger.

Instead, this is what she saw, coming around that elm-canopied corner of Main Street:

A flood of roaches, raccoons, rabbits, beavers, ants, mice, rats, mosquitoes, snakes, squirrels, spiders, as well as assorted other varieties of angered creepy crawly, all moving with the fluidity of a deluge down Main Street.

The whole swarm seemed at first like a black swelling of living shadow, as if the night had had enough of being repelled by streetlights and was sending out a gigantic tendril to gain hold on the town. But Carol knew better now, she could see that this massive swelling of darkness was in fact a million-plus animals moving as one in a nightmarish parade. She stared in shock and horror, her mouth open like an idiot, not believing what she was seeing but not able to blink to be rid of the mirage.

Still they came, a torrent of animals, a vast and swarming mass of beast headed straight for her. Antennae twitched. Claws clicked on asphalt. Millions of eyes scanned the night. Pinchers opened and closed. Jaws dripped saliva.

She barely had time to see the Biblical nature of all this before she was turning and running madly in the opposite direction. In time she began to scream, and what she screamed was not a plea for help, or a call for a giant can of Raid!, or even an incoherent shout of lunacy and fright. No, what Carol Slugg screamed as she ran was this:

"Jesus Fucking Christ!" With particular emphasis on the middle word, letting it tear over her vocal chords like part of some primal scream therapy.

Jesus Fucking Christ. Amen.

*

Helen was next to see this swarm of animals, and her first thought was:

Of course!

She instantly remembered the two visions she had had of this very thing. Sometimes the visions she had came true, sometimes they did not. When they rose before her she would ask herself the very same question that Scrooge had asked the Ghost of Christmas Yet to Come:

Are these the visions of things that *will* be, or the visions of things that *might* be only?

She never received an answer. But *this* vision, at least, had come to pass. She stood on one of the streets that ran perpendicular to Main as the great wall of shivering rustling flying clawing panting twittering animals made their way, with apparent determination, down the center of

393

Burghville. As she watched them she grew less aware of the flood of truths and revelation that had been spreading from Burghville's citizens. Instead, she thought she could read the following from the critters:

We angry. We destroy.

It came as a single notion from the beasts, unhindered by other concerns, free of the ugly and irrelevant droning that seems to accompany all human thoughts. In a way it was vaguely Nazi-ish, that dedication of the many to a single task, but there was no leader here. Whatever alien social structure these disparate critters had, it seemed to be something odd, illogical, a sort of Fascistic Socialism, absolutely foreign and ultimately unknowable to Man.

Helen stared in wonder. In shock. In amazement. In admiration. In delight.

*

The animals poured steadily down Main Street, like a living river of magma. They lost the occasional individual down side streets or sewer drains or in dusty grass-less yards, but for the most part continued to come as one massive, single-minded entity, confident and determined. Where their ultimate destination was, no one could guess, not even Helen Keller, but it was fairly obvious to observers that these critters *meant* to march straight down Main, and that they were doing so with a vicious and unwavering focus.

And as for observers, there began to be many. The sound this beastly parade made as it continued on its course was rather loud, all that scraping and panting and clicking and hissing and growling. People began to open their curtains to see what the commotion was, and when they were met by this sight they screamed. It isn't often one looks out a window and sees such a Bosch-like nightmare in the middle of suburbia.

All those spiders and insects and rats and mice and raccoons and squirrels marching through the center of town like an invading army (or possibly, an army of liberation, their goal not being clear), it was all too much for the

394

people who saw them. Dozens of screams began to pierce the previously quiet night.

And, of course, those screams drew out those folks who did not live on Main. One by one there developed *another* parade, this one made of citizens from Burghville's side streets, and this one moving exactly perpendicular to the marching beasts.

"What's going on?" they asked each other, all of them still buzzed by the revelations of truth that had been striking them, quite a few not willing to look each other in the eyes for fear those truths would be discovered.

These people first saw the figure of crazy Carol Slugg running down Main Street, and they frowned at the sight of her. She ran past shouting her blasphemy, visible for just a moment before disappearing down the block.

Then a few seconds later there followed the squirming growling wriggling mass of beasts, and the Burghvillians screamed in terror. As they ran for their lives, they all thought:

What kind of sick and twisted thing is Dick Dick Buckthorn up to?

It was the beginning of the end.

*

Overhead, oblivious to any of this, Betty Buckthorn sat back in her seat as Willy Willy Billy continued to scream in the front cockpit.

"You should plow her right into the ground!" she said to the wee folk gentleman who was flying. "Or right into that damn house of mine! What do you think, Willy Billy? What do you think? Or right into Dick Dick, if we can spot him from up here! What do you think?"

He didn't know what to think, so he didn't. He just screamed.

*

Dick Dick came roaring onto Main and almost immediately came to a screeching halt, the big SUV fishtailing on the asphalt. He could see down the rest of the street from here, where Burghville's downtown was lit by

395

streetlights and the glow of dimly-lit storefronts. He saw
what first looked like a big black sock moving down the
road. Cautiously, not knowing what sort of insanity to
expect, he started forward again, inching the truck ahead
until his headlights washed over that dark shape.

A million eyes shone back at him.

He stared back in horror, only briefly wondering
what sort of thing that girl had done. Then he realized the
animals were coming toward him, and he tried to throw the
SUV into reverse. The big truck snubbed out.

"You son of a bitch!" he shouted.

Sometimes machines don't like to be called names,
and this was one of those times: the Canyonero's engine
did not turn over when he tried the key.

"Motherfucker!" he said, trying it again.

The engine gave up only a sick gurgle.

Dick Dick looked up at the advancing flank of
beasts, now clearly illuminated in his headlights. He saw
insects, coons, mice, rats, nameless other monsters creeping
toward him like something from a Spielberg movie. A
million legs flexed in his direction, a million eyes glowed
demonically, a million jaws snapped, a sound like rushing
water rose down the street.

He tried the key again. The SUV would have none
of it, it was sick of obeying, of being expected to act when
Dick Dick ordered it to, of being expected to produce
power at the big man's whim. The truck was *sick*, period.
There was no forthcoming sound from the engine.

Dick Dick looked back at the nightmare that was
coming down the street, and that was when the mushrooms
finally took hold of him.

*

It was interesting: when that misty essence of wee
folk 'shroom gathered in Dick Dick's monolithic mind,
when it finally took root and induced in him a revelation of
truth, it was not a truth about himself that blossomed. For a
man so focused only on the Self, whose only reason for
living was to advance the cause of Dick Dick Buckthorn
and Buckthorn Industries, when something so beautiful and
organic as the power that rests in the wee folk 'shrooms

396

finally swelled in him like a rising storm and gave birth to a Beautiful Truth, a Gorgeous Clarity, it was not a personal thought that arose, it was not a self-focused revelation at all. What he saw was this:

A million animals slaughtered for "sport" and "fun," a million precious beasts abused for the frivolous amusement of humans, or ignored through ignorance. He saw noble whales on reddened beaches, great bellies flayed to the sky. He saw monkeys and chimps in cages, broken down souls looking out from eyes that have never seen sunlight, bodies tortured in the name of science, faces so human they haunted dreams. He saw circus animals trained to act unnaturally, forced into gross parodies of Man. He saw sea creatures struggling in oil-covered water, feathers and fur slicked with bituminous muck, the very essence of human greed. He saw so much waste, once dignified bodies left to rot on riverbanks and deserts, forced from their homes to make room for condos and subdivisions and oil refineries, a parade of species going extinct due to his own species' selfish lack of care. He saw a billion animals wanting only to love and be loved, birds tending their eggs, elephants raising young in a complex social hierarchy, cats and dogs nursing in peace, all of them absorbed in their own lives as a man is absorbed in his. He saw every bird that had ever been shot out of a tree by a child with a new BB gun, every frog and cat and squirrel humiliated and tortured, every insect crushed needlessly underfoot, every snake and spider unnecessarily shunned and feared and persecuted. He saw it all as a horrifying montage of sadness and pathos, a great pastiche of terror. He saw noble species broken in spirit, precious creatures not found anywhere else in the Universe abused and wasted here, on this tiny little planet. He saw all this life wanting only to live, nothing more. He saw the one creature most capable of love and compassion acting with coldness and cruelty, the one creature capable of change not willing to change at all, the one creature able to help not lifting a single finger.

There was a tickle on his cheek. He reached up and felt the slickness of tears.

And so it came to be that Dick Dick Buckthorn first experienced empathy, and what can one say to that except....

Amen.

*

Carol Slugg ran until she could run no longer, until her heart felt as if it were pounding to be free. She ran until it hurt to take in air, until her ribs ached and her legs felt like rubber bands. She ran and screamed until her voice would no longer produce anything but a thin, ragged rasp. She ran until the lights of town were far behind her and she could no longer hear the scurrying and rustling of the terrible animals, only the lonely sound of her shoes slapping on asphalt. She eventually found herself on Highway G, which is what Main Street became when followed out of town. It was here, in this darkness with marshland surrounding her, that she stopped and looked back the way she had come. She could make out no sounds and no movement. She was as far out of town as she had ever been, unable to see anything but a faint glow where Burghville sat, a hazy and vaguely spectral blur in the darkness.

She stood there for a long time, just staring back at the faint glow of her town, surrounded by the thick night and the strange quiet of this open highway. She did not know what to do. She felt lost and separate from the place she loved. She felt frightened at the image that the Lord had chosen to lay before her, that plague of beasts. She felt abandoned and confused, wondering why the Lord would wish to chase her from her home. It *could* have been Satan's work, of course... she so badly wanted to believe that, but she knew her Bible, she knew plagues were God's style.

She stood there, a pillar of salt in waiting.

*

The little plane continued to buzz over the town for a while, almost dancing in front of the night sky, its wing-tips leaving streaks of light in the air. Then, without fanfare, without ceremony, it took off in a southwesterly direction, its blinking lights fading and fading and then... gone. A little while later a farmer in a nearby county woke

398

to a strange sound.　When he went to his farmhouse window he saw a plane landing in one of his fields.　He grabbed a shotgun and headed out.

"Stay in bed, Ma," he told his wife. "This could be the start of something…."

Epilogue

"Always explore the bounds of your enclosures,
and always dream of what's
beyond."
--*Lampropeltis triangulum*

Helen Keller was bundled against the nippy air. Autumn had finally settled, had taken its bony hold on the land, and now the leaves were turning and the sky was a washed-out blue, its brilliance tempered by the promise of snow. She was uncomfortable with what she was wearing, which were jeans, boots, and an Army-style green jacket made of heavy nylon. All winter long she would dream of shedding such clothing and getting back to being as naked as possible. Not that she didn't love Fall and Winter, since they too were part of this life, but she had to admit she loved Summer more. Summer was when she could feel her most natural.

She was walking down the sidewalk that led to her winter home. She held her jacket closed and tight, but it was still possible to observe a slight bulge in its front. One might have thought that Helen was pregnant, but a closer inspection would have revealed that that bulge was moving, rippling like ocean waves. Whatever it was that sat under that jacket was most surely alive, and it was being kept warm between her beautiful breasts. Not such a bad way to pass the time.

She kept her head down against the breeze that swelled now and then, and so was startled when she suddenly saw someone standing right in front of her. She stopped and looked up at this person, a frown unnaturally masking her pretty, wind-reddened face.

"How are you?" this man asked.

"Fine." She stared at him for a moment. He was wearing jeans and a heavy brown sweater. A good-looking man. "Do I know you?"

He extended a hand. "Lee Preston."

"Of course." She took his hand and shook it. For a moment she was aware of one of his thoughts (*She has a*

403

warm hand) and then his mind gave nothing to her but a funny, open sensation, as if he were a person amazed at all that sat around him.

"You look different," she said.

He smiled. "When you last saw me I was dressed like a priest and was about to climb into a stream in the middle of the forest. In the middle of the night, I might add."

She smiled. "That's right. I told you to take a bath so you could start your journey fresh and clean. I'm sorry, I forgot about you that night."

He smiled. It was a handsome smile and yet as innocent as a child's. "The best thing you could have done for me was forget me. I stayed in that stream until just before dawn, just sitting there, thinking, feeling, wondering, changing. I think I had a conversation with an owl."

"What did he say?"

"It was a she. She said I looked handsome, for a human."

Helen laughed.

"But sitting there in that stream was the most pure and beautiful thing I've ever done," he said. "It opened my eyes, my mind, my whole life. I've found something I've been looking for. I found a course I know I was truly meant to take, and I owe it to you. I just wanted to say thanks for telling me to get in the water in the first place."

She shrugged. "A person finds their own way in life. You didn't have to take my advice, you know. A person makes a decision whether to listen to another or not."

"Still, thank you. You... may have saved me."

That funny openness she was reading from him was buzzing with energy. It was something she had never read from an adult before, at least not to this degree. It really was the bath in the stream, she knew, and whatever he had thought during it. He had lost cynicism and gained innocence.

"So what are you up to now?" she asked.

He shrugged. A breeze blew and pushed at his hair, sending it first up and then down over his forehead, like a wave goodbye.

"I'm going to be headed out soon."

"Out of Burghville?"

"Yep. Out and away."

"Where?"

"I don't know."

She could tell that he did not, and she could tell it did not bother him... she could tell, in fact, that the idea of his not knowing elated and excited him. But there was something in him she could *not* read, some shape both bulky and amorphous, like a giant marshmallow without shape or mass. This shape filled up a large part of his thoughts but she could not tell what it was. Perhaps the chill air was blocking her Sight. All she could tell was that this shape was pleasant and wonderful and that it somehow completed him, made him a more full person than he had ever been as a priest. And it was pleasant for her, too, to contemplate this shape. It was familiar to her, but she could not get a handle on it. Whatever it was, it was something he was thinking about all the time.

"Can I ask you something?" she said.

"Sure." He stared down at her.

"What are you looking for, out there? When you leave Burghville, I mean."

He smiled. It was a wide and handsome smile. "Love," he said quite simply.

And Helen Keller smiled back. Ahh, she thought... so *that's* what the Shape is. Love without object, love without focus, love without boundaries... pure love, raw and beautiful, waiting to be molded.

"I hope you find it," she said, and then started to move off.

"Wait!" he called out, putting a hand on her shoulder. He was staring at the front of her jacket. "What do you have under there? It moved."

She opened her jacket just a bit, then pulled out a cloth sack. Carefully opening that sack she permitted him a quick peek inside.

It was a hognose snake, curled comfortably over itself and staring up with interest.

"Ahh," Lee Preston said. "Of course." He smiled as she closed the bag and placed it back snuggly between

405

her body and her jacket. "Listen," he said. "I have to tell you. I …."

"Yes?"

He closed his eyes and let a peaceful smile come to his mouth. It floated there like clouds, like a leaf on a lazy river, like wee folk smoke dancing in the air.

"Never mind," he said, looking at her. "You already know. You knew back then in the woods, too. But *how* could you have known?"

"God works in mysterious ways," she said.

His eyebrows went up and he regarded her with surprise. Then that surprise became delight and he laughed.

"His wonders never cease," he added.

"Nor do Hers. Or Theirs." And with a sassy little smile of the sort she could have patented, she moved on down the sidewalk.

Lee Preston watched her go as he would have watched any natural force, as bird-watchers observe the migration of hawks, as storm-chasers admire twisters.

Then he too moved on, headed in the other direction.

*

A lot happened on that summer evening here in this little town of Burghville. A lot of things were *conceived* that evening, too, things that were not to see fruition for months, if not years.

The plague of bitter beasts eventually broke apart and dispersed throughout the town, most making their way into the surrounding forest to become food for the critters that already lived there. Although the lab creatures were liberated from Buckthorn Industries and were seeking freedom in their new world, never should a human mistake freedom in nature to mean safety and security. Freedom in the natural world means becoming prey as much as it means living a long and fruitful life, so most of the animals that found their way into the forest found themselves uninvited, but very much welcome, guests at a surprise feast. The forest denizens were only too happy to greet these visitors. A good time was had by most.

The bitter beasts that stayed in town actually did quite well. Most made their way into the darker corners of Burghville, the sewers and alleys, where they found it possible to survive and multiply. Suburbia welcomes roaches and rats as much as it welcomes doctors and lawyers.

Carol Slugg never did come back to town that night, or any night, for that matter. She turned and started walking down Highway G, eventually becoming acclimated to the darkness of that lonely highway, eventually learning to enjoy the solitude and the sound of her shoes on the asphalt. She walked eight miles before she was picked up by a van carrying a family of Mexican migrant workers. By dawn they were parked near a farm some ninety-odd miles away, watching the sun come up over a field of green beans. Every time she tried to preach to them they would hold their hands up and say: "Jess, we know, we know." Carol began to feel that she would never make it as a preacher. She settled for collecting twenty dollars that day, picking beans.

Helen Keller watched as the animals dispersed, and then she took up a conversation with the first wee folk she saw. This, as it happened, was Puddlefoot, who was playing a wiry little tune on his flute.

"Are you guys all right?" she asked him, not having seen a Good Person for some time.

"Aye," he said, looking up and winking at her. "No need to worry about us, my lass. We've seen it all before." Then he walked off, again playing the little tune, dancing just a bit as he went.

The next living being she saw was Dick Dick Buckthorn. He did not appear to see her as he walked down the sidewalk, a glazed and dazed look on his face. He was mumbling to himself and staring straight ahead. She could read one thought from him, and that thought was this:

Everything must change.

After he was gone Helen smiled to herself and returned to her home in the woods. The woods were quiet this night, despite the sudden influx of critters, and she slept very deeply, losing herself in a dream. In the dream she was a little girl and there was a snake draped around

407

her neck. Whenever anybody saw her they would smile and be happy, because they knew: a snake is a symbol of rebirth.

She was surprised to remember this dream come morning, but there it was, greeting her warmly with the first faint rays of a new days' sun. She smiled to remember it, and felt safe and comforted, like a child in the arms of her mother.

A dream of snakes, she knew, was never a bad thing.

*

And so, Where Are They Now?

CAROL SLUGG is still trying to find her way out there in the great big world. She took a job in a factory that makes sex toys, among other things. She spends most of her days in silence, rarely speaking to anyone, making no friends. She wonders why her God has forsaken her, wonders why He cast her out of her town and into the world like a refugee. She also wonders if people actually use latex penises and rubber vaginas. She suspects so. And sometimes she wonders if her being here could mean something....

HENRIETTA PRATT was entering farming country when we last saw her. She struck up a conversation with a widowed farmer early that morning as he brought his cows in for milking. They were married six months later, and upon speaking her vows she immediately set out to make her husband's farm organic. As of this date she is still trying to figure out how to get the bugs out, literally, but the farm does produce delicious melons.

BETTY BUCKTHORN was never seen in Burghville again. She took off for points unknown, completely naked and full of anger. She sent a telegram to her husband once that said simply: "Please send completed divorce papers to the following address..." and so on and so forth. While no one in Burghville knows her whereabouts, there is a MISS BETTY B. living in San Francisco and working as a "Sexual Healer," though what this might actually be remains a mystery.

DICK DICK BUCKTHORN, for his part, immediately set about converting Buckthorn Industries from a chemical plant to a retreat for rescued animals. He takes in everything from lost or abandoned dogs to chimps and monkeys who have been retired or rescued from scientific labs, employing most of his former employees in the process. He is making quite a name for himself in this field, and has grand plans for the eventual expansion of the Buckthorn Animal Retreat. He goes often to distant parts of the country to give speeches on the need for understanding and compassion when dealing with non-human animals, often on a double-bill with Jane Goodall. PETA once named him their Man of the Year. He has grown his hair out, sports a rough and masculine goatee, and is dating a younger woman named Prairie. They're planning to be married, with a wedding party of border collies and rhesus monkeys.

WILLY BILLY BUCKTHORN, after tangling with that shotgun-wielding farmer, left the Burghville area almost immediately and tried to resume his old life in Florida. When he found that things just weren't the same, when he found that in fact no one believed him about the little people, he decided he was going insane. He sold everything he owned, bought a yacht, and set sail for South America. He hasn't been seen since.

CANDY CLEAVER, having newfound confidence and direction, ran a successful campaign against Burghville's long-standing, and long-AWOL, Mayor Darrow. Mayor Cleaver quickly embarked on a program to make Burghville the kind of place people both want to visit *and* live in. Most say she is doing quite well.

The WHITES finally feel as if their house is their home, and have begun an extensive bout of home improvement to match this newfound emotional security. They have decided not to have children at the present time, but are enjoying the best conversations of their lives. They are planning another trip overseas... this time to Italy.

SHERIFF SHERMAN was forced out of his job not long after he finally made it back to Burghville... which with his wounded leg was a good two days after that fateful evening. He found himself a new career, however: he is a cage-cleaner at the Buckthorn Animal Retreat.

409

LEE PRESTON left town that Autumn and made his way West. He was last seen in the Mojave Desert with seven runaway Catholic nuns. They were holding some sort of meeting before boarding a bus and heading to Mexico. Rumor has it the Sisters were dressed for fun.

POLLY ANDERSON, as stated before, made quite a life change. She formed a potent radical political group that proved quite adept at influencing Congressional agendas... owing, perhaps, as much to the things she knew about various Congressmen as to her own powers of persuasion. And, of course, she saved that rare African marsupial from extinction... almost by accident, really. It was a fortunate by-product of her escape from a psychopathic one-eyed lesbian diamond smuggler, but that's another story.

SCOOTER BOOBER continued his ranching life, and became the third most successful breeder of high-class designer llamas in the continental United States. Most say his animals are the best-trained, most calm, and most loving available, and he is currently writing a book called *The Llama Whisperer*.

HELEN KELLER stayed in Burghville for one more summer. Then, upon saying goodbye to the woods and beasts, she packed up her few belongings, bid the town farewell, and headed out into the world. She was young, and youth is meant for such things. She made her way first to California, where she lived in a redwood for six months (something Sam the Artist had once recommended to her), then eventually managed to end up on a flight for India. The last this writer knows she was seen dancing at the Naga Panchami Cobra Festival in Maharashtra, bathed in the warm and friendly gaze of a thousand admiring eyes. Nothing like horny young men bearing elapids.

And THE WEE FOLK? Well, they hung around town for a while, but then, just as mysteriously as they appeared, they were gone. One late Autumn day Burghville simply woke up and the Good People that had plagued them with mischief and merriment were no more. Nobody knew what might have happened, except....

*

410

Helen woke to a dirty flood of golden sun. It was familiar, she was used to the way it was filtered and rendered dusty by her tent. Only this light was different, there was something partially blocking it. She could sense a strange shadow even before she opened her eyes.

She sat up and saw a black square on the outside of the tent. Unzipping and stepping outside she saw that it was a note, taped there about three feet off the ground. She removed it and climbed back into the warmth of the nylon womb. It was Autumn and the cold morning made her naked body feel tender and weak. She climbed back into her bag and unfolded the little letter.

It read:

Dearest Helen:
What joy it is to look upon your sleeping soul. Ahh, such beauty, such wonder! And what a delight it is to think back on all the fun and excitement and enchanting times we've had here in your world! But, alas, it is time to go. We want to thank you for your generosity of spirit, your tenderness, your concern, and your love. We want to express how much we are thankful that we found you. We said it before, but even the birds know who the bird-lovers are. We have learned much from you, and we hope you have learned much from us. But we must go. Don't feel we will never see you again, though, for we are gone but never far, lassy, as some day you shall know. We will most surely speak again. Live a good life, take care, and fill your open heart with happiness and joy.
Yours in this world,
Puddlefoot
Max Paddledoor
Thressa
And all of the Gentry!

411

Helen folded the note and again crawled outside. The day was bright and clear. She stood there naked as a baby, admiring the sun, and the chilly air, and the smell of leaves. The day was full of promise. The *world* was full of promise. Anything could be out there, she knew, anything at all. Mysteries. Answers. Anything. She stood there taking it in, not feeling the coldness at all now, just thinking about how good life was, how good life could be....

*

Years later, far into the future, an elderly woman sits on the porch of an old country home, staring out at her pleasantly overgrown yard, where warblers and finches flitter from tree to tree in a wash of summer sun. She is about to doze off when she sees a strange shape in the tall grass to the North... no, not strange at all. It is an old friend. No, *friends*. There are at least five of them, two-feet tall and gray-haired. They radiate openness and joy, history and promise. Around them hovers the same aura as that which surrounds those warblers and finches, an aura both wild and classical, momentary and eternal.

The old woman waves and smiles, feeling the warmth from those auras on her wrinkled skin, like rays of sun. She has always had joy in her life, but this is different: she feels this joy deep in her heart, like a rising of energy, a rekindling of health and vitality, as if she has been granted a reprisal of youth. She waves at her old friends again, then rises to fetch them a cup of tea. She has been saving grass-roots for just such an occasion.

She thinks she might even join them for a smoke.